MENAKA'S CHOICE

Kavita Kané is the best-selling author of *Karna's Wife: The Outcast's Queen* and *Sita's Sister*. She started her career as a journalist and is now a full-time novelist. She is a post-graduate in English literature and mass-communications and a self-confessed aficionado of theatre and cinema. Married to a mariner, she is a mother to two teenaged daughters and currently lives in Pune along with Dude, the overfriendly Rottweiler, Chic the friendly Spaniel and Babe, the unfriendly cat.

MENAKA'S
CHOICE

KAVITA KANÉ

RUPA

Published by
Rupa Publications India Pvt. Ltd 2016
7/16, Ansari Road, Daryaganj
New Delhi 110002

Sales Centres:
Allahabad Bengaluru Chennai
Hyderabad Jaipur Kathmandu
Kolkata Mumbai

ISBN: 978-81-291-3733-3

Seventh impression 2020

13 12 11 10 9 8 7

The moral right of the author has been asserted.

Printed at Saurabh Printers Pvt. Ltd, Noida

To my Prakash

Contents

Prologue:
Menaka's Daughter

The frightened deer disappeared into the thick darkness of the woods. King Dushyant gave a small sigh of exasperation as he realised that he would have to get down from the chariot and follow his prey on foot. But the King of Hastinapur was a determined young man; a nimble-footed deer certainly would not be able to defeat him. Tall and imposingly built, he was lithe enough to rush quickly through the thick glades, so as to not lose sight of the frisky deer. He heard, rather than saw, some movement behind a thick, thorny bush a little ahead, and swiftly drew his arrow and shot at the rustling sound. The deer gave a small whimper and crumpled down.

Before he could reach his fallen prey, the king saw a slight figure rush towards the moaning animal. It was a girl. He quickened his steps, drawn by a curious pull. She was a beautiful girl, her face hidden by a thick swathe of her ebony mane. She heard his footsteps and turned to look at him. Dushyant held his breath, finding it difficult to exhale. She was exquisite, her fair skin almost translucent, her dark and thick hair, tied in a loose bun, the way hermits do but some tresses had come loose, framing her oval face. Her large, deep eyes were luminous and were filled with rising distress. For the first time in his short, young life, the king felt a qualm of guilt; not for hurting the deer, but for hurting this lovely girl instead.

'What pleasure did you get by hurting this innocent deer?' she enquired, her eyes gleaming with annoyance. 'Is this proof of your great valour, o famous king?' she taunted.

Dushyant was rendered speechless by the maiden's beauty, but he noticed her proud nose and decided chin.

'You are a king, aren't you?' she spoke with controlled anger, making no attempt to smile or be gracious to his regal presence. She was vaguely dismissive of his royal stature and showed it.

'Yes, I am Dushyant, the king of Hastinapur,' he breathed in a hoarse whisper, 'and I am sorry that I have hurt your pet.'

'It's not my pet,' she corrected him tartly. 'But yes, all the animals in these woods are looked after with great love and kindness. We do not hurt those who live amongst us.'

Her curtness surprisingly made him bristle. He wanted to salvage the situation, and not just his pride. He tried to apologize again.

'In my exuberance I have hurt this innocent animal,' he started. 'Fortunately, it's not a fatal arrow, and can rectify the damage. I'll take it upon myself to nurse it back to health. Pray, fair maiden, where can I take this injured animal for further care?'

The girl looked at him suspiciously, not impressed by his request. 'He's bleeding horribly. I hope for all your changed, most kind intentions that he won't die,' she grimaced, openly critical. 'But yes, right now, you can carry him to my home. My father's ashram is close by.'

Taking the bleeding deer gently in his arms, the chastened king followed the girl, quietly. The woods soon cleared into a green expanse of a neat hermitage, studded by a cluster of thatched huts of various sizes. Roaming within them were animals of all types ranging from the wild bear to the gentle doe, each unmindful of the other. Fear ceased to exist here; and peace prevailed in the gentle rustling leaves of the thick trees, swarms of the kakar birds gliding over the banks of the River Malini and the shimmering waters where Dushyant could glimpse down to the riverbed from where he stood. He did some quick thinking.

This idyllic corner within the woods was obviously the home of the revered Rishi Kanva, who resided in this forest. He had heard about it, but the famed ascetic-scholar of law and philosophy was nowhere in sight.

'Where is Rishi Kanva?' he asked.

'He is gone away for a few days for some work in the city,' the girl replied. 'Did you venture so deep into this forest to seek his blessings, o king?'

'No, I had come to hunt,' he admitted sheepishly, reddening at the pointed look of stern disapproval the girl threw at him, 'and since I am here, I would not miss the opportunity to meet the great man,' he added reverentially. 'But pray, maiden, who are you?'

'I am his daughter,' she replied shortly, looking slightly mollified at the contrite tone in the king's request.

'My name is Shakuntala,' she added graciously, with a slight smile. 'Welcome to our ashram, though we do not welcome hunters here!'

Dushyant's embarrassment at her reprimand quickly gave way to disbelief and before he could stop himself, uttered an exclamation of swift surprise. 'His daughter?' he repeated. 'But Rishi Kanva is unmarried, revered for his single-minded pursuit to seek knowledge, and so...' he finished lamely, suddenly aware how rude and tactless he sounded.

The girl did not seem to mind his apparent thoughtlessness; she looked distinctly amused at his discomfiture, her smile gradually widening. 'Your information serves you correctly, sir. My father is unmarried, and he is a brahmachari. I am known to be his adopted daughter,' she explained.

The young king looked flushed. He was desperate to know more about this girl, but he found himself suddenly afraid that he would sound obtuse. The young, powerful king, famous for winning the bloodiest of battles, found himself battling with a surge of newly discovered emotions.

'Known to be?' he iterated, polite but uncertain.

'Yes, as almost everyone here knows I am not his daughter,'

she said with a wry smile. Her bright eyes suddenly dulled, clouding with an unread emotion. He couldn't fathom the reason, but he wanted to wipe the momentary grief darkening the girl's large, luminous eyes.

'I am the daughter of the most beauteous apsara, Menaka, and the greatest and the most powerful of rishis, Vishwamitra.'

'Rishi Vishwamitra?' repeated the young king, awestruck. 'The mortal king, who defied the devas as well as the rishis to attain supreme knowledge?'

The girl gave an imperceptible nod. 'He was known then as King Kaushik though, the mightiest king in the empire. But he gave up all for his great quest and ambition to become a Brahmarishi, the only mortal rishi to do so. He will become one eventually, courtesy my mother,' she said, her tone laced with pride, admiration and something else Dushyant could not decipher—anger, resentment?

'Today he is famously known as Rishi Vishwamitra,' she stated in courteous explanation.

King Dushyant stood speechless, too shocked to respond. This girl, dressed in simple bark clothes was the daughter of Vishwamitra, the venerable rishi who was feared and respected the world over; and Menaka, the most beautiful, bewitching being on Earth and Heaven, the celestial courtesan whom none could resist. *She has her mother's entrancing looks*, Dushyant thought, his eyes slyly raking over her shapely figure. He felt desire stirring deep within him. He knew then why he had been so besotted by her; he had fallen hopelessly in love at first sight, not with just her fresh face but her curt tone, her face lovely in defiance and the proud nose and the decided chin.

Shakuntala gave him a hard look. 'I am the daughter of famous parents. So famous that they were ashamed to claim me as their own,' she said flatly. 'I am their abandoned daughter, whom Rishi Kanva was kind enough to adopt and raise as his own. I owe him my life. I am named Shakuntala, meaning one who was brought up by the birds, the shakuns,' she said, waving to the flock of birds perched on the verandah. 'They looked after me since I was a baby. My mother used to leave me under the shelter of their wings.'

'Yet, she left you...' he said softly. 'But why was she so heartless?' cried the king passionately, wanting to draw the girl close in his arms, protecting her from further hurt. Her wilful spirit mingled with a certain fragile innocence was inexplicably moving, and he wondered what must have made her parents forsake such a lovely girl.

She gave a brittle laugh. 'They had their reasons,' she shrugged, her voice stilted. 'My mother was an apsara—she could not take me back with her to Amravati. My father had vowed to become the highest seer of all, the Brahmarishi, and a baby would have been a hurdle in his way...' her voice trailed uncertainly, the hurt evident in the subdued tone. 'Their love was supposed to be the most torrid, the most madly intense romance that shocked all. The devas despaired and plotted but yet they loved each other insanely, oblivious to the world, lost in their own...'

The girl's eyes filled with emotion, fastened in painful appeal on the young king.

'But their story is more than a tale of love and loss...!'

Creation

$\mathcal{S}$he arose diaphanously from the Ocean of Milk. Menaka blinked and looked around her. The sky was dark, a spinning, achromatic hue, the stars shimmering brighter than the distant, bigger suns. The Milky Way swathed in far above with the ocean churning (samudra manthan) below. It was a stunning contrast, both converging at some farther, hazy point.

It was the last day and she was the last one to appear from the zephyr of heavenly life. The devas and the asuras, temporarily united in peace and effort, had tirelessly churned the ocean with the magical herbs and plants for a thousand years now. Mount Mandar loomed loftily on the giant turtle Kurma, who bore its sinking weight and kept it afloat, and allowed itself to be the axle; the giant snake Vasuki wrapped around the mountain acted as a rope to rotate it as the devas and asuras on either side, pulled and lugged together in painstaking synchronisation to churn out the amrit—that nectar of immortality.

But the moment of triumph had been short-lived. The cup containing the elixir had been abruptly snatched by the asuras, ready to be consumed. But they had stopped to behold a breathless vision of a woman, stately and beautiful, her loveliness casting a spell of a hypnotic trance. Her quick fingers had been stealthier than her bewitching smile, her seductive gaze riveting them under her spell. She had deftly prised the precious cup from their convulsive clutch and vanished into thin, bewildered air. The cup was later retrieved in Indralok and returned to the delighted devas. Mohini had worked her charm once again.

Menaka laughed silently at the foolishness of the male gender; for all the might of the devas, toiling for years, it took the wile of a woman for one moment which had won them the day, the final war and that elusive elixir. Had it not been for Mohini, the enchantress form of Lord Vishnu, and her timely intervention of distracting the asuras, the devas could not have ever achieved immortality. First as Kurma and now Mohini, Lord Vishnu had come to the rescue again. The devas had promptly swallowed the elixir and had defeated the asuras to push them back to Patallok. There was jubilation all around; but the sea was still swirling slowly, wispy fumes effusing from the sluggish churning.

Menaka shivered, as she felt cold and clammy, a thin film of dew sheathing her soft skin. After all, she was the spirit of the cloud and water. Was she just a water nymph?

'You are more than that...' she heard a voice from behind.

She turned to see a tall, chiselled-face man, rather, a deva. Menaka recognised him instantly. He was Lord Indra, the king of devas, the most powerful heavenly warrior, the ruler of Heaven (Indralok), the dispenser of rain and thunderstorm. Menaka hid a smile; he was the man of all seasons, the veritable man of affairs, not excluding that of the heart and the flesh.

And an incorrigible trouble maker—not only for others but inadvertently for himself as well. It was because of this deva's ego that the whole episode of samudra manthan even took place. His careless arrogance had cost them their celestial kingdom and their divinity. The whole universe was in chaos because of this one man. As the story goes, Rishi Durvasa had gifted him a garland as a token of friendship. The egotist king that he was, Indra took it off and hung it carelessly over his elephant's neck. The pachyderm promptly tore it away, trampling on it. An incensed Durvasa, cursed Indra and the devas to lose their divinity, adding that they would have to earn it again, to realize the value of it. Losing his kingdom of Heaven, a distraught Indra rushed to Lord Vishnu, who advised them they would have to drink the nectar of immortality. But to obtain it, they would have to produce it first by churning it out from the ocean of milk—samudra manthan. As the task had been improbable for just the devas to undertake, they had to keep their ego aside and ask the asuras to help them in the mission; promising them, reluctantly, that they too will get a share of the amrit they churn out. And thus, for a millennium, the devas with the help of the asuras, had churned the ocean of milk to release the amrit.

Menaka looked at Indra with slight contempt; respect was one emotion this man would have to earn hard from her. But she had to admit he was handsome. Tall, fair with carefully-waved glossy hair and a white, ready smile, carefully prepared. But she noticed the weak, pointed chin, the sulky downturn of his thin lips. *Weak, spoilt and cruel*, Menaka warned herself immediately.

Indra smiled exaggeratedly, showing a perfect set of teeth, his eyes crinkling but the smile rarely reaching his eyes. '...You are an apsara, yes, Menaka, born from the water but never forget you are divine, emanating from the sacred ocean of milk.'

'So was halahal, the poison which was emitted while the ocean churned to asphyxiate both the devas and asuras,' she pointed out quickly. 'It was only when Lord Shiva drank it that the world was saved!'

Indra threw her a shrewd glance. She was sharp, unlike Rambha, Gritachi or Manorama, the other apsaras who had been brought forth before Menaka. He gave her a long, appraising look. She was also more beautiful than them. How, he could not fathom, though all of them had arisen from the same divine churning? Her loveliness was breath-stopping, and she had been created to have that effect. The sun was on her, bathing her tall, slender frame in a warm glow, making her soft, curvaceous body glisten. She was slim but delectably voluptuous, her long, slender neck over slight shoulders, her creamy, shadowed cleavage heaving slightly, her slim waist curving deliciously into flaring hips, the dimpled navel, provocative and alluring above a pair of long, slim legs, the thighs moving sinuously at the smallest movement she made.

Indra expelled a long breath and turned to look at her face.

It was as devastating as her firm, pearly-skinned, lissom body. She smiled mysteriously, her full, red lips, parted slightly in sultry anticipation. Her dark eyes were almost purple in their drowning depth, and were intent upon him, questioning yet sparkling with a suppressed mischievousness. They were heart-achingly innocent, yet strangely arousing.

Indra swallowed convulsively. She was born to distract, destroy and ravish. She was nothing like the other marvels which had emerged from the sea—Dhanvantari, the doctor of the devas; Surabhi, the divine cow; Parijat, the heavenly tree whose fragrance enveloped the three worlds; or Airavat, the elephant and Uchaivsshrava, the white horse, both which Indra had claimed immediately. He wished he had claimed her too, but he knew he could not. His wife, Sachi, would never allow it. *But heavens*, Indra thought ruefully, *Menaka is intoxicating. More than even Varuni, the devi of wine or Sri, the devi of beauty and fortune who had also arisen from the holy ocean. Was then Menaka, a sweet poison, like the halahal she had jestingly referred to*? The venom had turned Lord Shiva into Neelkanth—the blue throated one—as it passed down his throat and had not his wife, Devi Parvati, clutched at his throat, it would have spread through his body.

But she was Menaka, born of the mind, the imagination, Indra reminded himself, *from the mind of Lord Brahma, the Creator himself*. She was his daughter, not all beauty and bewitching charm only, but gifted with exceptional intelligence as well. *It would never always be the heady beauteousness with her*, he thought warily. Unlike the other heavenly apsaras, he would have to be careful with her.

He smiled at Menaka. 'Yes, you need to have a dash of halahal to be more like Mohini...' he trailed off deliberately, knowing Menaka would be quick on the uptake.

Menaka nodded slowly, assimilating the implication of Indra's words. Indra wanted her to take up the role of the seductress, the temptress of pleasure and lust, yet to woo intelligently.

'...and not just for the devas and asuras I presume?' asked Menaka with a husky laugh, looking at him through her thick, long lashes. It made Indra shiver with pleasure. Neither Rambha, Urvashi nor Tilottama had this effect on him. What was this woman made of?

He kept a straight face. 'Besides the asuras, of course, the men as well. Those mortals who hope to become immortals one day...' he added with a wry grimace.

'The kings and...umm, the rishis especially,' she nodded. 'They are the most usual threats to you, aren't they?' she simpered slyly.

Indra flushed. He knew to what she was referring to. His animosity for the rishis was well-known. And it was not entirely because he suspected them of ambitious motives or their potential power to conquer the world to usurp his heavenly throne. Menaka was smiling at him knowingly, a wicked glee hidden in her evident mirth. She was openly laughing at him, and he knew why. Her grin was taunting him of his scandalous sexual escapades with the women—the unsuspecting, beautiful wives of the rishis in particular. Menaka was openly smirking at his obvious weakness for them.

Indra's face darkened. 'The rishis are more dangerous than the mortal kings,' he said tightly. 'The kings have naked swords and naked ambitions; the all-knowing rishis are far more deadly with their tapas, their spiritual strength and arrogance. And help us, if we ever have both uniting against us!'

He looked down at the slow-turning Earth, a luminescent blue orb in the far distance below them.

Menaka looked down thoughtfully. 'That would be potent—a kshatriya and a rishi,' she breathed, her whisper hanging uncertainly over the three worlds.

☙

Satyavati stared at the two bowls of the rice pudding in front of her. One was meant for her and the other for her mother, Queen Ratna of Kanyakubja. Or rather, it was for the sons both of them would beget. One will be her son, the other her brother. Satyavati knew which bowl was for her. Her husband, Rishi Richik, the son of the famous Rishi Chayvan of the Bhrigu line, had planned it such. He had married her, a princess, but he was not too keen about the kshatriya blood from her royal lineage. He had created a special pudding which would make her conceive a son, who would be a remarkable rishi, a scholar like himself. 'Our son, formed thus, will be a seer of the greatest wisdom and learning, of the most severe ascetic penance and the symbol of tranquillity,' he told her with great pride and expectations. 'And from this carefully made sanctified food, your mother, the queen, shall beget the greatest among the kshatriyas, invincible and the most powerful, conqueror of all kings.'

My mother will be so pleased, thought Satyavati, with a sigh. She had had no child since Satyavati had been born twenty years ago, and she knew both her parents were pining for one, especially a son. She had begged her husband to prepare a special sacrificial food offering for her mother as well, so that both of them would have the son they wanted.

Her mother had looked delighted as she cleaned off the bowl Satyavati had given her. And she had returned to her kingdom, a happy queen, excited and full of happy expectations. Several months later, the glow on her face had spread, reaching ethereal proportions. Everyone gazed at the queen with wonderment, awaiting the prince to be born, but for one person. Rishi Richik was not to be fooled. He was puzzled and he knew from where to get the answer to his rising doubts.

'Which bowl did you give your mother?' he asked sharply.

'The one which you told me to—of which would be born the greatest of the kshatriya,' replied Satyavati, looking heavy but cheerful, as she ate the grapes from a bowl, which she knew were healthy for her unborn child in her womb. She touched her waist tenderly. 'And I had the one which will bear us the greatest rishi, the son you so wanted.'

Her husband shook his head. 'No, either you gave her the wrong one or your mother fooled you into taking the one meant for you,' said her husband sadly. 'But the consequences of such action will not be too pleasant...'

Satyavati paled. He continued softly, 'Your mother will give birth to a prince, your brother, who though a kshatriya will have the seed of the supreme and universal Brahma and shall become the highest amongst the rishis to eventually conquer the world and the heavens with his sheer wisdom. Because of this substitution of the pudding you, instead of giving birth to a brahmin, will beget a great kshatriya, powerful but cruel, the slayer of several kings of dynasties...'

'No!' exclaimed Satyavati in horror. 'No, no, please! I have done no wrong. Please don't let me bring a child to this world who would be a mass murderer! He is your son, o wise rishi, so let him be a worthy son of a worthy father—wise, kind and righteous.'

Richik gave his sobbing wife a pained look. 'Perhaps this is Fate telling us what is to come...you shall have a brother who will grow to be the greatest of all saints and scholars, and our son, dear Satyavati, shall be the bloodiest, unconquerable warrior!'

'Let that be our grandson, dear husband, not our son!' implored Satyavati, frightened tears coursing down her face. 'I don't want such a son! With your great powers, let me give birth to a brahmin of wisdom and kindness and let my grandson be that kshatriya destined to kill and conquer! I ask for nothing more, I beg for only this one wish.'

Richik smiled, giving a long sigh. 'My dearest wife, I shall do as you say. But there is no difference between a son and a grandson. But as you say, our son shall be a brahmin, our grandson a kshatriya. And the queen's son, your brother, shall be a prince, a king with sterling qualities, but destined to be the most feared and the respected of all the rishis, having all the attributes and wisdom of a brahmin; and shall devote his life to a war of not bloodshed, but a war of words and wisdom, will perform severest of ascetic penance to eventually become eventually a Brahmarishi, Vishwamitra—the friend, the teacher of the world. So be it.'

A few months later, as Satyavati rocked her sleeping baby in her arms, she knew his words had come true and would bear fruit someday. Though not the right one from the right tree, she felt a twinge of regret.

When Satyavati had confronted her mother, Queen Ratna had the grace to look sheepish and admit her subterfuge. 'I thought your husband would give you the best, and I wanted it for myself,' confessed her mother, '...the best crown prince, and then the best king.'

Satyavati felt a momentary stab of annoyance; her mother did not seem adequately contrite. And with mounting anger, she told the queen the implication of her folly.

'But that is not to be! All your cunning plan will come to nought,' the daughter retorted. 'My husband had planted in the rice morsel, the best seed of all the kshatriya energy but alas, it was me who had it and so will I have a wretch born among the brahmins. And you, Mother, have given birth to a prince, who though born to be a king, shall have all the qualities of a rishi. He will not remain a king, but become a revered rishi, devoting his life to knowledge and enlightenment. Not to rule empires,' she added bitterly. 'You, o queen, shall have all descendants who shall be brahmins and me, a line of kshatriyas! Mother, do you realise what you have done?'

The raw fury in her daughter's voice cracked the queen's regal composure. White-faced, she looked down at the smiling infant in the cradle, a thread of trepidation uncurling within her. Her Kaushik, with his sparkling eyes and flashes of temper, was named after his famous warrior great-grandfather, King Kusika. He was so unlike the quiet, calm-faced baby Satyavati was holding. He had been named Jamadagni—ocean of penance. But now her daughter was claiming that it would be her Kaushik who would grow up to do so. *Penance!* the queen shuddered. *My husband, King Gadhi, would never forgive me for what I had done. Nor would my daughter*, thought the queen worriedly. What had she done in her one act of foolishness? She looked down at the two babies, fear clutching her heart.

'Don't look at Jamadagni so sceptically, Mother. It is not him, but my grandson who will be born that feared kshatriya!" said

Satyavati, coldly. 'You have ruined everything for us!'

Kaushik gurgled loudly in his cradle, as if in merry agreement. He looked adorable, his huge dimpled grin already stealing everyone's heart. Satyavati picked him up, hugged him closely, in an affectionate embrace. He chortled noisily, looking up at the open sky, his small hands reaching for the sun. Her little brother would be someone all of them would be proud of some day. Recalling her husband's prophetic words, she knew this baby would one day become Vishwamitra, the most famous of all rishis. *But how*, she wondered, *or who would turn him from a king to a scholar, from a warrior to a saint?* And for a moment, she wished there would be someone who could change the course of events to come...

Paradise

*T*his was Heaven, Indralok, Swarg. And Amravati, its lavish capital, was the most beautiful city with Mount Mahameru towering over it benignly. It was the abode of the immortals, where they would live happily before the next incarnation; receive all the pleasures of living and loving, thought Menaka with a slight smile. Indralok was a place to assuage all wants and human hunger and to consummate all desires; where every hunger got satisfied, of the stomach and the senses. Be it from Kamadhenu, the wish-fulfilling cow who made sure that none stayed hungry. Or Chintamani, the magical gem which provided wealth and splendour. Or be it from the Kalpataru, the evergreen, everlasting tree that blessed all with health and harmony. And then there was sura—both, the wine and the music made and played by the gandharvas. And served by the apsaras—born immortal, deigned and designed to please and give pleasure, but never to seek it.

From the time the apsaras emanated from the azure vapours of the milky ocean, robed in ethereal shimmer, they had defined desire from a million emotions bewitching all with their arousing beauty, their radiance flaring up the world. They were the nymphs arising within the sunbeams, gleaming over Heaven, flashing in the sapphire resplendence of the sky. They were the sparkle of the sunrise and the dimming of the sunset, the coolness in the breeze, the haunting echoes of forests and fields.

We dwell in the life of the soul, smiled Menaka as she stepped out of the dance hall. As celestial courtesans, apsaras were known to inspire and arouse the mind to unusual thought and extraordinary creativity, the muse for many a poet, artist and sculptor. Yet lethal to whoever desired them. For that one whimsical, exquisite embrace, men, asuras, rishis and even the devas had flung their hopes into the rushing torrent of desire and battled it out to possess them. King Pururav did for Urvashi, King Kushnabh for Gritachi, Rishis Vibandak and Bharadwaj all had eventually surrendered to the stark sensuousness of their naked limb, destined to fall from their glorious ideal. The apsara was irresistible, the delight of life, the heady attraction of sensuous beauty, the mystic and the romantic. As was she.

As Menaka strolled down the columned corridor, she passed the royal court of Indralok—the intricately designed Sudharma Hall. If in the palace of the deva of Moon, Chandra, lived kind people without any woe or sorrow, in Surya's, the deva of Sun, golden palace resided those who kept their vows. But this was the most beautiful wing in Indra's palace, host to a world of heroes and scholars where often the shining hero killed in battlefield arrived, to be flocked by the apsaras who vied for his undivided attention. And unlike in the Puskharmalini Hall, in which Indra used to host the holy seers and ardha-deva, this was home to fun and feasting, with drunk devas and gandharvas sprawled on soft couches, their arms wrapped around smiling apsaras efficiently refilling their empty goblets, while some gyrated to their dance of seduction. In moral contrast, the stars and the Milky Way was the heavenly home for the rishis, saints and seers who lived and died on Earth, spiritually spruced. They never stepped into the wanton flamboyance of Indralok.

Heaven had its counterpart—the seven-tiered Patallok of suffering—and the mere thought of it made Menaka shudder delicately. Heaven was also seven-storied, the hierarchy defined by status and opulence. Indisputably, Indra's was the most fabulous, perched on the highest, whitest cloud. But this was not the seventh heaven that was Vaikuntha, Lord Vishnu's abode with Lord Shiva's Kailash and Lord Brahma's Satyalok. But how Indralok glittered! It was not just the throne of King Indra that flashed a fire of gold and gems. Every marbled column here sparkled with them, encrusted, to be touched and caressed lovingly. But they ceased to fascinate Menaka, herself cloaked in a shimmer of them. *Usualness spawns ennui,* she shrugged, *when you see, feel and wear them every day, novelty leads to boredom.* Beauty was everywhere here. She saw it, but barely registered it. Even the universal handsomeness of the devas and gandharvas. Everything here was beautiful, young and everlasting. She was surrounded by male beauty but attracted by none. Like the flashing jewels, they glittered, were admired but had ceased to attract her. But for one—her Vasu. She was to meet him now. She quickened her pace as she entered her palace, up the broad marbled porch and in her ascending steps, there was a joyous spring.

'It's only when you see ugliness, will you recognise beauty, my dear,' breathed Vasu in her ear, later, as they lay entwined in her bed chamber, hidden from prying eyes. 'And one day you will get to realise that. You have been indulged too long, too much with beauty to know ugliness. You are blessed!'

'I know,' she smirked. 'And valuing those blessings rests on us and the person we are. I take pleasure in your beauty, what more do I want? Or what more do you want?' drawled Menaka and turned around to kiss him full on his wide, smiling lips, her invading tongue wiping the grin off his handsome face, her fingers trailing lightly all over his smooth, muscled back. 'I know how to appreciate beauty,' she whispered and pushed him away slightly, to allow herself to look blatantly at him, her roaming eyes travelling over the entire length of his lean, sculpted frame.

Vishwavasu, the vigourously sensual king of the gandharvas, was said to be the most handsome of all, more than even Indra or Kama, the deva of love. He was fair, with thick, curling gold-tinted brown hair and light brows blending beautifully with his amber eyes, his straight, thin nose rising elegantly over full, sensuous lips. It was a perfectly proportioned face, with a wide, clear, un-furrowed forehead, high cheek bones and a smooth, strong jawline. *No imperfections here*, Menaka gazed indolently. *He was by every instinct suave and polished.*

Vishwavasu allowed Menaka to strip him with her eyes. He was used to her brazen appraisal; she did it to tease him. But there was neither arrogance nor vanity when he gazed back at her, his eyes tender. But they rapidly darkened to a molten gold as Menaka pushed him on his back, her roving eyes replaced by her feathery fingers and moist, marauding lips, which played a delicious game on his body.

'My great musician, philosopher and scholar, you may be a good student of Rishi Yagnavalkya, but keep aside your theologies when you are with me,' she whispered, enjoying watching his eyes clouding with rising passion, his breath coming in short, quick gasps. 'I do acknowledge beauty when I see it, uhm...here,' she gurgled, tracing one slim finger along his face, down his neck, across his chest and flat, clenched stomach and moving lower to his thighs. He trembled.

'...here and here...' she said huskily, her flicking tongue etching a damp outline over his full, exquisitely shaped lips, his jutting chin, sliding down his sinewy, strong neck, to the wildly beating pulse at the base of his throat. She paused deliberately, softly kissing the pulsating beat in the small hollow, feeling his pounding heart under her. She tasted his smooth, broad shoulders, her nails digging deep into his taut back. '...and here!' she murmured as his muscles tightened in desire. 'I do love beauty!'

Her searching lips followed the hot trail left behind by her flirting fingers, scorching his skin, and making his body writhe with a burning, inflammable passion. Through half-lidded, lust-laden eyes, he saw her, felt her moving, sensuously slithering further down, her lovely face flushed, her mouth still smiling wickedly, her hair fanning out in glorious abandon. He groaned, moving in slow, quickening rhythm. This was heaven...

'O God!' he exploded thickly, grabbing her hair and pulling her up to his dry, throbbing lips. She smelled of him, tasted of him.

'Not God, it's me. Menaka,' she smiled calmly. '...worshipping beauty. Pleased?'

'Please!!' he whispered back.

She gave a small laugh, and proceeded to oblige him all over again. Each time she made Vasu realise in rapturous wonderment what it was to be made love to by her. And why all the devas were jealous of him, particularly Indra.

Vishwavasu was also known as Devagandharva, but for Menaka he was Vasu, her lover, her husband. It was an odd word in Swarg. Apsaras did not marry, but Menaka had. They did not love, but Menaka did. She loved Vasu. And she had dared to marry him.

Not that gandharvas wished to marry or commit to a permanent relationship, though they had a marriage ritual named after them. The gandharva marriage was the sole witness to lovers performing a private, secret wedding of love and vows, without the blessings or consent of others. But Vasu had wished, wanted and wooed Menaka unlike the other gandharvas, who never allowed themselves to get besotted. They were too vain and self-loving. Vasu loved Menaka with a rare and strange possessiveness. Everything was shared in Heaven; you could not possess anything in this land of plenty. You could have everything, but own nothing.

Indra had not taken too kindly to their news, secreted to him at a judicious moment by Rambha, the queen of apsaras. Stroked by her malicious tongue, Indra had, in conformity with her motive and expectation, been sufficiently furious.

'This is Indralok, there are gandharvas and apsaras who love and make love but never marry!' seethed Indra, looking at Menaka with rising disbelief. 'Both of you are available to anyone who have the strength to claim you—you have been made beautiful, young and immortal—but for the pleasure of everyone. Not just yours! There is nothing like private marital bliss here, it doesn't exist! How dare you break the rules!' he continued vehemently, turning furiously on Vasu.

Vasu looked at him equably, as handsome as ever but there was a sheen of happiness on his face that made him radiant. Indra felt a stab of jealousy or was it plain, unadulterated rage? Vasu had been his best friend, his closest companion, and he had betrayed him, never once uttering his secret. Indra now regarded him as a wary foe, never to be trusted. The two now faced each other, serious with open hostility.

'You, Vishwavasu, should have known better! You were, after all, part of our plot to separate Urvashi from her love, that mortal King Pururav,' he paused, glaring at Vasu. Both controlled their anger, and Menaka was surprised and alarmed it was already so strong. 'You know that in this heaven only erotic love can flourish and not personal romances! Yet you acted presumptuously and for that I pronounce...'

'No, please, forgive us. I am as guilty as him!' Menaka intervened swiftly, knowing Indra's wrath that would pour down on Vasu alone, but he could never gather the strength to hurt her. Would Vasu be expelled from Indralok? But Menaka came to a quick, shrewd conclusion—Indra could not oust Vasu alone, he would have to throw her out as well. Indra would dread even to contemplate such a thought. He would have to punish them both or spare them. If they were guilty of the same crime, they would have to share a common punishment.

Menaka had been prepared to face Indra's ire, gathering that single deadly arsenal. Her lethal charm was her defence and her weapon that she had famously employed to beguile so many men before. It was Indra's turn this time. But she didn't have to do much. One long, imploring look from Menaka had melted Indra down instantly, dissipating his jealous anger.

'I am to blame for this. I have violated the moral principle of my duty as an apsara,' she started slowly, gazing straight and sufficiently pleadingly at Indra's incensed face, arresting his anger. Her voice was soft and sweet. Menaka was a fine singer as well and knew how to modulate her voice, with the right throes and pathos. It was filled with the right dose of remorse and self-acceptance.

'I broke the boundaries set up by this world and favoured one man over others. I did it. I seduced him, because I wanted him!' she bit her lip, her eyes still riveted on Indra. 'I fell in love, o king of the devas, I couldn't help myself and I saw to it that

Vishwavasu, your king of the gandharvas, was as besotted with me—not just to have him, but to own him, to keep him forever. For that, I committed the next unthinkable crime—I married him! I had to. It was like a fever, burning me, consuming me and I wanted to live in this fire forever,' she cried, raising her voice just enough to show her desperation, her helplessness.

Indra looked on impassively, but his eyes glittered with jealousy.

'Our passion was quenched but never died and to save ourselves, we got married!' she continued. 'Again, it was my decision, but I did it for you, for the devas, for Amravati...'

Indra looked puzzled and Menaka saw her chance to swiftly explain. 'How could I make others happy if I was miserable? And so I married Vishwavasu so that I could stay happy, and keep all of us happy too. My desires should not shame me—and I desired Vasu enough to marry him, to have him for myself,' she saw Indra purse his lips. 'Fortunately I chose someone from our world as my mate, not a mortal, not a rishi, not a deva. I did not over-step my position and I chose a gandharva. Someone who could also understand the restrictions laid on an apsara but large-hearted enough to share his wife with others and serve you, my lord,' she said sapiently, her voice still beseeching. 'By marrying Vasu, I shall not shirk from my duties, I promise. I shall carry on what is expected from an apsara. I am a celestial woman and our desires are vast!' she added, with a clever flourish.

Menaka was quick to see that Indra's anger had cooled down as quickly as he had flared up. He could never resist a good story involving lust; he had done it often enough himself.

Indra allowed her words to convince him; they were like drops of cool water on the leaping flames of possessive jealousy. Menaka was not just one of the apsaras, a courtesan in his celestial court whom he loved to watch. With each sensuous sway, sinuous movement and her smouldering glance, she could dance away his blues. She intoxicated him with her mere presence. Indra knew he wanted her constantly by his side, he couldn't take his eyes off her, he could not survive without her. She was like a whiff of life, setting his blood on fire.

Indra grudgingly smiled. He had forgiven them, Menaka concluded with silent glee, chewing nervously at her lower lip. She smiled back ingratiatingly, her charmingly coiffured head tilted gracefully, her face glowing with undisguised relief, rushed to Indra and grabbed his hand gratefully. She had him now. He could never resist her touch. Thanking him again profusely, with limpid eyes and a lilting laugh, she retraced her steps and joined Vasu, her hand slipping into his. She wanted to laugh aloud victoriously, but she reined it in with a gracious smile. She had won her argument.

Rambha, who had witnessed the entire charade, looked on disbelievingly, her darkly kohled eyes smouldering, the corners of her full pout, momentarily turned down. Her displeasure was evident as was her sultry gorgeousness—dark maned and dark-eyed, she was tall, full-bosomed with vigorous, pleasing curves which she flaunted defiantly. Nor could any man stare away from the delicious expanse of her deep, dark-honeyed cleavage. But she was always cleverly well covered, the sheer, flimsy angavastra revealing more than it hid, to allow more than a generous peek. And she took vain care of herself. Her heavily-kohled and well-traced lipstick spoke as much as the confidence with which she moved, swaying her flaring hips to an erotic roll.

Indra was a fool, but only where Menaka mattered, she fumed silently. *He thought Menaka had allowed him to have an established and recognised right over her. She blatantly used him and he could not see through her deception.* Rambha forced a smile, temporarily defeated but making a genuine effort of jovial tolerance. She had tried to open Indra's smitten eyes, hoping he would throw the lovers out in a bout of violent jealousy, but Menaka had seduced him with convincing words instead. That was where she always won. Menaka did not need to use her luscious body to allure, her charm and wit were powerful weapons of enticement. She had wooed and won yet again. Rambha swore savagely and vowed, *one day I will throw my most beautiful rival out of heaven.* She threw Vasu a baleful glare.

Vasu witnessed that glance, missing nothing and did not hesitate to voice his apprehension once Menaka and he were alone.

'Rambha will never give up scheming against you, Menaka. I guess you gathered that it was she who snitched about us to Indra,' he commented, as they lay sprawled naked and spent, in the soft grass, under the cool shade of the profusely fragrant jasmine tree in her garden. 'You ought, we ought, to be more careful.'

Menaka shrugged. 'Careful? Why? Thankfully, it's out in the open and we don't need to be discreet anymore,' she moved closer, wrapping her arm around his waist.

She glanced up at him. He seemed worried and Vasu was a man of calm disposition. But he was tense today, she could feel it as she lay close to him. She could feel his thigh muscles tense and quiver, his hands closed in a tight fist and his clenched jaw.

'She cannot forgive me for having you. Simple,' drawled Menaka carelessly, hoping to reassure him. 'As the queen of the apsaras, she thought it was her right not to lose you to a lesser apsara like me! She got Nalakuber instead, and Tumburu. She is favoured by both.'

Vasu was not convinced. 'She already has the best!' he protested, grabbing her wandering fingers splayed over his chest. 'Tumburu is a maestro amongst the gandharvas with the best voice in heaven, which even Narada is said to be jealous of! And Nalakuber is the son of Kuber, the deva of wealth.'

'But she doesn't have you,' said Menaka. 'Or, did she? And didn't like to give you up?'

Vasu smiled, 'Shh, never discuss past amours with the present one...' placing his finger on her lips.

'So, you did!" she exclaimed, biting hard on her lip, scorched by a sudden flame of jealousy.

'Menaka, you well know that apsaras and gandharvas have no norms to flout. We can move from one to another,' he paused, holding her chin. 'But then there are those rare occasions that one becomes a favoured lover, a friend, a consort...' he said lightly, his thumb caressing possessively over her full lips, forcing them to part as she tasted it, sucking softly. '...like you are for me.'

'For now?' she teased, gently nipping his probing thumb.

Menaka put it as a question, but suddenly she realised it was more a statement of the status of their relationship. Nothing in Heaven was permanent, nothing to be possessed, to be called your own. It was yours till it savoured—be it power, love or lust.

Vasu smiled lazily, quite unfazed by the jealousy lacing Menaka's voice, 'You have your share of admirers too, witch,' he whispered, nuzzling her ear. 'And I am not talking about just Indra,' he said.

Menaka frowned, pulling at her lip, as she wondered whom he was referring to.

'Ohhh, you mean Uranyu,' she said smugly. 'I am not reluctant to admit that we were once together, but we drifted apart...' she shrugged indifferently.

'He hasn't!' retorted Vasu. 'He's still smitten by you, following you with his sad, waiting eyes. He makes me feel terrible!'

'It's a choice I made,' she laughed, almost callously, pulling up her loose mane and coiling it dexterously in a neat knot. He always found it strangely arousing, the way she swept up her hair to expose her smoothly rounded shoulders, her bare back and her long, slender nape. 'Just like you had a choice—you once chose Rambha over me, I have realised that now, but too late. We always have choices—how we select them, make us.'

'Or unmake us,' sighed Vasu, kissing her exposed nape, his hand slowly snaking down to cup the rising soft swell of her full breasts.

He turned towards her, leaning forward so that she was confronted with his warm smooth arms, lightly covered with golden hair, his strong neck and his beautiful face. He still appeared uneasy. He was not anxious about the other gandharva's unrequited love for his wife. Rambha was the more dangerous rival. He could not forget the venomous look she had reserved for Menaka.

'But, be careful, Menaka. It's more than just about me or her sexual conquests,' he warned, shaking his handsome head slowly, a frown pleating his wide forehead. 'It is about her jealous ego, which not me but you have hurt! She resents you—your beauty, your charm, your popularity—and your proximity to Indra. She is your queen, but she has no control over you—the strings are held by Indra whose lavish patronage and obvious fondness for you are legendary. Clearly, you are his favourite and he makes no pretences about it. He is obsessed about you, altogether blinded, Menaka. I saw him today—he's putty in your hands!' he said as he trailed his lips along the soft curve of her neck. 'He can't bear to lose sight of you even for a moment. That's why he'll never let you go, whatever you do! And you know well that, don't you, my Menaka?' he murmured savagely, his fingers gripping her inner thigh, deliciously silky. 'They say Indra sprang a thousand eyes so that he can keep looking at you wherever you go!'

'Is he watching me now?' she smirked, rolling away from him in the grass, to sit up and peer around. Vasu smiled as she sat up gracefully and looked around her, stretching her slim arms, uninhibitedly thrusting out her full, firm breasts, the curve of her bare back forming a supple arc.

'He might be. I am sure he has his spies,' grinned Vasu, his eyes drinking in the stark beauty in front of him. But his eyes were serious. 'You are his weakness and that makes you so powerful,' he reminded her. 'Menaka, you are just not the most beautiful apsara, you are the most powerful too. And that is what Rambha is scared of. Do you realize that?'

'Power is only potent when you use it,' she retorted, slipping languorously on top of him, soaking in the sensation of his bare skin against the entire length of her body. 'And I am not interested in employing it in anyway or on anyone.'

'You don't? You did it superbly with Indra today and you are using it on me right now...' chuckled Vasu, closing his arms protectively over her, resting at her waist. 'And you full well know you can twist your hold on Indra, always.'

'It's my way of managing him—he's such an egotist with hardly any moral courage!' she said dismissively, looking down into his worried eyes. 'His ego needs to be watered consistently.'

A sudden thought struck him and Vasu's smile slipped a little. 'Heaven forbid the day if he ever gets disenchanted with you! That would be your last day in Heaven. Our last day in Heaven,' he corrected, his head thrown back, his thick hair tousled and his forehead marred with frown lines. He looked gorgeous, but she wanted to wipe that anxious frown from his face.

Menaka shook her head, her face close to his. 'It's not just some silly infatuation on his part; Indra needs me, he will never throw me out,' she remarked with casual entitlement, but her lips were frozen in a tight smile. 'Let's not waste our energy thinking of them—there's nothing as exhilarating as making love under an open sky!' she sighed, bending her face down to kiss him slowly, teasing his lips. 'Don't stress, darling, that day will never come, I assure you!'

Vasu hoped so, fervently. But a small fear stayed within him.

Kaushik sighed contently. Everything was as he had hoped them to be. His kingdom Kanyakubja was expanding, he had won all his wars, subjugated his enemies and his subjects were happy and his empire was prospering every day. He was his father's son and his forefathers as well—the great kings, Kush and his son Kushnabh, the famous rajarishi. He had to better the royal legacy they had bestowed on him. Good was a mediocre word, he disparaged derisively. To outmatch his ancestors had been a fierce, devouring ambition consuming him all through his growing years. It was not easy being the son of King Gadhi; his father had been a wise king, as great as he was righteous. Kaushik had inherited that throne but he would have to do more, colossally more.

Kaushik stirred restlessly.

'What's the matter?' his wife Hemavati asked patiently. She was used to her husband's changing, sharply varying moods. He was temperamental, often lapsing into moody silences or uneasy restlessness. She cast him a long look. He was deep in thought, his swarthy face marred by a deepening scowl. Just a few moments earlier, he had seemed happy, smiling all though the morning. She looked at him again. He was attractive but not good looking. He could not boast of the smooth, good looks of the devas but it was his very ruggedness that made him so magnetic. He was tall, looming under everyone, his piercing, small, tawny-speckled eyes always alert over eyebrows thick and shabby. It was his strong and hooked nose that gave him a certain character, lending him an air of relentless ruthlessness. Above his deeply cleft chin, his lips, now pursed in silent contemplation, were full and generous and they smiled readily, dimpling engagingly each time he did so. That and his husky voice were what made him so hugely popular—both with the subjects and his queens, Hemavati observed affectionately. His wide, dimpled smile was disarming, capable of wooing anyone, allaying the strongest hostility. It was what made him an extremely likeable man, his bouts of temper and arrogance notwithstanding. His hard, craggy face appeared obstinate, almost sullen, when he was unsmiling, like he was now. His whole, solid, tall frame, with his head jutting forward aggressively, his square jaw clenched, his tawny-brown eyes unblinking, carried an appearance of remorseless ferocity.

'What is the matter?' she asked again. 'You have just returned after winning a war, so what's troubling you so much, so soon?'

'I need to start for another battle,' replied Kaushik, after a long pause. He had been wondering if he should divulge his war plans so soon to his queen. He knew she would get upset, she always did, which made him impatient. She had married a king after all. *The king of all kings*, Kaushik smirked, correcting himself. *An emperor.*

Hemavati's smile slipped from her serene face. 'Not again,' she uttered before she could stop herself, knowing fully well it would annoy her husband. She cursed herself silently, knowing that she should learn to deal with him better. *Like his other queens Renu and Sheela did*, she thought sourly. *Either they are wiser or I am more possessive.*

'My father thrust upon me a certain responsibility,' said

Kaushik shortly. 'I have to go beyond that—I have to make his kingdom bigger and stronger than what was given to me.'

Hemavati shook her head. 'You were a king but now you wish to be a monarch,' she argued. 'You want to rule all. But when will these conquests end? And for what, for whom? For our son? Or just to slake your ambition?' she shot back, the angry disappointment evident in her voice.

'What sort of a queen are you, who does not want her husband to be the mightiest of all?' Kaushik looked annoyed now.

'A disgruntled queen!' she retorted. 'I would rather be the only queen of a humble king than be one of the many queens of a grand ruler!'

Kaushik looked at her in disbelief. 'What are you complaining about now? That I don't love you because of my other wives? Marriages, you should know by now, my dearest Hema, are essentially political alliances and...'

'...and that you married them so that you can have prized trophies. Yes, but it does take away my right as your wife. I have to share you with them!' she said.

'I can handle anything, but a jealous wife!' he exclaimed exasperatedly. 'Here I am thinking of how to plan another campaign, and you, my dear, are crying over your marital rights! You are my chief queen, what else do you want?'

'You,' she cried. 'You could get killed in those bloody wars you so love! But I am crying not for me,' she said, her temper suddenly losing its steam, as she was flooded by a new wave of anxiety. 'I am arguing for us. For you. Me. Our children. Our family. Give us some of your time!' she said, pleading. 'I don't want to lose you!'

Kaushik was quick to notice her change of emotion. He had hurt her, again. Her unhappiness made him feel more restless, less guilty. He could not change himself. Nor could he make her change her outlook. He glanced at her. She was an attractive woman, tall, honey-toned, elegantly regal with her dark, sombre eyes and straight long hair, which she never allowed to tumble loose. *It could have softened her chiselled features considerably*, he thought. He liked her immensely, her frank, almost outspoken, views, her smooth graciousness, but it was an innate respect which dominated his feelings for her. Not love, as she often complained. Kaushik felt impatient, he had no time or the tendency for love. It was a draining emotion unlike lust. War and women, he smiled indulgently, was what he fought and sought for.

'We have everything—wealth, power, fame, family and most importantly the love and respect of our people,' said Hemavati, quietly. 'What more do you yearn for? Whom are you competing with? Yourself? You know you are the best. You have far surpassed your father and your grandfather,' she added astutely, knowing well his consuming desire. 'You are a just, kind, caring king. You have distinguished yourself as the mightiest warrior, so accomplished in the art of warfare that no one dares to challenge you. You are brave, fearing none, neither enemy nor the eternal. You are unvanquishable. So what, Kaushik, do you achieve in challenging kings and provoking war? What is this pathological urge to hanker for higher success each time?'

Kaushik's lips thinned in a displeased, stubborn line, his eyes scanning the view outside, from his palace verandah. His kingdom was much farther away than the distant horizon. And it would not be boastful prevarication if he claimed that he had given his people everything. His was a prosperous kingdom. Like the heavenly Amravati, it was the land of plenty. Yet he wanted more—solely to give his people more. It was not just about acquisition. Attaining gave a brief flush of power, but giving lent him a greater sense of controlling influence. He wanted to be known as a king by virtue of the people's support. Not just by the kingdoms he subjugated. *Hemavati would never understand this*, he realised, with a slight shake of his head.

Feeling a familiar quiver of excitement run through him at the scent of war, Kaushik knew what he must do. He had to simply goad his design into deed. He would send orders to his Commander-in-Chief to meet him in half an hour to discuss the coming military blitzkrieg he intended to initiate.

Hemavati almost read all his thoughts aloud. Kaushik was

again leaving for war—his mind seemed to be made. Would he return safely to her?

'Is it your insatiable greed for power?' she persisted softly. 'What more do you want to conquer?'

'I was born a king,' he said quietly. 'But as an emperor, I want to rule the world. And I shall have it.'

Trouble in Paradise

Amravati was the everlasting realm of endless joy, conveying the idea of an eternal city and it held good to its promise, where none residing here would ever come to pass. Like this city, Menaka knew she had everything—beauty, youth, immortality, love and a strange hold over men. Yet there was a strange hollowness in her contentment. Or was she suffering from the problem of plenty. Maybe she had too much of everything? Menaka could vaguely fathom, nor could she decide, leaving her restless, which was quick to show in her dance movements that morning.

Kama who was discussing some new steps, was quick to discern the change in her. 'Why are you so distracted?' he asked sharply. 'You don't seem focussed these days!'

Menaka bit her lip at his open reprimand.

He looked visibly annoyed, his usually good-humoured face marred by a frown. Menaka rarely made a mistake; she was a quick study, absorbing each word, each gesture and each step he taught her. 'Making love was not a mere expression of sexual abandonment,' he dismissed derisively. 'It was creativity—creation and expression. And an evolved craft, a skill, an artistry perfected by practice and patience.' And Menaka had both, power and prowess.

'Submerge your personality, take on a new one when you dance and you lead the man to the final act, but not before building up that sexual tension first through each move, each gesture. There is no touch yet. Excite him with a look, your body language—dance is the expression for that language!' he was saying. 'Be sexual—master that sexual escalation! No words, it's a physical game—raw and fluid! Be sinuous, sensual, sensuous, shameless!'

Menaka sighed, feeling suddenly drained. As the deva of Love and Lust, a more apt definition for him, as Menaka thought dryly, Kama with the gandharva Tumburu and Rishi Muni, taught the apsaras to master the art of dancing as a craft of seduction. They were the dancing nymphs, the heavenly courtesans trained to be proficient in the sixty five-odd ways of making love.

'Your dance has to be tantalizing!' shouted Tumburu impatiently. 'You are one of the twenty six apsaras hand-picked by me and Kama to grace Indra's court. Each one of you represents a performing art. Remember dance is sensuality and seduction blended subtly. And it's not just about showing flesh and flaunting your body only—that anyone can do. You are artists, you are courtesans skilled to make certain, special men happy, to bewitch the strongest, to weaken the toughest—they can be mortal man, asura, deva or rishi!' he hollered, waving his arms to quicken the tempo. 'Men have always been susceptible to a woman's beauty: it's their weakness and to hide it, some get aggressive. Sexual aggression arises out of this male vulnerability to female sexual power. They are both fascinated and frightened of it. It is often sought by the men through degradation of women to make up for their lack of this sexual power. Be warned, o apsaras, for they think you to be powerful and tempting, yet weak when it comes to sexual aggression. You must avoid violence, know how to tame it, yet sustain the desire, inflaming the lust but controlling the fire. This is how...'

Menaka could barely listen to her guru's words. She felt ill, another odd and a rare experience in this land of the immortals. There was no death and disease here, but then why did she feel so physically unwell. Her legs were cramping badly, her back ached and her full breasts felt painfully tender. And it was not because of their torrid lovemaking that morning. A flashing image of them together quickly uncoiled—Vasu's lips moving hotly over her bare flesh, touching her, drawing out her very being with his exquisite mouth, making her weak and wet with mad desire. She shut her eyes as she was feeling dizzy again. And it was not because of the sequential spins of the dance. She staggered and Kama quickly rushed to her side, helping her sit down in the nearest chair.

'There is something wrong with you!' he said anxiously observing her pale, damp face.

'Give her time to get back her breath,' said his wife Rati. 'Open the windows to let in some fresh air, and she'll be fine soon. You continue while I sit by her side,' said the devi of desire, giving her perplexed husband an assuring smile.

Menaka took in some long breaths, feeling the queasiness evaporate slowly. She looked at Rati gratefully.

'Thanks so much but I am being silly,' she laughed shortly. 'I need to continue practising my footwork,' She got up quickly but another spell of giddiness forced her to sit down again. She felt uneasy, almost tasting the bile in her mouth, her throat constricting violently.

'Just lie down here,' said Rati sharply, pointing to the settee. 'And don't move for a while. Try to gather your wits and strength. Rest.'

Menaka obeyed meekly and settled down in the settee. 'What is wrong with me?' she moaned with a flash of annoyance as another wave of nausea swamped her.

Rati gave her a long, hard look. She was her tutor, teaching her new tricks of the love game, particularly the versatile sexual positions the art of love making demanded. Menaka was a quick, innovative learner, adding her bit and stamping it with her distinct individuality. No wonder, she was the most coveted apsara with the devas, and not purely for her exceptional dancing skills alone. *Vasu would know better*, she smirked. Glancing at Menaka's wan face, she instinctively knew what was wrong with her. Menaka seemed unwell for almost a fortnight now and that was unusual. No one fell ill in heaven. But Rati was not sure if she could tell her; if she should. But it would be better if she heard it from her, and not Dhanvantari, the celestial doctor. He would promptly inform Indra and all hell would break loose in heaven. It would be safer for Menaka if he came to know through her, and not from some third person. But for now, Menaka needed to be enlightened of her state herself.

She saw Menaka cough up another dry retch.

'I think you might be pregnant, Menaka,' said Rati, gently touching the listless figure, huddled in the settee.

There was such a long pause, Rati wondered if Menaka had heard or if she had fallen asleep in fatigue. But Menaka was staring at her, with her pale lips and her lustrous eyes looking suddenly bleak. She tried to speak, but she felt once again the bitter aftertaste of bile in her mouth. The truth tasted more bitter.

'Pregnant?' she repeated hoarsely, pulling her lip with clenched teeth. 'But apsaras don't get pregnant!' she shook her head in bewilderment.

'They can, and they do,' Rati corrected her. 'Urvashi has had Rishyaringa from Rishi Vibhandak and nine sons from King Pururav and Gritachi, and had daughters from King Kushnabh...'

'But they were conceived to lure them!' refuted Menaka hotly, the colossal weight of her new reality crushing her.

'No, apsaras can never procreate from lust. They have to be in love. Like you are,' said Rati. 'Apsaras are nymphs of lust and desire, they cannot beget without love. But then, neither do they know what love is. They are not supposed to fall in love. But you did, Menaka,' Rati reminded her softly.

At her words, Menaka, even as she floundered in despairing confusion, smiled wanly in swift agreement.

'Yes, see this is the wonder called love. Not lust,' smiled Rati. 'Lust is for the now. Love, I'm afraid, is more lasting, it lingers long and sure.'

It was not a question, it was her observation. Rati had seen Menaka in the throes of lovemaking—fierce, frantic and fully in control, devouring her man in deliberated desire. She had been taught by her after all. But when love touched Menaka, she unwittingly, blindly thought not with her sharp mind but her lost heart. That was not what apsaras were supposed to do. For, they had no heart—apsaras were trained to be heartless. They were meant for quick pleasures—like lust, power and wealth—giving instant, momentary joy, but fickle and unstable, slipping away from grasp. They could not be faithful; they had faith only in themselves and their consummate skills. They did not love; they loved themselves more. They followed neither their hearts nor heads; their whim leads them. They were taught to be selfish and pitiless: they cared for their selves. But Menaka had dared to stake her heart, wager her chances, sure she would she win. But now...

'Am I to suffer for this transgression?' whispered Menaka, her voice dry, her face waning like a withering flower.

'Love is punishing,' sighed Rati.

And I shall be punished, Menaka thought dully, pulling long at her lower lip. She struggled with rising emotions but panic seemed to overwhelm all reason. She had to inform Vasu. And Indra would have to be told too. She gave an involuntary shudder as she realised that the time for reckoning had come.

Kaushik stared at his army spread far across the hilly terrain. They had won the war. There were smiles, shouts and jubilation, but Kaushik was a worried king. He knew the victuals were fast depleting and he had no wish to return home with a hungry army. There would be pillage. Kaushik shuddered; he hated plunder and unnecessary violence. His sharp eye caught a comforting sight at the far end of the flowing river. Kaushik narrowed his eyes. It appeared to be an ashram with tall, thatched huts neatly lined and visible even from a distance. He gave a sigh of relief. Possibly he could ask for some food grains. He glanced again at his army—dusty and tired. Kaushik decided he would personally visit the ashram.

As he rode across the valley, through the green fields towards the ashram, Kaushik could feel the warm breeze and the descending calm. *It must be the ashram*, he smiled as he spurred his horse into a faster galloping pace. The ashram was as neat as he had observed from the hills. And well populated with the rishi's disciples.

'Whose ashram is this?' he asked a young man.

The young man looked at him disbelievingly. 'Rishi Vasishth's,' he stated stiffly. 'Are you a stranger in this land?'

'Yes and I would like to pay my homage to the great rishi,' replied Kaushik, flashing his disarming smile, softening the peeved man immediately.

'Follow me, o king,' said the young man pointedly, guessing correctly Kaushik's royal identity. 'Guru might be busy with his prayers, but he shall definitely see you. For all his greatness, he is the most humble man.'

Kaushik had heard of Rishi Vasishth. Who had not? He was one of the Saptarishis—the seven of the holiest rishis. The patriarch of the Vedas and the Upanishads, he was famously known as the Brahmarishi not solely because he was the manasputra—the adopted son-disciple of Lord Brahma—but for his astute knowledge and selfless penance.

He might be a mighty king but Kaushik was filled with a strange diffidence, as he was about to meet the great rishi. He had several of them at his royal court as well, and they accorded him the respect due to a king. They listened to him, but now, in this humble ashram, he would be seeking help to save his starving army. It was an unequal equation and it was not a very good feeling. Kaushik was feeling distinctly uncomfortable as he approached the Brahmarishi.

Rishi Vasishth came out almost immediately. He was tall and thin, an old man, yet sprightly and brisk, his long strides belying his age. As he approached close, Kaushik got to see him more clearly. His face was lined, but his skin was translucent and fresh, glowing with a strange aura which was reflected in his grey, gentle eyes as well. His head was a crown of silver hair, as sparkling white as his long, flowing beard. His hands were folded in respectful salutation.

'Greetings, King Kaushik! Welcome to my humble abode,' he smiled through his luxuriant beard. 'Were you passing by and decided to rest, or is it that you seek my blessings, good king?' he added with a twinkle in his grey eyes.

Kaushik liked the elderly rishi instantly. His student had surmised correctly, Vasishth, the greatest of all seers was a humble man—with a sense of humour, Kaushik acknowledged with a wide smile of his own.

He returned the greetings and bowed low to the guru. 'I seek both sir—your blessings and some rest!' he said, in his deep tenor. 'But it's not just for myself...' he paused, again hesitant to ask for help.

'Yes, good king?' pressed Vasishth kindly. 'I shall give you all the help I can.'

Kaushik decided his ego was smaller than the enormity of the situation. 'I come for food,' he said simply. 'Not for me but for my starving army waiting in the valley below. If you could kindly give us some provisions or food grains that could sustain my men for a while?'

His words came out in a quick rush as if to let go of them swiftly. He had made a sincere plea; his first and it was not as difficult as he thought it would be.

Vasishth's initial look of surprise gave way to a growing admiration. 'O king, if you had asked for help for yourself, it would have been selfish. But you first saw to the needs of your people, your men, your army. And the fact that you personally came here, speaks highly of your generosity. Serving your people and not your self-interest is your priority. That is the sign of a great king.'

Kaushik shook his head. 'I did nothing extraordinary. I have to look after my people,' he replied solemnly. 'It is a worried man who has come to your ashram, not a king.'

'There is no cause for further worry, good king. Come, call in your troops! Your army shall be well fed!' replied the old man heartily.

It was Kaushik's turn to look surprise. 'Feed an entire army?'

he exclaimed in astonishment. 'I came to ask for a few sacks of grains to sustain through the day but...'

'But do not fret, o king, you and your army can rest and eat for however many days you want,' assured Vasishth. 'I have enough food—yes, enough to serve your army! Please bring them. My ashram shall play the good host.'

And an hour later, Kaushik was forced to believe what the rishi had assured him of. He did feed his army, thousands of his grateful men to a venerable feast, hosted personally by the rishi's wife, Arundhati, who saw to it that each and every soldier had had a full meal. Kaushik was dumbfounded and perplexed. How had this man managed this extraordinary feat? Kaushik inspected the ashram again. It was small and neat, with a tiny cookhouse. Yet, within a matter of a short time, the old man had been able to serve a full-fledged meal to his starving men. He had not touched a morsel himself though.

'Why are you not eating?' asked Vasishth, breaking into his bemused thoughts.

'I shall have with you, sir,' replied Kaushik politely.

Vasishth shook his head. 'I am fasting today. You go ahead and have your food. I am afraid it won't be as rich and lavish as the feast in your palace but it will do well for a hungry man!'

'Men!' corrected Kaushik with his amiable smile. 'I cannot help being impressed how you managed to serve the troops. I should thank your wife, the revered Arundhati, for being such a considerate host. And also my apologies for all the inconvenience I caused.'

Vasishth guffawed loudly. 'No, my dear son, though I would not be what I am because of my dear Arundhati, for this, pray, I cannot give credit to her! The splendid meal served to your men, has been provided, not by my wife but by my calf Nandini,' he chuckled. 'We affectionately call her Sabala. She is the daughter of Indra's celestial cow Kamadhenu, and he gifted her to me. Like her mother, Nandini is also a wish-fulfilling cow; she provides me with everything!'

As they were talking, Vasishth led him to the fabled calf.

Kaushik stared at the fascinating creature. At first glance, she looked like any other calf: as humble and incongruous as her surroundings. But as he looked longer, he noticed the silken, glowing sheen, the soft, golden eyes shining with unusual brilliance, the aura of radiant light drawn around her, and the serenity she emanated.

'She can give anything?' Kaushik could not hide the amazement in his voice.

'Oh yes, anything! Or else how could I, the poor rishi, serve you the feast in gold dishes?' laughed Vasishth. 'Do you wish for anything? You can ask her right away and you can have it—even from Amravati!' he added with teasing glint in his old, grey eyes.

Kaushik returned the laugh heartily. 'Even Menaka?' he quizzed, his dimple deepening, his eyes half-laughing, half-mocking. And before he could contain his amusement, the beautiful nymph appeared before him. The smile died in his eyes, his laugh cut short. *Menaka, whom even the immortal devas would die a thousand deaths to be with*!

Kaushik's throat had gone dry. He was not sure if it was because of the breath-winding, smouldering beauty in front of him or the second miracle of Nandini. He blinked, expecting the ethereal apparition to vanish. But Menaka stood close, a tiny smile teasing her lips, her eyes softly alluring, widening in an innocent stare. He instinctively licked his dry lips and managed to shake his head, slowly smiling in dazed astonishment.

'I can't believe this!' he exclaimed, consternation and desire deepening in his tawny eyes. He felt an unrestrained excitement. This was madness.

Menaka sniggered. It was fatal, leaving him strangely smitten.

'I don't wish for anything, I was jesting!' he said, regaining his senses, his usually measured, sonorous tone, unsteady. He bowed politely to the waiting apsara. He heard her laugh huskily again, watching her dissipate in the cool air, thick with tension. She was gone, as quick as she had appeared. Kaushik felt a strange wrench.

He turned to the old rishi. 'We were hungry and you fed us well. And I am indebted to you for that. I don't want anything more,' he repeated evenly. He felt rash and foolish, and all he wanted to do was leave this ashram as quickly as he could.

'That's a wise king—one who doesn't wish for more!' smiled the old man gently.

↡

Menaka, gnawed at her lip as she picked up her troubled thoughts again. She touched her waist lightly, suddenly conscious of the tiny weight she carried within her. She had yet to tell Vasu.

Vasu took in the news more pleasantly than Menaka had expected. He was beatific. His eyes lit up swiftly, his smile broadening into a deep, hearty laugh of joy, exploding with enthusiasm, which Menaka could not muster. So much for motherhood.

'Imagine, Menaka, having a child...our child!' he cried, his voice quavering with wonder. 'It is ours—our love, our own. But you don't look too happy?' he asked, suddenly aware of her tight face.

'I am scared,' she answered tersely, clenching her lip between her teeth.

Vasu was quick to read her rising apprehension.

'You are worried about Indra's reaction?'

'You should be too,' said Menaka quietly.

Vasu looked at her confidently. 'You will be able to persuade him this time as well,' he assured her. 'He cannot say no to you, Menaka, you know that.'

'Vasu, can't you see what's going to happen? He may allow us to have the baby, but he won't permit us to keep it. Indralok has no place for children and connubial complications! You should know that—this is not the first child you have fathered!'

Vasu flushed. 'But it always remained with the mother, if not me.'

'Because, she was not an apsara! An apsara cannot keep her child. And I am not an exception Indra would overlook. He will be more furious because *I* did it!'

'No, he wouldn't do that!' grimaced Vasu. 'He can't be cruel to you, and an innocent baby!'

'Vasu, Indra is cruel!' she cried. 'You should have realized that by now. He wouldn't be the king of the devas but for that! Haven't you seen how unscrupulous and insecure he is?'

'Yes, but we are not talking politics here!' exclaimed Vasu.

'It would start an undesirable precedence!' said Menaka. 'He doesn't want husbands, wives, babies and families here. Just apsaras and gandharvas to make music and love!' she added, unable to hide her bitterness.

'So what do we do?' asked Vasu, gently taking her hand in his. The fingers were clenched and he could feel the tension in her closed fist.

'The pathetic part is that we can't do anything!' she said helplessly. 'We are at his mercy.'

'He might banish us...or we could both leave Amravati...' began Vasu.

'To have a life together with the baby? Where? On Earth—Prithvilok—we can never survive there!' she said violently, staring incredulously at Vasu. 'Even in my wildest hope and fancy, I cannot consider that as a solution! And do you think Indra would ever allow it? He'll never let go of either of us. He won't set us free!'

Vasu shook her shoulders. 'Then what do we do?' he demanded fiercely. 'Let go of our baby?!! What sort of a father am I who cannot protect his own child?'

Menaka nodded slowly. 'Because you are not meant to be a father. Nor me a mother. We can conceive but never foster a child. You have fathered other children, Vasu, haven't you?' she looked wistfully at Vasu. 'But were you allowed to bring up any? They were looked after by rishis or childless kings. We are but a gandharva and an apsara, destined to give pleasure to all but ourselves. And it is in such a Heaven we live.'

'Hell you mean,' he lashed out. 'And we have yet to inform Indra...' continued Vasu bleakly.

Vasu hoped he would be kinder than he thought him to be. But Menaka had no such illusions. Sadness did not exist in heaven. But it had been borne now—in her heart and Vasu's. Was her heaven turning into hell?

War and Defeat

*R*eturning to Mahodaya, his flourishing capital city, King Kaushik could not stop thinking about Nandini. And when he thought of her, his thoughts trailed back to another unattainable being—Menaka. He was filled with sudden restlessness when he thought of both. They were both impossible to possess...and he wanted them.

His minister had just delivered the news that his northern kingdom was suffering from an acute drought. Kaushik felt a cold, mounting rage possess him. Drought spelt famine. The river had dried up, the crops had failed. His people were dying with hunger. Kaushik ordered food grains to be sent there, but he knew it was a short term solution. All he could remember in his abject frustration was the feast he had at the ashram of Rishi Vasishth; and the gentle-eyed calf Nandini, who had provided those endless rounds of meals to his famished troops. And then he thought, *I could feed my dying people too.*

Kaushik made a quick decision. He would return to the ashram and ask for the rishi's help again. He needed Nandini. With that thought, his temper cooled off quickly, his mood and intention improved vastly. He immediately set forth for Vasishth's ashram with his customary small band of soldiers.

Vasishth was tending to a yagna with Arundhati and a few disciples. He was surprised to see the king. 'This is indeed unexpected! But, pray, make yourself comfortable!' said the old rishi. 'For what purpose has the busy king visited my humble ashram again?' he asked.

Kaushik had the grace to flush in embarrassment, but it was a moment of unpreparedness. He decided to speak honestly about the purpose of his visit. 'I am sorry that I have come here unannounced, but it is a matter of urgency that I had to meet you. To ask for a favour, again,' he paused.

Vasishth waited, allowing Kaushik to explain further, but he was quick to notice the changed demeanour in Kaushik. This wasn't the hungry, desperate king, requesting to feed his army, he had met last time. There was a different hunger—a wilder desperation about him.

'My kingdom in the north is reeling under a severe drought, and my people and cattle are dying from the famine,' started the king, in a deeply grim voice.

Vasishth nodded. 'Yes I hear the river has dried up, not fed by the rains for three consecutive years. But why come to me? How can I resolve this problem?' Vasishth looked slightly bewildered. 'You wish that I perform a yagna to appease Lord Indra and bring forth the rains?'

'No, we have tried...it's too late for that too,' said Kaushik, and decided to come straight to the point. 'I request you earnestly to please spare me your Nandini so that I can take her with me to the north. She can provide food and succour to my starving population; be their benefactor, a saviour,' he said fervently.

Vasishth stared at Kaushik in sheer disbelief. 'But she hasn't ever stepped out from this ashram! She cannot live without me or Arundhati...'

Arundhati nodded desperately, about to intercept but thought best to remain silent. The king did not seem to see reason, eyeing their calf, frequently and furtively.

'Then please accompany us and help those in desperate need there!' Kaushik was quick to point out, his tone impatient, sounding almost harsh.

'O king, I am too old to travel. Nor can I give you my calf

as she is a gift. You never give away a gift—it is an insult to
the patron and the gift as well,' replied the rishi quietly. 'But I
suspect there is more than what you claim to say. Is it that you
yearn the calf yourself?'

Kaushik flushed at the old man's shrewd astuteness. 'If you
can understand the urgency of the situation where thousands
of people are dying of hunger, can you not help by giving me
Nandini?'

'There is a difference between borrowing and usurping,'
countered the rishi.

Kaushik's tanned face became mottled with rising fury. 'I
am not a thief! I am ready to pay you a rich price for her,' he
retorted. 'You name the price and it'll be recompensed.'

'So, your intentions are not as honourable as they seemed,
are they?' said Vasishth scornfully. 'My Nandini is family, I cannot
sell her. Nor would I gift her to you,' he said.

Kaushik realized Vasishth was being courteous but stubborn
in his refusal. He would have to find a different argument to
tackle him.

'But I am the king of this land, sir, and everything you have
belongs to me,' he reminded him softly, his tone silky smooth
and dangerous. 'Including Nandini.'

Vasishth's face hardened perceptibly. 'I know my rights as
a citizen of your kingdom,' he said. 'I have to either leave your
land or obey you. But if you look closely, you shall notice that
my Nandini does not tread on your land as she walks, as she is
always an inch above the ground.'

Kaushik whirled around to look at the calf closely. She looked
back at him, her eyes soft and steady. She bent her knee slightly
to prove what her master claimed was true. She was an inch off
the soft hay she was supposed to be standing on.

The slow anger simmering inside Kaushik, threatened to boil
over. 'I have no time for your wise words,' he said brusquely.
'But as your king and yes, as your honourable guest, I request
you again to hand me over Nandini.'

'You have me in a moral quandary, King Kaushik, forcing

me to do something that I despise. I cannot refuse you because you are my king, my protector,' he mocked. 'And also my guest, I cannot refuse a guest either. So, I shall allow you to have the calf, if she is willing to go with you.'

Kaushik felt a thrill of jubilation. He now had Nandini!

'Get her here!' he ordered his men.

His men lead the calf to where Kaushik was waiting. She looked up at him with her big, melting, soft, brown eyes. *She is beautiful*, Kaushik thought, smiling jubilantly.

'Why are you smiling, king?' asked the rishi, smoothly. 'Are you imagining all that this calf will give you—untold wealth, land, gems and glory? You said you have everything, yet you covet her as a means to acquire more. What is that more? Heaven? The throne of Lord Indra? Immortality? The pleasures of Amravati? Menaka?' he added derisively.

Kaushik flinched, and the rishi instantly knew the king's secret desire. 'I know what you desire,' continued Vasishtha relentlessly. 'But you need to ask Nandini if she wants to go with you. Because unless she is happy and willing, she will not fulfil your wishes or desires.'

Nandini shook her head violently and retraced her steps, closer to the rishi.

'You have your answer, king!' It was the rishi's turn to flash a triumphant smile. 'She does not wish to go with you. I cannot comply with your request.'

Kaushik knew he had no further arguments to justify: the enlightened guru had defeated him with his words. So strong was his desire that he decided to take the step he might have detested otherwise.

'Never mind! She doesn't need to come with me. I can always pick her up or sweep her off her feet!' he replied laconically. Saying so, he lunged forward and pulled at the rope tied around Nandini's neck, trying to drag her by his side. Nandini pulled back strongly, digging her heels firmly in.

Vasishth was taken aback at Kaushik's blatant peremptoriness. 'King, this is asinine! You are exercising unwarranted power over her! She doesn't want to come with you,' reiterated Vasishth.

Kaushik did not bother to reply, offensively self-assured. He tugged at the rope more viciously. Nandini gave a soft whimper. She looked at both Kaushik and Vasishth pleadingly.

Arundhati made a small movement of protest. 'Please, sir, don't drag her away against her wishes. It is assault, it is disrespect!' she implored.

The passionate protest broke through the haze and the king stopped, and politely bowing his head, he said, 'I need her very urgently, kind lady. Nandini can save my kingdom.'

And he pulled at the now fiercely disinclined calf, again. Nandini gave a soft whimper.

'Stop it! You can't force your way into my home and snatch her away like a common plunderer!' said the rishi, more forcefully. 'I had supposed you to be a wise, young king looking after the welfare of the state and people!'

'That is exactly why I am doing this!' retorted Kaushik. 'I need her to feed my dying people!'

'If that was the true reason, I would have gladly lent her to you, but knowing you well now, you would have never returned her to me. That was never your intention. You want her solely for yourself, to assuage your ego, your greed!'

'I have everything! What more do I want?' sneered Kaushik.

'To possess the ultimate—a wish-fulfilling cow. It is the ownership that gives you the sense of power. She would be another of your coveted possessions you could flaunt, providing you with all the things you lust for!' he paused, meaningfully. 'King, remember she has to do it voluntarily. Will she listen to your requests?'

As if on cue, Nandini tugged harder at the rope and wrenched it from Kaushik's clasp. She fled towards the closest barn.

'Catch her quick!' Kaushik ordered his men, and they rushed after her. The initial few were unsuccessful and another motley soon joined them to catch the calf. They could not either. Soon, the remaining soldiers joined the pursuit.

'What do I see? A brave king is trying to harm a helpless

calf?' jeered the rishi. 'This is not hunting, foolish fellow, this is force! You are abusing your right as a king.'

'Spare me your words, old man,' lashed Kaushik. 'Let me handle her.'

The rishi shrugged and continued to watch the show of royal strength. Nandini gave the panting guards a hard chase. The scene would have been comical, if not for the graveness of the situation—a hundred sturdy soldiers scuttling after a nimble-footed calf. The soldiers soon started looking exhausted and each heaved a secret sigh of relief when Nandini stopped scampering around. *She must be tired too*, Kaushik thought with a smug grin. But suddenly she darted a shower of arrows on the unsuspecting soldiers. Before they could reach for their swords, the arrows pierced their heart, killing them all instantly.

Kaushik's smirk slipped, wiping the cheer and colour off his face. He stared at the innocent-looking calf in disbelief. She had just killed a hundred of his men.

He felt a searing fury, seeing the dead, limp bodies of his men. Mad with grief, he charged towards Nandini. He clenched the hilt of his sword, but he could not unsheath it—he could not kill the calf, as that would defeat the purpose. But it might intimidate her, and with furious deliberation, he withdrew his sword from the scabbard.

But the calf was prepared. She unsheathed another blast of arrows at Kaushik, ripping the brandishing sword from his hand. Kaushik was used to heavenly warfare, he had mastered it. He sent forth cannon of fireballs. *Every animal is scared of fire*, he thought sourly.

But before they reached Nandini, they were reduced to ashes. Kaushik was stunned. A mere stare from the old rishi's eyes had crumbled the fire into fine ash and glowing embers on the ground!

'Enough! Don't touch her!' said Vasishth cried out, struggling with his anger. 'She is under my protection. Not that she needs it—you saw how she just destroyed your army! Don't make the mistake of assuming all who are meek and mild are weak, o king. She stood up against your exploitation and she could have killed you too. But as you're a king, we give you the permission to walk away,' he condescended.

'She killed my men!' breathed Kaushik, through clenched teeth, his eyes crazed with mortification. 'They were obeying my orders. She could have confronted me instead! You old fool, you shall regret this day!'

Vasishth's face shone with a benign calmness. 'I spared you so that you live another day and repent your actions! But the next to turn to ashes will be you, King Kaushik, if you do not leave my ashram right now! Go! Without Nandini,' he added pointedly.

His placidity incensed Kaushik further. Kaushik felt himself go hot, then cold as a fire seem to kindle and sweep over him, raging deep inside. He was not sure if it was wrath. Or humiliation. Or grief. Or all of it. He had never felt so powerless before, so helplessly incapacitated, deprived of his strength, pride and dignity. 'One day I shall return as a person equal to you, if not better in all manners. For that, I shall strive and do everything in my power,' he vowed, looking at Vasishth and his serene-faced wife, Arundhati, who looked at her husband with troubled eyes.

The old rishi remained unaffected.

Slowly Kaushik turned away, promising himself he would return some day. To seek his revenge.

✦

Indra glared at Menaka and Vishwavasu in shocked silence, yet seething under the emotional impact of their revelation. They had confessed to their crime that they had dared to beget a child in Heaven. Indra was more taken aback by their impudence than the severity of their folly. But he had been a fool; he had allowed it to happen.

'What do you expect me to do?' he asked at last, his eyes scathing, on Menaka.

'To let us keep our child,' she retorted bravely.

Her docility was misleading; there was a certain discourtesy in her request making it sound defiant.

'Menaka, you have gone too far this time...' said Indra

dangerously. 'And you know it.'

'No, I didn't know I would have a baby,' she said. She looked up at him, her eyes large and earnest. 'I didn't. I would never lie to you. I never imagined that I could ever have a child...apsaras do not, do they?'

Indra's lips tightened. 'Don't question me, Menaka! You give me the answers!' he barked.

Menaka folded her hands. 'I have no answers. It is not upon me to have them...'

'That's some noble talk after all what you have done! You have been consistently disaffected, resisting authority and in spite of knowing the rules here, you broke each one of them. No, Vasu, don't interrupt and rush to her defence...I want to talk to her!'

Indra raised his arm in admonishment. Vasu was forced to keep quiet, but Indra noticed the smoulder of fury in his eyes.

'You were created, Menaka, to please, to appease. You are not to have a "personal" life. You belong to us. You know that. Yet you decided to fall in love...of all the people, with my friend, the Devagandharva, Vishwavasu. And you were clever enough to make him fall for you. But that's not difficult for you, is it, Menaka? You can make anyone do that!' sneered Indra, his face reddening. It was an ugly flush.

'We love each other. Neither of us forced each other to do that!' intervened Vasu quietly, with a simmering heat in his voice. He knew he would have to keep peace, but he couldn't allow Indra to accuse Menaka unfairly, in jealous spite.

'Ah! The lover to the rescue! What do you know of love? What is love between a gandharva and an apsara but not lust? Divine lust!' he said with a derisive laugh. 'It is just a simple sexual passion between the two of you and I permitted because it was just that! Yours is no marriage, however much you would like to believe that!' jeered Indra. 'It is a temporary, convenient relationship. You were meant to enjoy, not beget children! And Vasu, my dear fellow, she doesn't need your assistance. Menaka knows how to look after herself. But don't you think both of you have been excessively assumptive?' asked Indra, his hands at his waist. 'Both of you have created enough mischief by being the lovers. Do you realize how the equation has changed drastically within the apsaras and the gandharvas? You should know that, you are their king!' said Indra scathingly. 'And you, Menaka, are supposed to entertain us, and not private liaisons! You may have got secretly married the gandharva way with just the Kalpataru, the celestial tree as a witness, but this marriage in Heaven is a sham and yet I allowed it because of my indulging weakness!' he turned his wrath again on Menaka. 'You well knew you could get away with it. I should have banished you then and finished the matter once and for all but...' he paused, taking a long breath. 'But, I didn't. And again, you took advantage of me, Menaka, and now have the temerity to carry Vasu's child! Apsaras are supposed to seduce mortals, those avaricious kings and ambitious rishis, not my people in Amravati. That was your biggest crime and I was foolish enough to allow it. No longer, dear,' he said, his eyes hardening perceptibly.

'I shall leave Amravati,' said Menaka quietly, looking straight into his eyes.

The moment she said those words, Indra knew that he could not bear to let her go. However much he hated her at this very moment and was furious with her. However much she had betrayed him, he could not imagine her not being here with him.

'No, you will not,' he said quickly, his words coming out almost like an angry plea. 'You can never leave Amravati...'

'Nor can Vasu,' said Menaka. 'He is the gandharvas' king, you cannot banish him!'

Indra knew Menaka had put him in a fix. He would have dearly wished to throw Vasu out from his heavenly abode, as he was the cause of all this grief. But Indra also knew he was helplessly cornered and could not hurt Vasu with the protective Menaka fiercely standing by his side. He would handle Vasu later, but right now he did not want to let go of Menaka but neither could he allow her to have her say.

'I have erred and I shall bear the punishment. It is best I leave Amravati with the baby,' repeated Menaka, and without waiting for Indra's permission, turned to leave. She knew she would be stopped even as she took her first step.

'You dare defy me again, Menaka! You won't go anywhere but stay here!' shouted Indra.

'And I cannot let go of my child,' said Menaka softly.

'You can't have everything, Menaka. You have your love, your husband, but you cannot keep your baby here. Heaven does not allow it...'

'It allows the devas to marry and beget!' persisted Menaka. 'How will my child be different from their's?'

'Because you may be an immortal apsara, but you are not a devi!' retorted Indra.

She went white, her face drained of colour and forbearance. 'The heavenly harlot you mean, never a wife, never a mother!' said Menaka, with a twist of her lips.

'There are no whores in heaven!' roared Indra. 'You are an apsara, not a harlot!'

'By ratifying it, does not mean it is acceptable' she cried, 'to me!'

'By ratifying it, there is no stigma!' he raised his head and said sharply, accusing. 'No one can dare call you or any apsara a whore. It's a cheap word coined in Prithvilok, not here. There is no disgrace, no infamy in being an apsara. I have sanctioned seduction here and it is beautiful. Don't sully it with ugly words from the mortal world.'

Menaka leaned forward, confronting him and insisted, 'Say it, lord. Admit it. And that's what I am, a reluctant seductress. To make love, to lure, but not for my own pleasures. A woman of lust but who cannot love, wed or conceive. Your land of great wealth and wantonness does not favour social equality...!'

Indra looked incensed. 'Here each one has a role to function, a duty to do. Yours is to entertain and amuse...'

'And flirt and woo, and seduce!' refuted Menaka. 'To allure and exploit men, that's it! You made me a woman that glorify beauteous creation, yet so rudimentary. I am that beautiful, eternally young woman who believes she lives with the blessed in Heaven. You gave me all the weapons of love, sex and desire but disarmed me of my capability of conscious choice and decision. Why? I can be a woman, but never a wife or a mother. Just a sexual slave. A whore,' she repeated forcefully.

Vasu thought this was the end; Indra had gone white with fury. 'Seducing dangerous men to save the world is not whoring it is salvation!

'Salvation!? Dangerous men? Dangerous for whom? You?' scoffed Menaka, her tone soft and even. 'There is a difference between making love and making intrigue! To use my sex appeal to exploit men is intrigue! Engaging in sexual intercourse with a covert motive is not just intrigue, it is whoring! *You* make me do that! *You* make me compromise myself for *your* gains. *You* use me not just to lure men to have sex but to entice them away from their goals, to lead them astray. It is seduction at its worse. It is not an option I have, it is an imposition. And yet you deprive me of my right to freedom to love and beget and rear...if you made a woman, why then can I not be a mother too?'

Indra gave her an incredulous look, his eyes flinty. 'Right? What rights?' he thundered. 'Don't humanise our world, Menaka! Emotions play no part in your life, be it love, pain or grief. They are just words. You are beyond all such weakness. Yet you choose to embrace them and so you suffer! Don't beg for mercy or your child, Menaka. You were told what you are essentially and always be the temptress and nothing more. The dancing nymphs can't have babies!' said Indra, with a disparaging curl of his thin lips. 'You can have your baby here, but you can't keep it. As the tradition goes, the children of apsaras are handed over to celibate rishis of Prithvilok as their surrogate fathers or some king.'

'Misbegotten and deserted by us!' retorted Menaka.

Vasu stepped forward. 'I am the father. I am ready to leave Amravati and look after my child,' he asserted.

'I have had this debate long enough,' said Indra impatiently. 'Both of you stay put here but the baby goes.'

'Or...?' challenged Menaka, desperate for some sort of reprieve.

'I shall forcibly throw the child out from here!' countered Indra, his voice dangerously soft. 'Don't try me further, Menaka.'

He stared down at her with all his accumulated arrogance of power over her. She stood straight, unflinchingly, her eyes shining with anguished rage. Indra felt a sense of fear, of deep loss. Had he lost her forever? He felt the tension in the air, her inarticulate cry of pain as she struggled with her emotions.

'Please!' she beseeched, her voice faltering, her composure cracking. 'Please!!' she cried wildly, screaming that single, desperate word of appeal again, sinking slowly to her knees, her head bowed in defeat.

Indra was speechless. Vasu looked ashen. Menaka was grovelling at his feet. Her imperious insolence seemed to have crumbled, as the woman of brazen beauty and pride was imploring him on her knees, stripped of her ego, her dignity, herself, her soul. Indra was filled with a smug glow of self-congratulation. He had broken her.

'I so feel for you...' he began. 'I feel your beauty, your passion. I feel your love. For Vasu,' he said smoothly, but he couldn't hide the savage edge. 'I feel your yearning. I feel your despondence,' he said, unmoved. 'But yes, Menaka, I will give you a choice...' he paused for the desired effect. Menaka looked up at him, hope rekindling in her despairing eyes. 'You can give up your child or ...' again he paused dramatically. '...or give up Vasu and this Heaven, which you hate so much. Which one will it be?' he asked silkily.

The utter stillness of Menaka was like the stillness blanketing the room. Everything seemed to have come to a halt. She remained immobile, she couldn't breathe. She felt the moments drag out her scrambled thoughts. Slowly expelling her breath, clenching her fingers into tight fists, her face waxen, Menaka got up falteringly, to face him, her eyes dry with the fire burning within. He had forced her into a situation, where a favourable outcome was impossible; she was bound to lose whatever she decided. His offer was a sham but she knew she had a choice to refuse. Our choices and nothing else, she realized grimly, shape our fate—hers, and that of her child, of the man she loved.

She found it hard to swallow as she was forced to voice out her decision. 'So be it, Lord. I shall abandon my baby once it's born,' she whispered, her voice strangled. She looked at him with an emotion Indra could not decipher.

He saw her whipping around and striding out of the hall with the elegance and grace only she could muster. He felt like gloating; he had taught her a lesson but in his heart he felt a strange dull ache. She would never forgive him. But an inner voice goaded him further, *would I ever be able to forgive her?*

'See to it that she never lays her eyes on the baby when it's born,' he told Vasu dully. 'If she holds it, she'll never be able to let it go. Spare her that pain.'

Vasu pursed his lips. 'You could have done that if you had wanted to.'

Indra shook his head. 'Vasu, don't hide behind her and dart arrows over her shoulder. I can throw you out right away so don't try me either. You know we are no longer friends. But both of you will pay for this someday...'

Vasu looked at him steadily. 'We already have.'

Revenge

$\mathcal{K}$aushik was a changed man. Hemavati could sense it. He had lost his peace, his quiet, his smile—the winning smile that could otherwise woo hearts and win arguments, without stringing a single arrow.

She didn't need to ask the reason for his disquietude—he was still mulling over his defeat. Hemavati hoped his gloom would soon lift. She knew he was a mercurial man, with his erratic twist of temperament: willful one moment, gentle and kind the next. He had a quick, short, unpredictable temper; but she had never seen him so silently livid before, a simmering extreme, cold fury refusing to bubble out.

'The more you brood over it, the more it'll upset you,' she consoled. He was a stubborn man, with a tenacious unwillingness to yield.

'Have you ever experienced humiliation?' he asked quietly, with a tremble of suppressed rage in his baritone.

Yes, she thought, *each time you go to your other wives, I feel the same.*

'It must be a helpless feeling,' she said instead. 'It is not the incident but the importance you give to it that is tormenting you. You won't allow yourself to forget it.'

Kaushik shrugged his broad shoulders, which were taut with tension. 'I shall not allow myself to dismiss my defeat so easily. The old man has to pay for what he did.'

Hemavati looked at her husband with exasperation. 'What did he do wrong?' she countered. 'You were in the wrong. You tried to seize his calf and he protected her from you. Don't let your ego cloud your judgement,' she said. As soon as the words were out of her mouth, she realized her mistake, as she saw Kaushik flush, his tanned face darkening in remembered anger, clenching his jaw to cut out an angry retort.

'You are one of the fairest people I know,' she added soothingly. 'But you are a king. You made one mistake of coveting the unattainable, while trying to forcibly take away something which wasn't yours. Don't make things worse.'

'How am I making things worse? By my arrogance?' said Kaushik, frostily. 'Or by my power as a king? No, my dear, I have realized that this royal power has its limitations. I couldn't win over the old rishi because I am a king, it gave me defeat instead. I will give up my power that weakened me...' he said slowly, articulating each word with cold precision and intent.

Suddenly, there was a strange stillness in his tall frame: his back straight, his face carved in stone, his head flung high in innate arrogance. As he kept thinking about his sudden decision, the tentacles of the thought took deeper root, and his face shone with determination as he made up his mind.

Hemavati felt a small knot of dread unfurling inside her. 'What do you mean?' she gasped, dreading what he would say next. 'Give up your power? You mean you will forfeit your throne?!' She stared at him in incredulous horror.

Kaushik nodded slowly, his eyes suddenly tranquil. 'Yes, I shall not be accused of abusing my royal rank. I have decided to relinquish my crown and kingdom!'

She could not believe what she was hearing, but she was aware of the rising fear in her heart; Kaushik was coming to some momentous decision that would devastate their lives.

'Stop, please, this is not some battle you are planning! Be serious, you cannot not be king to spite a rishi! What about your responsibility to your kingdom? And why? Because of this unreasonable ire towards that rishi? Humility, not humiliation is your only succour. This mad desire for revenge will be your downfall! Why can't you let it go?' she pleaded. 'Rishi Vasishth has a habit of moving from one kingdom to another—he might have left ours by now. He is sure to have dismissed the incident from his mind. So should you. Why are you bent on seeking vengeance at the expense of your family, your crown, your kingdom, your people?' she implored, quickly pressing on his weak point. 'They need their king. Kanyakubja needs you!'

Kaushik smiled, but it was not a pleasant smile, but a grimace of contempt. 'I am a king of what? A kingdom, an empire? It is just a tract of land I inherited from my ancestors, a line of famous kings. It is a piece of land peopled by its subjects, populated with nobles, ministers, merchants, the poor and the needy. I rule over these people. I have power, wealth, love and respect. And yet I have nothing...' he pronounced. His eyes glittered with a strange gleam. 'I do not have the power to subjugate a rishi or his calf. They boast of heavenly power, a power greater than royalty. And I too shall have it...' he paused, inhaling a deep breath. 'I shall have it,' he repeated, his voice dangerously soft.

'I shall do penance to seek and earn the celestial arsenal that will destroy Vasishth, his holy calf and his army!' he said calmly, his voice matching the sudden serenity in his speckled, molten eyes. 'This defeat made me aware of the limitations of royal power: it is a mere trap. What I need is siddhi, the tapo bal—the great yogic power of penance. My solace, salvation and strength will be in meditation till I get what I want,' announced Kaushik, his voice rising slightly, almost strident as if it was a promise he was giving himself. 'I shall invoke the blessings of Lord Shiva for unlimited heavenly powers and weapons...'

'No, please you can't!' Hemavati cried, holding his hand desperately. 'One should invoke Deva's blessing for a good cause, or it becomes a curse! You are a visionary kshatriya, can you not see that this pointless rivalry, this stubborn need for revenge will be doom for all of us? You are asking for the unimaginable! You cannot forget your duties as a king, as a husband, as a father!' The mere thought tore her crazed mind. 'You can't leave us...

who will look after us and Kanyakubja?'

'Our sons will,' replied Kaushik. 'Andhark is old and wise enough to take up the crown. He will serve the people well. And he shall have his brother Madhuchand to help him. Don't you trust him?'

'Yes I do. He is a good boy and will one day be a good king. But that day is not now. We need you. I need you! Oh, I love you—you can't be so heartless...' she wept, her stricken eyes reflecting a terror and grief that could not be washed away with the tears coursing down her ravaged face. Kaushik closed his eyes; to shut off the image of the wild grief. Her world was crumbling around her with each word he uttered and all she could do was watch helplessly as she was being interred forever in the darkness of the future. His dream was her nightmare.

'Please, please, don't go, don't leave me' she implored, her hands folded together in a gritted grip, ready to cower at his feet. 'I won't be able to live without you, don't forsake me for your ambition, Kaushik. I am your wife, don't play with our lives. Think, consider just for a moment, me, our son—you cannot abandon us!' she cried piteously.

Kaushik stood implacable, his face as hard as his voice. 'Yes, I have failed you, but I would rather take on a slur as a heartless father than a failure. Better to be known as a heartless husband than a humiliated king,' he said, his hands clenched by his side. 'This is my mission now.'

'And what about us?' she repeated, her expression frozen. 'You are ruthless enough to desert us for your noble, selfish cause.' It was not a question: it was her bitter accusation, flung straight and hard. 'You are a coward, a loser who cannot handle his pride punctured,' she accused, her eyes flashing through her unshed tears. 'You would rather hurt the people who love you them heal your hurt ego! You talk of attaining knowledge and wisdom, but you are one of the most morally reprehensible man I know. A man who forsook his family for fame!'

Hemavati wanted to wound him as he had hurt her. Angry words were her only weapon in this battle to win him back, to save herself. Pale and trembling, she was beside herself with rage and grief: rage at his callousness and her naiveté in loving this man. And grief, for she was going to lose him forever; and she knew that he would never return.

And in the thickening haze of pain, she recalled what her sister-in-law Satyavati had once warned her as a bride—one day Hemavati would lose her husband, not to death, but to a strange prophecy that haunted the royal family. Kaushik, though born a prince and brought up to be a king would renounce it all to become a rishi...

She had giggled then, in her silly innocence, assuming it to be an extension of the older woman's fervid imagination. How could a king ever become an ascetic? How could a warrior give up power and his arms for knowledge? But one look at the tall, determined man, silhouetted against the setting sun, she knew this was he.

And through her fast falling tears, Hemavati realized that that day had arrived.

❡

Menaka lay exhausted, waiting to be shown her baby. She could barely recall the baby cry its arrival in the world. She did not remember holding it. She did not know if it was a boy or a girl. But she had yearned so strongly for a girl all this while that surely it must have been a daughter. *She was her daughter, and she would be lovely*, Menaka thought drowsily, without a pinch of vanity. She had already discussed the name with Vasu: Pramadvara, the cautious and the careful. *Unlike her mother*, she thought bitterly. The moniker would be a sharp reminder of her carelessness, her callousness. From this moment onwards, she would have to endure the stigma of being branded as a heartless mother, who had abandoned her child. She could confront all, the people and the accusations, but would she be able to face herself? Menaka tightly squeezed her fists in suppressed pain, her nails biting into the soft flesh. She had not yet seen her new born child and she would have to relinquish it.

'Where's my baby?' she asked Tilottama in a hoarse whisper. The light-eyed Tilottama, who was her closest friend among the apsaras, gave her a reassuring smile and said, 'I'll fetch Vasu.'

Menaka frowned. Something was wrong. Tilottama was never evasive.

The sight of Vasu entering her room gave her swift solace. He was here; he would know.

'Where is she?' she asked eagerly. 'Why haven't you let me see her yet?'

'Because you are not to see her, Menaka. Ever. It wouldn't do you any good, would it?' said Vasu hollowly, his eyes vacant.

'What do you mean?' she asked frantically. 'Why can't I see her?'

'She's already been given away.' It was a bald statement, torn from his lips.

So, it *had* been a daughter, Menaka thought miserably. But she was gone, without Menaka getting a single glimpse, or without holding her close. *I will not see her ever again*, her heart lurched painfully at the thought.

'Why?' she whispered bleakly. 'She was to be sent away anyway. Why could you not let me keep her for just a little while?' she beseeched, feeling another deep stab of pain. Or was it anger? 'How could you snatch away that experience from me? It was my only moment with her.'

'She was not ours any longer,' said Vasu wretchedly. 'The sooner the better! She was too beautiful to let go...' Menaka heard the catch in his voice. 'You could have never been able to give her up had you laid your eyes on her. I couldn't have made you suffer more. You could not have handled it.'

Menaka gave him a sharp look, afraid to believe what she was thinking. 'You were scared that I would leave you and Amravati with her,' she guessed, reading his thoughts. 'That's why you decided to give away our baby quickly!'

Vasu had gone white. 'You make me sound heartless. Menaka, I am her father!!' he muttered. 'We could have never kept our child here in Amravati. Were we ready to leave heaven for our child, Menaka? If you have the courage to reply to that question, you have your answer.'

Menaka bit her lip to stifle the pain and guilt surging through her. 'Where is she now?'

'I left her at Rishi Sthulkesh's ashram.'

'Did you speak with him? Didn't you let him know she was our daughter?'

'I did. But we are not her parents any longer, Menaka!!' he retorted forcefully, giving in to his own pain at last. 'I simply spared you that guilt of handing your child to a stranger; it breaks you! I wouldn't wish it on anyone, so how could I have made you bear that pain?'

'Don't decide for me, Vasu! I won't ever get to see her. I won't ever know her. You have snatched her and her memory which I could have cherished as mine,' her voice broke. 'Oh, Vasu, I have abandoned her!!' she sobbed. 'I had a choice...!'

'It was a wicked ploy!' raged Vasu. 'How could you and the baby have survived?'

'Just as she will now, all alone...'

Vasu did not reply, but he held her close, his arms protectively round her, letting her weep against his chest. The silence in the room was punctuated by her broken whimpers. She stopped abruptly, barely sensed him holding her, stiff and straight. His silence sparked off an erratic storm of fury in her.

'You were following Indra's instructions,' she accused through her tears, making a shrewd guess. 'As usual,' she added caustically.

Vasu paled. 'You are upset...'

'But I mean what I am saying!! It was by Indra's suggestion, you did not allow me to see my Pramadvara,' she stated emphatically, colour rushing to her blanched face. By uttering her name, Menaka felt she had some right of possession on her. But she knew it was futile. Her fury escalated, as did her grief. 'And you listened to Indra, you did it!'

'I did it to spare you the pain...' he started helplessly, taking her trembling hands in his, caressing them to calm her. But she just grew angrier.

'And he did it to hurt me!' she shot back. 'And you agreed to it. Vasu, he used you again. He used you against me. One day he will tear us apart!! I cannot forget the look in his eyes when he saw us together. He pretended to accept it, but he never shall! He will see to it that we are never happy with each other!'

Vasu shook his head. 'He can do it only if we allow it to happen!' he muttered fiercely. 'You are doing it right now— by over-reacting to a decision which we had already decided upon. It was unavoidable. We have had this discussion so many times before; we had a choice and we decided we cannot keep Pramadvara, *our* child!' he said deliberately, calling her by her name for the first time but accentuating each word with cruel emphasis. 'Accept it, Menaka, and don't hope on Indra's well wishes. We are no longer in his favour and he will attack someway, someday. Yet you would rather accuse me unfairly. That's driving us apart!'

Menaka noticed his anguish for the first time.

'I ought not to blame you,' she mumbled, her eyes reddened and filled, and she determinedly blinked them clear. He gently took her tear-stained, crumpled face in his hands and said, 'Don't allow him to come between us, please. That is what he is doing. I say it for the last time—I did what I did to save you, in whichever small way I could. Not to hurt you, never that! Yes, I followed his orders but for your good. I listened to him for I could hear your pain...'

'But that is what Vasu always does, does he not? Always obey Indra!' rang a voice loudly through the length of the room. It was harsh and strident, laced with enough bitterness to make Menaka realize its owner immediately. It was Urvashi.

Vasu stiffened and abruptly got up to leave. His face was pale, his eyes tired. Menaka felt a twinge of guilt. *He must be suffering too,* but in her selfish grief, she had blamed him solely for their misfortune. She bit her lip and tugged at his hand to stay. But he gently prised away from her clasp.

'It's best I leave now,' he murmured, placing a soft kiss on her lips.

Menaka kissed him back fiercely to assuage her guilt, not wanting to let go of him. But she too knew that it would be better for him if he left right away, if he had to save himself from Urvashi's barbs. Vasu would never be able to face Urvashi with a straight face after what he had done. Or rather, what Indra had made him do.

Menaka quickly wiped her tears, feeling the warmth of his lips imprinted on hers and looked warily at the approaching woman. Urvashi had a languid grace, but her walk was a deliberate sway, rolling her slim hips with each stride, her shoulders straight, her heavy breasts thrust out in defiance. She was supposed to be the most beautiful of the apsaras, for which she was equally loved and hated. She was also the most sensually explicit of them.

Urvashi, as her name spelled—the one who controls her heart. Ironically, she had done the most unlikely—she lost her heart to a mortal. King Purarav of Pratishthan was so besotted by her that he was ready to leave his wife and his kingdom and Earth for her. But he was not permitted to live in the Heaven. Urvashi, taken in by his ardour, who would rather marry an ardent lover than a brave warrior did not seek his power of weapons but his power of words. Pururav proved to be an articulate lover, poetic in his thoughts. She agreed to live with him on Earth, but on two odd conditions. That he take care of her pet sheep. And that he was never to appear nude in front of anybody but her. It was her clever way of keeping him with her forever, to ensure that he remained loyal and never go back to his first wife or take another. The besotted Pururav did not think twice before making the promises. They got married and lived blissfully for several years on Earth, till the day Indra started missing his apsara. He had to have her back. Once he got to know of the two unusual conditions laid down by Urvashi, he took his friend Vasu in confidence, and plotted a plan around it. Vasu along with other two gandharvas stole Urvashi's pet sheep in the middle of the night. An alert Pururav was quick enough to discover this and rushed out of the bed to chase the thieves. By creating a bolt of lightning, Vasu managed to wake up the sleeping Urvashi to make her see her husband running naked after the fleeing gandharvas. One of them, of which, she recognized as Vasu. Quick to infer what and how it had happened, Urvashi was forced to leave her broken-hearted lover behind and return to Heaven. But she still had not forgiven Vasu, relishing those moments when she could make Vasu feel miserable for the dubious role he had played in the subterfuge. Today seemed to be one of those sadistic moments again.

'I hope you suffer the same pain you made me endure!' shouted Urvashi at Vasu's retreating figure as he left the room.

Menaka flinched. 'By saying that, you are cursing me as well,' she said weakly.

'No, I am not. You cannot protect him from the crime he committed,' said Urvashi. 'However much you may love Vasu, I want him to suffer...that wily coward!'

'That's a more apt description for Indra,' retorted Menaka spiritedly. 'Vasu was merely following his king's orders. Indra wanted you back and made Vasu do the dirty work.'

'Vasu was his friend. They were in this together. And besides, Vasu, like Chitrasen and Tumburu, is one of the most influential gandharvas,' argued Urvashi. 'He is the king of the gandharvas, he is the son of a powerful man, he is a maestro, a master philosopher, and the leading singer with that heavenly voice! Mortals even pray to him after Agni and Chandra—he is a ardha-deva and the only immortal gandharva in Heaven!

'The women of Prithvilok do—as per the marriage ritual, for he represents love,' sighed Menaka, tying up her hair tiredly in a loose knot. 'Vasu could never have hurt you, if he was in a position to decide. He is too kind-hearted, you know that, Urvashi. He did what Indra forced him to do. Vent your rage on Indra, he's the culprit!'

'But Vasu is as powerful. He could have dissuaded Indra; Indra listens to him!' said Urvashi. 'Today when he is suffering the same, he can see Indra for what he is. That is my sweet revenge, Menaka. He is facing the same pain and helplessness that I did when they forced me to leave Pururav and come here!'

'But Indra still goes free, who makes him answerable for what he did?' charged Menaka, her lips pursed in grim determination. 'Vasu was not responsible for your heart break, Indra was. He wanted you back, and that's why he made that elaborate plan. Can you stand up to him and hurl the same accusations you are throwing at Vasu? You too are powerful, Urvashi. You, who could make the twin devas—Mitra and Varun—have children through you, yet you cannot challenge Indra!'

Urvashi tightened her lips. Menaka knew she was not as ruthless as she made herself out to be. All she wanted was her to be more kind to Vasu. 'It was because of you that Mitra and his Varun, the devas of the oceans and rivers, could have children like Agastya and Vasishth, through your powers of the ayoni sex. They were born from water pots after the devas discharged their semen by your mere presence! You were so moved by the love of Varun and Mitra that you agreed to be the surrogate mother of their children. Can't you be more kind to us too?'

'Can I, Menaka?' asked Urvashi, her face hard. 'Can I make myself forgive Vasu ever? But I guess I need no longer be malicious. His close friend Indra is doing the needful! Indra cannot digest your temerity that you loved and married Vasu. His jealous anger makes him spread ugly rumours that your daughter was born out of wedlock. Wedlock?! When did apsaras have weddings and wedlocks?' sniggered Urvashi hollowly. 'And he will keep hounding you. Not allowing you to see your child was an act of petty revenge. He'll keep at it, but will you or Vasu be able to take it for long? He just took away your child, but can you do anything about it? Will you?'

'No, I can't,' admitted Menaka with painful resignation, her jaw clenched. 'And nor could you all these years. That's why you lash out at Vasu in your impotent helplessness. You can have him only to blame. But I won't forgive Indra. Never. And not make him forget it either.'

Menaka took a deep, strong breath, trying to control her grief and composure. 'But will I be able to? It's so not true. We keep lying to ourselves that we are in heaven and we have everything.

We have nothing but youth, beauty and immortality; blessed to live on for years and years with our fears and insecurities, achieving what? For whom? We are but assorted pieces of his property, to be taken and tossed, just entertainers serving his lordship Indra. We have no choice, no voice, yet we are to sing paens for him!'

Urvashi took Menaka's tight fists in hers. They were cold and clammy, trembling with an inner rage. 'Then sing happily, as that's the reason why we were created—to be happy and make others happy. You are upset because you had to give up your baby,' she said. 'But Menaka, why burden yourself with motherhood? It's not for us. We are not for nurturing; we are to here nourish something else—sex, sensuality, pleasure—different words to describe our job. Loving and bearing kids are not parts of them. I had so many children; not just from Pururav but others as well, on Indra's orders. But though they were left motherless, they are happier where they are—with their fathers or the adopted parents.'

Menaka did not look convinced, her face convulsed in silent grief, swollen with tears and pain.

'We apsaras are supposed to be free and unconfined in our choice. We make love and leave. That is our motto. Live by it, Menaka, or you shall suffer untold, unnecessary grief. Devas, rishis, gandharvas, and mortals are merely different types of men. Men!' scoffed Urvashi. 'But they all come crawling to us for pleasure; give them that, but don't get saddled by them or their offsprings. Sport with them and have fun, why endure the blame or guilt of imposed morality? Neither family on marriage subjugate us. We have no husband, no sons, no daughters, indeed, no relations. We are apsaras, free and carefree!'

'But she was our child, Urvashi. Mine and Vasu's!' cried Menaka.

'Vasu has had other children. He knows what it is to let go. Just as I did,' said Urvashi calmly. 'It's new for you. That's why you are so effusively maudlin! And be sensible, if you had kept the baby, what future were you going to give her? Let her grow up to be a courtesan like us, a singer, a dancer, a...'

'No, don't say it!' cried Menaka swiftly, biting her lip.

'An apsara,' reiterated Urvashi with vituperative vehemence. 'Our children are better off with some celibate rishi or a childless king. They will either grow up in knowledge or wealth, neither of the status we can bestow on them!' her smile curled in contempt. 'Heaven does not breed children, only apsaras to spread love in this everland of passion and abandon.'

Menaka gave a brittle smile. 'And the swiftness of divine retribution.'

Call to Challenge

*K*aushik looked at the weapons in his hands—the celestial arsenal gifted by Lord Shiva. After years of penance, he had achieved what he had so desperately wanted. Lord Shiva, while presenting him with divine protection of the heavenly artillery, had blessed him with a new title—Rajrishi.

'Stop your penance now, as you have gleaned enough knowledge. It's so severe that's it burning my body,' Lord Shiva had said with a wry smile. 'You have my benediction, o Rajrishi Kaushik.'

Kaushik waited, as he stood outside the ashram of Vasishth. The sky was a purple darkness before dawn but Kaushik could see the contour of each hut in the ashram. He had come armed with his new weapons and renewed intention to defeat Vasishth today. He shot his precursory arrow, Pashupatastra. It hit a dry hut immediately, engulfing it in flames, which then hungrily spread to the adjoining thatched huts. Kaushik expected the old man to rush out, but he did not. But his disciples did, shouting in terror. Some rushed to their guru for help.

Vasishth had noticed the body oil that he was rubbing on his wrinkled skin was getting unusually warm. From the corner of his eye, he saw the orange flames leaping high from the window. And through the smoky haze, he observed the wispy silhouette of a man. He immediately recognized who it was—Kaushik. Vasishth surmised what was happening. A disciple rushed into his room and screamed, 'Move out, sir! The ashram is on fire! We need help. Who will save us from this inferno? It's spreading like wildfire!'

'Calm down, son,' said the old rishi, his voice as serene as his face. Observing the tranquillity in his eyes, the disciple found his panic subsiding. 'No one shall be harmed. Just remain calm, and see that the animals are not frightened.'

The disciple nodded his head vigorously, as relief flooded his face on hearing his guru's assurance, and rushed out to follow his instructions. Vasishth strained his neck to see how high the flames were raging. Almost his entire ashram was ablaze, but first he needed to douse the spreading fire. Too sticky to get up and attack the culprit, as he was in a state of undress and oiling himself, he glanced around in his hut. He spotted his weathered seven-knotted bamboo stick, standing stolidly against the flimsy mud wall. He leaned over and threw it outside.

'That stick should teach him a lesson or two,' he muttered and got back to oiling himself more vigorously.

Kaushik hurled the Agnisastra, sparking a conflagration in the surrounding trees. Suddenly, he spotted a stick thrown out of Vasishth's hut. Curious, he looked at the seemingly harmless stick absorb the inferno in a giant swallow. Kaushik stared, dumbstruck. *It was not a knobby, old bamboo stick, it had become the Brahmadanda*, he thought.

Kaushik decided to use the Vayuastra to fling the stick far away but the Brahmadanda stood straight and sucked in the blowing wind, to allow a cool breeze to blow on Kaushik's red, heated face. Next was the Santapanastra but that too got gulped down ignominiously by the Brahmadanda. He tried all heavenly armouries, one after the other in quick, desperate succession, but each felled before the might of the puny Brahmadanda.

Kaushik had been saving his last weapon in his hand, the Brahmastra, for he knew the potency of its destruction. He touched it lightly, and his mere intention sent a shiver through the three worlds...

'What is happening?' shouted Indra, as his court of Amravati physically shook and Menaka's dance came to a standstill. Indra looked more shaken than he would allow himself.

'A mortal, a king called Kaushik has been given the Brahmastra by Lord Shiva and he intends to use it...!' explained a visibly worried Lord Agni.

'How did a mortal attain the Brahmastra, and I didn't get to know about it??' demanded an incensed Indra.

That is because you were chasing petty issues like spying on Vasu and me, scoffed Menaka, silently. When she tried to remember Kaushik, she saw a face flash across her mind. *That tall hulk of a king with Rishi Vasishth, crackling with raw animal magnetism*, she remembered faintly. *And those sullen, golden speckled eyes and dimpled smile, gazing at me with open adoration.* She had been amused then; but from now she would keep the name and the man in mind: he was the man Indra feared. *The mortal king, who is capable of rattling him up and the three worlds*, she mused.

'And I presume there's no one to stop him?' asked Indra furiously.

'Possibly, Rishi Vasishth himself with whom he has sworn an undying rivalry may...?' said Agni dubiously. Looking down from heaven, he prayed that they would all survive this man's vengeful fury.

Kaushik was not to be mollified. The fact that all his divine weapons had failed him, made him more determined. But a stray thought struck him, *would he survive if he struck the Brahamastra?* Before he could fathom an answer, he had shot the deadly weapon, hurtling the world towards anarchy...

The moment the Brahmastra touched the wiry stick, it froze to dripping icicles, disintegrating and dissolving into a small, shameful pool of melted water on the grass. The Brahmadanda stood straight and steady, having defused the most lethal heavenly weapon, saving the world from possible annihilation. It seemed to straighten up with a new purpose—to attack the offender.

Kaushik felt mortified when he realized that he was going to be beaten by a bamboo stick. *And I stand beaten again*, he thought, as waves of humiliation washed over his vengeance. Vasishth had not used a single arrow, or any celestial weapon, but a bamboo stick, which through his superpowers, had transformed into a Brahmadanda absorbing years of Kaushik's penance, his perseverance, his tapas. It was as invincible as its master.

Kaushik saw Vasishth standing at the doorway of his hut, staring at him serenely. There was no anger, no remonstration, but Kaushik could feel the heat of his gaze. It had not been superpowers; but the supreme power of yogic penance. It was simply his strength of the mind, his Brahmabal; and his Satvik prowess, the might of the gentle which was more powerful than all the weapons, one that could make a mere bamboo stick into a formidable weapon. He might have been bestowed with the title of the Rajarishi, but Kaushik rued about what he was lacking. All he possessed was the vestige of a royal hauteur, his Rajasbala, the power of the dominance and passion. What he needed to earn was that strength of the mind, a more severe tapo bal like Vasishth's; he would have to become a Brahmarishi like the learned rishi.

Kaushik stared at the distant figure, who made no move to approach him. But their eyes clashed and Kaushik felt a familiar flicker of revengeful anger. *This was the man who had vanquished me, twice.* And Kaushik made himself a new promise, *I would defeat this man, with powers matching the rishi's. I would become a brahmarishi one day.*

❦

'Have things sorted out between the two of you?' asked Menaka, resting more comfortably against Vasu's broad shoulders, running her fingers absently over his chest, her long, loose hair spread out. She was thinking, chewing her lips more relentlessly than usual. She admitted to herself that she was anxious to the point of being agitated.

Vasu did not reply. He was brooding as well, his amber eyes troubled but he did not want to upset Menaka. He felt a strange sense of foreboding, which was rising fast into a panic.

But Menaka sensed it too. The animosity between the once good friends, Indra and Vasu, had not dimmed over time as she had hoped. Indra, in his superior status was more virulent of the two and demonstrated it amply in public. Both seemed to be competing as for the same prize—her. But Menaka was not conceited to assume she was the sole reason for their conflict. It went deep; it was a friendship curdled in bitterness and betrayal.

Indra was a man with extreme consciousness of his identity. He could not suffer contention of any kind; he always had to be the winner, but it had been Vasu who had won her. Indra's essentially entrenched anxiety made him feel doubly insecure. Jealousy often stirred with his inflated feeling of pride in his superiority to others, specifically Vasu who was regarded with more favour, approval and affection by all. And he portended a more grievous threat—Vasu was becoming almost as powerful as him.

'I have decided to ignore him...' sighed Vasu, running his fingers in her hair.

'Even his daily insults?'

'Yes, because they are words of a jealous man; they don't affect me. And anyway, what can we do, Menaka?' he shrugged his bare shoulders, his arms tightening around her. His fear of losing her gripped him in a tight fist.

'He resents me. We have lost his favour, and all we can do is endure it. And no, Menaka,' he added with a strained smile, 'your charms don't work on him, so don't even try attempting it. It will make him all the more furious and resentful.'

'He is sulking and I had hoped he would come around by now. Like I did,' she paused, stifling a painful thought of her forsaken child, which still made her heart bleed. 'What are we to do?'

'Nothing, as I said,' warned Vasu. 'He is a spiteful person and he will keep needling us. It's his purpose and pleasure. He is a sadist. Let's not spoil it for him.

Menaka nodded doubtfully. 'I wonder why Indra is how he is. Why is it that even the most powerful remain insecure and vulnerable? They have everything, yet nothing but a niggling neurotic fear.'

'They lack maturity and confidence,' said Vasu, thinking of his former friend. 'They need to be constantly assured, either by false pride or people. Often, you'll find them surrounded by mediocrity, people who never challenge them.'

'Because they are mediocre themselves! Arrogance and foolishness make an insufferable pair!' she said. 'Indra has got corrupted by his position. He won't last long...'

'Who'll throw him out?' asked Vasu bitterly. 'Oh, to have an intelligent, wise king! It's a dream to work under such a leader, free from fear or doubt, easy in mind and manner, inducing and bringing out the best in you. Indra was like that once...' he sighed. 'And I feel guilty that I helped Indra become the monster he is now...'

'You were friends,' she immediately corrected. 'That's why he is so vindictive. He cannot bear to see us together; it goads him more,' she said thoughtfully. 'He thought we would soon part ways as it happens with the others. But we did not. We got married and had a baby. Rambha, is said to be with Tumburu, though some insist she is with Nalakuber. But whoever she is with, she is smart enough not to have a love child. We did, Vasu, and that was the final act of betrayal. Indra lost a friend and his apsara.'

'His favourite apsara, no less! Yes, he knows he has lost you,' agreed Vasu. 'He got back Urvashi from Pururav but he has not been able to get you back.'

'I am too modified for his likes!' smiled Menaka, without humour. 'I cannot be his chattel, I never was. He knows I am yours.'

She said it simply and with such whole-hearted honesty that Vasu felt his heart lurch. It was not desire; it was a deep emotion of infinite tenderness. He touched her face lightly, and he felt her tremble.

'He can't lord over you either. Unlike the other gandharvas, you are immortal like him and the other devas. But he won't be able to harm you, will he?' she added anxiously, clenching her lip tightly with her teeth.

'He cannot kill me, but he can banish me from Indralok...' his voice trailed uncertainly, his handsome face marked by a slight frown.

Menaka snorted dismissively. 'Can he? You are powerful and popular, not an ordinary gandharva. You are their king, the son of the earlier king. You are the shining gem of his court, a musician, a rare spiritualist, a philosopher, the master of the art and the science of illusions, a master of the Chakshushi you learnt from Lord Chandra. Could you not use it on him to bring him to his senses?' she asked.

Vasu laughed half-heartedly, his face still strained. 'I wish, but I should be going,' he said, leaping from the bed. Menaka's eyes followed his naked beauty greedily, her heart missing a beat.

'I have to meet him at the court right away, but I shall join you for the dance recital later. We make a formidable pair, my feisty nymphet, and we shall create magic as we always do!' he kissed her, tugging at her lower lip. 'Don't bite it so often, you'll eat into it someday. It's mine!'

She pressed his head down on hers, fingers in his thick, curling hair. But he released himself eventually, albeit reluctantly.

'What sort of an apsara am I that I can't seduce you back in bed?' she said in lisping coyness, chuckling throatily, her face thrown back invitingly, uninhibited in her nudity, the silk sheets bunched up under her.

Vasu laughingly shook his tousled head and left their bed chamber. Menaka stretched, feeling drowsy, languid in his lingering warmth on the bed...

She woke up with a rude start. There was a jolt; she had felt the tremor, shaking the bed to bolt her awake. Was it Kaushik again? At whom had he thrown some divine weapon this time? If rumours were true, he was the biggest threat to Indra now. His tapas, stretched over decades, was worrying the devas. After his confrontation with Vasishth, he had earned extraordinary powers over time, and it seemed that he was intending to create a separate Heaven for his friend, King Satyavrat, in retaliation for being thrown from this heaven by Indra!

Strange what jealous rivalry can make a man do, and Menaka could not help retracing her thoughts to the rivalry brewing between friends-turned-foes Indra and Vasu, Rambha and her,

Rishi Vasishth and King Kaushik. For Indra, it was bringing out the worst in him, but for King Kaushik, it was encouraging him to aim for the best. He had been dismissed as a mere mortal dreaming of the impossible, till he had shaken the world by creating his new galaxy and openly challenging Indra. Was this jolt another reminder to Indra of another universe he had created? Indra must be in an apoplectic frenzy...

Amused, Menaka dressed up quickly, taking care to tie her bun neatly, but allowing a strand to stray on her face in a tantalising manner. It was time for the dance rehearsal and both Tumburu and Kama would be more shocked than disapproving if she reached late. She was known for her stringent punctuality. People who were not on time were those who did not respect their own time nor others. That was her staple argument with Vasu, who was infamous for his tardiness. He was supposed to join in later for the recital as the lead singer. Her dance and his music formed an unsurpassable combination that was another reason for common envy, especially for Tumburu and Rambha.

Menaka was almost at the doorway when Tilottama came rushing in.

The sight of her in the bedchamber took Menaka by surprise. She was her dearest friend and was the quietest and the gentlest of all the apsaras, though ironically she had been born solely for death and destruction. Having been created by the heavenly architect, Vishwakarma, himself from til—sesame, the smallest bit and the best of everything—gems and all the qualities of the three worlds, Tilottama was exquisitely and dangerously unique. By the divine order of Lord Brahma, she was so made to destroy the two inseparable demon brothers Sunda and Upsunda, who had dared to overrun the world and heaven. By making both of them fall in love with her, she had breached a rift between the twins who otherwise shared blood, bed and brides. The brothers fought each other fiercely over her, eventually killing each other. Such was the power and beauty of Tilottama.

But right now the apsara looked unusually pale, her dusky loveliness afflicted by an anxious uneasiness. Menaka was more surprised at her distress than her unexpected entry; she rarely arrived before announcing herself, more as a discretionary courtesy in case Vasu was around.

'I was going to come to the court anyways, you didn't need to come to accompany me,' Menaka started but her smile disappeared as she noticed the shifty wariness in Tilottama's troubled eyes. 'What's the matter?' she asked sharply.

'It's Vasu...' swallowed Tilottama with some difficulty.

The way she said it, told her all. Menaka had not known such a great fear as the one which clutched at her heart at that moment. What had befallen him?

'It's Vasu and Indra!' repeated Tilottama in a rush. 'They had a violent argument after Indra accused him of being a drunk debauch. Angered, Vasu challenged him...'

But Indra can never kill Vasu. He was immortal, Menaka thought was quick relief. But what had been the challenge for?

'Tilottama, please start from the beginning...' said Menaka consolingly, trying to stem her own mounting trepidation.

'It started with Rambha. She complained in the court that Vasu always came drunk for the music lessons...'

'Say that again??' Menaka could not believe her ears.

'Yes, she cried foul that Vasu had been indecent to her in his drunken stupor several times and demanded that Indra take action against him,' continued Tilottama. 'Rambha got the support of some other apasaras who too voiced the same accusation against Vasu...'

'Was Urvashi one of them?' asked Menaka, with a sinking feeling. This would be her chance to avenge Vasu.

'I wouldn't know. She wasn't present in the hall.'

Menaka bit her lip. 'Indra pulled up Vasu and confronted him,' recounted Tilottama. 'Vasu was at first indignant, protesting strongly for his innocence, and when Indra refused to believe him, he furiously demanded a trial to clear the allegation. Indra refused and Vasu charged Indra of a plot to frame him, accusing him of being the instigator. Indra flared up and threw his Vajra at Vasu...'

Menaka stifled a gasp. The Vajra was Indra's divine thunderbolt. *It was deathly, with momentous consequences, but it could not have killed Vasu,* Menaka thought with renewed hope. *Vasu could never die.*

'It didn't kill him,' said Tilottama, voicing Menaka's dread. 'But it drove Vasu's head and limbs into his trunk turning him into a monster—a one eyed, big mouthed monster with long arms and a huge belly. Indra cursed him to be the headless torso monster Kabandh, to roam the forests of the Earth. It was so horrible! He writhed in pain, begged for mercy, screaming in agony; death would have been deliverance! But Indra was unmoved and cursed he will continue to suffer on Earth. Vasu's gone, Menaka!' cried Tilottama.

Menaka stood white and still, waves of agony crashing over her, unbroken by any vestige of anger for Indra or Rambha. All she could feel was a cold numbness. Vasu was gone, fighting till the last; driven away, as she had always feared. But now the fear had dispelled; suffusing her with a gush of anguish that she found herself drowning in, with nothing to save her...but herself.

She fought to control the tumult of emotions in her, drawing in herself the strength and the power to determine and direct her raging emotions, resolutely denying herself to succumb to kinder impulses, like crying.

Dry-eyed and trembling, she started walking towards the court.

'Don't, Menaka! Don't go to the court! Everyone's too stunned!' warned Tilottama. 'It was intentionally timed during your absence, before your morning dance performance at the court.'

'Indra spared me that!' she said bitterly. 'He is too much of a coward to have me witness it!'

'You are his weakness!' said Tilottama quietly. 'He can never let you go. So he threw Vasu out! Each of us apsaras have been alternately banished or cursed, but you. Have you wondered why, Menaka? He protects you, defends you...'

'...and yet he is the one who has hurt me most!' retorted

Menaka fiercely. 'He is a monster! I don't want him! But I can't be free of him!!' she cried desperately, her body racked with dry sobs.

Tilottama nodded her head. 'Vasu tried to free you from him, and Indra in his mad jealousy threw him out. Menaka, he wants you to be solely his. You are his, his best.'

Who brought out the worst in him? Wasn't it because of me that he had made his friend into his foe? And cursed him to a life of perpetual indignity and ugliness, disgrace and misery? Death would have been kinder, but not Indra. She raised a trembling hand to her face, covering it with her hands, to shut out the flood of grief overwhelming her. It crashed on her, taking her down in a whirl of darkness, she wept.

But as the tears burst violently, coursing down her stricken face, a determination grew; it grew all the way from her cold mind to her weeping heart: Indra and Rambha would not get away. A person is made by the places in which he lives; hers was Indralok and Menaka would follow its law. What goes around should come back. But it would be no Heaven, it would be Hell. They would have to pay for this deceit.

Clash and Confrontation

*A*fter Several weeks and numerous entreaties, Menaka, with deliberate, slow steps, proceeded towards Indra's palace, finally heeding to his call to attend court. She was oblivious to the long looks she received and whispers in the court as she walked towards the palace, staring listlessly ahead of her. She strode past piteous glances, stony-faced guards and a thousand gem-crusted pillars that eventually led her to the glittering resplendence of Indra's court.

The path, which she usually walked twice a day, seemed excruciatingly long and far that day. That was now the chasm between her and Indra. *I would not leave it to any deva or Fate; vengeance would be mine*, Menaka promised herself as she walked towards the Sudharma Hall. That would be her measure of peace. As was the drowning darkness of pain which was hers now, the agony that was slowly tearing her apart, allowing her some soft moments of memories but even that was a hungry longing for something past, for someone lost. Vasu's tender mouth fastened on hers, his amber eyes laughing down at her, their warm handclasps, his voice lingering in her ears—were they her only reward left now? *So be it*, she decided as she entered the hall.

The moment she entered, there was a stifling, ear-splitting silence. Everyone looked aghast, some had the grace to look ashamed. But she had eyes only for one. Indra was sitting on his throne and looking smug, with his wife Sachi. Menaka's eyes dispassionately noticed how Indra's fingers were clutching her hand.

'Welcome back, Menaka! My court has been deprived of your beauteous presence for many days. I presume you have heard of your *husband's* misdemeanour,' he started. 'My heart bleeds at the shame you must be feeling on this dastardly act of his; and that could be the reason you could not show your face in the court.'

'Yes, and I also heard of how wonderfully you meted out justice,' said Menaka coolly. 'The devas are applauding.'

Indra smile slipped. 'Vasu got a punishment that befitted a contemptible drunkard! He dared to harass Rambha, the queen of the apsaras! '

'Vishwavasu was your closest friend once. You knew him well,' she reminded him, dryly. 'Did you not notice this drunken lewdness when you decided to make him the king of the gandharvas? Was your friendship so deep and blind so as to overlook your friend's shameful flaw, and yet make him one of the most prominent gandharvas of your court? Instead, you, o king, deigned to cover up for this degenerate friend and made him your collaborator, assisting you in all your plans...' Menaka paused, throwing a lengthy look at Urvashi which made the entire court stare at the apsara. Urvashi remained silent. *She would*, thought Menaka bitterly. *Silence was her accusation, her retaliation against the perceived wrong wrought on her.*

Indra caught the glance, his face darkening. Sachi restrained a warning hand on him.

'You were not the only ignorant one, dear Menaka,' said Indra evenly, trying to appear unruffled. 'I too did not realize that he could stoop so low.'

'For your ignorance, and for sheltering your friend for so long, poor Rambha had to pay an ...er... uncomfortable price,' agreed Menaka, icily. 'She claims that a drunk Vasu made an indecent advance. It's her word against his. Who are we to believe?'

'The victim, of course!' retorted Indra. 'Besides Rambha, there were others too who voiced their protests.'

Menaka nodded slowly. 'Drinking to work is an unforgivable

offence and the subsequent behaviour more so.'

'You should know better Menaka, he came straight from your room,' intercepted Rambha hotly. She was looking buxomly beautiful as usual but there was a glow of triumph that made her large kohl-lined eyes shine with a satiated gleam. 'He used to reek of drink and you!'

'Sex, sexual exploitation, sexual slavery and now we hear of a drunker sexual assault in our Amravati! And yet, we know how to tackle even the most lecherous of devas...!' Menaka paused pointedly.

This time it was Sachi who flushed a deep red.

'We apsaras indulge, and often endure their amorous proclivity by believing that it's their right to use us. We were created for that, to give pleasure, to seduce, remember? Wine women and inebriation is our culture, and if you say he reeked of wine and me...' she rounded on Rambha. 'How would Vasu dare to even look at you when he had me?' she challenged.

Rambha paled under her smooth, sultry skin. 'You should have asked him that when he was exposed!' she flared.

'But I wasn't here, was I?' shot back Menaka. 'I was not called to court when Vasu was accused and tried by your hearsay. Why and how was it that all the other apsaras were present in this court except me?'

'Because you would have argued for him like a faithful wife, without seeing the fault lay in your husband,' interrupted Sachi, trying to temperate the rising tension of the hall. 'Wives are often blind to their husbands' faults.'

Menaka smiled mirthlessly. 'You said it,' she agreed with elaborate acquiescence. Sachi glared at her.

Menaka continued, her beautiful, porcelain face a frozen mask of cold contempt. 'But now, if I accuse Tumburu of the same offence Vasu was accused of, would I too get justice?'

Rambha physically recoiled, and Tumburu was too dumbstruck to respond. There was a collective murmur of indignant horror.

'Menaka you are going too far!' snapped Indra. 'Tumburu is your teacher, you are his disciple; don't slur the relationship.

He is a learned musician, the lead singer of my court, the best in the three worlds...'

'So was Vasu. He was more than that,' she retorted smoothly. 'He was knowledgeable in philosophy, the scriptures and spiritualism, a student of Rishi Yagnavalkya. So like Tumburu, we cannot fault Vasu of his divine knowledge but for his dubious intentions. So why is that you, o king, believe Rambha and not me when I accuse a gandharva of the same crime? Why will I not get my justice?'

'You have no proof.'

'But Rambha's accusation was proof enough? Or were those lying words of the other apsaras used to substantiate a blatant lie?' taunted Menaka. 'But mercifully, I have proof. Tilottama alleges the same against Tumburu. She says he used to be disgustingly intoxicated when he taught her,' said Menaka, ignoring the collective gasp of horror behind her. 'Ask her,' she invited, pulling the petite apsara by her side.

Tilottama nodded. 'Yes, he has tried to do that several times,' she said clearly, her voice unfaltering and hard. 'If Rambha hadn't been brave enough to complain against Vasu, I would not have had mustered enough courage to voice my complaint too. In his druken state, Tumburu has fumbled all over me on the pretext of explaining various postures of dance...'

'That's preposterous! I have never done that!!' shouted Tumburu, his face red with mottled fury. 'This is the most heinous accusation. I am innocent; everyone knows that! I have never looked at a woman with disrespect but right now I do. These women, whom I am ashamed to call my disciples, are brazenly lying!!'

'If we are lying so was Rambha and the other apsaras,' countered Menaka, feeling a twinge of pain. *Was this how my Vasu had protested his innocence in this full court, in all his helpless earnestness, screaming desperately for justice, begging for a kind, merciful ear?* Menaka shuddered at the thought.

She saw the look of shame on her teacher's face and said, 'It is a sin to assail the reputation of a good man. Rambha did that.

She trivialized sex and made it into a weapon to strip a man of his honour, his pride, his very being. That is an assault too; not what Vasu is accused of; but what Rambha did to him. And to illustrate my argument, I did just that. I publicly confess to my crime—that I falsely accused Tumburu to prove Rambha wrong, and Vasu correct. I attacked your reputation, slandering it with my false allegation,' she bowed her head, folding her hands in respect and request. 'You are my guru and that I cast this aspersion as a means of defence is unpardonable. If you can, please forgive me for what I did. I stand humbled...' she said, 'and humiliated by their act of malice, they ruined a man to a terrible curse, disgraced him in the face of the three worlds. And for this, Vasu was punished for their lie by the king,' she added accusingly.

Menaka turned to look squarely at Indra. 'So how do I get my justice?'

The court lapsed in an abrupt silence, no one daring to voice their thoughts, doubt or disapproval.

'How will Vasu's name be cleared?' persisted Menaka. 'Will I get my Vasu back? Can you undo the curse on him to bring him back to heaven?'

She waited for Indra to reply. She was met with a belligerent silence; the stillness so deafening that she could almost hear Indra gulping nervously.

She continued relentlessly. 'Rambha is the culprit, o king, not Vasu. And so are you!'

Pandemonium broke loose to be reined in only by Menaka's next words.

'And if you cannot deliver justice to me and my expelled Vasu, then I announce right now, right here, that I refuse to dance in this court till Vasu returns,' she enunciated crisply. 'My lord, I came here today in respect to your order to see me in court. From henceforth, I shall not attend this court, your royal orders or the expectations from me as a heavenly courtesan notwithstanding. You are not my king!'

Indra could only stare back at her in incensed disbelief, struck speechless.

'This is gross treason!! How dare you question the king?' exclaimed Sachi, springing to her feet, her face livid. 'Your open defiance has been indulged too long and will not be tolerated any longer. For your insubordination, you should be banished!'

'I am ready for that,' said Menaka simply. 'I shall readily leave Amravati. But I shall not entertain anymore in this court, till Vasu returns.'

Sachi was taken aback. The last threat had failed; Menaka was undaunted by the prospect of the proposed banishment. In fact, Sachi wondered suspiciously, that she seemed to want it. *Was Menaka deliberately leading the conversation to force her expulsion?*

Indra realized it faster than his wife; Menaka had cleverly laid down her terms. Now it was he who would have to choose— expel her from Heaven for her defiance or let her remain here on her conditions.

'Should I leave, my lord?' mocked Menaka, derisively provocative and relishing his obvious discomfiture.

The court was waiting for his answer, his final decree which would define his power and authority. Either way, Indra knew he was beaten. Menaka had amply proved to all those present in his court that it had been out of his petty spite that he had thrown out Vasu, not as a noble gesture of justice for a wronged woman. And that Vasu was not the offender, but he was. Just as Menaka had efficiently demonstrated that it was she and Vasu who were the victims, not Rambha.

'No,' he said haltingly. 'No you shouldn't leave my court. You are an apsara, whose duty is to be in Heaven...'

'Which I shall *not* be doing; I shall *not* perform or dance till the day Vasu returns,' she reminded him.

'Did you hear that, her sheer impudence?' fumed Sachi. 'Throw her out!'

'Yes, please do!' challenged Menaka. 'I shall be rid of this place that has no shame, no remorse, no scruples. You call it my impudence, o queen, but what I am battling for is not only justice but dignity! It was my husband, my lover, who has been wrongly accused of the most despicable crime—drunken misbehaviour!

His reputation damaged beyond redemption, beyond a fair trial. This innocent man has been cursed to a life of horrible, undignified existence by your husband, Devendra, the king of the devas. I, as his wife, can only protest. It is not defiance; it is a demand for justice.'

Her voice rang soft and clear, echoing loudly within the lofty walls of the hall. Menaka stood there pale and proud, her head high, her eyes glowing with a fierce brightness, her voice low. Not once, had she raised her voice.

'Yes, you will get it. By staying here,' said Indra quietly. 'On your terms.'

A restrained furore broke through the long hall, everyone shocked but relieved.

'I, the king, realize my grave mistake and I cannot reverse my actions and its effect,' he continued bravely.

But he could not fool her. Indra was trying to save face, making best of the worst. He was grappling for the last semblance of dignity and a credibility she had made him lose.

'By allowing Menaka to stay, I shall recompense for the great wrong I did to her...'

'And to Vasu?' she prompted. 'How do you plan his return?'

Indra swallowed convulsively; he was trapped again. She was forcing his hand and twisting it around. 'I cursed him and I cannot annul it,' he said evenly. 'But I shall speak on this with the Holy Triumvirate—Lord Brahma, Lord Vishnu and Lord Shiva...' Indra recognized the gleam of warning in Menaka's eyes and he hastily added, 'I assure you, Menaka and everyone else here that Vasu will be released from my curse as Kabandh by an avatar of Lord Vishnu himself who is to be born on Earth soon.'

'And he shall be welcomed in full glory as the king of the gandharvas?' she persisted.

Tight-lipped, Indra nodded and the court broke into a murmur of appreciation. Menaka expelled a long breath, the confined, raging tension slowly ebbing. Indra would not be able to go back on his word. Hopefully, he would be getting his share of penalty as well. A drastic cut down of his bulk of power, she thought savagely, mentally enumerating the list of curses Indra had endured himself, yet he was impervious to correction or contrition.

Menaka saw Indra approaching her.

'You think you just won?' asked Indra snidely.

'After losing everything, I have nothing more to lose, so how have I won?' she riposted with a false smile. 'By proving to all what you are? What you did was not surprising; you always felt threatened by Vasu and wanted an opportunity to get rid of him. And you manufactured one. But what was despicable was that you used Rambha and a lowly allegation. You couldn't have stooped any further!' Naked contempt flickered in her eyes as she stared back at him with loathing. 'You have always used sex as a weapon through us apsaras. Call it temptation, enticement, but it was always consensual sex; we seduced, we did not force anyone against their wishes. If there was force, it was you who used it on us ordered us, victimized us in the name of our heavenly duty . But what you did today was not exploitation but dishonouring and denigrating the very act by using it as a tool to assault someone's character. *You* violated Vasu. And his reputation!'

'Don't be so righteous, Menaka! It doesn't suit you. Agreed I made Vasu a victim and I don't regret it, I got what I wanted!' he snarled, his lips drawn back to show his teeth in an ugly grin. 'But you, my dear, have not been victimized. You are an apsara. You keep forgetting that, meant for all but wanting to favour only one—Vasu. That's why the conflict of interest, and ahem, conscience and honour!' he gave a short laugh. 'But now you won't get Vasu for a long, long...er...long time,' he reiterated, his eyes bright with fury.

'He will come back...' she assured him benignly. 'And I shall wait for him forever. But to you, I shall be right here; you can see me but never touch me, you can hear me but never listen to me singing. You *cannot* have me!' she hissed, bending closer, smiling. 'You will pine for me every single morning and evening, each time during the dance presentations, visualising my moves, fantasising about me, wanting me but never having me! I'll be there but I won't be dancing in front of you, just watching the fun: your discomfiture, your yearning. I shall never dance for you again, my lord, till Vasu returns. We were a team, we were lovers. I shall never make you forget that. You'll miss me...and Vasu!' she added cruelly, her smile sweet, her eyes bitter. 'I'll make sure of that.'

Looking at her, her face so close to him, hot and flushed, her eyes burning, her lips curved delectably, her breasts heaving with each short, angry breath, Menaka seemed exquisitely excited in her wrath. Indra felt strangely aroused and a sliver of fear sliced through him. This woman was his bane yet he shamelessly wanted her.

'Is that your punishment for me?' he said with a gruff, uncertain laugh. 'I am still king and I can do more harm than good... still.'

'You cannot harm me further. But I can. And I shall not exhaust effort or energy putting a curse on you. You are not worth my hate either, only contempt. Hate is too wearying an emotion to waste on you! You will get what you beget...' she said, with an indifferent shrug. 'But a day shall dawn, my lord, when you will be stripped of all what you are so proud, so vain and insecure about your throne, your power, Amravati, Indralok, your retinue of apsaras and gandharvas and...your wife,' she worded with slow, measured deliberation. 'Till then, revel in being a silly dictator.'

Indra reddened unpleasantly. 'The curse of an apsara is too low to work!' he sneered with an uncomplimentary smile.

'Is it? Tilottama once cursed King Sahasranik; and you know what happened! He had to endure the pangs of separation from his love till she forgave him,' Menaka reminded him tartly. 'But I shan't waste breath or bane on you, you are not worth either. But remember what I said, these are words of a woman whom you have made to suffer—you snatched my child, you took away my love,' her voice trembled but hardened instantly. 'It is not a curse, it's a warning.'

Heaven and Earth

Kaushik hoped he had paid off his debt to his friend. King Satyavrat had looked after his family and his kingdom when he had relinquished them all to take up his new path. His higher goal, as Hemavati called it, bitter and sarcastic. That path had been long, hard and unending. He had still not got what he wanted. But with the recent episode of Satyavrat with Indra and his intervention, Kaushik was adorned with a new title—Vishwamitra, the friend of the three worlds—investing him with prestige and power enough to challenge both Indra and Vasishth. *To prove both of them wrong, I created a new universe, my own Heaven,* Kaushik gloated with vicious satisfaction.

It had started on a small note, on a wisp of a truculent wish. King Satyavrat of Kosala of the Ikshvaku royal dynasty, his long-time friend, stated a strangely vain wish. Proud of his good looks, he wanted to enter Heaven in his best mortal form—alive, while possessing his youthful life and handsomeness so as to best enjoy the wondrous pleasures promised by Indra's Heaven. He voiced his intention unequivocally to his royal priest, Vasishth. The rishi was initially amused, dismissing it as one of his conceited whims and explained patiently to the king that he was asking for the impossible. Living people were not allowed entry in Heaven, handsome or not. He would have to die to get to Heaven, and there was no other way. Satyavrat's royal request turned to threat but the old family priest did not budge. Incensed, the young king flounced off to seek help elsewhere, even requesting the rishi's sons, but they all flatly refused. The incident took a nasty turn when Shakti, the eldest son of Vasishth, annoyed at Satyavrat's egotistic vanity, turned him into a chandala named Trishanku, for his last three sins—greed, ego and disobedience. Devastated, Trishanku limped his way to Kaushik for help. Kaushik gauged the situation at once; he could aid his friend as well as believe his long sought purpose. This would be his new battleground. Trishanku had given him another opportunity to defeat his rival. Defying Vasishth, he would pave way for Trishanku to enter heaven.

Kaushik knew what he had promised his friend would be his biggest achievement that none could ever surpass. He would not be just disputing Vasishth's decision, he would have to defy the devas as well. Indra, he knew, would not take it kindly. He would have to put all his powers and knowledge to work, calling upon Agni, the deva of fire and Vayu, the deva of wind, specifically to start with an extraordinarily potent yagna. With his nephew Jamadagni, Kaushik began the grand rites to forge a celestial path for Trishanku's entry into Heaven

Trishanku did but his delight was as ephemeral as his vanished good looks. He was promptly kicked out from the Heaven by an indignant Indra. As Trishanku came hurtling down back to Earth, Kaushik made Trishanku pause mid-air. Now in a belligerent mood to take on the world and heavens, Kaushik decided that if Trishanku was not allowed in Indra's Heaven, he would have to make a new one for Trishanku. Kaushik knew he was pushing himself and his ambition to the extreme, what he was seeking was impossible, something that none had dared to accomplish. With Jamadagni, he sat at the mahayagna, formulating, actualizing, chanting...

And as days lapsed into weeks, Indra to his growing horror saw an unbelievable sight. Rishi Kaushik was forming an entire universe, a parallel galaxy with a new set of stars, constellation, solar systems, a generous sprinkling of life to thrive there, and a clone of Indra to rule it!

'How can we have two Indras?' Indra begged to Lord Brahma, who had come down to see the new wonder. A mere mortal had been able to achieve this miracle—man had made Heaven!

Kaushik faced Indra, with a smug smile of self-congratulation. 'We shall have two Indras because you, lord, did not allow Trishanku to enter yours,' he snapped. 'Your Indralok is biased, segregating on the basis of caste, colour and country. My Pratishristi—this new universe—will be just and egalitarian, welcoming all, respecting all, promising salvation to all. Merit not entitlement will be considered.'

Indra hated Kaushik's tone, the malicious magnanimity of its content, but remained silent, not daring to aggravate him further.

'It was through the reluctant assistance of Lord Agni and Lord Vayu that I could transport Trishanku to his new Heaven,' continued Kaushik imperiously. 'But you, arrogant king, you threw him out because he was a dark and dirty and an untouchable, spurned by the rishis, cursed by Vasishth's son! Even your heaven is dictated by the terms of certain rishis and kings!'

'No, no! I did it as he was a living person,' protested Indra loudly. 'I could not allow him to enter the land of the immortals, however beautiful and tempting it might be!'

'...and so I manufactured another, my own human! And a lot kinder than yours!' shrugged Kaushik.

Noting Brahma's embarrassment, Vishwamitra decided to downplay his victory and agreed to Brahma's request to call off his mahayagna, which was about to set off the fourth galaxy in his Pratishrishti. Visibly impressed, Brahma thanked Kaushik and bestowed him with a new name—Vishwamitra, the friend and philosopher to the universe.

Indra was none too pleased, but he secretly sighed in relief. So did Trishanku and the stars twinkling serenely in the new Heaven. The heavenly war was over. It was a reminder of what a mortal could achieve.

Today the world knows me as Vishwamitra, he thought with a faint smile. He had inched closer to his goal. *Someday, Vishwamitra would meet Vasishth on an enlightened battlefield where the old rishi would himself hand me the title of Brahmarishi, just as Lord Brahma had done.*

Vishwamitra looked around him, casting a good-humoured eye on his surroundings. He had been invited to the rajasuya yagna by King Ambarish, along with Jamadagni and Agastya, the revered rishi from the south of the Vindhyas. The Suryavanshi king had made the grand preparations. A huge platform for the yagna had been constructed close to the sacred River Sharayu.

Suddenly, Vishwamitra narrowed his eyes. He could not believe what he had just seen. There was a young boy tied to a post on the platform.

'Why is a human sacrifice being made?' he thundered, appalled and visibly angry. 'A rajasuya is meant to be a celebration, an announcement to the world and your subjugated kings that you are an emperor. So why the heinous act of a human sacrifice?'

King Ambarish looked crestfallen. 'The *yagna pashu*—the sacrificial animal—had disappeared...' he paused uncertainly. 'We searched for it for hours but as a last resort, considering the supreme status of this yagna, a Brahmin boy was recommended, best suited for the occasion.'

'A human!' barked Vishwamitra, still looking aghast. 'Sacrifices as rituals are in human, be that of a man or an animal. Man, as the highest animal, is supposed to be the preserver of other species. But what you, as a king, are doing is appeasing to your barbaric bloodlust!'

Ambarish quailed at the fury of his words. But Vishwamitra quickly realized why the sacrificial animal needed for the great yagna had disappeared and by whom—Indra. Only that dastardly king of the heavens, insecure that Vishwamitra would get more powerful to stake the heavens again, could trump such a ruse.

'Who is he?' snarled Vishwamitra, laconic in his ire.

'He is the son of a poor Brahmin, who agreed to sell his son for the sacrifice, for some food and cows...'

Vishwamitra shuddered with the thought, *how is it possible for a father to sell his son?*

'And as a king you allowed this?' asked Vishwamitra

contemptuously. 'To save your honour, you are ready to sacrifice another life; one of your subjects to whom you primarily owe yourself. That is the first duty of a king,' he reminded the king caustically. 'A good king.'

Vishwamitra shook his head. 'I shall not allow any sacrifices—this is abominable! You are a king of a civilized world are you not, o emperor? There shall be no bloodshed here especially an innocent one's. This is not war!' he berated, fuming. 'Free that boy! And bring him here...!'

The boy was immediately released. Frightened and trembling, he ran to Vishwamitra and flung himself at his feet.

'You saved my life!' he muttered, tears flowing fast down his thin, wretched face. 'You are my saviour!'

'What's your name?' asked Vishwamitra kindly.

'I am Shunasef, the youngest son of Rishi Richik and Satyavati. There is a famine in our land and we have barely anything to eat. My family is almost dying of hunger...and that is why I agreed for the sacrifice, hoping my death might do some good for my family!' he sobbed.

Vishwamitra whirled around to give King Ambarish a glare that could reduce him to ashes. 'What sort of a king are you? There is a famine in your land and you think of a costly rajasuya yagna to flatter your ego? How noble an accomplishment is that? Your foremost concern should be to look after your people, not yourself!' he exploded, incensed. 'And instead of helping this impoverished family, you allow an inhuman barter for your miserable prestige and honour? How poor could you be, o famous king, of your famous clan? You are not fit enough to be a human, leave aside an emperor!'

Glancing at the tearful boy, Vishwamitra turned his relentless eyes on King Ambarish. 'Do you know who this boy is?'

'The son of Rishi Richik,' the king stuttered.

'...and my nephew, my sister Satyavati's son,' said Vishwamitra grimly, 'and the younger brother of Rishi Jamadagni, who is right here for your yagna as well.'

The king's face drained of colour and mortification.

Vishwamitra turned to Jamadagni. 'Did you not know your family was in such dire straits?'

Jamadagni looked perplexed in his evident shock. 'I have not seen them for years since I took this path of enlightenment...'

'And what an enlightenment we have received today, have we not, my dear nephews?' mocked Vishwamitra, his tone as dry as parched earth. 'Let's start the yagna, Jamadagni, and lets try to make the devas of the oceans, seas and rivers understand that sacrifices don't augur well for the devas as well!'

'But he is to be sacrificed. Lord Varun will be angry if I don't!' pleaded a frightened King Ambrish.

Vishwamitra cast him a shrivelling look. 'Oh, is that so?' he said nonchalantly. 'Then we need to protect this boy and get the Lord down to Earth himself!'

Cutting short any further argument, Vishwamitra continued, 'I shall teach you a mantra, boy, say it, understand it, and mean it,' he said his tone gentle but firm to the trembling waif. His deep, soothing voice seemed to calm the boy and he nodded his head, and started to repeat the mantra after Vishwamitra. The mantra slowly unwound from the knowledgeable tongue of the rishi, echoed by the staccato repetition by the boy. It went on for hours: the sun dimmed, the wind went still, the birds stopped chirping. Yet the yagna went on as Agastya, Jamadagni and Vishwamitra, three of the most venerated rishis started the yagna with renewed flourish, chanting a long mantra.

And soon through the rising flames of the yagna, Lord Varun appeared, his hands folded, his head bowed low in greeting and succinct subordination to the great rishi's wishes. As he graced the yagna with his divine presence, all could merely stare in disbelief.

'Vishwamitra, because of you today this king has hopefully realized the meaning of the word sacrifice. It does not mean to offer up as a ritual, it means to give, to selflessly endure a loss,' enunciated Lord Varun. 'He did not do this nor did he keep his word. He asked for a son, he got it and used a yagna at the expense of someone's life to propitiate the devas! What he needs to propitiate is his conscience...' he smiled and blessed Vishwamitra and Shunashef.

Vishwamitra put an arm across the young boy's shoulders and announced in the holy assembly, 'By the grace of Lord Varuna I have received you, Shunashef. You are now my son and hereafter I shall call you Devrath.'

The stricken King Ambarish prostrated himself before Vishwamitra.

'I have severely erred. I placed my false pride before an innocent life. I failed as a king and betrayed my subjects to neglect, famine and self-interest,' he cried. 'From henceforth, I always shall remember this lesson. O great Vishwamitra, you have opened my eyes and you are indeed the friend of the world!'

Vishwamitra smiled; he was now Vishwamitra, the earthling had made his own Heaven and got down the devas to Earth.

♀

Menaka looked blankly at the white, serene face of the inert girl lying on the straw bed. This was her daughter, Pramadvara, who was dying, hovering more towards death than life. This blue-lipped, blanched girl could not be her, Menaka kept telling herself over and over again. Time and emotions had stopped. She felt nothing but numb, her heart drained. There lingered that crushing feeling that she had failed her daughter. She could not console herself anymore that by leaving her, she had done the best for her. How could things have been different?

She was beautiful, as Menaka had always divined her to be. Her remarkable resemblance to Vasu filled Menaka with renewed grief, making her miss him. She was her father's daughter; she had inherited her father's golden skin, the gossamer, delicate translucency of heart-shaped face. *But she was so young. How could she be dying*? Menaka was confused, as she did not know what death was. She touched her daughter's clammy, limp hands, feeling the seeping emotion of life ebbing away, the blow yet savage to make her aware of the brutality of mortality. It was as agonisingly helpless as the grief of not having Vasu any more.

Menaka looked bewildered. *Pramadvara is our daughter—mine and Vasu's—so she ought to have been immortal too, right?*

Menaka had not realized she had spoken aloud her anguished query.

'No, Pramadvara was raised on Earth by us, so she is a mortal like us too,' said Rishi Sthulkesh gently, his lined face crumpled in grief. 'That is why a snake bite proved fatal for her.'

'...and now she is dying,' said Menaka dully.

'Yes, and that's why I sent you a message so that you could see her before...' his voice broke. 'We will need to do her last rites,' wept the old rishi.

Menaka stared down at the ashen face of her daughter. This was not the last time she would be seeing her, it was the first time. This was the first time she could touch her, hold her. Menaka touched her arm hesitantly. It felt ice-cold. Menaka shivered.

'But how can she die when I, her mother, am alive?' she said in a broken whisper.

'You cannot fight Death. It is inevitable,' murmured the rishi. 'I have been trying to explain the same to poor Ruru, whom she was to marry next week. The young fellow has gone mad with grief. He cannot accept that she is dying. But we tried everything to save her...!' the old man choked, weeping disconsolately.

Menaka felt an old guilt bubbling inside her. This was the parent of her daughter, under whom her baby had bloomed into a beautiful girl, instead of her.

Sthulkesh regained his composure and wiped the tears from his tired eyes. He turned to another grey-haired rishi. 'Pramati, please console your son Ruru. He is challenging Yama, the deva of death, to exchange his life for Pramadvara's. That is crazed wishfulness! Please bring him back to his senses...!'

'But where is Ruru?' asked Menaka urgently.

She was informed the young ascetic was deep in the forest, lamenting his lover's death. Ruru, like her daughter, was born from an apsara, Gritachi who had left the new-born son with the father Rishi Pramati. Just as she, Menaka had deserted hers in selfish instinctiveness. It was their second nature—self-preservation.

Menaka knew she had to reach Ruru, before Yama deigned to listen to his plea. The other devas were already touched, moved by his grief and it would not take much time for Lord Yama to agree to Ruru's strange invocation. It should not happen, Menaka hoped fervently.

Menaka caught sight of the young man. His face was ravaged, his eye twin pools of despair, and he was weeping unabashedly. Was this pain? Was this mad, senseless anguish? Is this how a mortal writhes in agony? Menaka trembled at the sight of his raw pain: he was ready to die for his love.

'Ruru, I can understand your sorrow but I cannot bring her back to life,' Lord Yama was trying to pacify the young rishi.

'But I cannot live without her!' cried Ruru, distraught, his cry of hopelessness, stirring Menaka's cold heart, her frozen mind. She had long gone numb since the day Vasu had been driven away from Heaven. She had started living like an apsara as was expected of her—cold and heartless, warming all with her mere presence, hot and passionate, fervid and fiery in her erotic intensity. Yet cold and dead within, inanimate, and as deprived and destitute of love and life as was her daughter now.

But right now she was a mother trying to save her child's life.

'Neither can I take your life for hers, Ruru, as life cannot be exchanged,' Lord Yama was saying. 'I cannot let you die for her.'

'But I can, can I not?' interrupted Menaka, slowly approaching Yama, looking squarely at the Lord of Death. 'I am ageless. I cannot die and so I can give some of my life to my daughter, can't I?'

Yama looked flummoxed.

'I am immortal,' she persisted. 'I cannot be subjected to death, but I have enough years of life to donate to my daughter whom I bore from Vasu, an immortal as well.'

'True, but what you are asking for is unheard of—an immortal bargaining for a life!' exclaimed Yama. 'You are taking disadvantage of the boon of the infinite life that has been blessed upon you.'

'I don't know what to do with it,' implored Menaka. 'I have

too much of it. Can I not give a bit of my living breath to my dying daughter?'

Yama looked helpless. He had never dealt with an apsara, this creature of exquisite beauty, wooing with words, wrangling for her life with her reasonable logic.

'You cannot deprive Ruru of his life. It is not done. He is a mortal! But you can take the life of an immortal, of the undying for we apsaras know no death!' argued Menaka. 'I cannot die, so my life I can breathe into another, my own child! Give me this just one right as her mother!'

Ruru threw himself at Yama's feet. 'You could not comply to my wishes as I was a mortal, who cannot haggle for life and death,' he said. 'But this fair maiden can. She is a mother, pleading for her daughter's life. My lord, you cannot deny a desperate mother her one wish.'

Yama looked at Menaka suspiciously, but not without a grudging admiration, 'Yes, I guess, if Vishwavasu had been here, he would have done the same; and as a powerful gandharva, I could not have denied him,' he rued. 'Nor can I now. As her mother, Menaka, I grant you your wish.'

Justice does prevail, Menaka thought with amazed jubilance. Down in the ashram, Pramadvara woke up from her deep sleep, fresh and beautiful as ever, eager to get married to the man she loved. Staring into her moist, grateful eyes, Menaka could only smile back tremulously as she embraced her daughter for the first time, swamped by a sudden swell of happiness, an unfamiliar feeling since long. She had learnt the value of life, the essence of living and of death as well. She had thought she had died a little when her baby had been taken from her or when Vasu had left her languishing, alone in Amravati. But today, as she had watched the still face of her daughter, Menaka witnessed the physical demonstration of death, its brutal eventuality; of what it was to be without life, without a breath in your body; to be lifeless. And in deference to death, preceding all her previous emotions, Menaka herself resuscitated, rejoicing in her immortality, feeling the rush of a joyful, revitalising energy. Of what it meant to be full of life, to never die, to be everlasting.

And with that had welled another new emotion of lasting experience: of being a mother. It had been just for a day, but it meant a lifetime to her. She had touched her Heaven.

☙

Vishwamitra was in Heaven. He stood looking at the grand portal of the Sudharma Hall. This was the nerve centre of Indralok, where power was brokered, peace negotiated. Vishwamitra knew what power was, what it evinced and what it connoted. As a king, Vishwamitra had worn the crown easily on his head. Carrying the crowning glory of Vishwamitra though had not been as easy. Possibly because it was hard gotten and not a privilege handed down to him as his royal legacy. Or perhaps, because he had earned it, a fact which still rankled many. He was proof what man can accomplish when mind is set on purpose. He wanted to be a rishi, the enlightened one and he had achieved it. And it is through this deed that the awed whispers had grown into a resounding echo making a legend of him, the inspiring hero. He was neither just an ambitious king nor an opportunistic rishi, he was Vishwamitra.

His contemporaries were mostly disgruntled seers who did not miss a chance to demonstrate their displeasure. Vishwamitra was an oddity, almost an outcast amongst them, more hated yet grudgingly respected. Some boycotted courts which he attended, walked off from a yagna in a rude huff, openly questioned him, his credentials suspected, or brazenly insulted.

But not today, Vishwamitra swore grimly, as he recalled his most punishing moments. He stood before Indra's lavish hall where all the devas congregated. He had been invited here by the devas themselves. *This is where all is decided, all is plotted, all is devised to make and break the world*, he mused. Indra himself had come down to receive him with a smile and salutations. But both were hollow. Vishwamitra could feel his dislike and he was more amused than alarmed. The last time he had seen him, he had left Indra in a dire dilemma, forcing him to acknowledge

Vishwamitra as Vishwamitra. That was one ego he had loved disseminating.

'I welcome you to Indralok, dear sir. This is your first visit here,' said Indra pointedly.

'Yes, Devendra, and certainly not my last. I shall keep coming often whenever there is a conference next,' replied Vishwamitra cheerfully.

Indra's smile was fixed, never reaching his eyes. Lord Varun interceded and received him with all honours. It had been because of him, that an invitation had been addressed to him, as a show of obeisance to Vishwamitra's reigning superiority which he had presented to the world by forcing the deva of the seas to come down to Earth at the rajsuya yagna of King Ambarish. Varun seethed silently at his disgrace at the hands of this very rishi, but escorted him graciously and made him sit in an exalted seat. It was a gesture of their defeat and Vishwamitra's victory.

Vishwamitra looked around approvingly: he was in very good company. The seven great rishis were present, eyeing him a trifle suspiciously except for his nephew Jamadagni. They were the Saptrishis—the seven great Brahmarishis born out of divinity. They had been ordained the order of the Brahmarishi too through divinity, by Lord Brahma himself. Unlike him who would earn it through his purpose and perseverance, vowed Vishwamitra. He would win his war as a man, he did not need the devas or divinity.

He was the sole mortal sitting amongst these divine seers—Bharadwaj, Gautam, Atri, Kashyap and Vasishth. He noticed Rishi Brihaspathi, preceptor of the devas and several others, were eyeing him with visible doubt. What was a the Rajrishi doing here? Their discomfort made Vishwamitra feel comfortable. He was basking in their jealous resentment.

Then there were the six of eight dilplakas as well—Indra, Agni, Yama, Varun, Chandra and Kuber—seated in the assembly, seeming strangely edgy. Was his presence so unnerving?

Vishwamitra knew he added to the divine assembly a special lustre, not simply because of his achievements but in spite of it. Clearly, he was not very welcome but they had been forced to acknowledge him. Both the devas and the rishis resented his climb to self-achieved greatness. Unlike them, it was not by birth but by the virtue of worth, he was sitting amongst them.

Vishwamitra relished his fame. And he meant to enjoy it, the scepticism notwithstanding. This was his hour of glory. The discussions soon flowed, often expanding into amiable debates, each rishi wary of the other, not prepared to ruffle ego or argument. Vishwamitra soon found himself getting bored with the meek acquiescence of each other's ideas. Indra had started the debate on how difficult it was to remain true and to keep to the truth. Fine man to talk, scoffed Vishwamitra but kept his face expressionless.

'There is none in the world who can follow truth faithfully,' he was saying. Many heads nodded wisely, except one.

Vasishth spoke out in his soft, soothing voice. 'Do not generalize, Devendra,' he said. 'Truth is hard to seek, but harder to sustain. Even the devas cannot follow it!!'

For once, Vishwamitra agreed with him but he made no motion to show it. Indra had the grace to look slightly bemused, taken aback at Vasishth's blunt appraisal.

'I would not agree nor approve of your sweeping statement. Is that an argument or for effect?' asked Vasishth, sarcasm soft but sure in his voice. 'The asuras are famous for their lies, the devas are infamous for mocking it but for the mortal. He is the most honest amongst all.'

'The mortal?' interjected Vishwamitra, raising one brow. 'They are forced to lie at every step. Call it circumstance or convenience, but for a mortal speaking truthfully is a task, imposing and impossible.'

'I beg to disagree, Vishwamitra,' retorted Vasishth, accentuating on the 'mitra' to emphasize that they were not friends. 'Man lives by truth in his daily living.'

'Which man are you talking about?' sneered Vishwamitra. 'The poor man who is more worried about how to feed his family and get the next meal in? Or the weak, who is too scared to speak the truth in fear of some inflicted torment or torture? Or the greedy who will lie to amass more? Or the powerful and the rich for whom both a lie and a truth have a price, without knowing its value but to be bartered away? Truth is for sale, to be bought only if you can afford it. And not many mortals are so enriched. And so which man are you talking about?' he repeated, sardonic.

'King Harishchandra,' replied Vasishth. 'He has been known in the seven worlds for being truthful. He never deviates from the path of truth.'

'Trishanku's son!' Vishwamitra laughed. It was an open affront. 'But dear sir, besides he being your protégé, you are his royal priest, why are you advocating him so earnestly?'

Vasishth looked sufficiently chagrined.

'How dare you accuse me!' seethed the elderly rishi. 'Yes I am the royal priest of King Harishchandra and I was their priest even during his father's time when Trishanku came up with the absurd idea of entering heaven alive! A silly wish which you encouraged...'

'But which I achieved!' riposted Vishwamitra smoothly.

'You did not pamper a silly king, you played with the law of Nature, the fundamentals of Order and Creation!' argued Vasishth.

'...to create a pantheon! Do you grouse that?' challenged Vishwamitra.

'What you did was wonderful!' berated Vasishth scathingly. 'But you did it to pamper egos of that stupid king's and more importantly, yours! And to assuage both was folly, a childish attempt of self-aggrandisement; you were ready to fool with the Universe!'

'Can Universe be created out of folly? I thought it was out of wisdom,' remarked Vishwamitra, his voice suddenly soft and dangerous. 'The devas did it. So did I.'

'It's always about you, your ego,' sneered Vasishth. 'You wanted to prove you were great and that's why you picked on Trishanku and agreed to his whim. And now you argue with me because your ego does not agree. You pick on my words, accusing me of nepotism when I claim that Hrishchandra is the epitome of truth and honesty in this world.'

'But what is the proof?' countered Vishwamitra.

'His very existence. He is a living example of Truth. Harishchandra is not just a king, he is a righteous man, who has sworn to the path and he shall never veer clear from it, come what may!'

'I doubt it. No man, however extraordinary, can carry the weight of honesty for long. He eventually lies to save himself, if not his soul, his life!' said Vishwamitra dismissively. 'There is no one in all of the seven worlds and the universe and beyond who can remain honest all the while. He will lie, he will be defeated by the burden of truth. And this great king you mention, your king, your protégé, is no exception.'

The devas looked distinctly uneasy now, the rishis were too stunned to interrupt. This was no more a discussion, it was a confrontation. The only person secretly pleased was Indra. He was waiting for his chance to strike. He had to fuel this conflagration into an inferno of words and war. By making the two rishis fight, he would be able to save his Heaven. He would take his revenge on that imperious Vishwamitra; he would vindicate his humiliation. He would ruin him.

'Two great minds are in discussion here,' he intervened silkily. 'It is difficult to agree or disagree with them. If what Vasishth says is true, Vishwamitra needs to confirm it.'

Indra's words whipped the usually calm Vasishth into an impotent rage. 'You ask for truth, Vishwamitra!! You arrogant young man, you ask for proof, then go seek it yourself!' roared Vasishth. 'You prove me wrong about Harishchandra and I shall bow down to you!!'

Vishwamitra loved challenges but this one was a do-or-die dare. Either he won or the old rishi lost. He had to pick up the gauntlet.

'Yes I shall,' he vowed, his voice full, deep and loud. 'I shall prove to you that Harishchandra too is but a mere mortal who can succumb to the travesty of truth. I shall prove this man a liar!'

Vishwamitra walked out, his head high and his determination resolute. He had to make Harishchandra speak one lie to make true his win.

Plan and Proposal

*O*ndra was not sure whether he should call for Menaka or go see her himself. He was in trouble, and only she could help him. This feeling of helplessness made him feel weak and angry; and he wanted to feel neither in her presence. She abhorred him; her disdain and discourtesy publicly demonstrated at his very royal court was the proof of that. But it was a daily punishment for him—to see her but not go near her, to look at her and see the contempt stark in her cold, violet eyes.

But he had to see her; the situation was such. He finally announced his presence at her palace, with more trepidation than hope.

Menaka looked as breathtakingly beautiful as always, and as forbidding, not offering even the smallest smile of graciousness in his presence.

'I presume you must be in the worst of trouble, or you would not have come to meet me,' she started, her words terse. 'Let's make it quick and brief. Who is your new prey I am to stalk? Or better yet, who is the individual I am to bed—not that I'll agree to either'

Indra winced. Menaka could be brittle when she wanted, her soft, sweet voice hardening on each word she uttered.

He swallowed. 'Kaushik,' he said. 'He goes by the name Vishwamitra these days,' he could not help adding acidly.

Menaka's face remained expressionless. 'Vishwamitra, who created the new pantheon to spite Rishi Vasishth,' she said thoughtfully.

'No, to spite me!' retorted Indra.

'From what I hear, his grouse is against the revered rishi. It has nothing to do with you, my lord. It is a fight between the two rishis,' said Menaka. *Trust Indra to get overanxious*, she scoffed.

'Vishwamitra does not aspire to be the king of this Heaven, but he wants to be a Brahmarishi like Vasishth. And he soon will be one, I am afraid, evident by the way he is going!' she said. 'If a mortal can create another heaven, who will stop him from becoming a Brahmarishi?'

'Me,' said Indra, self-importantly, keeping his hands on his hips. 'I have to stop him or he'll ruin my Indralok! He had the temerity...'

'...and the brilliance,' she interposed mockingly.

'...to create another Heaven and Lord Brahma permitted it and crowned him with a title—Vishwamitra—instead!' ranted Indra, his handsome face pinched with anger. He turned to look at Menaka and said, 'You have to help me stop him!'

'Me?' asked Menaka in genuine amusement, stretching her long legs languorously with feigned indifference. But her interest had sharply piqued. Indra needed her, and she could very well use the opportunity to her advantage. 'And why would I do that?'

Indra looked at her with anxious eyes. 'Yes. Only you can stop his madness. He has been meditating for years acquiring the knowledge and collecting power only the devas can possess. His tapas is so great now that the heat is burning up Amravati! And only your beauty can consign his tapas to oblivion. You will have to be his salvation and ours too!'

She shook her head. 'The devas think they have powers. They haven't earned it like this man has. And why worry about Vishwamitra's salvation? He doesn't need it or your Heaven. He is capable of creating his own. He is no longer a lesser mortal; he is more powerful than a deva. But that's your worry, is it not, my lord?'

Indra threw up his hands in despair. 'Yes! If Vishwamitra seeks for more, he is going to create an imbalance between Earth and Heaven...'

'Between Man and Deva,' she corrected him sweetly 'He has proved that Man doesn't need deva!'

'Exactly! Man will become deva, and thus his impertinence needs to be checked. Vishwamitra has to be stripped of his powers, drained of all his spiritual might and strength; and only you can do this!'

Menaka remained silent but she was listening avidly, allowing him to vent out his frustration and fear.

'When he devised his Pratishrishti, I had to come down to Earth and beg him to desist,' riled Indra, with obvious resentment. 'He didn't listen to me, but fortunately agreed to Brahma's request for which he has been declared as a Vishwamitra, revered and feared in all the lokas, all the three worlds. Since then, Vishwamitra has acquired an unsurpassed radiance from his rare siddhis, one so phenomenal that when the time will arrive for him to leave his body, the devas and I are worried how to receive him in Heaven and in which dimension we can place him...'

'But he doesn't need your Heaven, my lord,' she repeated, watching the colour leak from his face, making it appear unpleasantly blotchy.

Indra stopped pacing in the chamber, his annoyance flaring, no longer a mere irate flare of temper but a deeper, sicker worry that was eating into him. Menaka could recognize the signs; Indra was a very worried man. And Vishwamitra was his new obsession, his growing, unfeigned terror.

'He has to be stopped,' said Indra, his fist clenched. 'He is getting too powerful. Only you, Menaka, can subdue him' he admitted sheepishly. 'I have no one else who can do it better than you.'

Menaka looked on knowing where the conversation was leading.

'It's time for him to break! I need you, Menaka,' he appealed.

'I need you to go down to Earth, seduce him, sap him entirely of all his powers and find a way to trap him into domestic bliss on more permanent terms.'

Menaka froze, letting Indra's words sink in. 'You mean have a baby?' she asked coldly. 'Like I had earlier?'

'No, not like your's and er...Vasu's' he said with some difficulty. 'More like when Urvashi had a son from Rishi Vibhandak—love and leave. Have a child from Vishwamitra, leave him and saddle him with that responsibility. You come back to Heaven, having saved the world.'

Her hard face softened into a small smile. 'And having saved you, my lord,' she said, bluntly. 'Such a lofty task! But why should I do all this for you?'

Indra looked taken aback.

Menaka looked up at him steadily. 'And why only me? Any other apsara can do it. Vishwamitra has to be seduced so completely that he is a finished man, crippled of all his powers, right? It's not new to any of us, so why assign this task to me? Urvashi has done it before, ask her.'

'Because only you possess that intoxicating mix of beauty and intelligence to make him–surrender. Vishwamitra is not an easy prey,' warned Indra, hoping to incite a challenge in Menaka. She could never resist a challenge.

Menaka gave a mirthless smile, refusing to rise to his bait. 'Absolutely,' she agreed. 'He is a dangerous man to contend with, so, why are you putting me in danger? Or is that your plan?' she asked shrewdly. 'Vishwamitra is no fool to get so easily seduced by sex and lust. He will see through me immediately. And knowing his infamous temper, he is sure to put a curse on me,' she paused meaningfully. 'Is that what you want?' she asked softly.

'Of course not, you know I can never lose you! Never!' replied Indra heatedly. 'You are too precious for me to lose you. I can't even let you go out of my sight,' he said. 'But I have to risk it, and I do know that only you will be able to lure him away from his mission.' He said it with a strange sincerity, placing his trust and hope on her.

'But why should *I* help you?' she repeated.

Indra had the grace to look ashamed.

'I need you,' he said shortly, but there was desperation in those three words.

'To do your dirty work, to clean up the mess you have made, to lure, to entice, to sleep with your enemy so that you win and get more powerful,' she said. 'Why should I do that? I refuse to be your slave, your whore of Heaven.'

Indra hated the word 'whore', especially when she said it. *Menaka is not my whore*, he screamed silently. He hated it when anyone even glanced at her. He recalled his days of agony when she was with Vasu. He had thrown him out, but he had lost her as well. *Now I am throwing her to that Vishwamitra, that raunchy king*, Indra thought with a grimace. He loathed the thought but he had to do it, and if Menaka refuses, he decided that he will have to force her.

'I am still your king. I order you,' he said simply.

Menaka raised a quizzical brow. 'You can't order me, remember? I don't perform for you any longer so why would I agree to your sleazy seduction games?'

'Because you are the best! And I need you!!' he repeated fervently. 'Is this your way of getting back at me? Making me grovel and beg?'

His words misted a double image in her mind—of her begging on her knees for her baby and Vasu screaming for Indra's mercy. None had been given justice. She had lost both. She could do the same now. But by refusing him, how would she gain?

'But if you still decline, I shall be forced to send someone else...' he shrugged. 'Hema, maybe. Or probably Tilottama, she reduced the asura brothers to a bloody pulp!' he grinned briefly. 'Or Manorama. Or Saudamini. If not you, I have to get some apsara to get through this man...'

But he knew he was fooling himself. There was none like Menaka—smart and sensuous. She was made out of love—the sand and the sea, moulded, miscible, entwined forever. She permeated from the life source of all living things—air and water had sculpted her as the most deadly in her magnificent loveliness. *Oh Menaka,* he sighed, *I have seen what you do to men; devastate without them even knowing what had struck them. Your beauty left me parched, thirsting for more.* Indra watched her. Even in her grief, she was ambrosial in her gorgeousness, arousing an insatiable hunger. Her thick mane, long, wavy cascading like the ripples through water, flowing down her creamy shoulders and not pulled up in a knot as she often did in careless gesture. Her lush, luscious lips, which she had a maddening habit to chew, so ravenous to touch, to taste, to devour and eyes the colour of wine, what man could possibly resist their intoxication? *Certainly not Vishwamitra,* he scoffed. He wanted the plan to succeed and Menaka was his best bet. He would have to let her go, just this once, he promised himself. He had never let her out of his sight till now and it was with heavy reluctance he was carrying out this deed. He turned his attention to what Menaka was saying.

'By throwing the other apsaras names, do you hope that I shall be prompted to jealous action?' she asked wryly.

Indra was known to use such tricks, pitting one against the other, dividing them to maintain control over them all.

'But I want you, Menaka, not the others. Only you can handle Vishwamitra, who right now is one of the most powerful men on Earth. Only you can bring him down to his knees, with your wile and winsomeness.'

'Literally,' Menaka gave her deep, husky laugh, urging Indra to silence that delicious gurgle with his lips. 'You are right, though, I don't think I can allow them to snatch away my assignment. I shall do it,' she said slowly.

She noticed the look of surprise and delight on Indra's face. He made no effort to hide it.

'I have nothing to do here anyway,' she shrugged her slim shoulders. 'I am bored, my lord, and this Vishwamitra sounds like a very interesting man.'

'Oh he certainly is!' he exclaimed with an irate frown. 'Supremely arrogant, proud and rude...'

'You are not making him sound too encouraging for me to

take him on,' remarked Menaka. *And he sounds like he is describing himself*, she thought with dry amusement. Proud people had one weakness: vanity. But she had no intention of divulging it to the man who was its personification. She smiled encouragingly instead.

'But that's exactly how you can hook him!' countered Indra swiftly. 'His superior manner and haughtiness has a chink. He is essentially a kind man, moved always to the quick by some sad story of pain, loss or tragedy—you can always trump up one!'

'You mean to be the veritable damsel-in-distress?' she said. 'Yes, it always does work so wonderfully with men. They are surely gullible to tears, a little sniff, a pretty pout and that coy batting of the eyelids,' she derided. 'And a peek at the cleavage is always irresistible with the promise of such a prelude! But this time, with this man, I am not too sure...' she looked thoughtful, her lip between her teeth. 'Seduction is an art best practised on those who are vulnerable. A lie or some sob story is not going to work, he'll be able to recognize me for what I am. Don't underestimate his yogic powers to perceive the true nature of people,' she warned. 'He'll catch me in a second, and that would be the last of me!'

Indra frowned. This was going to be more complex than he had figured. Menaka by pointing out the errors, was making their plan sound weak. But she was sharp by deleting possible ambiguities, Indra knew she was making their case stronger. That was what made Menaka so refreshingly different from the others—she always used her exceptional intelligence to work out her schemes of seduction. And other schemes as well, he thought dourly as he recalled how efficiently she had dismembered him bloodlessly in his own royal court.

'I have to go to him as Menaka,' she explained, tracing her thoughts carefully. 'No lies, no pretence, no subterfuge—nothing for him to suspect or surmise. Even a hint of suspicion, you will have your enemy at your heavenly threshold.'

'So how do you propose to arouse his sympathy and the requisite sentiments besides having sex, of course?' he asked.

Menaka grimaced. Indra could be so conspicuously tasteless.

'I shall introduce myself as who and what I am—Menaka, the banished apsara,' she stated her plan. 'I shall convince him that I have been thrown out from Heaven by you as a punishment for having dared to love the Devagandharva Vishwavasu and sired a child from him. And how you cursed him and recount all what you did to extract all the needed sympathy,' she purred, her voice cruel. 'That way, there is no untruthfulness in my story.'

Indra flushed under his fair skin. 'You don't have to supply all the details,' he said abruptly.

'But that's exactly what would make my story convincing—simply because it is true! Even if Vishwamitra rechecks my story, he won't suspect any deceit or dishonesty,' said Menaka. 'Remember you cannot fool him, my lord, don't ever make that mistake.'

Indra nodded his head slowly agreeing with her cautious wariness but her next words surprised him considerably.

'I would like to take Kama with me.'

Indra brows shot up in amazement. 'Are you so unsure of yourself?' he asked sardonically. 'Menaka, just a look from you makes any man lose his senses and come running to you!'

'But not this man, my lord,' she refuted stoutly. 'He is no fool to go after some woman, however gorgeous she may be! He's a wary man, always on his guard, marked by keen prudence and sharp caution. That's why I need Kama, to use his love darts. Also, I shan't dance to seduce. It is sure to incense him!'

Indra looked incredulous. 'Menaka, but that is your forte, your best tool!' he exclaimed. 'You entrap, you woo, you win men with your sensuous moves. You are the best dancer who knows how to wield her power over men, however tough or even if he is praying! You know that and use it ruthlessly. You make them see your body, your flesh, your movements suggesting the wildest, firing their imagination, making them yearn for more, wanting more, wanting you!'

Menaka knew this, and Kama had been an excellent teacher. A certain movement of the eyes, suffusing it with the right emotion, a tone of voice—husky, exciting, helpless, wretched, or simply a sigh—or a slight touch of the hand on the shoulder or the hand but never outright eroticism. *Make the men think you like them, they will immediately assume and account for you of being special, exclusive. Meant just for them. Men could be such fools*, she thought.

'But that shall not work on Vishwamitra,' she dissented, with a firm shake of her head. 'If I try to break his tapasya, he will see through my intentions immediately—not as a desirable woman but a mercenary seductress, an enemy out to destroy his tapas. His open eyes will see all this, and curse me or reduce me to cinders because of the treachery! But Kama,' she dimpled a knowing smile, 'should ease matters up considerably if he were present at the scene. His love arrow would be a safe shot.'

'So you have these two conditions—Kama and no dancing,' said Indra, watching her nod. 'Fine, though honestly I still think you can do it on your own. I am more confident about your magic than his. How do you plan to do it?'

'We shall figure it out and let you know the details,' she affirmed, effectively cutting him short.

Her laconic reply meant the discussion was over. Indra pursed his thin lips in evident displeasure. But he did not want to push her either. Menaka was known for her imperiousness but her whimsical moods had got more pronounced since Vasu's expulsion. *Damn, that man. He kept intruding into her thoughts. He was still clearly not out of her mind and heart*, Indra gave Menaka a probing look. She had moped, she had mourned, she had rebelled, she had outsmarted him, and she had avenged her grief. *Or had she?* Indra felt a coil of uneasiness. Was Menaka up to her tricks again? He had been pleasantly surprised when she had fallen for his plans so willingly, though, as an afterthought, Indra discerned, it had been she who had controlled their conversation and the intended conspiracy. He had assumed she would give him a hard time considering her unveiled animosity for him since the time he threw Vasu out. *So then, why had Menaka complied so easily? Was this her ruse or her revenge?*

Hunt and Hunted

*W*hy had she agreed to help Indra in his plot? But Menaka knew her answer—it was not her revenge plan or a ruse. It was her only chance in a desperate attempt to escape from Heaven. But how could she escape and where could she hide? She had seen Earth, had witnessed its lushness and life's temperance when she had held her dying daughter in her arms. Pramadvara had survived and was happily married to Rishi Ruru now, but Menaka had witnessed more than the meeting of two happy souls. She had learnt more about life and living than what she had in the beautiful realms of Indralok. She had seen the anguish and ugliness behind the earthly loveliness, but Menaka was ready to live in this beautiful world of pain, joy and emotions than the unending chasm of celestial longevity, with its long, empty years without Vasu...

Menaka could not bear to stay in this Heaven anymore, and Indra would never let her go. She had hoped he would banish her for her impertinence when she had publicly disgraced him in his court, laying open his malicious intent and design. She had won instead—her revenge as well as everyone's respect—but had lost her chance to leave Heaven. Vishwamitra would be a legitimate opportunity of escape and she would have to see it went well, she reminded herself. Indra fortunately was unaware of her treachery, yet.

She glanced at Lord Kama. He was as handsome and dapper

as always, with his jade green eyes and ready smile. Today, as his task commanded, he was carrying his long bow made of sugarcane, the ends of which were tied not by the usual taut cord, but a string of tightly-lined honeybees. There were just five arrows in his quiver, each one decorated by five different fragrant flowers—jasmine, the white lotus, the blue lotus, the mango tree blossoms and the flowers from the Ashok tree (Kama's favourite), which many considered the symbol of love and desire.

'Will those love arrows be enough?' she jested.

'With you around, Vishwamitra should not need even a single shot!' he chuckled. 'You have planned it out well,' he said, visibly impressed. 'I liked the intricate story, woven with those omissions, you intend to use on him. It will save you from getting caught with outright lies. That will make the pretence easier for you and convincing for him.'

They were proceeding to River Mahi, along which was Vishwamitra's ashram.

'Where's Rati?' asked Menaka, fairly surprised that Kama's wife has not accompanied him as she usually did in such assignments where 'love had to strike...and penetrate,' as Rati had wickedly remarked.

Kama and Rati had an interesting love story of their own. A young Kama, who was instructed to spread love in the world by Lord Brahma after his creation, was trying out the potency of his love arrows. In misdirected enthusiasm, he tried some at Brahma and his sons to make them all fall in love with a lovely maiden Sandhya. Little did Kama know that Sandhya was Brahma's daughter. Mortified by the incestuous feelings her father and brothers had suddenly developed for her, Sandhya committed suicide. Aghast at the tragedy he was inadvertently culpable for, Kama prayed to Lord Vishnu for repentance, who resurrected her to be reborn as Rati to Prajapati Daksha (Brahma's son). Rati eventually married Kama, the one responsible for her death as well as her new life. *She was his true love*, smiled Menaka, thinking strange about the ways of life and love, and karma. *Did apsaras and devas have any karma to answer to?* Menaka bit her lip in quiet thought. They were still accountable for their actions although they might be spared the cycle of life and death. They had to live out their mistakes, their penance and punishment. *As Vasu was doing...*Menaka blinked, forcing herself into the present.

But the incident had taught Kama one lesson certainly. He was now elaborately diligent on whom he used his love arrows. Possibly that was the reason why he was carrying just five arrows in his quiver.

Kama grinned. 'Rati said I won't need her with you around! Why do we need three to seduce one poor Vishwamitra, was her argument. Anyway, I am sure you must be well prepared with the preliminary work on him?'

Menaka nodded, chewing her lower lip absently. 'Cannot afford to be lax, or I shall get caught!'

'Which would mean that we will be turned to ashes or monsters, or stuck by some other curse!' he winked, but his smile slipped the moment he saw the changed expression on Menaka's face. He saw the quick flicker of grief, and Kama cursed himself for his insensitivity. *She was still in love with Vasu, and has not come to terms with the loss.*

The thought worried him further. It was not going to be a one-time seduction with Vishwamitra but a prolonged amour. Menaka had to make Vishwamitra fall in love with her for him to be so besotted, so distracted and so doomed in her love that he lets go of his mind and mission. Would she be able to play her part convincingly as Vishwamitra's beautiful nemesis from now on? He did not want to lose Menaka. She was his favourite student and Kama still could not reconcile with Indra's deviousness in making her suffer unduly over Vasu. That had been unpardonable.

'In this new game of deception, will you be able to pretend to love Vishwamitra?' he asked her quietly. 'Making and faking love are entirely different. Lust is quick. Love is not. It is a more sustained, exhausting emotion even to sham!'

Menaka hunched her pretty shoulders as if preparing for the onslaught, ready with her answer. 'I can feign love well. I know what is kaam and what is prem—lust and love,' she gave a faint smile. 'As you once taught us, there are various stages in love. Love starts at first sight, the visual contact. Then comes the desire, when both the hearts and the minds are in flux, full of intense thoughts and hopes, followed by determination to get the lover and your love reciprocated. Disinterest with the world, appetite and sleep are the smaller symptoms but triggering a certain rebelliousness, a madness in love. Then comes happiness and its consummation. Last of course, is the end of that love—either through separation, betrayal or physical death of the lovers. I know it,' she paused, staring down at her empty hands. 'I prefer the pretence. Real love is too painful to live with, Lord Kama. I nearly died once and it would be suicidal to live through that pain again,' she said stiltedly, her frozen face warm with heightened colour and an unspecific emotion. 'Let's go to Vishwamitra's ashram fast. I want to catch him before he sits for another long round of meditation.'

⍦

Vishwamitra could not stop feeling angry with himself. If he could control the stars, could he not control his black mood? Vishwamitra felt a slight sliver of memory swishing past his troubled mind. Brahma's words echoed back to him, 'Vishwamitra, the day you rein in your arrogant temper, you will find the path you seek. That is the day you might become a Brahmarishi.'

After all what was so difficult about controlling anger—direct and determine the cause. But why could he not fulfil such a simple task? He had made a new galaxy, forced the devas to come to Earth, been invited to Heaven. He was getting close to his dream...

He was stopped by a soft taunt: he had yet not been able to prove Vasishth wrong about the incident regarding King Harishchandra. It rankled, gnawing his mind—would Vasishth vanquish him again?

Vishwamitra's eyes flew open, glittering with querulous animosity. He could not meditate or concentrate on simple thoughts. He got up, agitated. The day was almost dying to its diurnal end, the tangerine vividness of dusk flaming the sky. Another quick bath would do him good and refresh his mood. He strode rapidly towards the stream. He stepped into the cool waters of the River Mahi to sweep a long plunge in the stream, feeling the irritation seeping out of his troubled mind. The water of the river was more bubbly and vivacious than the mighty River Ganga or the calm River Saraswati, though each originated from the same source. Rivers were like humans too, all sprung up from the same wellspring but each formed their own course, flowing through different lands but meeting a similar end, emptying their waters, irrespective of their power and volume, into the same sea. *Man should learn a lesson or two from these rivers*, smiled Vishwamitra as he took a deep breath and swam deftly underwater.

He came up invigorated, and with swift, firm strokes started swimming back to the bank. He stopped midway, registering for the first time his changed surrounding. The place seemed to be exploding with colour and the fragrance of flowers hung heavily over the trees and bushes. *It wasn't spring yet*, Vishwamitra frowned. It was as if the season had changed overnight. Possibly he had not noticed it, immersed in his own thoughts. He shrugged but could not help noticing to his surprise that this stream where he had his daily swim was quite a pretty sight. He should get more close to Nature and learn to value its innate exquisiteness—the thick woods, the eager creepers clinging, the branches sinking low, pregnant with swollen fruits and the vivid cluster of sweet-smelling flowers, the trickling stream from the clear, rushing cascade of the nearby waterfall. Vishwamitra's alert eye thought he saw a quick flash of movement and he instinctively moved towards it.

Vishwamitra heard rather than saw her. It was a lilting hum, soft and sweet, lulling his senses yet wanting to hear more, wanting to know who the owner of this beautiful voice was...

His breath stuck in his throat, it had gone strangely dry. His eyes widened in shock and rising wonder as if it could not take in any further the sheer beauty he saw standing in front of him. *Menaka*, the name tore silently from his screaming mind. *What was she doing here?* She was bathing under the waterfall, her wet garments cleaving to every luscious curve of her slithering body lending it a translucent sheen. The sheerness of her wet sari revealed more than it was meant to conceal, clinging desperately trying to clutch and cover her supple, straining body, under the sluicing shower. He saw the exposed length of her long legs, and as his eyes fervidly travelled up, he drank in each curved contour—the shadowy folds below her dimpled navel, her slim waist curving deeply to the sensuous swell of her softly heaving breasts, the skimpy, upper garment soaked through, slyly uncovering the nakedness of her dark nipples straining against it.

He swallowed spasmodically, tearing his eyes away to flick upwards. Her wet face glistened through the thick swathe of her long, dark mane curling over her bare shoulders, the damp tendrils making a trail of falling drops down her white neck to the deep cleft of her cleavage. She was a vision of exquisite pleasure, her beauty almost painful to behold. He thought he was falling head long, pulled down in a swirl, drowning in her beauty...

She seemed startled at the sight of him emerging from the stream, her dark thick-lashed eyes widening, softly lucent yet intense in their radiance, submerging him in a whirl, drawing him to her, filling him with an uncontrollable emotion.

'Menaka?' he managed to whisper, recalling when last he had seen her. In Heaven, while he was leaving from India's hall in an angry huff, but not without glimpsing her wan, lovely face as she stood forlornly in the balustrade window of her palace. He had not believed his eyes, then nor now.

She stepped out of the waterfall, nodding tentatively, startled that he had recognized her, keeping her smile shy, her eyes unsure, but knowing that he was already hers. Her charm had been kindled. She had to work on him subtly now. She paused, feeling a fleeting sense of shame. She closed her eyes in silent prayer for what she was about to do was unforgivable.

'Mercy, o rishi. Forgive me for what I am doing. I am but a weapon of destruction wielded by someone else.'

She opened her eyes to hear his deep voice again, hoarse

with desire.

'The apsara?' he asked incredulously with a flash of a smile.

Menaka nodded, shivering. It was not the cold—it was his gravelly, low-pitched voice, yet so deliciously deep in tenor. She noticed how his smile changed him completely. It was almost boyish, taking off years from his hard, craggy face, the spreading smile, crinkling his solemn eyes, lighting them up in a warm glow. For one who was accustomed to the good looks of the devas, this man was severely lacking in them, she observed critically. Yet, she liked what she saw. He had a predatory sensuality making him seem overwhelmingly tall yet lean, the ribs showing neatly through his broad chest narrowing down sharply to a well-defined abdomen and a narrow waist. He was bare-chested with a skimpy loin cloth slung dangerously low at the waist. And it was as revealingly sodden, she observed wryly. She glanced up at his face. She could not see much of him because of the thick growth of his beard and moustache over a strong, hooked nose and deep set, sullen eyes. It was his unexpected smile and the rich baritone that had warmed her heart so insidiously, making him immediately attractive.

And he was huge in height, which she found disconcerting. She was tall herself but she felt quite dwarfed and had to tilt her head high to look up at him. From far he looked younger than he was, lean and tall, with his thick beard and unsmiling, swarthy face with the pronounced nose. But when face-to-face with him, he looked older—the tawny eyes were touched with the annihilating eternity from which he had come and to which he would go. His body was stiffly controlled, tense and recoiled in animalistic restraint. The only sign of nervousness he showed was a slight pulse in his cheek, through his tangled stubble, where you might have expected a deep crease whenever he spoke. It beat more impatiently when she moved closer, his jaws clenched.

'I think I have lost my way,' she started tensely. 'I was thirsty but the waterfall was too tempting to splash in,' she added sheepishly. 'I am sorry, I didn't realize I had intruded into your ashram.'

'But what are you doing here?' he asked his eyes narrowing, not leaving her face even for a moment.

Menaka licked her lips, feeling suddenly nervous. She saw him tightening his jaw. *Was my charm wearing off that he had started cross examining me? Would Kama have to use his love arrows after all?*

'I am an apsara banished from the heavens by Indra,' she said softly, with the right catch in her voice. 'I have been wandering for long till I inadvertently reached your ashram. I apologize again and I shall leave this place immediately.' She turned abruptly, pretending to retire, giving him an ample glimpse of her firm, smooth back, glistening invitingly.

'No, please, wait,' said Vishwamitra hastily. 'I did not mean to be rude, but was wondering why an apsara should come down to Earth...'

'Unless she had been ordered to distract a rishi,' she completed his line for him. This man might be well aroused with desire for her but she had aroused his suspicions too, Menaka rued, biting her lips. Again he seemed to stare at them, mesmerised as they moved with each word she uttered.

'No, sir, I have no such power. I am an apsara exiled because I was foolish enough to love the devagandharva,' she paused deliberately for effect. 'For our temerity, my husband Vasu was cursed to be a monster on Earth and I was thrown from Indralok...'

Menaka tried to keep her face straight, but Vishwamitra noticed how she clenched and unclenched her fingers.

He cast an appraising eye, his brooding eyes thoughtful. Menaka steadied herself against his scrutiny, hoping she had the right look of dejection that would slowly melt him.

'Vishwavasu was turned into Kabandh, a monster who now terrorises the people in the forest of Dandaka,' he supplied and Menaka glanced at him in visible surprise. He knew. As she had known and warned Indra, Vishwamitra was using his psychical powers to crosscheck her. He could not have been fooled by some weak tale of tragedy. Nor easily seduced through dance, she thought sardonically, as had been Indra's plan.

'Yes, this is our punishment we have to suffer,' she sighed, her lips trembling, weaving her fingers in agitated restiveness.

Vishwamitra could not take his eyes off her moving lips, wanting to taste their moist softness. He was standing taut, upright, his clenched fists resting at his side, his mind still obtuse with the surprise of finding her here, talking to him as if she had known him all her life. He gritted his jaw, nervous she would again turn away to leave but he would be helpless to stop her. Everything about her was exciting, from her glossy hair to her small bare feet. The sight of her had stoked a spark inside him that had never been touched off by any other woman, neither by his three wives. But this vision standing in front of him now had thrown him flat, defeated, igniting a flare of a dangerous conflagration, smouldering in him a fervent flame drying his mouth, pounding his heart, leaving him hot and breathless.

He stood motionless in the purple dimness of late dusk, gazing at her, his blood was racing, the rush pulsating painfully, starkly aware that he had never seen a woman he had wanted so badly as this one.

'You can stay for a while...' he faltered, not sure of his words, his intentions any more. He was standing not too close to her and he moved a step towards her, filled with a mad urge to touch her, hold her and crush her to him, aware of the faint perfume emanating from her drenched body, dewy yet powerful, and heard her quick, gentle breathing prompting the rise and fall of the soft, full swell of her breasts. For perhaps that one short, frozen moment everything around him went out of focus.

The sky darkened and a mighty gush of wind almost staggered him off his feet. Menaka's angavastra had been blown away with the gust, and the woman stood magnificently nude in front of him. There was nothing left for his feverish imagination to conjure. He found he could not breathe, his eyes riveted, burning wildly. He should have gone after her wind swept clothes but he seemed rooted to the ground, transfixed, bewitched. She was looking helplessly at him, her eyes large and luminous, her furtive hands attempting to cover her bare breasts, backing slowly away from him. Her move pulverised him into action and he lunged to stop her, grabbing roughly at her wrist, pulling her towards him, his other hand holding her strongly by her tiny waist. He could feel her bare body, soft and silky moulded against him and he felt a rush of blood, his face flaming, he descended his lips on her waiting ones, crushing hers, kissing her deeply, desperately drinking in her softness, as if he could never let her go.

Menaka had been prepared for his kiss, but she had not prepared for what she felt. The touch of his frantic fingers hot on her skin burned through, waking a fire in her, his tongue urgently prising her lips to invade the softness of her mouth, trailing a blaze inside her. She recoiled in deep shock and intense pleasure. A searing, hot rush of desire deluged her, making her cling to him, clawing her nails deep into his bare, bronzed back. He roughly pulled her down to him, his lips locked hard on hers, his breath coming fast, his fingers grabbing her hair, one trembling hand kneading the supple softness of her breast, turning and pushing her against the wet sands of the river bank, his hard thighs pushing her legs apart, the gentle water lapping around their writhing bodies, his marauding lips at her throat, her shoulders, her breasts, driving away the last of her remaining thought...had she seduced him? Or had he?

ꙮ

Three shadowy figures watched Menaka and Vishwamitra from the distant woods.

'That's a job very well done!' beamed Kama. 'And I didn't need to use a single arrow. All I had to get done was make the ambience prettier and more conducive. As I had said, one Menaka is enough to seduce a universe of rishis! And of course, Vayu here did his bit too—the wind howling, and swishing off of her clothes was a masterstroke!'

'That was Menaka's brainwave too. No saint or scoundrel could resist such a temptation!' laughed Vayu, his narrow, weakly good-looking face, appearing less solemn that it often was.

'Apsaras and their siren call!!' sighed Kama. 'The rishis seem to have a special affinity for Gritachi. First it was Rishi Bhardwaj, then Pramati, from whom she had Ruru,' he joined in the laughter.

'She happens to be related to Vishwamitra,' quipped Vayu. 'She married Kushanab, the rajarishi, Vishwamitra's grandfather! All these rishis, the all-so-enlightened, but go silly at the mere sight of an apsara!' he said contemptuously. 'These men seek refuge in celibacy to claim they are immune to female sexual charm.'

'That's why the apsaras were created to distract and to destroy!' grinned Kama, 'through the most primal human instinct, lust.'

Vayu smirked. 'Kama, the apsaras, like you, are symbols of lust. And Man seems to be particularly susceptible to the many lusts, the lust for sex, lust for power, lust for land, lust for acquisition, lust for knowledge, which made that high and mighty Kaushik to call himself Vishwamitra. Yet he succumbed from his higher goal by the simplest of all temptations, a woman's sexuality! He has finally met his doom or is it paradise?' he chortled at his own weak attempt at humour. 'He dared to command me to transport his friend Trishanku to Heaven during his mahayagna...' he recalled with a scowl, his thin lips pursed. 'Now it will be he at her command! She will make him her slave—lost and unable to free himself! We have got rid of him at last!'

Kama gave Vayu a long, searching look as a thought struck him. 'You hate Vishwamitra for another reason too, don't you?' he questioned astutely. 'You had once tried to seduce the daughters of his ancestor—King Kushnabh and Grittachi. But the princesses had rebuffed you and furious, you had entered their bodies to deform themselves. They were finally rid of you when Rishi Brahmadatta touched them and they regained their lost beauty. He eventually married them, getting what you never got, the princesses' hand in marriage. Wonder if Vishwamitra was nasty to you to teach you a lesson for what you did to them?' Kama asked with undisguised amusement. 'You and Vishwamitra go a long way back, Vayu!' he chuckled wickedly, 'So that's why you readily agreed to help Menaka, to get back at Vishwamitra! But what you claim is correct,' Kama agreed with a relieved smile. 'Vishwamitra will be hopelessly addicted to her.'

Indra broke the mounting tension. He was barely listening to their banter.

'Why did you not employ your arrows, Kama?' he asked sharply.

Kama looked nonplussed, filled with rising perplexity. 'But it wasn't necessary!' he protested. 'Menaka enticed him at first sight!'

'But I want you to shoot one arrow at her,' said Indra, grimly.

Kama and Vayu gave him a look of disbelief. 'But why?' demanded Kama. 'Menaka is a miasma of love and lust and longing. Why does she need it?'

'I want her to fall in love with Vishwamitra.'

'That's absurd!! It will ruin the entire plan!' asserted Kama. 'He is to fall in love with her, not she. She needs to be in control, to manipulate him. If in love herself, she won't be able to hold sway over him and accomplish her given task.'

'I want her to forget Vasu,' replied Indra, through gritted teeth, 'so make her fall in love with Vishwamitra!'

Kama was taken aback; he was not expecting such a volatile reaction or this unexpected turn of plan.

'It does not work that way, my lord,' he tried persuasion, recovering from his shock. 'Let's not tamper with our original plot; it is infallible. And you have the proof in front of you! You just witnessed how the great Vishwamitra fell for her like an infatuated boy!'

So did I, dear fellow, thought Indra with a grimace. 'Do it!' he barked. 'I know what I am doing!'

Kama looked undecided but his jaw was set in a stubborn line. Vayu decided to intervene. 'Please my lord, we have laid out the perfect trap. If we make Menaka fall in love, it would turn ugly. Remember what happened with Urvashi and Pururav? You have already removed Vasu from her life; give her time, she will forget him! But if it's Vishwamitra, we really don't know how he would react, what he can do!'

Indra frowned; what Vayu argued was making sense. Vayu was a cautious fellow, wary when to make a breeze willow up into a gust of storm. But Indra also well knew what an implacable foe Vishwamitra would make. Who had suffered it worse than Indra? But the threat of Vasu's return dangled close and Indra wanted Menaka to forget and forsake Vasu forever. This was his only chance.

'Shoot the arrow at Menaka, Kama,' he said imperiously. 'Now!'

He gave an ugly grin.

Kama reluctantly removed one arrow from his quiver. Closing his eyes, praying that it would do more good than harm, he shot at the couple in the distance, not knowing on whom the arrow had landed...

Love and Lust

$\mathcal{V}$ishwamitra was a stranger no longer, he was her lover. Menaka glanced at the naked length of the man sleeping beside her, trapping her with his bare leg straddled over hers. But it was she who had trapped him. She was Menaka, who made the man she made love to scream and writhe in passion, exhorting him to heavenly heights, making him beg for more. She was here to master his mind, break his will; and his heart, if need be. *But that would be easy*, Menaka smiled lazily as she watched him, his large, heavy arm flung across her in unconscious possessiveness. She belonged to him, but only for the time being and as an erotic hirudinean, sucking away his vitality each time he made love to her, taking it in, slowly draining out his virility, his strength, all his powers he so possessed.

But this man *was* different. *So unlike Vasu*, she thought. He was almost brutal in his lovemaking, his hands tearing away her clothes, grabbing her by her hair and pulling back her face for his hard lips to taste and crush hers. His brutishness strangely aroused her, contrasting it immediately with Vasu's smooth, skilled lovemaking.

With a husky laugh, she had pushed at his shoulders and slowly taught him how to be gentle, allowing the tenderness to flow in his passion. 'Get to learn the art of undressing,' she laughed, tugging gently at his waistcloth, her hands sliding lower, guiding him to a new unfettered world of elated rapture.

'Removing clothes is like casting off your armour, leaving you defenceless and vulnerable to assault. You are making love not war, my rishi-warrior. I'm not an opponent to be subdued; I am your lover to be enjoyed,' she whispered against the rising crescendo of his groans, his ragged breath coming in quick, uneven gasps.

'Release me!' he screamed thickly, his eyes blazing, pleading with her as she smiled, her triumphant face looming over his, contorted in endless ecstatic torment.

But he too flamed her in a raging fire. Each time he was in her, she felt the power of him—the hot, abrupt, emphatic rush expelling lividly inside her. She felt that she was reborn each time, and that he was suffusing her with an energy she could not decipher or define. She felt she was ablaze, the flames licking fast, coursing into every cell, spreading an inner inferno in her, slowly incinerating her, yet pulsating her with a new forceful vitality. It fascinated her by the power he had in him and the power she wielded on him. It was almost symbiotic; both feeding on each other, both revelling in the same fire.

But Vishwamitra was insensible to either, too deep into her to register that she was extorting him to lust and concupiscence. He considered her his lover, his companion, his woman who made him his meals and warmed his days and nights. He had known her now for just a month, but she knew he had never been more in love with any woman than he was with her. The tempestuous days they spent together had made his love for her grow to a degree that she knew he could not do without her. He had to exert a great deal of control not to show his feelings, but he couldn't hide them.

Not that he was a gullible man. Menaka recalled how well she had to enact her sad tale to convince him of the validity of her seemingly sorry plight.

'Indra is a beast!' he had said hotly. 'I always knew him as a pompous fool but what he did to you...he is wicked!' Vishwamitra remarked angrily. 'Why did you wait for him to throw you out? Could you not have escaped?'

'No,' she sighed, lifting her arms and clasped them behind her head. He could see her breasts lift and strain against the thin fabric. 'He would have dragged me back to Heaven even if I had attempted to. Except for Rambha, none of us are allowed to step out of Heaven to roam the universe. Urvashi used to slip out quite often. But once, she was attacked by some asuras and she didn't venture out again,' she explained, shifting beside him and keeping her head on his shoulder. 'King Pururav came to her timely rescue. That's how she met him.'

'Who can resist a damsel in distress,' he drawled, softly stroking her nape. 'Like you. Did I come to your rescue or was it you who rescued me from an empty life?'

She brought down his lips to hers, thinking that as most of her story was true, it made it smoother for her and easier for him to believe it, his sharp sixth sense notwithstanding. Lies of omission—as Kama had called it—that subtle art of lying, while withholding a certain crucial element of truth. Artfully portraying herself as a pawn to Indra's vicious games, she had tugged slyly at his heartstrings, evoking sufficient sympathy and his innate sense of protectiveness. He had promptly offered her his home.

'Have I frightened you again?' teased Vishwamitra as his shadow fell on her and she moved in quick alarm. 'You have this funny habit of being easily startled as a frightened doe!' He looked at her ashen face, his smile slipping. 'What are you scared of, Menaka?' he asked gently, coming from behind her and slipping his arms around her waist. She felt a frisson of pleasure. Was it his touch or the tenderness in his voice?

'Indra?' he guessed intuitively as she stiffened against him.

'He banished me, but I live in that dread, that he might return to take me back...' she whispered, turning around in his arms to face him, her eyes wide with suppressed fear.

'That he will, most certainly,' said Vishwamitra in a hard voice. 'He thinks he owns you and he won't let you go forever. This banishment is just a punishment to teach you a lesson. He will take you back.'

Menaka could not stop a small gasp of horror. 'No,' she said violently, tuning her voice to rise slightly in panic. 'I don't ever want to return to that hell. No, no, no!' she cried, making her body tremble in anticipated trepidation. If Bharat Muni, her guru of Natyashastra, had seen her now, he would have been proud of her fluent display of histrionics.

Vishwamitra placed his hands on her shaking shoulders. 'You don't have to go anywhere. As I said, you are safe here. You can stay with me forever...' he assured her, tightening his hold, 'as my wife. Will you marry me, Menaka?'

She stepped back, her face pale. 'No! I am already indebted to you for all what you have done. Yes, I shall stay here as your lover, your friend, a housekeeper who will keep your home, make you your meals; but please, not as a wife. Don't elevate me to such a high status that I am ashamed of it. I am but an erstwhile apsara and you are the famous Vishwamitra. Don't degrade yourself into marrying a humble woman like me.'

In her feigned humility, lay a more mercenary motive. Her unique power was her ingenious eroticism, her willingness and ability to express in wild amorousness; she was sexually intriguing, stimulating, exciting. Marriage might kill it, replaced with bored familiarity. Or it could strengthen their relation. Either way she could manipulate her own sexuality, using the passion she incited as a weapon to wield over him, to assault and weaken him. It was her expression, her emancipation; but his imprisonment from which he would not be freed.

'I love you, Menaka,' he said, his eyes soft and pleading. 'Be my wife.'

She had used all her cunning and guile to escape one prison, to gain her freedom. She had run away from Heaven and had no intention of getting caught into another net of lulled security. She would not allow herself to be wooed and won by some passionate love of a man. She would entrap him instead, careful not to get trapped herself. She refused to submit to the temptation of love and marriage. It was stifling making her hard to breathe and live. Just like Heaven had been.

'I shall be yours, forever,' she replied, looking deep into his eyes. 'But please don't ask me to marry you...it'll only complicate what we are, what we have...'

And thus, she kept him on hold. She was his, but he would keep yearning for her, wanting him to possess her completely, own her rightfully. So much that he would be ready to take on anyone, even Indra and all the might of the devas. She would use him to save her from Indra. Vishwamitra was her weapon, he was her shield. In Vishwamitra, Menaka had shrewdly perceived his gentler, humane side. For all his sharp temper and sharper tongue, his arrogance and ambitiousness, Vishwamitra was a caring, conscientious man who could not stand to see anyone suffering, not just her. It was that kindness, his quality of being warm-hearted, considerate and sympathetic that was his mortal weakness. She had deviously wielded it to the hilt.

Menaka recalled Kama's words of caution. 'Never show any sort of questionable motive or suspicious behaviour. He is your prey, you are the predator. But make him feel he is yours— your man, your lover, your protector, your soulmate. Know his vulnerabilities to pin him, to determine the tactics you would need to use on him later. Conceal and be covert, let it be the double motto. And don't rely only on your sexual wiles, lies and coercion work admirably. It's not just your beauty that is going to get him, you need to work on his mind too. Most apsaras merely use their body but you need to use your mind too and never your heart. So, be ruthless enough to have no qualms of causing hurt and harm to the man. You have to be indifferent, insensible and irresponsible. You are meant to destroy him.'

Destroy this beautiful man? Menaka tilted her head sideways, to look at Vishwamitra closely. His face had a strange serenity, absent otherwise when he was awake and frowning. Possibly because his eyes were shut; they were his most fiery features dominating his face and his personality. They seemed to be in a deep dream now, the thick, dark lashes resting contently against the tanned skin of his face. He was unconventionally attractive. His nose was as high and mighty as his ego, flaring in temper which needed no provocation. His lips were full, hot-blooded and generous. They were hard, mobile and aggressive when he talked and kissed. She smiled, looking down at the bruises on her shoulders and the soft swell of her breasts. He had a firm, square jawline hidden under his beard. She would have to persuade him to remove the thick bristle, she decided, touching it lightly.

His eyes flew open, wide and alert; the hazel flicks turning to dark mahogany as daylight and realization seeped into them. He smiled and her heart lurched. He wasn't supposed to affect her; but she was affected by him. She moved closer to him, feeling his warm skin against her unclothed body, pushing one slender, bare leg between his, her toe caressing the inside of his ankles. She brought her face very close to his, making him want to kiss her. So, he did, long and deep.

'You have woken up late! And you missed your dawn meditation, again,' she murmured in mock accusation, pushing herself up slightly so that he could catch a glimpse of her bare, fair flesh. He reacted the way she had expected him to. He cupped her breast, his lips closing over the taut nipple. She sighed in pleasure—it was genuine, not exaggerated as she had intended. She moaned softly as he sucked harder.

'I overslept again. How you exhaust me!' he muttered indistinctly, his voice thickening with quick desire. 'I don't know when the nights end and the days start, witch!'

She laughed, leaning far back in the bed, exposing her full form, with an air of ribald luxury. She did not want him to think too much, yet spur him to a frenzy of fevered imagining—entwined limbs, heaving hips, tossing thighs, their glistening twisting bodies contorted in consuming passion. He had to get driven and dependent on her. Their unbridled lovemaking had to become a habit, a raw need, a reflexive pattern of their daily life.

Keeping that thought in mind, she languorously slithered over him, wondering which position Rati had taught her, and which could be excitingly reinvented...

Vishwamitra was struggling with his beard, or rather the removal of it. Menaka glanced at him with amusement. She got up and took the blade from his hand.

'Let me do it,' she smiled, 'before you scar your face any further!'

She put her cool fingers on his wrist.

'Another wouldn't make much difference, I have enough of them from all the wars to never let me forget I was once a king!' he replied.

'Exactly! You are brandishing this blade as if it's a sword!' she said. 'Stay still!'

For the next few minutes, there was silence as Menaka neatly clipped at his chin and jaw. 'Hmmm...better,' she murmured, twisting the small, gilded mirror at him.

'I did this for you,' he said. 'Not so ugly really, am I?' he grinned running his hand over his relatively smooth cheek.

'Oh, so you do have a dimple on your right!' mocked Menaka. '...and even a cleft in your chin!' Her eyes sparkled with sudden merriment. 'Tsk, all those good looks hidden away under that filthy beard!'

She could not resist placing her slender finger on the deep indentation of his chin. Vishwamitra caught hold of her wrist, his eyes darkening. She swiftly replaced her forefinger with her lips, her tongue darting deep in the crevice. He felt himself tremble; this woman could make the slightest gesture seem erotic.

'Go! You meditate in the woods while I get to practice some singing!'

She put her hand on his bare arm, gently pushing him. The feel of her cool fingers sent a hot wave of blood crawling up his spine. She got up and walked away from him, her each movement sinuous.

She had a voice as gorgeous as her. He loved to hear her sing. It soothed him from his fears, his troubled thoughts. He no longer worried about how he could get back at Vasishth. It seemed so long ago, so futile. *What a dull destitute emotion this bitterness is; it sapped the life out of you, leaving just an empty moult. Menaka had leased me a new life.*

When he was young, love could not have stopped his ambition. Now it was altering his thoughts, his outlook and his daily schedule. He had been a disciplined man, as a king and as a rishi, for whom work was the highest priority. His meditation usually used to begin before dawn, and however late he might be, he would read the day's work over in his mind and sleep on it. The habit of meditation was the basis of real knowledge, he believed and practised it religiously. Love had left everything undone. He was making love to her through the day, sometimes for days together. He was a man in love; it was quite easy to return to work even under such neglected hours. As long as the spirit is happy, it inspires one to work and to endure any discipline. Like it did now when he could hear her lilting voice, floating through the wood. It encompassed him with a strange sense of peace, lulling him into another world.

Vishwamitra recalled how Vasishth had looked at his wife Arundhati—each time, his eyes would soften with affection and admiration. She was his ardhagini—his equal partner in love and learning. Together they took upon themselves to heal the world, to enlighten all with knowledge and wisdom. They had been blessed by Lord Shiva as the ideal couple, naming the sixth star of the constellation after them, as a symbol of their love and reverence. And in ultimate respect, Man at the marriage rituals, expected the bride and the groom to look up into the skies to search for that sixth star of Vasisth-Arundhati, and pray for the same kind of love, trust, respect and happiness between them.

He had married three women, but Vishwamitra was honest to admit he had not been in love with any of them. They were his queens, his wives, the mothers of his children. He had made love to them and many more, but he didn't love them like he loved Menaka. She was the love he desired and trusted, his belief for the future, the one with whom he intended all possibilities of fulfilment.

Vishwamitra had been surprised that a friendship had stirred under that heady mix of lust and love, perhaps nothing more than a companionship in mutual loneliness. He was lonely by habit, she lonely in her tragedy.

'What will you do once Vasu returns to Heaven?' he could not stop himself from asking, dreading the answer. *Would she leave me for Vasu*, the thought often haunted him. 'He won't find you in Heaven when he returns.'

'Nor can he come down searching for me,' she replied, her voice laconic, her face tight. 'In Heaven, nothing is for keeps, particularly relationships. Morality is for the mortals, not us. We enjoy the moment and move on. What I had with Vasu was rare and exceptional, but clearly not meant to be. Indra saw to that,' she said pragmatically. 'And I refuse to live on hope any more that Vasu might come back, that he'll still love me. Hope is often just a consoling thought, our naive disclaimer, retracting the possibility of a certain reality that we don't have the power to change.'

She did not look bitter in her beauty, and the cynicism had not corroded into her but given her an unyielding strength, difficult to perceive. It had been a trial by ordeal and he knew she avoided discussing her past. He did not want to push her.

'I don't think so far, so ahead. Like you can. What do *you* see?' she asked instead.

Those words made a conspiracy out of their association. They gave him a queer, bitter-sweet sensation. 'The future is not ours to hold,' he said.

'You don't want to tell me,' she said quietly.

If she had but known it, he would have given her anything if she had asked him for it; that's how far gone he was.

But Vishwamitra gave shook his head slightly and she smiled back, both content in the comfortable silence. They were fellow strangers in a friendly sense of companionship. He always seemed to find something agreeable about her which made him talk more comfortably than he ever had.

'Did you not feel guilty deserting your wife and children?' she parried cautiously, as if reading his mind. 'Don't you feel you wronged them, that you need to go back to them?' Men always liked to talk and she liked to hear, as she gauged from her immense store of masculine experiences. She moved to make place for him to sit next to her.

'I honestly think I didn't love them enough to miss them,' he replied shortly, 'I am a selfish man. I shan't deny that. Like you cannot deny being a selfish mother, who deserted her child.'

His bluntness was like a slap, sharp and stinging. She started to say something, but was interrupted by him.

'You cannot do anything about it now, it's too late to turn back,' he gestured.

'It's never too late to make amends,' she suggested.

He shrugged, he could not care less. He had found her, and he did not want anyone or anything more. They disagreed often but as the days went by, he realized he *liked* her, very much and very intensely. She knew everything about him.

'Indra couldn't stop talking about you. He was obsessed! You were his rival, his enemy, his usurper, the fiend he could not get rid of!' she said, tracing her finger along his jawline to the inside of his ear lobe.

'He hates my guts,' he retorted blandly. 'But then Indra hates everyone who has guts. He doesn't have much to boast about!'

She confessed she had even read his books. Vishwamitra did not know whether to be flattered or suspicious, but he was impressed. 'How do you know about the Vedas?' he asked curiously.

She bit her lip as she often did, her small white pearly teeth digging deep into the soft, pink flesh of her full, lower lip. He found it maddeningly cruel and distracting.

'Vasu,' she said softly, almost a whisper.

'Yes, I heard he was a philosopher,' nodded Vishwamitra. 'And a master illusionist. That is not easy. It takes years of meditation. And it's the best wonted secret of the devas not yet revealed to Man.'

'And you don't desire to go after it?'

'Right now I am chasing you, sometime later perhaps...' he said pulling her hard against him, his lips searching hers. A touch of a smile and amused gurgle stole from her white throat, her lips half parted, her hands moving down his muscled back, stirring new sensations, her beauty reaching his aroused brain. And under the open sky, on the hard ground, with the trees swishing in gentle agreement, they made love—tenderly and roughly. When the moment came, hot and gushing, he saw her smiling triumphantly, revelling in his subjugation. And then he would put his hand gently over her tremulous, smiling mouth, to stifle that soft shriek for fear that the silence of the woods would carry it far. And he would hear himself too, that groan torn from his pulsating throat, screaming for more, collapsing in her arms, his face buried in the fragrant curve of her neck...

He lay naked beside her and watched her interminably, as though she might vanish and he might never see this again—her ebony black hair spilling over like an inky night, her smudged lips, the heavy breathing marked by the rapid movement of her voluptuous breasts, and the vision of her luxuriating in the exhaustion of victory. They were alike; love was a conquest. So was making love.

He was on his back motionless, his head flung back, hands damp and clenched, his heart beating fast while he stared at the vast expanse of swaying trees, clouds and the distant horizon. In the hard light of the moon, the land was lit up for miles. There was no sign of anyone out there, no animals, nothing. They might have been the only two people left in the world.

He gazed sideways at her lovely face, touching it lightly.

'May I call you Kaushik?' she had asked tentatively.

Vishwamitra was taken aback. No one called him by that name any more. It gave an immediate effect of intimacy. But that is what he truly liked about her; he found himself treated as a normal being rather than a revered seer. He was getting a little tired of the awe he inspired in people. She treated him like no woman had treated him before—without passing any judgement, evaluating him without any expectations.

'I'm not being impertinent,' she clarified quickly, assuming his pause as reluctance. 'I can't call you Vishwamitra, it's too lofty! I would be overreaching myself. I want to be with you, the man; not the famous king or the brilliant rishi. For I am but an apasara who knows just two things—to sing and dance. And yes, to seduce.'

Vishwamitra sighed, *she refused to believe in her own beauty.* 'Yes you do that wondrously,' he chaffed, but he looked at her solemnly. 'Do you know what your name means?'

It was Menaka's turn to be puzzled. 'My name?'

'Menaka means borne from the mind. You have been born from Lord Brahma's mind when you were created during the samudra manthan. You are his daughter,' he explained. She looked as delectable when surprised and he saw she was too stunned to respond, slightly amused at her ignorance. 'That is why you have a clever mind and the talent of an artist. You call yourself a courtesan, but singing and dancing is not just entertainment but your expression of creativity. You are an inspiration to many. But you too can be lifted by thought and emotion when inspired. Do that.'

Menaka blushed. It was a lovely sight. She bit her lip, her eyes suddenly bashful. 'I have been called beauty of all sorts and I know I am that,' she remarked with a resurgence of her old flippant confidence. 'But brains...well...' she chewed her lips and laughed self-consciously. 'Never!'

'Are you sure? That is why a gifted, intelligent devagandharva like Vishwavasu fell in love with you. And that is why I love you,' he said quietly. 'Not just for your loveliness. For me, you are the Menaka for all that it means.'

Menaka swallowed. His words moved her to an undefinable emotion. This was not how it should be, she told herself frantically. He was to be besotted with her, spurred by unreasoning, foolish love. But he was affecting her, overwhelmingly.

'And yes, you can call me Kaushik!' he grinned engagingly, breaking her confused thoughts. 'A mere mortal, your slave.'

He admitted he was enslaved, tied with the servitude of love and longing. He knew he longed for her even when she was with him, lusted for her shamelessly. If he woke randomly in the night, she immediately filled his mind and abandoning sleep; he thought of her while she lay in his arms, soft and silky against him. When he saw her interacting with the animals and the birds and the flowers in the forest, he saw in her a radiant happiness and her way of touching them with her hands, as though she loved them. He thought, *Was it because she was an apsara that whatever she touched she could seduce?*

He knew he was in love with her, but was she in love with him? He wanted to believe it. Like a man possessed and in love, he would try to get her, to speak a little more than the truth. But would their love last? Be as pure and lofty like Vasishth's and Arundhati's? That this romance would never end, that one day they should marry.

He loved her for her honesty. She had often disconcerted him by her bare truth. But when it came to marriage, she strangely kept silent, almost mysterious, driving him mad. He wanted her assurance, he would have liked to hear her saying those wonderful words of living happily ever after. But she did not. Possessiveness wells out the tenderness of responsibility; he wanted to be her husband, not just a lover, responsible for nothing. He had proposed to her several times and each time she had refused. Not that he doubted her but it made him restless, desperate to have her completely.

'Why,' she teased, 'anyone would think you were in love!' she exclaimed.

But that night, resting in his arms, laying across his chest, she had said softly, yet so suddenly and unexpectedly, 'I have never loved a man as I love you, and I never shall again.'

He heard it with incredulous, incandescent happiness.

Love and Lies

'*I* have never loved any man as I love you, and I never shall again.' She smiled faintly and stopped. And yet she could have sworn it was just then that she fell in love, at that very moment when she saw how her words brought an inexplicable tenderness in his dour, dark eyes and lighting up his face with happiness; when she felt it spreading warmly all over, melting her heart, freezing her conscience. She thought, *how happy I can make him and how easily. I would like to keep him happy forever.* She was sure she was in love with him. She was not lying when she had said it. It was that swift surging sense of a free woman, an individuality, an openness, an admittance of feeling that she knew might later make her feel glad and miserable.

She realized she was smiling again. That genuine, upward curve of the lips, after so long a time, uplifted so many emotions, so many hopes, filling her with a new found elation as she watched him sleeping in his new found bliss. He moved, still foggy with sleep and the contentment of his dream. He felt that dream warm against him, soft and supple. He woke with the gladness of her last, ringing words still resting on his mind, and within minutes of waking her voice excited him more, dispelling any doubts, unreasonable fears. He had never known a woman before capable of altering mood by simply speaking in her soft and lucid voice. Or when she touched him and put her hand on his, she created at once the absolute trust he had lost, and felt bereft with every separation.

'Marry me,' he whispered, stroking her long neck. She turned her face, turning her head in shock. She had not said those words easily last night, for a quick invitation to seduction. But he had treated them to persist in his intention of marriage. Menaka felt a wave of shame slowly rising within her, smothering her in a tide of confusion.

'And that is an order, not a request,' he said kissing her open mouth, her lips still gaping in surprise. He slipped his tongue between her parted lips, pressing his hips against her, pressing his hardness against the silken softness of hers. Breathing unevenly, he crushed her to him. She was now in his blood, as deadly and as dangerous like a disease. He didn't want her to go.

She returned his kiss instinctively, shock giving way to pleasure, luxuriating in the enormity of the proposal. But she could not allow herself to forget that she was deceiving him.

'But you are married!' she said, pulling away from him.

'Yes, I am married; I married thrice!' he smiled. 'But so are you,' he reminded her.

Menaka's eyes suffused with sadness. She had almost forgotten Vasu. Her pale, stricken face made him curse himself.

'No, don't look so forlorn,' he cupped her face gently in his large hands. 'Both of us have our past. We can't change it. But I love you. I want you like I have never desired anyone else. And I need you. I want to marry you; be my wife, my partner in our love, our friendship, our companionship. Is it too much to ask for, this marriage of ours?' he asked, his eyes burning intensely with hope.

She felt a hard lump in her throat, like a pebble stuck, almost choking her. She could not bear to see the earnestness of his love in his eyes, hear the pleading tone in his voice. It was excruciating. She was not just deceiving him, but herself as well. Her sham had made her exploitative and devious of her own feelings.

She quickly bowed her head, hoping to hide her gnawing guilt and shook her head slowly.

'Is that a no for this question, or no again to my proposal?'

he quipped.

He was afraid she would refuse him, he was afraid he would lose her someday. She was an apsara, a celestial being; and he was a mortal. He would die one day, she would never. He would grow old, she would not. They had been together for more than four years now, but not once had she regretted of having left Heaven for Earth. She was much happier here, she insisted. And he believed her, believed her each time she kissed him, made love to him, took care of him.

The same old dread struck him. *Would Indra take her back once he came to his senses?* He would challenge Indra, like he had done once before. This time it would be another Heaven he would be fighting for.

'Can a mortal marry an apsara?' asked Menaka dubiously. He heard the fear, the tinge of cynicism in her voice.

'It has happened before. My grandfather married an apsara called Gritachi. They lived happily ever after.'

Menaka gave him a look of genuine surprise. 'I thought Urvashi and Pururav were the only ones!'

'It was true for Urvashi and Rishi Vibhandak. But then, that wasn't love, it was deception,' said Vishwamitra, his lips curled in contempt. 'She fooled the poor man, had a son from him and dumped them both to rush back to Heaven after doing the needful—cheating the rishi of his years of hard work, his yogic achievement and above all his love and his trust! What a thorough...apsara!' he mouthed venomously.

Menaka flinched, his words stinging like a lash. He had said 'apsara' like a filthy expletive. Watching her blanched pallor, Vishwamitra was immediately contrite. 'I was talking of Urvashi; all apsaras aren't as heartless as she. Nor are they like you,' he said taking her hands in his. They were fair and fragile against his large, hardened palm. 'These hands have done a lot to me, a lot for me...you cook, you wash the clothes, you sweep and you swab—can you conjure any apsara doing this? You have made this hut a home!' he gently kissed each finger of her hand. 'My dear, you are not an apsara, you are the lady of this house, my homemaker, my strength. Even a king's palace although filled with all the gold and wealth and servants, is destitute without a wife. A house without the wife is as desolate as the wilderness in the forest. You, as my wife, are my home. Menaka, would you be that wife of mine? And please don't refuse me again...each time you break my heart, but never my resolve never to propose to you again!'

Menaka knew he was struggling with his emotions under that forced wit.

'But I guess my love is loftier than my ego, so here I am asking you that same question—will you marry me?' he gave her a quick, boyish grin, his eyes teasing. 'We have lived a long time in sin and now I wish to wash all of it away by a dip in that holy river outside and marrying you immediately afterwards! So?' he raised a quizzical eyebrow, waiting.

She bit her lip and then smiled, which slowly warmed his scared heart. 'Yes!' she said, laughing away her last doubt.

After that, all seemed a happy blur. They were going to get married in the afternoon. He had informed her that Rishi Kanva, an old friend of his, would be performing the wedding rites. It would be a simple ritual, he had stated.

Not like the gandharva wedding she had had with Vasu. Her heart contracted. *Where was he, how was he?* Menaka could not but help remembering her first wedding and she felt again that shadow of sadness and guilt. How readily was she marrying Kaushik. How easily had she forsaken Vasu. Was that how grief was, the ache dulled through time? But she had not forgotten him because she constantly made an unconscious comparison between the two men. Their physical appearance, their demonstration of love, their lovemaking, their attributes...it was silly, if not morbid, and that was her way of keeping Vasu alive in her waking memory. She needed him as an anchor to her past, she quaked at what was to come. Her present was Kaushik but did she have any future with him? She had once lost Vasu, would she get him back? Would she have to choose between the two? Or would she lose them both?

She felt restless, her initial burst of happiness seemed an

illusory bubble. She scrambled from the rock on which she was sitting and got up. She saw Kaushik still at his morning swim; his tanned, muscled body knifing through the silver spray, his powerful strokes beating against the eddy of the river waters. She was to wed this man today. She determinedly shrugged off her shroud of sadness and promised herself she would do her best, give him the best.

For the first time she wanted to dress up. Not for the ulterior purpose of seduction, a small voice taunted her, but for herself. She did not have much, she didn't want much, just a handful of fragrant flowers to deck herself with. She could gather them from the bushes she had planted all around the ashram, the flowers exploding with colour against the lushness of the forest, perfuming the air with their heavy, lingering fragrance. She hummed unconsciously as she plucked the flowers, mostly jasmines. The tiny, partially open, milky buds were her favourite, pure in their whiteness, emanating a quiet, erotic scent that none could resist.

She was a quick but a meticulous dresser. It was a long time since she had dressed for herself. She peered in the small, gilded mirror Kaushik had got her, probably using his magic powers, as she often teased him. He had found her trying to catch her reflection in the moving water stored in the small brass vessel. The following day he had gifted her hand mirror—his first gift—and she had been touched at his unusual tenderness. She stared not at her reflection now but at the mirror, intricately gilded. Just like her, decorative and deceptive. *No*, she said fiercely, *it was not pretence.* It never was but she had run away from it, fearing she would get hurt all over again. She had seen him not as her conquest, not her quarry, but as a means of escape, a fresh lease, a new hope. He had become her saviour instead, saving her from herself. Through last night, long and wakeful, her confession of love kept mocking her, her confusion giving way to culpability, waking her up to a new misery. *Had I seduced him as I had been instructed or had I done it to save myself? Or had I wanted him for myself all along? Did I have a choice or had I been free to decide?*

Or was that me falling in love?

She buried her face in her hands, not able to look at herself in the mirror anymore. Could she not be a better being, a woman more worthy? She was marrying him today, marrying his love, his trust which she was betraying each day she lived with him.

❧

The love arrow must have pierced Menaka, as I had hoped it had not, thought Kama as he strode into Indra's hall to divulge the latest news he had heard with a sinking heart. Yet, he was happy for Menaka. She deserved some happiness at last. But he was not too sure how long it would last. Indra would not allow it.

'I presume you have heard Menaka got married to Vishwamitra,' he pronounced to Indra. 'They wed some days ago.'

Indra kept silent, but Kama knew he was none too pleased with the news. It was taking enormous effort on his part not showing it. But Kama was unexpectedly furious too today, for an entirely different reason.

'Are you enjoying rubbing it in?' asked Indra shortly.

Kama needed that one straw to hang on to his anger. 'You made a mess of this!' he exclaimed angrily. 'You made her fall in love with him and now they are married, all because you wanted to distract her from Vasu. That was the most convoluted reasoning!'

Kama's annoyance was almost bordering on the impertinent, but Indra allowed it as he did with his close friends. *As he had once with Vasu*, he thought. Kama was the only one now with whom he could discuss his most private, if not his most devious thoughts.

'Menaka was the perfect choice to destroy Vishwamitra,' continued Kama, heatedly. 'She had the charm, the wile and the gumption to carry forward our plan and return quickly to Heaven with the result we wanted. But none of this happened. She managed to entice Vishwamitra, but got unnecessarily involved herself with the man, courtesy your brainwave!'

'It proves the strength of your arrow, Kama!' said Indra dryly.

'Agreed it was not a wise move on my part...'

Kama snorted in obvious derision. 'You almost lost Urvashi once. But now you have certainly lost Menaka to Vishwamitra. He scored over you once again,' he added bitingly.

Indra pursed his lips tightly and tried to ignore the barb. 'Tell me how you can rectify this mistake. I am sure you must have thought about it too.'

Kama looked incredulously at Indra and said, 'You really believe in simple solutions don't you? You make a mess and we clean it!'

'Enough!' Indra barked. 'I am asking for an answer, not your opinion!' But seeing Kama's uncooperative face, he decided it would be wiser to restrain his impatient irritation. 'How can we bring Menaka back?' he asked his tone a shade softer. 'You know I can't do without her. She has been gone long enough, it's been more than four years. By now, she was supposed to have had his baby and dumped it with him and come back. She should have systematically demolished him by now. His power now dissipated, he cannot hope to recover his spiritual strength ever again. Vishwamitra has been reduced to a lovelorn fool married to an apsara. Just shows how desperate he is about her!'

'And she about him!' Kama tartly reminded the king of the devas. '*That* is the problem.'

'Kama, you are here to solve the problem,' replied Indra, with exaggerated patience.

'I can't make her fall out of love, if that is what you mean!' riposted Kama with a mirthless smile. 'If that could be done, you would have forced me to use some potion or some arrow on Menaka when she was grieving for Vasu. The fact that she has been with Vishwamitra for so long magnifies the problem, and intensifies the emotion,' he sighed. 'Seriously, I don't think she wishes to return. Also, Vishwamitra won't allow it. I had warned you, he is a terrible enemy to have.'

'Not anymore,' retorted Indra. 'He has lost all his powers, remember? Her job is done, she better come back!'

Kama looked at him doubtfully. 'How?' he asked instead. 'She is an apsara in love. It was you who made her fall in love with him. She is now his, completely and truly. Unless you kidnap her the way you did with Urvashi. Urvashi never forgave you, Indra. Beware, Menaka would be worse. You can't break her heart again, even you can't be that cruel! She was always your favourite plaything, your prize trophy whom you used shamelessly! Indra, be a little kind to her.'

'Oh, stop being so soft-hearted!' said Indra impatiently. 'She belongs here...'

'To you, you mean!'

'She belongs here,' repeated Indra. 'She can't be with him forever!'

'But that's what she hopes for!' warned Kama. 'She wants to be with him now. You made it so happen.'

But a flicker of doubt kindled in Indra's churning mind. *Had this been her plan all along to use the seduction of Vishwamitra as a ruse to escape from me and never return?* He felt the first stirring of anger, awakening in him his dormant streak of vindictiveness. She wouldn't dare...

'I thought you would have the answer!' snapped Indra, feeling suddenly unsure. 'I gave her time, trusting her to do the needful!'

'Urvashi married both Purarava and Rishi Vibhandak,' Kama reminded him tactfully. 'But Menaka is a shrewd seducer. For her, when a thing is done as decided, it is done: remorse dies with the act. She doesn't allow emotions to interfere with her work. That's what I believed of her till now, but then, you made her fall in love!'

'Possibly this marriage might be her ruse?' Indra sounded dubious. 'Kama, I think it's best you go and meet her. Tell her she is wanted back in Heaven.'

Kama was not too sure about Menaka; love had conquered and vanquished even the most manipulative woman. And if Menaka had fallen in love with Vishwamitra, Kama knew even he could not undo it. It was time to meet Menaka in person. But he recalled his own words of warning to her—the best of battles were won by deceit.

Man and Marriage

$\mathscr{M}$enaka felt the dampness of dew on the unbridled grass under her feet; savouring this pleasure each morning. A soft, chilly breeze swept against her body. She inhaled the intoxicating fragrance of the wild flowers in full bloom. *This was the beauty of Earth*, she sighed wantonly. For all its beauty, she had found Heaven stifling. For a land promising everlasting life, everything seemed cold and sterile, even the colours and the fragrance of flowers were beautiful but soulless. Unlike Urvashi who frequented Earth in nocturnal furtiveness, Menaka had encountered the wonder of Earth for the first time when she had to rush down for Pramadvara. After the shock and joy of saving her daughter from the verge of death, Menaka had found mood and mind to investigate what the mystery of the Earth was all about. Its lush beauty was magnified in her mind's eye with its paradoxical harmony of warmth and sadness, pain and violence, beauty and ugliness. Yet Earth was her Heaven now; her home with Kaushik, the thought quickly drawing a hint of a smile.

'You seem to be enjoying yourself here,' she heard a voice saying. She whirled around, recognizing it before she could see the face of its owner, dread streaming into her heart. Kama stood under the dark shadows of the mangrove. Menaka was startled, unable to mask the fearfulness stark on her face, as she realized—Indra had sent him.

'You look gorgeous, as always!' Kama smiled back at her warmly.

Menaka relaxed perceptibly, her apprehension subsiding, her face breaking into a lovely smile.

'You can't flirt with your student!' she laughed, but as the laugh dimmed in her eyes, she came straight to the point. 'You took your time coming down to check on me.'

Kama's smile sobered immediately. 'Indra was expecting you back a long time ago. When he heard you had got married, well, you know him, he went into a spin...'

'...and ordered that I return at once!' she prompted.

'Yes.'

She shook her head.

'You can't or you won't?'

'Both. I am not Urvashi, who got bored soon enough of Earth and mortals.'

'Menaka, you know Indra can forcefully drag you out of here!'

'He won't,' she retorted coolly. 'He knows he will have to face Kaushik...Vishwamitra,' she corrected politely.

'Vishwamitra is a spent force,' dismissed Kama, shrugging. 'Indra can vanquish him now.'

'Don't underestimate him, Kama. He is not as powerless as you imagine him to be,' she warned. 'He's in meditation now.'

'That must be your doing again. Your guilt won't allow him to go into complete ruin. Either way, Menaka, only you can avoid the confrontation. You have done your work here, admirably enough. Now quietly come back to Heaven. Please.' Kama looked at her solemnly, he rarely beseeched. 'You will only get hurt. Let go of him, Menaka. He was never yours to take. He was the target, you were a strategy.'

'I was the causality, as is Vishwamitra,' she accused. 'You made me do it!'

'So was I, Menaka,' he said helplessly, blurting the truth he could not contain any longer. 'Indra forced me to shoot that one arrow at you, for you to fall in love with Vishwamitra.'

Menaka froze, her eyes widened in shock. 'But that wasn't the plan!'

'It was Indra's plan, so that you would forget Vasu.'

Menaka nodded imperceptibly, still too stunned to speak. A thought struck her. She frowned. 'Did that arrow hit me, Kama, or Vishwamitra? He was already under my spell...' her voice trailed uncertainly.

Kama paled. 'I am not sure. You seemed unsure too. And yet...' he started, bewilderment dawning on his face.

Menaka seemed unfazed, her face grim. 'I fell in love with Kaushik nevertheless,' she paused. 'I have accepted it. It is time you and Indra did. And I shall not leave him and I don't want to return to Heaven. Ever.'

There was her former fierceness back in her voice as she announced it. Kama was subdued to argue any further. The scheme had gone all awry. Menaka was made to fall in love with Vishwamitra, his arrow notwithstanding. It seemed destined. Why? Menaka was supposed to be the providence to change the future of Vishwamitra, the means and the reason for his fall from glory. She had fallen a victim herself.

'Menaka, I understand your feelings, you love him too much to let go of him,' he said finally. 'But you shall have to come back to Amravati one day. If not today, perhaps later, but it is inevitable.'

'No.' Her refusal echoed with a stubborn finality.

'You know you won't get away with it,' he said quietly. 'Indra will force you to come back!'

'He wouldn't dare!' she replied scornfully. 'He will have to face Kaushik first!'

'Courtesy you, Menaka, Vishwamitra is no longer as powerful as he used to be. And Indra knows this and shall seek it to his advantage. He can kidnap you without Vishwamitra's knowledge like he did with Urvashi. What will you do then?'

'Kaushik will get to know immediately where I am and who the culprit is, and then there will be war!' she said. 'As I warned earlier, don't underestimate his spiritual prowess. He is a man of purpose, and such men are dangerous.'

Kama laughed shortly. 'Purpose? Does he still aspire to be a Brahmarishi, Menaka?' he quizzed with a brief smile. 'He was great once upon a time. You undid him beautifully.'

Menaka flinched.

'You have dissipated him entirely—his disembodied spirit, his potential divinity. He is but a lesser mortal now,' Kama continued relentlessly. 'You made him lose himself in your love, but you lost your heart as well. Was it my love arrow or the magic of the mortals?' he questioned. 'I have heard mortals make terrific lovers.'

Warm colour suffused her translucent skin, and to Kama's amused surprise, he watched Menaka blush. It was a rare, exquisite sight, making her appear all the more exciting, delicately beautiful, her thick lashes hiding the sudden shyness in her eyes. She looked the picture of femininity, shorn of her celestial etherealness.

'Urvashi used to often complain that Pururav used to make love to her so often through the day that it exhausted even her!' he teased, a twinkle in his eyes. 'Does Vishwamitra outdo Pururav?'

Menaka could not utter a retort. She blushed more furiously, trying not to visualize images of Kaushik's raw passion, hot blood pounding in his veins; his short, ragged breaths fanning her face as she made him pant and moan; his eyes wildly ecstatic; his lithe, sun-bruised body crushing her voluptuously under him; the sweat running wildly down his bare, broad chest; the warm clasp of his hard-boned hands as he pinned her down, muttering thickly through parched lips; his tongue snaking hotly in her wet, soft mouth...Menaka shut her eyes. Mortals were dangerously, excitingly different; for one, gandharvas and devas didn't sweat, mortals did, Menaka thought inanely, instantly comparing Vasu's skilled lovemaking with Kaushik's brutish passion.

'So, what's your next step? Conceiving a baby with him?' Kama's curious question cut her short rudely. Menaka collected her wild thoughts together.

'That was what Indra wanted,' she retorted.

'Selective obedience, eh? You will do it, but not for the reason

Indra wants. You want to have a baby from your lover, don't you? You have no intention of dumping the baby with him or leaving him. You want to have this one sweet happy family!' snorted Kama. 'But be forewarned, Menaka, it's a dream you can never make real.'

'It's my escape from Heaven!' she said fiercely. 'I am fighting for some sanity. If that what happiness is, I want it.'

'And what when Vishwamitra gets to realize you tricked him? That you were a part of Indra's plan?' mocked Kama. 'He loves you because he believes you. But he still doesn't know the truth. The moment he does, he will throw you out himself!'

Menaka clenched her fingers into a fist, refusing to allow Kama tap her innermost fear. 'I agree Kaushik still doesn't know about my deception. But who will tell him?' she challenged. 'You? Or Indra? Even if both of you divulge the secret, he won't believe either of you!' she scoffed openly.

Kama stood silent, amazed at her confidence. 'Because he believes me more. I have told him that I was banished by Indra. He was convinced because there was an element of truth to validate it. He loves me enough to protect me, to fight for me. And the moment Kaushik comes to now that Indra is to take me to Heaven, he will assume that it is by coercion. I won't have to spell it out to him; he knows I have been victimized by Indra. So, it's your word against mine!' she added pointedly.

Kama gazed at her in a new light. 'You had it all neatly planned, didn't you?' There was a hint of silent admiration in his voice. 'You used both the men.'

Menaka looked back at him defiantly.

'That's why you agreed to "help" out Indra. The conceited fool that he is, Indra did not realize you were using him to get away from him. You employed his plan as a weapon against him. You made him a victim of his own design. Like Vishwamitra, you made a fool out of Indra too.'

'I had to, to save myself.'

'He won't like it. Not one bit,' warned Kama. 'And he shall retaliate, vindictively. I pray for you and Vishwamitra. Bless you both!' he sighed. 'So with what message do I go back to Indra?'

'For now, tell him this marriage is a ruse, the next step of the plan' she answered promptly. 'He'll believe it, I assure you!'

Kama could not help smiling. 'You are wicked!'

'I know him too well,' she agreed. 'He'll fall for it, smug for another few years. Till then, I can stay with Kaushik,' she said wistfully, biting her lips.

'You are living on borrowed time,' he cautioned. There was something dangerous and remorseless in her optimism.

ψ

Where was Menaka? *Busy with her morning chores, presumably.* Vishwamitra made a mental note of expanding his ashram. He should have more disciples, more attendants so that he could teach and she could have some help. But the thought of having strangers in his paradise daunted him. No, life was perfect here with just him and her. She was not in the hut. *Must have gone for her daily evening swim,* he thought. She never missed it.

'Me-na-ka!' he called, spacing the syllables with an unrestrained urgency, suddenly scared that she might have left or been taken away.

There's nothing discreditable about jealousy, thought Vishwamitra as he spotted Menaka finning in the river with all sinuous grace. He considered jealousy as the mark of true love. But he prided himself for not being a jealous man. He had never felt threatened, possibly because he always had everything. He was everyone's envy. He never nursed a jealous thought, till he met Menaka. He was either tortured by the fear of Vasu's memories or Indra's possessiveness. He believed her completely, but dreaded he would lose her to one of them one day.

The water looked welcoming. Soon, he was in the water with her. She certainly could swim. He went in after her, but he saw it was hopeless to attempt to catch up with Menaka. After a while, she turned around and came back, almost as fast as she had gone out.

She circled around him, her face wet and glistening. 'This

is one thing I am better at than you!' she grinned victoriously.

He turned on his back and stared up at the big moon. The water was warm, but he wasn't in the mood to appreciate it. He was impatient for her to finish her swim and come out or else he wanted to make love to her right now in the water. As if reading his mind, she teasingly swam away from him, came back and then slithered beside him, her body slippery, her hands at his thighs, her lips deliciously wet on his, her tongue moving over his face, his ear, into his mouth, which had gone suddenly dry. She was touching him everywhere, her silky hair swirling, blinding him; he thought his heart would explode. He heard himself groaning as she pushed him under water, their wet skins stuck together. But he knew her body well, his hands grasping her waist, thrusting himself deep inside her, waves of ecstasy crashing on him. Outside, the water laved gently around them and sometime later, they came out of the water, gasping, their bodies still entwined, drifting in the warm water. They stayed afloat in satiated silence, their fingers touching, enjoying the water, enjoying while staring at the stars above in the inky, cloudless sky.

'You are fascinated by the stars aren't you?' she murmured. 'The universe, the constellations, astronomy—that's why you could create a galaxy...'

'I discovered more than created!' he laughed lightly. 'All Man has to do is search Nature and he'll find Deva everywhere. But Man has yet to discover much, much more and he will keep on searching, never give up...and so, what did *you* do today?' he glanced at her languidly.

'After the day's gruelling dance practice, this swim did me good!' she sighed, slowly catching her breath. 'And yes, like a good girl, I was practising the classical, not the erotic variety!' she mischievously assured him, her tongue exploring her smiling lips. 'Soon I'll find myself punctuating our conversations only with swarams and shlokas, guruji!'

'Am I a better guru than Lord Kama?' he grinned in the darkness.

'More exacting! I completed my target of thousand whorls,'

she grimaced. 'Fortunately, Bharat Muni and Tumburu had taught the geometrical aesthetics of the classical dance movements,' she said, stretching her long legs, her feet neatly splashing. 'I could recall all the adavus I had learnt from him, and soon everything fell pat into place. There is a logical progression in the steps. In our erotic dances, we have to innovate and improvise, but we have to be anchored in the roots of classical dance. Or, we can get lost. As we often do, had it not been for your timely instruction,' she touched his shoulder lightly.

'Were you not ever taught the spiritualism in dance?' he questioned, his eyes serious. 'Dance is a philosophy. I want you to discover that and excel in it. It's the embodiment of sensuality and spirituality, an expression of the divine, and that should be reflected in the dancer's outlook at life as well,' he said. 'Music and dance cannot be plain entertainment. The performer spreads an energy, peace and calm that is almost scientifically defined. Both in dance and music, the way sound is used is important, be it the ragas or the movement and the more you get deeply involved, it ushers a certain degree of meditation. It explodes into a completely different dimension of experience.'

Menaka absently stared at the twinkling stars above. 'Yes, I have heard Lord Shiva, one of the best dancers, always carries a drum with him because it is symbolic of the rhythm of life.'

'Dance *is* the rhythm of the body. And it's not just in the beat of the heart,' explained Vishwamitra. 'Every fibre, every pranik nadi, every chakra, your pulse in the body has its own tune. There is a whole science about sound and body movement. That dance is a spiritual release, using body language, words and music, ornamentation and emotions to communicate the inviolable.'

Menaka nodded. 'The nine emotional essences of Indian drama, the natyashastra, go with dance as well—the erotic, the humorous, the compassionate, the fierce, the heroic, the fearful, the disgusted, the wondrous, and the peaceful,' she said. It was not just his voice, but what he said that mesmerised her. She looked forward to such discussions, even if they were in the middle of a river! He was a scholar but he never made her feel inadequate. He coached her instead, often without she even realizing it, gentle but insistent.

'Bharata Muni has taught you your drama and music well too!' he chuckled. 'Good lord, please don't spell out those 6000 shlokas of the natyshastra now! By the way, do you know how the muni got his name? 'Bharata' is a generic name, an acronym for the three syllables—'bha' for 'bhava', that is mood, 'ra' for 'raga', that's melody, and 'ta' for 'taal' which as you know means rhythm.'

'Oh!' she looked surprised. 'I would have teased him if I had known.'

'Teased?' he raised an eyebrow in amusement. 'I have heard he is an irascible disciplinarian. You can charm him too, can you!'

Menaka giggled. 'He's a little odd... demanding an exact conformity to perfection, always. Once he almost spelt out a curse on Urvashi while she was performing the Laskhmi-Narayan dance, where instead of saying Purushottam for Lord Vishnu, she blurted out Pururav's name!'

'That's what love does to you!' smiled Vishwamitra. 'See, you have made me your slave and master both! And that you are training so beautifully under me!' he teased, stroking her feet with his toe, his touch and the water, making the fatigue ebb away.

She nodded, biting her lip.

'Don't do that!' he said spontaneously, placing his forefinger between her lips, easing out the lower one to see the slight teeth marks on it. 'See, how you mutilate it!' he said exasperatedly.

'You are a very good teacher, do you know that?' she said softly, in shy admiration. 'Sometimes I wonder whether we apsaras ever had all this in mind when we danced. Is shringar supposed to be sensual and spiritual? Are grace and beauty the only two elements of dance? But you taught me that dancing is like performing for the Lord, with no audience looking on, no music, just the song of faith in your heart. It was just the dancer and his inner self, the highest order of divine quality. Like when I perform for you,' she paused. 'You are my Lord. You are my guru.'

Vishwamitra was about to protest but the strange intensity

in her voice silenced him. She straightened up, placing her hands on his beating chest. 'Bless me that I never corrupt my art from henceforth.'

He held her gently by her shoulders. 'You are an apsara, there is nothing corruptible about that. It is your profession, not a sin.'

Menaka moved her face. 'But it is. That was what I did!' she refuted. 'You showed me a new path, a spiritual insight which I did not have.'

'Because you were never taught so. That's what Indra has reduced you to an artiste, not an artist!' he frowned.

'A seductress,' she said quietly.

He nodded. 'Exactly, that's how he has made you define yourself. You are an artist, Menaka, all apsaras are. They are prolific proponents of art, not dissolute dancers entertaining vulnerable victims! But that does not mean what you did till now was unrighteous or unchaste. Why do you think so?' he asked in mild exasperation. 'Is this your misplaced humility? You are neither inferior nor unworthy. You are a celestial being, Menaka, you were born divine, from the mind of the purest,' he stroked her neck. 'And you are my inspiration, my strength. How more can I explain that I love you, respect you and am so proud of you.' He placed his finger under her chin and gently turned her head to his to gaze searchingly in her eyes. 'I meant every word I just said. I want you to believe them.' He pressed his lips on her brow, almost in veneration.

His probing tenderness evoked a painful emotion, that same cold haggard fear, arising from her deep sense of inadequacy. Regret gnawed frantically. She wanted to look away from his earnestness, from her embarrassment but she couldn't move her face. He was holding her firmly, forcing her to face a truth—was she worthy of his love? She was an imposter; she had feigned situations, she had pretended what she wasn't, she had faked her identity. She had changed her demeanour, her personality, her intentions. She had fooled him and herself. But one truth she could not hide was that she was in love. Menaka returned his gaze as fearlessly as she could, mustering all her moral courage to look into his honest eyes. 'I do. I love you. I am so happy that I am scared, afraid that I might lose it all someday, lose you and my Heaven.' And she knew she was not lying to him.

Game and Gamble

$\mathcal{S}$he felt his presence immediately. Menaka looked around her surreptitiously, all her senses alert. She knew Indra was hiding in the shadowy glades, tucked away from ordinary sight. Fortunately, Kaushik would not be able to sense his unwanted presence in the woods; he was in deep meditation and would not come out of it for another few days. She had been gently persuading him into following a more disciplined routine for the past many months. Not that it assuaged her guilt, her restless shame and the agony of seeing a great man wasting all because she had undone him.

Indra must have panicked at Kaushik's renewed round of tapas and had rushed down to keep his eyes on her. The figure in the shadows sprung into shape against the defining morning light of the sun. Indra's smile when he greeted her was supercilious—smug but deigning to be gracious.

'You seem to have made another Heaven for yourself here,' Indra started. 'When do you intend exchanging this one for the original?' he smiled faintly, but his eyes were hard as diamonds. 'And I don't want any argument, Menaka! It's will be almost eight years now since you have been wasting time with him! I have come to specially escort you back home.' He looked belligerent, ready to take on any fight from her.

She had played this scene in her mind a thousand times those sleepless nights. She knew how Indra would behave, and thus had her plan all set. She found herself praying that it would work. Her happiness hinged on this one.

'I won't argue with you, my lord. I know how powerful you are,' her tone was subdued. 'But I beg you, please let me stay! I love him. Don't take me away from him...'

Indra felt a thrill of pleasure. He was making Menaka beg again.

'Falling in love with him has made you lose reason!' he remarked instead, yet pleased.

'I don't have the will in me to fight you anymore. I lost the last time. I surrender, this time not for my sake, but for Kaushik. I would do anything for him!' she said, making it sound like a confession torn from her.

'But please let there be no bloodshed!' she implored dramatically. 'I agree to leave him but I don't want you to harm him like what you did to Vasu.'

Vasu, he thought with distaste, *she had dragged in that wretched man again.* But there was no rancour simmering in Menaka anymore, just an unusual suppliance. Indra seemed to be luxuriating in her cowed submissiveness, her spirit broken under the brutality of his power which seemed to terrorize her. She took a few steps as if to meekly leave right away.

'Is that why you did not come at his ashram and openly take me away?' she asked innocently.

'I am hiding here in the woods for I wanted to discuss this with you first,' Indra retorted indignantly, his vanity instantly bruised. 'I did not want to confront Vishwamitra blatantly. There is no need to. This was a subterfuge and shall remain so. You shall leave as quietly as you arrived in his life.'

'Let's leave before Kaushik realizes I am gone,' begged Menaka, with the right cadence of grief and acquiescence. 'He'll go mad with fury!'

'You were to take care of that—make him so weak that he could never dare challenge the devas ever gain. Why has it not been done yet?' demanded Indra, unsettled and unsure about his enemy's untold powers. 'Or did falling in love make you weak too?'

The moment he said it, Indra realized he had owned up his mistake. He had made her fall in love with Vishwamitra but could not revert the damage. He was caught in his own trap. He recovered quickly, choosing a swaggering show of courage over admittance of fault.

'You are quite the martyr, aren't you?' asked Indra, with malicious glee. 'Ready to come back with me, instead of spitting fire as you always do? Love did make you weak this time, not strong.'

'I know now I can never win with you,' she agreed, with unbearable falsity. 'I would like to stay back and be with Kaushik, but I know you won't allow it. I won't fight you, I'll leave Kaushik for his own good.'

'His good?!' questioned Indra.

Menaka nodded, looking up at him with none of the defiance he was trying to prod.

'It will break my heart but it'll protect him from your wrath,' she sighed in painful sufferance. 'He won't give up without a fight, and I want to avoid that. So, please let's leave before he wakes from his meditation. He will, however, soon guess where I might be...' She kept the words hanging in the thickly scented air of the forest.

Indra eyes narrowed. 'He still holds divine power?' he exclaimed, scowling. 'I thought he was a lost cause by now.'

She shook her head helplessly. 'He is too great a rishi to be trounced so easily. It couldn't have happened in a blink!' she replied, employing the common inference that Indra's single blink was equivalent to a mortal's lifetime.

Indra paled slightly under his fair skin. 'I don't want further war with that man! That is why I planned this scheme in the first place. I was roundly reprimanded by Lord Brahma the last time and want to avoid any further complications...' he looked obviously bemused. 'You haven't told Vishwamitra more than what you were supposed to?' he questioned tersely.

Menaka's eyes widened with feigned horror. 'Why would I reveal our deception?' she managed weakly, lacing the word 'our' with a soft, conspiratorial tone as if they were partners in crime. Indra relaxed immediately. She continued pleadingly, 'If he comes to know my truth, he'll put a curse on me. It's best if I leave with you now!'

Indra paused, frowning. 'Yes, you have been with him long enough! How many more years do you intend to be with him? It cannot be forever!' he added bitingly. 'You well know that.'

'I do, oh, I do. I cannot allow myself to forget that I am a creature of Heaven. I don't belong here, but my heart shall always belong here,' she gave a spurious sigh, her eyes stricken, wringing her hands agitatedly.

Menaka took her time adjusting her angavastra nervously over her shoulders. Indra followed her unhurried movements closely, entranced with her beauty in all its simplicity and frugality. She was not wearing a single piece of jewellery, yet she glowed. She could still take his breath away. *Oh! How I have missed her. I have ached for her mere presence—her dazzling smile that lit up her divine face and the world, her heavenly fragrance as she walked, her trim hips rolling to a mesmerising sway, her husky laugh gurgling from that slender white throat, she biting into her crimson, luscious lips. Heaven was hell, without her. And I want her back,* urgently, his mind screamed at him. And that she was ready to come back with him made it a lot easier. He had been taken aback at her willingness, even suspicious but Menaka had changed, he realised with a start. She was more docile, more resigned. There was a softness in her strength, Vishwamitra had tamed her in his own way. *The mortals have their own magic,* he surmized with a smirk. She looked decidedly mellowed and matured. The fight had gone out of her, replaced by a rare wisdom. He liked her better this way so easy to mould, soft to hold. He tore his mind away reluctantly and focused on how they would head back.

'You seem to have wisened up, Menaka,' he chuckled, 'not that foolish woman in love anymore.'

She ignored the jibe, biting into her lip to restrain her contempt to well out. She would have to play her part carefully now. 'Exactly, I would rather leave him than witness the bloodshed!'

She saw Indra flush with pleasure; he considered her acknowledgement of his power to destroy as a compliment.

'But bloodshed there will be, my lord,' she warned. 'I always knew I had to return to Heaven, but will Kaushik allow it?' she paused cautiously. 'He is bound to be angry. He will either curse me or curse you. Or both,' she adjoined slyly, milking Indra of his biggest fears—living through a curse. The last one uttered by Rishi Gautam on him for copulating with his wife Ahilya in the guise of her husband, had made Indra an object of public ridicule. Gautam had castrated him and punctured him instead with a thousand vaginas to quench his vigorous prurience.

Indra pursed his lips, to stop them from trembling. Menaka was not sure if it was fear or anger. 'Vishwamitra still has enough yogic powers in him to curse us?'

'Yes and to challenge you as well, I warn you again, my lord,' she reminded him quietly.

'I thought he was well and truly finished!' he mumbled. 'How much more time do you need to put him out?' he asked, exasperated.

'He still meditates on and off...' Again, it was a lie of omission. Indra would not know and should never know that it was she who had pushed Kaushik to take up his tapas again. 'And to prise him out of the meditation completely, he needs to be a busy family man, not just my lover...' she implied, stretching a long thread to a sane argument, a possible way of convincing him. She pretended to think hard.

Indra stood straight with his arms akimbo, his favourite pose in aggressiveness, waiting for her response.

'Possibly my novelty is wearing off?' she tittered nervously. 'That's why he has got back to his meditation?'

'No, I can't believe that, he's too much into you to think of anything else. You physically tire a man, Menaka, not bore him senseless!' Indra was quick to retort. 'The fact that he is back to his old ways is dangerous. It will stoke his old fire and keep the embers of ambition burning,' his brows furrowed darkly into a deeper frown, unaware that was what Menaka intended to induce

Vishwamitra to resuscitate his dying dream.

'Exactly,' she said earnestly. 'And if I have to have him more for myself I have to have a larger power over him. I have to stay with him, keep him so occupied that he is bound to me forever... oh, I have it' she said in mild relief. 'As you once said, I need to have a child from him!' she stated, the words delivered with the right impact they was meant to contain. They had the desired effect—Indra's frown disappeared, now completely convinced that she was so vulnerably cornered herself that she was ready to connive with him again. They would have to subjugate the great rishi together.

'You were right, my lord, let me have his baby to fetter him. To trap him in the domesticity of marriage,' she said with a dawning smile as if good sense had prevailed upon her at last. 'He will be bound to the child, not just me. So when I leave him eventually, he will be saddled with a baby and be forced to forego his tapas, his quest, his mission, to nurse the child instead.'

Indra wore a smug look. 'I had told you this before!' he paused, a frown marring his handsome face. 'But why didn't you have a child from him by now as instructed?'

'He didn't want it,' she lied quickly. 'He wanted me all for himself. But I'll have to trick him now. Make him want a baby, but that would take time...'

Indra was still scowling.

Menaka persisted. 'The baby would also blunt his wrath and grief when I leave him,' she continued, piling up her assertions, offering them more as evidence and making them appear less specious. 'Vishwamitra would not dare think of confronting you or the devas when he has as baby in his care. It would remind him of his responsibility and distract him from his revenge. Am I wrong?'

'Or, from what I can see, he is so insanely in love with you, that when you leave him, it will certainly break his heart and he'll give up on everything—you, his damned mission, and hopefully his own life too!' swore Indra. 'But that's wishful optimism. A baby, as I said, is a better plan. But will you be able to leave man and baby, Menaka?' he asked, with an unpleasant grin.

'I have done it before, you made me do it, and I have suffered sufficiently for it,' she said generously, suffusing her voice with tears and allowing him the pleasure to gloat. 'This time I want it be less messy, for all our sake.'

Indra looked pleased that she had figured out a solution even though he would have to wait a little longer for her to return to Heaven. But Menaka's brow was delicately puckered, still pondering hard.

'But the dilemma here is not what I want or what you can do...' she said. 'It is what we cannot stop—Kaushik. How do we rein in his unleashed fury? He'll wage a war. The moment I leave, be it now or later, Kaushik is sure to resort not to just revenge, but he shall be back with a stronger purpose than before, won't he?! Earlier it was war with Vasishth, but now it shall also be you too, my lord. He will not forgive you for what you did. Ever!'

Indra felt a coil of fear uncurling inside him. 'What are you saying?' he asked, his eyes narrowing.

'That he will go back to becoming a Brahmarishi with vengeance the moment I leave him!' she declared succinctly. 'I know him too well, he won't be heartbroken to give up on everything. Rather, he will be like a hurt animal, thirsting for blood. You will have an old formidable enemy rankling you again knocking on Heaven's door, my Lord,' she insinuated looking adequately aghast, her voice tremulous. From his white face, Menaka guessed she had alarmed him supremely and Indra was now close to panic.

'But you have a choice,' she said ingratiatingly. 'Either you take cudgels again with Kaushik as he restarts his efforts to become the most powerful Brahmarishi or...' she paused deliberately, 'leave me with Kaushik to keep him in check, forever.'

She allowed her words to sink in. She had played out well, goading him, enticing him though exaggerated promises and persuasion and finally scaring him just enough to provoke him into agreeing with her. She had him completely in her grip, and she would twist him as necessary. Make him writhe and wriggle

and wrench in agony as he had once done to her. He could still
do it if she ever relaxed her stranglehold now. She wanted to
get rid of him, never to see him again.

'So how would you prefer it, my lord?' she asked humbly.
'That I leave now for Amravati or that I forever remain with
your enemy to rein him in, removing your obstacle forever?'
She waited expectantly for his answer, her fingers playing with
the end of her angavastra.

Indra took a long moment to retain his equilibrium. This
woman had outwitted him again. Naked rage flickered across his
face. His fingers flexed but he barely managed to control himself.
Menaka watched him with vigilant eyes, relishing every moment
of his frustration. He was caught in his own net of deceit.

'You crafted a wonderful plan, dear,' he hissed through
clenched teeth.

'Did I?' her eyes widened in mock surprise. 'All I did wrong
was to fall in love with my prey, that was not my intention,' she
said artfully, her voice a pleading whisper. She had him there
again; Indra would never admit to his ploy or that he had foiled
his own plan. *Let him roil in his regret*, she thought smugly.

But Indra knew what would happen next: Vishwamitra would
be like a loose, crazed animal, lusting for revenge and blood. Only
Menaka could control him now. He had to decide—to take her
away with him or lose her. He looked at Menaka uncertainly.
He was not sure if he could credit Menaka with the genius he
suspected her to have. He had made the blunder, not she. She
had followed his orders even that of falling in love. To demolish
one monster, he had created another who could destroy him
instead. Menaka, the deadly seductress, had lured him into his
own trap. And he did not know how to get out. He was stuck
in his own decision. He would have to let go of his weakness
to make himself stronger. Or both would destroy him some day.
He would have to let Menaka go.

'Yes, my lord?' she asked, thrusting the knife deeper. 'What
should I do?'

'Stay here and rot in this goddamned hell!'

Birth and Worth

$\mathcal{K}$aushik was a man of habit. The routine of his day had stayed the same for all the ten years they had been together, and Menaka had grown accustomed to them. Usual, almost mundane, but it made her feel protected, calm and comfortable.

Menaka could not have been happier. She had driven away the last of the lurking shadows of doom. Indra would not bother her any more, she was safe. And she was pregnant. This time there was no emotional chaos in her mind. The symptoms were startlingly the same—the morning nausea, the day long sporadic spells of dizziness, the tight, tender tingle in her breasts. But this time she was enjoying every moment of it.

'Apsaras make love, but when they make babies, they are in love!' Rati had once said. Was that why she had taken so long to have this baby? Was her love for him now complete, free of fear and deceit? The baby was the truth of their love, the culmination of his yogic energy having the potency of decimating the another world had created with her unadulterated love, cleansed of the last trace of stealth. They had made love a thousand times, a thousand nights through dusk to dawn, days coalescing into nights. Yet, Menaka could single out that frozen moment when she must have conceived. She had felt it that twilight hour, before the sun had soared to announce a new dawn of another day. She had felt the hot, raw rush of his passion and energy gushing into her, burgeoning that seed of new life, which would imbibe the potent with the pure, the best with the beauteous, someone special. Menaka touched her waist lightly, a small smile on her lips.

It was an enjoyable secret that she had not yet divulged to Kaushik. Her smile slipped fast, she felt a sudden surge of apprehension. *How would he react? Would he resent? Get annoyed? Or be simply deliriously happy as she was now, kicking her feet in the warm water of the running stream.* She was sitting at her favourite place—the huge boulder by the river, watching the frothy water tumbling over each other in apparent haste, swirling joyously along the tide. *Much like life itself,* she pondered, *taken by the tide, to drift along, pulled and drawn in a certain direction, the spatial relation often meandering between something sought and the course it eventually took. Or was it?* She hadn't been allowed that luxury. She had clawed, fought, conspired and connived to chalk out her Heaven on Earth. She had created her own Heaven too, like Kaushik had. She stared in the tumbling turbulence, gurgling at her feet, the cool noise calming her, to assure herself the possibility of normalcy.

'You'll catch a cold if you play in the water any longer, that's what kids are often told!'

She jumped at his deep baritone right behind her, warmly caressing her nape, his large hands spanning the small of her waist. She swivelled around, her smile blinding him.

'You finished early!' she beamed radiantly. 'We might catch the sight of the sun setting.'

She leaned against him, her head resting comfortably on his broad chest, his arms around her waist. She heard the birds chirping away busily as if to rush home to their nests. Menaka sighed deeply, she was home, here in in his arms. Suddenly she felt no fear, no dread, no relentless doubt. There was a strange calm, soothing and blissful. She closed her eyes and inhaled him, savouring their togetherness.

'I am going to have our baby,' she murmured contently, her whisper gently floating in the breeze. She felt him stiffen, unconsciously tightening his arms around her. She did not turn around, but patted his hands resting on her flat stomach, her eyes shut, a smile warm on her lips.

She felt him lowering his head in the warm crook of her neck, his lips on her bare shoulders. 'Oh Menaka!' he groaned. 'How much more happy can you make me?'

Menaka felt a quick sense of relief. She twisted her head to gaze up at him. 'I was worried that you might get upset,' she confessed.

'And why would you think so?' he asked her quietly. 'Don't you know me by now?'

She shook her head slowly. 'No,' she muttered. 'I know you as you are but not as what you would be otherwise, other than what I suppose or expect.'

'And you supposed and expected that I wouldn't take too kindly to this news?' he repeated.

Menaka chewed at her lips. 'Why Menaka? Don't you trust me?'

'I do, it's just that ...' she hesitated. 'I was just being silly.'

'No, you were insecure.'

Menaka looked away, the same old dread tearing at her heart again. She clasped her hands around her knees and pulled her knees up to her chin.

'You are scared that I shall leave you if you have a child?' he guessed shrewdly. 'That I would abandon you like my wives and sons in Kanyakubja?' His lips tightened.

Menaka flushed. 'All these years you have been living in that fear?' he questioned, his eyes darkening with an indescribable emotion. 'Is that what you think of me as a person?' It was a statement, not a query.

'It's not because of you, it's me,' she explained earnestly, placing a hand on his big, tanned one. 'I was dreading you would think I would use the baby to trap you...'

'Do you have such a poor opinion about yourself or do you think so poorly of me, Menaka?' he said, raising her face by her chin with his finger. 'As for me, agreed I left my family. I was selfish, inconsiderate and driven by one mad ambition. But that's all changed now. I left my kingdom for myself; but I have left my sanyas for you,' he sighed, his thumb gently rubbing along her slender neck. 'How can I ever leave you, my darling? How can you ever fear that?'

Red hot guilt seared through her. Menaka closed her eyes to hide the pain. He took it as a sign of placation, to invite him to kiss her. He did, clamping his lips on hers, his tongue moving demandingly in her mouth.

'I want my baby to grow inside you,' he muttered thickly, running a hand over her soft stomach. 'How would I not want it? It would be a part of me inside you, a part of us becoming a whole—our baby. Oh Menaka, ours, ours, ours!' he cried intensely.

The echo of his impassioned cry kept ringing in her ears for a long time.

⚘

She was cooking his favourite meal—roasted brinjal with lentils. He watched as she bent over, stirring the pot, humming. In her voice was distilled a small world of her own—the aroma of the meals she prepared, the perfume of the parched Earth as she watered the plants, the fragrance of the flowers she decked so carefully in her hair, the swish of the pot as she carried it all the way up from the river—it was all music; when she hummed softly, it was music to his ears.

She looked much heavier, the bump visible now. But she was as exquisite, perhaps more. It was not just the heat of the fire that made her face appear flushed and glistening. She was radiant, her fair translucence seeped in a soft, strong sheen of pink, shining with happiness and health. Her bun had come loose, and she impatiently tied it, pushing the thick swathe of hair off her smooth, white neck, her fingers moving dexterously to form a quick coil. As always, the flash of exposed slenderness of her neck fomented a clamp of desire grinding at his guts like the tide at the seas.

Sighing, he got up to help her take out the food. He frowned noticing the small portion of the meal prepared. 'Are you planning to skip your meal again?' he asked sharply.

'I really don't feel like eating, the smell of the rotis makes me feel queasy...'

'So don't make them! I'll have rice instead,' he shrugged. 'But that doesn't absolve you from missing meals. Wait, I have got you something.'

He walked up to the doorway and came back, holding a basket. Menaka looked curiously as he fished out some fruits, holding out some in his hand.

'Peach and apricots!' she squealed, her eyes lighting up. 'Where did you get them?! And in this season?'

'Rather in this land!' he said, busy washing them in a bowl of water. Wiping them neatly, he pushed one in her ready mouth. She almost gobbled it down, the juice trickling down the corner of her lips onto her chin. He was sorely tempted to lick it away but he wiped it off with his thumb instead, proceeding to caress her delicate jawline.

'So you were hungry!' he smiled tenderly.

'Just for these!' she said sheepishly, popping another, her pink tongue between her teeth, licking the edges of her wet, juice-soaked lips.

'More?' he said, fascinated by her moving mouth.

'Hmm...yes, more and more! Like making love!' she twinkled, slurping on the juicy fruit. A thought struck her, and she stopped midway, the half-eaten apricot still in her hand, her smile slipping.

'You spent the whole morning getting these?'

'Yes, like you did cooking this meal,' he replied. 'And cleaning the house.'

She suddenly looked grim, the sparkle dying in her eyes. 'You did not meditate again. It's been a week!' she accused. 'I have noticed you have been getting up before me and collecting water from the river and washing the clothes before I can do it! I am not sick, Kaushik. I can do these chores still. You need not miss your prayers and morning meditation.'

He did not reply. But she had got her answer. He was off his routine, one which she had tried to impress on him with her alternating attempts of persuasion and pleadings. She felt a double sense of defeat and disappointment unfurling within her, leaving her with the feeling that he did not want to do it, but she was forcing him.

'Why, don't you want to be a Brahmarishi anymore?' she asked bluntly.

He did not answer immediately. Menaka thought he was ignoring her but he returned her fixed stare, unperturbed.

'No, I am longer interested in becoming one.'

Menaka reeled as if he had slapped her, her face drained of colour. *No!* She screamed in her stunned mind. Her mind went blank, his words shouting back, 'I am no longer interested'. He had given up, surrendering his all for her, to her, because of her. *As had been planned*, a voice taunted her. Menaka had achieved what she had started out for. That he become her slave, forsaking his all. The temptress who had been set to lure him away from his dream. She had killed his ambition, his drive to succeed, his hunger to excel. He had been left with no desire for anything but the all-consuming one for her. She must have intuitively seen it coming, and that is why she had sought so desperately to make him resume his work, to make him see reason and to rekindle that fire in him. To bring him back to his spiritual odyssey. But she had failed. Because she was the cause of his failure. His dangerous enchantress, as he often teasingly called her, had enticed him to his doom. Now even when she wanted to help him rise and recover from his fall, she could not for it was she who had made him stumble from grace and glory. She had ushered his downfall. She had ruined him.

But she had to try, she could not give up on him, she could not allow him to give up on himself.

'How can you yield so early?' she challenged. 'You aspired once to be a Brahmarishi. Your goal was to be another Rishi Vasishth, better him one day...'

'Vasishth has his Arundhati for strength. I have you,' he said simply.

Raw shame leapt at her throat. 'No, Kaushik, no! Don't put me on such a pedestal! I am not worth that respect.'

'I have you, I have never been happier and I don't want more!' he said. 'Can't you understand, Menaka? I have never been more content, more at peace than what I am today. And it's all because of you. Why should I aspire for anything when I have my world, my heaven, my universe here?'

Menaka shook her head frantically. 'You were the greatest of kings, but you relinquished your throne, kingdom, fame, wealth for that one great dream. You gave up your family for it. You suffered the insults of the rishis, endured the worst of penance to get to be what you are today, a unique scholar boasting of knowledge and power greater than the devas. You proved the seers that you were unequalled—a warrior who thirsted not for war but for wisdom to become a rishi out of sheer virtue. All for what? To come to this...to this nothingness?' she cried. 'You can't!'

'But I have,' he said calmly. 'I realize I was arrogant in my ambition, foolish in my quest and I want no more of it.'

'You proved that man could do anything if he had the will. You, a mortal, defied the devas. You wiped out their arrogance, their divine power by usurping their Heaven. You threatened them with the prospect that Man might not need Deva any more. You proved man could make his own Heaven. You brought the devas down on their knees. You did this, Kaushik, you! And that's why you became Vishwamitra! How do you forget this??'

He smiled, noticing how she could look excitingly beautiful even with a frown pleating her smooth forehead, her eyes glittering angry sparks, her cheeks flushed a warm pink.

'You just said it, Menaka. Man makes his own Heaven. This one with you is now mine. The one I created was out of my ego, my arrogance, my thirst for power. The one which I own now, is out of love, *our* love, Menaka. And I prefer this one!'

Menaka could not believe her ears. Horror quivered through her body.

'You are the only mortal rishi of the seven holiest rishis— the saptarishis—born from divine power. You created your own divinity. Lord Brahma himself acknowledged you as the great Vishwamitra, you cannot disappoint him! You cannot defeat yourself, your purpose! Kaushik, you can't give up all what you once sought for, what you gave up the world for!!' she placed her hand on his arm, hoping touch could bring him back to his senses.

He stayed silent but his silence did not mean acquiescence.

'You were to be a Brahmarishi,' she reminded him again, hoping to goad him. 'That rare, extraordinary one who has realized his supreme self, to attain that elusive consciousness bliss as the highest reality, to receive the highest divine knowledge— the brahmajnana. You were to be the liberated being aware his brahman, the infinite atma, his true inner self. You, oh Vishwamitra, are the only man, the only rishi, who got elevated to the position. You rose by merit to prove that that brahmin status can be earned and is not entitled, to tell the world that it's not birth but worth which determines the outcome of one's life. You were on the way to be a Brahmarishi till you met me...' she broke, choking. She swallowed, recovering her breath. 'You have come so far, your goal is within reach, then how can you simply shrug it away, Vishwamitra?'

'Don't call me that!' he said sharply. 'You have never called me by that name, so why do you taunt me now? I am Kaushik for you.'

'You are also Vishwamitra,' she reminded him, harshly. 'If you forget that, it's a shame!'

He tightened his lips, his face showing the first trace of temper.

'Why does it bother you who I am, what I was, Menaka?' he asked coldly. 'Isn't it enough that we are happy together, that we are going to have our baby? Why are you ranting about tapas, vidya and enlightenment? I have resigned to the fact...'

'What fact?' she asked dismally.

'That to be a Brahmarishi, tapas and sexual intimacy do not go together,' he said quietly. 'You have to choose one of them. Pure tapas involves meditation done for self-realization done in total solitude, secluded from society and family. He has to become an ascetic, indifferent to worldly pleasures to pursue his spiritual goals. That is why I had to leave my family. Attachment hinders tapas. It is the fire that burns within, that is needed for the yogi to achieve that enlightenment, to foster that immense self-control...'

And I have killed that self-control, she realized, remorse knifing through her.

He continued, 'A rishi needs a ruthless single mindedness and his focus is solely on wisdom and integrity. He has to discipline his body, mind, desire and character, keep complete control of them and finally act without any selfishness or thought of reward. I have realized I can't do that anymore, the Brahmarishi goal itself was a reward I aspired to satiate my ego. I did it for all the wrong reasons.'

'This time do it for the right reason,' she beseeched. 'Don't let me or our child stop you. We shall wait for you here. I am yours, Kaushik, I shall wait for you forever.'

'I tried doing tapas, Menaka, as you bullied me into it, but all I could think of is you and our new-earned happiness. And then I wondered, why am I being so greedy? I have everything and I would again be foolish to give it all up for some egotistic ambition of mine. This goal suddenly seemed hollow!'

'Your goal is your dream, Kaushik. Among the highest good of all is self-realization. It is a rare feat, you know that,' argued Menaka. 'You were achieving the inconceivable. You had made the impossible possible! Kaushik, go away from here, far away from me and this place and seek your dream, and come back to me as a Brahmarishi. Then I can say that I am fit enough to be your wife as Arundhati is for Vasishth.'

'But this time I choose you and our child over my mad need for power. I don't want it, I want you. I cannot have both! '

'You can have both, Kaushik. Are not the other six Brahmarishis married? They balanced asceticism and celibacy with family life. They had children. I beg you, do what you are destined for and I shall wait for your victorious return. Come back to me as a warrior who has won his battle, the Brahmarishi who has conquered it all.'

He gave a smile, that same devastating, heart-stopping smile. 'But Menaka, I am not that man anymore. I don't wish to be that man anymore. He was a conceited, self-centred, power-hungry, revengeful, despicable egomaniac. I have changed; you changed me for the better. Don't you want me as I am now?'

'You are destined for greatness!' she cried. 'That is why you became Vishwamitra from Kaushik. I love you, Kaushik, I always shall. But don't stop loving yourself, for what you could be,' she persuaded, floundering in frustration. She was not merely losing the argument, she had failed to win. She had, inevitably, won Indra's war for him, but lost her own battle. Yet she would not allow herself to surrender, still desperate to convince him, cajole him, and counter him. But he was such a stubborn man: obdurate in his belief and implacably in love.

'You made me a new man, Menaka,' he said, taking her face in his hands and kissing her softly on her forehead. It was almost like an act of reverence. Menaka shut her eyes to stem her shame. 'You are the one who showed me a better, simpler, peaceful world. You are going to be the mother of my child. What more could a man want?'

'Ambition,' she said forcefully, her face flushed. 'A drive, an aspiration, a dream!'

'I have it, standing right in front of me. You are all that and more,' he whispered, his eyes tender, worshipping her. 'Don't send me away. I have come home, Menaka. You are my home.'

Menaka's face went white. Why did each word he uttered pierce straight at her guilty, unworthy heart? Because he loved her absolutely for the person he believed her to be preserving his love for real—undying and without forsaking. He would rather forfeit the world, his ideals, his brilliance, his future to keep her with him. His love was forever hopeful to his unswerving soul.

She hated herself for what she was doing to the man, of what she had done. She had brought down a great man to his most shameful nadir as he grovelled in his love for her. She had snatched his future from him to gain her present, but her past stalked her. Her remorse, her shame no longer permitted her to continue her pretence. She curled her fingers into fists, what had she done to him?

Mother and Child

'Menaka has given birth to a daughter!' said Kama, his face expressionless.

Indra looked moodily around him; the hall had long since lost its charm since Menaka's absence.

'Another girl is born to an apsara,' he shrugged nonchalantly, but Kama knew his casual lack of concern was deceptive. Indra could never be indifferent about Menaka or any of his apsaras, they were all his chattels. Some viciously called them his concubines, as he was more possessive about them than his wife. Kama smiled cynically. Sachi might be his queen, his consort, but even she had to endure the indignity of seeing these beautiful women around him.

'But that's a myth that apsaras give birth only to girls,' said Kama. 'Urvashi's Rishyaringa and Grittachi's Ruru are famous sons! Not that the daughters can become apsaras or can they, my lord?' he asked sardonically,

'At the rate we are losing the apsaras to mortals, we might need to create a new tribe of them!' interrupted a harsh voice. Both men swivelled around.

Rambha stood glowering at the doorway in her sullen glory, oozing a hostile sensuality.

'We had lost Urvashi for a long time, and now Menaka's gone! My lord, it's time this Heaven permitted babies to be groomed into apsaras and gandharvas,' she added scathingly. 'We hardly have any now.'

Kama winced. Rambha was clearly referring to Tumburu's recent ouster from Heaven and Vishwavasu's, not that she was particularly affected by the dismissal of the latter. But Tumburu, strangely, was now suffering the same fate as Vasu. As Kuber's favourite, Tumburu was often heard singing from the lofty, craggy hills of the Gandhamandan, the abode of the deva of wealth. But suddenly, he found himself out of favour of his divine patronage, offending Kuber by not presenting Rambha at the said time of performance of her dance. He had been cursed to be born as the asura Viradha to the giant Jaya and wife Shatahrada, a huge terrible creature with two long arms and a fierce face. But the unpleasant truth was that Kuber had placed the curse for a personal reason. None too pleased with their raging romance, he had found a sure, shrewd way of eliminating a rival for Rambha's attention as his son—Nalakuber too was in love with Rambha.

They were dramatic in their likeness—Vishwavasu and Tumburu. Both gandharvas, both in love with apsaras, their love for whom had proved to be their doom, and both cursed by their friend-benefactor devas to live in hellish misery.

But justice was poetic too, and this time it was Rambha who suffered. Like Menaka, she too had lost her lover through a curse, and the cruel irony was not missed by anybody. But Rambha refused to be the weeping widow; she was a woman on the warpath, much like Menaka had been when she had grieved for Vasu, but there was difference. Menaka had taken her revenge on the man responsible for her tragedy—Indra—and not wasted her fury on others, even Rambha although she had plotted against her. *But Rambha would make Heaven hell now with her wrath*, Kama was sure.

'Now what, Rambha?' grimaced Indra. 'Don't tell me you are missing Menaka! You were never too fond of her anyway and now that she and Vasu are gone, you should be the happiest person around in Heaven. So why are you complaining?'

Because Menaka has earned her share of happiness, and not

she, but Kama remained quiet.

'Menaka has had a baby girl I hear. Does that mean she returns to Heaven or continues with her conjugality with that mortal?' asked Rambha, contempt laced with venom. 'I am acutely short of apsaras now to entertain the whims of devas, rishis and the like! And even I have to admit, Menaka was one of the best, to have been allowed to let go so easily,' she glared.

'What do you want me to do?' Indra looked weary, the lines dragging on his face. *He aches for her*, Rambha thought viciously. Did she truly want Menaka back to make her own life miserable? Or did she wish Menaka in Heaven just to spite her and ruin her last chance of happiness?

'Why don't you kidnap her as you did with Urvashi?' suggested Rambha.

'And we'll have a bloodthirsty Vishwamitra at our doorstep, because this will be the first place he will check out after scouring all of Earth!' snapped Indra, annoyed at the foolishness of her remark.

'You and all the devas can throw him out, can't you?' she parried, unruffled by Indra's show of temper. 'You could overpower him.'

'A war in Heaven, Rambha?' asked Indra testily. 'I shall lose my crown forever for that foolish temerity. When was the last time Heaven was attacked? It won't be a vile asura or an over-ambitious king we would be fighting, but a righteous rishi. We'll earn the wrath of Lord Vishnu, Lord Shiva and Lord Brahma collectively, and this time neither of the Trinity will lift a finger to help us because we have created this mess.'

You have, Rambha itched to correct him.

'Will she be coming back?' she asked briefly.

'I am not too sure,' said Indra weakly. He knew if he worded an outright 'no', Rambha would fly into a jealous frenzy. She was already a snarling snake, ready to strike These apsaras were a handful. And he simply failed to know what they may be thinking next. He did not know how to handle them, he thought savagely. Menaka, for one, had completely trumped and trussed him.

'If Menaka does not return, I have just nine daivikas now to present before you and the devas. The other thirty-four are the worldly laukikas, better at entertaining the dead heroes welcomed here than being seductresses. Also, unlike the daivikas, they are not immortal nor can I make them so. In short, how do I replace Menaka?' she challenged him.

'Let's wait for some time and then we'll see,' said Indra dismissively, wishing she would go away.

'Either get her back quick or find me a replacement,' pronounced Rambha, flouncing away in all her imperious hauteur.

Indra knew he could not postpone the matter any further. Heaven needed another apsara urgently. But he did not know what to do. He did not have the power to create them. Apsaras were divine creatures created during the making of the samudra manthan, and Menaka had been one of the last to be created such. Tilottama had been born by the divine architect Vishwakarma, on the behest of Lord Brahma. The birth of Urvashi was more intriguing.

Indra recalled how he had sent two apsaras with Kama to distract the sustained penance of the revered rishis Nara-Narayan who were meditating in the Himalayas. Unaffected by Indralok's apsaras, Narayan had instead casually plucked a flower and placed it on his thigh from which emerged a woman so ravishingly beautiful that the other apsaras were left aghast. This was the tempestuous, temperamental, torrid Urvashi, who had been gifted to Indra once the meditation had been completed. And since then, she had always occupied the pride of place in his court, which brought Indra back to his problem. Heaven was currently running short of apsaras and gandharvas, with Vasu and Tumburu gone and Uranyu, another gandharva, was almost good for nothing these days. He was pining painfully in Menaka's absence. How many men would she inebriate forever in her love?

Indra turned to Kama, exasperated. 'Don't you have any potion that could undo love and make the person come back to his senses??!' he ranted. 'I started this game which is coming back to haunt me!! I have sent umpteen apsaras on umpteen assignments on umpteen rishis, but never have I faced such a dilemma!'

'...because you never used the love arrow on the apsara herself!' retorted Kama.

Indra had the grace to flush with embarrassment. 'I simply traded one problem for another,' he sighed ruefully. 'But, Kama, do you know of any way to get Menaka back? She has me neatly cornered. She left me with a choice between a warring Vishwamitra or Heaven without her; for it's only Menaka now who can keep him away from both, his self-destruction and our destruction as well. Can you think of something?' he turned desperate eyes at his friend and accomplice.

Kama hid a self-satisfied grin. *Menaka had won after all, ensnaring Indra into a predicament in which a favourable outcome was impossible; he was bound to lose whatever he did.*

'It is a ten year liaison of love and passion, it cannot be undone unless one of the two decides to do so,' Kama said noncommittally.

It was a well-orchestrated, happily-ever-after love story that Menaka had cleverly planned; the twist being she had never imagined she would fall in love herself. But she had turned an unforeseen hurdle into an advantage. She now held the dice in her hand.

'I wish I could expose her,' growled Indra, his manner uncharacteristically flustered. He liked to be in control of every situation. Menaka had trounced him completely. 'But letting Vishwamitra know of Menaka's true colours, would more likely burst a blood vessel than break his heart! He's sure to put a curse on both me and Menaka. There seems to be no way out!' he added glumly.

Kama was secretly enjoying Indra's discomfort. It was a rare vision to behold: his brows furrowed, the arrogance drained, panic etched on every line of his face, his long thin nose turning pink with furious mortification at this irreverent turn of events.

'You have lost her, Indra,' he said quietly. 'Give her up.'

'I am reconciling,' acknowledged Indra with an angry shake

of his head. 'But I need to look into Rambha's request too. From where am I to get a new apsara? I cannot create one. Only Lord Brahma has that power of creation!'

'And Vishwamitra,' Kama could not resist pushing in the jibe. 'He has one Menaka already and he would certainly not help you creating another!'

Indra glowered, not amused. 'I'll be forced to go to Lord Brahma, who hates indulging in such mundane affairs, as he calls it! The last time he intervened was when Trishanku's Heaven was created and he was more livid with me, while Vishwamitra swept away with all the honours including that fancy name! I don't dare to go to him again. Kama, so now what am I to do?'

'Nothing. It's out of our hands,' shrugged Kama. 'Let's wait and watch.'

❧

'What do you intend to name her?' murmured Menaka, watching the baby basking in the early morning sun, gurgling comfortably at the cautiously sniffing deer. 'We can't keep calling her by some warbled nicknames which sound more like affectionate snorts.'

Vishwamitra laughed, his eyes riveted on his daughter, her tiny legs kicking in the air. 'She's one strong girl. And unafraid of the animals or the big birds around her,' he observed.

Menaka followed his glance. A flight of shakun birds were circling low around the baby as if to ward her off from the dangers of the outside world.

'Shakuntala,' she said instantly, moved by the strange sight— the brown-plumed birds chirping in tune with her daughter's chortle.

He looked startled, but slowly his surprise gave way to a widening smile. 'Yes, it suits her perfectly—Shakuntala,' he repeated, rolling the name with carefully spaced syllables. 'Also the eternal beauty. Though now she appears more as Nature's child to me, she seems to attract all the animals and birds from the forests!'

'Hmm, eternal beauty, is she? I assume that's courtesy my

beauty with some of your brains?' she teased.

'And your goodness too,' said Vishwamitra, his eyes serious. 'It's more important being beautiful from within.'

Menaka felt the familiar sliver of guilt pricking her, she quickly lowered her lashes.

'A daughter,' he sighed. 'I always wished for one and now I have her!' he said and picked up the baby to cradle her. He did it smoothly, settling her snugly in the crook of his one arm, while using the other for supporting it. It was a cosy contrast—the burly giant of a man holding his tiny baby, cooing softly to the soft, fair, upturned face. 'My sons can rule my kingdom, but my daughter will rule my heart. She is my princess. But she will be a queen, destined to be the mother of the greatest emperor, whose name the country will bear.'

Menaka was strangely moved. She gazed at them, her eyes thoughtful. 'It's amazing how much humans are capable of loving. Of planning your future despite knowing that it's all going to be taken away. You believe in the permanence of love despite the impermanence of time in your hold. That's what I find a miracle in you humans!' she said. 'Though being immortals, nothing is permanent for us.'

'Possibly because we are bound by Time and Death, we realize the value of life, and the briefness of it,' he agreed.

'Or that's why you are meant for Earth, and me for the Heavens!' she remarked, cryptically.

He glanced at her quickly, noticing her sudden brusqueness. 'No, *you* are my immortality, Menaka!'

On cue, their daughter wrinkled her pretty face to howl a lusty, indignant cry.

'Give her to me, she's hungry,' said Menaka, her smile stilted.

He obediently handed his daughter to her. Menaka seemed oddly whimsical. The sunlight coming in through the thick shade of the tree to light up her profile, suffusing her with an inner beauty as she nursed her child. It was a picture of contentment. Words ceased and the long silence was punctuated by the sound of the strong suckling gulps of the hungry baby.

'Do you know this is one single time that you are bereft of all your sexiness?' he observed, smiling but his eyes sombre. 'You are sitting here, half nude in front of me and all I can see is a mother feeding her baby. It is a beautiful vision. Motherhood might define a woman, but it determines the essential quality of a man as a father, to make him decide upon definitely on his new responsibilities,' he said, his voice and eyes strained with emotion. 'I have been a father before but Menaka, you made me realize the true essence.'

Vishwamitra abruptly bent down his head to kiss her smooth brow. Again that act of respect, not of lust.

Hot colour fanned her face, suddenly self-conscious. Vishwamitra assumed it to be a blush. It was a stain of guilt, of her self-loathing. Each sincere word he uttered in all his adoration, wrenched at her bleeding heart.

Watching him walking to the river, she lifted her thick hair off her shoulders with a movement that hinted oddly of despair. *I don't deserve him*. Menaka gave herself a harsh, mental shake. She would not brood while feeding the baby. She looked down at her little girl, suckling with tightly shut eyes, intent and content in action. Menaka remembered the first time she held her, bawling and bloodied, snugly swathed in a muslin cloth. She had felt a rush of emotion, and she felt it each time she held her daughter, feeling the warmth of her small, slight body nestled in her arms, her tiny heart thudding strongly against hers.

She had been deprived of this bliss the first time she had had a child. Was that why Vasu had done what he had to do? So that she could not experience what would be snatched from her, of what she would be deprived of forever? To have a child and abandon it; how more wicked could an apsara be? Why had she been created thus—to solely be the seductress; to love, to make love, to enjoy the intense pleasure of consummation, to conceive a child, to have the power to give it life, spirit and strength but to never experience the coalesced love? What sort of a woman was it who had arisen from the miasmal vapours emanating from that milky elixir which was life-giving yet taking the very spirit of life and loving?

But why, Menaka had kept asking herself that question, *did she fight with Vasu, battle with Indra?* And each time she had been defeated by its answer—she had been denied that right, deprived of motherhood. She had not been allowed to ever set eyes on Pramadvara, her first child; to see her blossom from a baby to a little girl, from a girl to a maiden; not until she was struggling for her last breath, dying in her arms. Menaka could never forget the terror, the palpable grief tearing into her holding the dying girl, rocking her so as to breathe into her some life again. She had begged for her life and Yama had yielded, sharing a slice of her immortality into Pramadvara's limited years on Earth. Her daughter now lived on her borrowed years. And that was when Menaka had experienced the joy of giving, of being a mother.

Motherhood was an unearthly metamorphisis for her. She recalled Urvashi's words, 'Apsaras are not meant to be mothers.' If the world commonly entitled a mother to be one who does not demand, who does not take, but feels it her privilege to give, Menaka knew she and her like had corrupted the definition. A mother could be evil, conniving and cruel. Apsaras had proved to be so. They were just an enticing, abstract desire gratifying the senses of beauty, sexually free, blithe spirits, which was what she was, Menaka reminded herself. They were made from the mind, but of beautiful body to give pleasure through the appetites and passions of lust, not to be tamed by the burden of motherhood. This hedonism was empty in seeking its fulfilment—without qualms which were neither immoral nor amoral, recognizing no law but their own that was the fulfilment of their own being. In their world of beauty, morality did not inherently exist and values were abstractly contrived. But Menaka had found herself in a new world of paradox—a free woman with no choice, torn between mind and beauty, truth and lies, pleasure and duty. Ideals of all sensuousness defined her; that was why she was made to be a dancer, a singer, actress, musician, a courtesan, the consummate lover, but never the mother, never the nurturer because that was not in her spirit.

Would I have to abandon my child again? The dread had been deepening, tearing through her anguished mind. The self-condemnation of being a heartless mother was about to be validated again.

Menaka touched Shakuntala's soft curls, patting her head. She pulled her close, deciding, *no, she could not let go of her.* Her mind admonished her otherwise. Her child would have to pay for her sins. She was a fraud, who could no longer shy away from the lowliness of her crime, from the accountability of her action. By leading a life of lies, her loving was a lie too, so fragile without hope and trust. Would her daughter hate her too? Menaka looked again at the sleeping baby. *Would I be betraying her as well as Kaushik? Just because I am cursed to be an apsara, dangerously seductive without heart and soul?*

Virtue and Entitlement

'Why do you brood so much while feeding the baby?' asked Vishwamitra curiously, as he sat on the bed watching her nurse Shakuntala. That seemed to be the highpoint of his life these days, the most enjoyable part of the given experience.

'That silence speaks of the mother-child intimacy,' she said simply. 'It's like we are talking!'

Shakuntala had gone to sleep, and Menaka put her gently in the cradle Vishwamitra had made from the wood of a forest tree.

'And what does that logical and causal connection say?' he smiled.

Menaka did not return the smile. 'That why her father did not go for the royal ceremony of King Harishchandra,' she said, her tone slightly terse. 'You turned down another invitation to perform a royal yagna.'

It was not an accusation, it was a confrontation, Vishwamitra realized with a sigh. 'Yes, because I had no wish to go there,' he shrugged, nonchalantly. 'Come here, now that you are free.'

She did not obey him, casting him a cold glance. 'But you are one of the very few who can perform such rites,' she argued in hushed tones aware of the sleeping baby. 'You are the Vishwamitra that every powerful king wishes to have in his court for your blessings and wisdom.'

'There are others who could do the needful...'

'There are just a few of them to be counted on the fingers of one hand,' she reminded him. 'Just like there is only one Brahmarishi called Rishi Vasishth.'

Vishwamitra ignored the taunt but was surprised at Menaka's malice. She rarely had a mean tongue, more likely to be brutally honest than spiteful.

'Let's not get into it again,' he said wearily, getting up quickly to his feet.

'Don't run away from the answer, the issue won't run away either!' she said.

He stopped, swinging around to give her a look of exaggerated patience. 'You seem to be in the same surly mood again and I don't wish to quarrel any further!'

She started to her feet, following him outside in the verandah.

'I am asking you, not quarrelling!' she whispered loudly in exasperated frustration.

Vishwamitra turned, his face furious. He reached out, grabbed her wrist and jerked her to him. She fell across his chest, her back arched, her face close to his as he bent over her.

'Answer me!' she hissed, refusing to be intimidated.

'I'm not made of stone,' he swore, the blood hammering in his temples. 'I am tired of your little games! You crook your finger and I come running. Not so! Menaka the apsara you are, you well know how to use sex as a weapon. You pick these arguments and don't allow me touch you for days! Why?' he demanded. 'Because you are peeved? You are disappointed in me?'

He tried to get his mouth down on hers, but she began to struggle and he found her surprisingly strong. For a long, horrible moment he tried to subdue her, fastening his lips hard, thrusting his hips against her, pinning her by the wrists. Then she got one hand free and pushed him away violently.

The shove brought him to his senses. His breath came out raggedly. He glanced at her, her lips bruised, gathering the folds of her sari with as much dignity she could muster. Her push had been hard, but he was still savouring the softness of her hand against his chest. He missed her touch, reminded of the accusation he had just flung of not allowing him to make love to her. She did not do it often these days, seemingly busy either with the baby or household chores. She was angry with him now and he knew he had hurt her. He was ashamed at his sudden brutality. He stood motionlessly staring at her in anguish, his breathing fast.

'I am sorry,' he murmured, gently holding her waist and pulling her close. He gently placed his mouth on hers, but they remained stubbornly shut.

'You are to meet your disciple Devrath soon,' she muttered through clenched teeth, disengaging herself from the imprint of his lips, the burning intensity of his body. But he did not let go of her wrist, persuading, almost pleading. She could feel his nerves jumping under her hand. He was like a man with fever.

'That same Shunasef whose life you once saved from being sacrificed at the altar when you were Vishwamitra,' she prompted pointedly.

He dropped his hand angrily. 'I *am* still Vishwamitra!'

'Are you?' she tilted her head to give him a grim look. 'When was the last time you met your disciples? Where did you last teach them? Where is that ashram now? This,' she said, pointing at the lonely hut in the woods, 'is not an ashram. It is a boudoir!'

Vishwamitra went white and Menaka wondered if she had gone too far. But there was no anger, his eyes looked wounded. She clenched her lips between her teeth, hating herself for hurting him.

'It is not an ashram, the seat of learning, but just a hut, Kaushik,' she said, more gently. 'The home of an ordinary man with a wife and child.'

'And I am not ashamed of that,' he said quietly, but stubbornly.

'It should be the school of wisdom and high thoughts,' she said. 'You don't need to be ashamed of either. Or neglect one for the other.'

'The same way you are ignoring me these days, and no, Menaka, the child cannot be an excuse for your reluctance, my supposed ineptness is,' he said.

Menaka did not make an attempt to refute him. She stood straight in stony silence.

He grasped her arm savagely, his fingers biting into her soft flesh. 'The charm is wearing off, is it?' he glared into her unwavering eyes.

'Yes,' she said brutally. 'You are not the man I once admired, the one who aspired to be a Brahmarishi cannot be claim to be even a simple rishi any more. He does not teach, learn or educate the world as he is supposed to. He is but a husband, a father, a lover,' she added contempt naked in her voice.

She saw the quick flare of fury burning in his eyes but it dimmed to a glower. 'A lover who perhaps doesn't entice you anymore? Am I lacking in your expectations or are you more ambitious than I first imagined to be?' he said caustically. 'Clearly I as a husband and father to our child is not enough for you, not my love, not my respect not my ...'

'You earn that respect, Kaushik! I loved you because you were someone, the famous Vishwamitra. Can you call yourself that now?'

He studied her, hard faced. 'But how does it matter to you who I am, Menaka? What sort of love is yours that it changes so soon? Which wife does not want a husband who dotes on her and their child, tell me!'

'I am telling you what I can see that you are a great man, wasted, and I can't help but loathe it!'

'Because I didn't meet Devrath? Because I deserted my disciples? Or because I did not attend King Harishchandra's yagna?' he raged, his voice trembling. 'But with what face would I go to them—their guru who is the lover of an apsara?' he shot back furiously.

Menaka did not reply, her face pale, biting hard into her lips to cry out. He had inadvertently blurted the truth. That he could not face the world because of her. And that is why he had resorted to hide in his den of love, passion and denials. The great Vishwamitra had surrendered to the charms of an apsara and the world was laughing at him. She clenched and unclenched her fingers, trying to hold on to her pain.

The silence between them seemed to stretch, thickening with

tension, screaming in its stillness.

'Then, all the more reason for you to regain that respect, not from me, but the world you are so ashamed to face,' she said evenly. Tears of pride and pain pricked behind her lids.

Vishwamitra looked haggard, his pallor ashen. 'I am not ashamed of you, Menaka! You are my wife.' He took her hand, kissing her fingers. He could not let go of her. His eyes looked contrite, hating the words he had uttered without thinking.

'You are ashamed of yourself, Kaushik, but your love for me hates to admit it. But, Kaushik, I can never be Vasishth's Arundhati or Kashyap's Aditi, just a Menaka who seduced a great rishi. The world will never see me as your wife!' said Menaka, her voice hollow. 'But we are not talking about me, it's about you. You are that enlightened man who mastered the knowledge none has done before, ready to defy devas and the greatest rishi of all—Vasishth. Go, seek your path, your glory.'

She turned away abruptly, lifting her hair off her shoulders in a nervous gesture he had come to recognize. Vishwamitra shook her by her shoulders, his fingers digging hard in the softness of her flesh. 'Dont' you get it, Menaka? I love you!' he said thickly, emotion deep and grave, his eyes desperately imploring. 'Isn't that love enough for you, for us? I don't want anything else, but you!' he breathed, kissing her wildly. 'I don't aspire for the world because you are my world. I don't care for what they think, for I care only for you! I cannot live without you, my Menaka!' he muttered, burying his head in the softness of her neck. 'Is it too much to ask?? Be kind, Menaka, don't be so hard on me,' he said, his mouth on hers.

And as she heard the fevered desperation in his voice, lost in love, lost from reason, Menaka knew she had to be hard on him. Not kind, but cruel. People are wicked in the madness of hate and revenge, she would have to be wicked in love. Menaka, while using love as an asset, knew of its limitations. It was the fairest of human ideals, a deluding splendour dazzling the mind and the senses which neither appeared dim and dull. The brighter the love, the duller it's death. Apsaras, Menaka reminded herself painfully, lived in perpetual dread of this, preferring to slip away when their love shimmered brightest. She would have to do that—leave him, not to save herself but him.

Hers was a destructive kind of love. Love was an emotional choice one was not free to decide or determine. But she couldn't shake the shackle of her identity as the courtesan, the lover of an important man. Menaka both in her earthly likeness and divine similitude, had desperately sought the other role on her, as a wife. With both Vasu and Kaushik, it had been a furtive assertion, a dignity she could never flaunt. For a while, as Kaushik's wife, she had enjoyed her status but she could not stay further to experience the fall of a mighty man. He was unmindful of it, content in his gained happiness. He was a lost man. And it was only she who had to find his way back for him. Even if it cost losing him forever.

⚡

Vishwamitra was playing with Shakuntala when he saw Devrath walking towards his hut. The boudoir, Menaka had called it harshly, he recalled wincing. It was his home, not his ashram. Not because his disciples and Devrath were reluctant to study here but because he did not want them here. It was that simple. He did not want to share his world with theirs. It was to be just him and Menaka, and now Shakuntala, he smiled looking down at his little daughter splashing in the river water.

'Good wishes for the day, my lord,' said Devrath, bowing low with folded hands.

'And what is it that brings you here today?' asked Vishwamitra kindly. He carefully pulled Shakuntala from the lapping waters and perched her on his broad shoulders, immediately extracting an indignant squeal from her. She was six months old, curious and had an opinion for herself. She wanted to be put down and her father obliged, smiling indulgently. Shakuntala's expressive chortle mixed with his stentorian laugh and the little girl, unfazed with its booming loudness, cheerfully started to play with the darting rabbits. Devrath could not help noticing the cloak of formidability his guru had shrugged off. Vishwamitra looked intent, talking with him but keeping a keen eye on her; like he did with his students, strict but kind.

'King Harishchandra wants your presence for the rajsuya he is performing...' he began.

Vishwamitra swiftly cut him short. 'His family priest is Rishi Vasishth. Why does he want me there too?' he frowned. Harishchandra reminded him of his unfinished challenge with Vasishth. He felt an age old familiar, forgotten resentment rising within him. He wanted to run away from it, from the same old churning emotions that name whipped in him.

'He has invited all the leading rishis of the country. How could he not call you?' said Devrath. 'And you are his father, Trishanku's oldest friend.'

'I am not interested, Devrath,' said Vishwamitra shortly.

'But what do I tell them??' Devrath asked in genuine bewilderment.

'That I am busy elsewhere,' Vishwamitra shot back tersely.

Devrath flushed, looking clearly uncomfortably.

'You don't need to lie for me,' said Vishwamitra curtly. 'Tell them I am busy with my family. That is hopefully honest enough for you?'

Devrath flushed again. 'Everyone knows that, sir,' he muttered.

Vishwamitra felt a flame of anger licking him. 'Is that not decent enough? Devrath, I don't wish to go there, and if you are so embarrassed to explain my true reason, you can think of a viable one. Is that all?' he snapped dismissively, glaring at him with grey contempt.

Devrath was reminded of the old arrogance that made his guru the man he was. It was back again, faint but assertive. 'It is your son Andhark, sir...' he started hesitantly.

The expression on Vishwamitra's face immediately changed, from feigned indifference to genuine worry.

'What has he done now?' he asked sharply.

Devrath took some time to gather his thoughts and courage to explain the crisis. It had always been a difficult relationship

between him and his guru's oldest son from the very first day
they had been introduced. Andhark had not welcomed Devrath as
Vishwamitra's disciple or as his newly adopted son. Madhuchand,
the second son, had taken it more graciously.

'Andhark is the king of your kingdom. He is harassing us, our
ashram, our people,' said Devrath briefly, knowing his teacher
would gauge the full implication.

'He dares!' flared Vishwamitra.

'He dares because you are not there to stop him,' replied
Devrath quietly.

It was Vishwamitra's turn to feel the hot flush of
embarrassment. His hand closed to a large fist, clenched at
his side. He did not want to know any of this—not about
Harishchandra, Vasishth, or Andhark and his arrogant ambition.
He sighed. He would have to find a solution right away.

'Leave his kingdom, his forest and seek a place for the ashram
elsewhere,' he ordered.

Devrath looked unconvinced. 'But where are we to flee?' he
questioned. 'And why are we fleeing? Andhark shall follow us
everywhere wherever we go.'

'No, he's a bully. He won't dare to attack another kingdom.
Go to Magadh. The king will give you patronage once he knows
you are my disciple, I assure you,' he averred.

'Meanwhile, tell Madhuchand to attack Andhark, and rebel
against his own brother. Andhark does not deserve the throne
handed down to him,' he pronounced, his tone clipped, but
Devrath could hear the hint of disappointment in his guru's voice.

'The time has come for war. But it will be civil war, one
brother against the other. Make it as peaceful as possible. No
violence,' he reiterated

Devrath could see the traces of old King Kaushik resurfacing,
his face hard. Vishwamitra said 'Don't involve the army, the
soldiers. They shouldn't be fighting or dying for their king's
arrogant foolishness. Andhark is a coward like most bullies.
Madhuchand does not retaliate for respect for me. Now I say
so, let him usurp the throne. Better still, take a letter from me,

it would be a neat, bloodless coup.'

Devrath looked visibly relieved. 'I shall return with your letter and hand it to Madhuchand himself,' he agreed.

'Andhark had once accused me of being unjust when I made you my chief disciple,' smiled Vishwamitra sadly. 'He forgot he was himself patronized because he was my oldest child. But it was my second son from my wife Sheela, who proved to be a better person. It just proves that right by birth and hierarchy *is* wrong. Privilege cannot be heritable. Entitlement should be by virtue and talent; it gets to be morally unjust if founded on birth and wealth or class. And who should have known better than me?' he sighed tiredly. 'I fought to become a Vishwamitra, fighting prejudice and discrimination because I was a kshatriya aspiring to be a rishi. Today I am. But I encouraged nepotism in my own kingdom. The son of a king, becomes a king. No he does not. Unless he proves himself to be a good one. He might be privileged to be born a prince, but not a king. It is not his right. Let Andhark know that!'

'Don't blame yourself, sir, one cannot hold the action of one's offspring as his own.'

'Thanks for the kind words, Devrath, but I am to blame for this mess. I left a kingdom, my people, my subjects to a young boy...'

'Because you trusted him!'

'He seems to be living up to his name. Andhark. I had named him as he would dispel darkness. He seems to be darkness himself, bringing blight, not light.' Vishwamitra shook his head grimly. 'I traded my kingdom for my ambition. That was my fault,' he said unforgivingly, his eyes staring into the distance, glittering with suppressed emotion.

Devrath recognized the same dispassionate tone of before. His teacher was a kind, just man but not kind enough to forgive. He would not spare even his family. He was a hard man to please, harder to appease. And he could be vicious to those who failed him, especially those whom he loved unquestioningly but got betrayed instead. Devrath shuddered inwardly, feeling sorry for Andhark. *Help that man who was ever at his mercy.* He could never hope for any.

Crime and Confession

$\mathcal{S}$he would tell him her truth today; she had been procrastinating for too long. Indra's visit had validated her last doubt—Kaushik would never leave his sanctuary of her love to return to his former fame and glory. His home was with her and their daughter, and he would never forsake it for a better, bigger world.

And she would have to do it for him, Menaka bit hard on her lip, suddenly fearful of the option she had decided upon. She would have to turn his love into hate, which wouldn't take much time or effort. All she had to was reveal the truth about herself.

Menaka curled her hands into tight fists and thrust them in her eyes to stem the burst of emotion. *Give me the strength to hurt him, please, give me the strength to bear to see him hurt*, she prayed. And give me the courage to take on his hate. Yet within the heaviness of her heart flickered a small flame of hope. *Would he forgive me for my deception and accept me again?* It was a mad hope which danced treacherously in her mind to fleetingly lighten her heavy heart. But she killed it immediately, as she would kill their happiness. She had to leave him to set him free. She was the shackle fettering him from his path of high honour, but no longer.

She looked down at her sleeping daughter. She could not tear her eyes away. This might be the last time she would see her. She instinctively pulled her close to her thudding heart, to shield her from the storm she was about to unleash. The knot of dread was throttling her.

She heard him enter the hut and she quietly placed her daughter in the cradle, her heart lurching painfully. The moment had arrived. She sensed him behind her, circling her waist with his arms. She felt menaced by his nearness. He lowered his head to kiss her bare shoulder, nuzzling closer to trail his lips over her the smooth skin of her shoulders and move up to her long neck. A wave of warm pleasure coursed through her, her flesh crawling with desire. She sank in it, closing her eyes. Her unspoken words floated insidiously. She turned around, his breath winnowing her nape. She stiffened, straightening her back with renewed purpose and looked up straight into his eyes.

'I need to tell you what I could not all these years,' she said slowly, though she wanted to rush through her confession. He stared at her, baffled, his smile freezing. Would it be the last time she would see him smile?

'I lied to you. I am an apsara but I wasn't banished from Heaven by Indra,' she took a deep breath and continued, not taking her eyes from his transfixed face. 'Instead, he sent me here to seduce you. You were my mission You were a threat to him and to distract you from your meditation, I was to make love to you, make you love me, lust for me. The scheme succeeded. You neglected your years of penance. You fell in love with me,' she swallowed spasmodically, '...absolutely as was planned.'

She had said it. She had blurted it out. She waited for him to respond, with bated breath. Instinctively, she bit her lip, clutched her hands in a tight clasp as if to prepare for the blow. He stood frozen, letting her words wash over him, immobile in thought and action. His face slowly blanched of colour, his skin ashen and his lips bloodless.

Time stood still, so did he as he allowed each word of hers to percolate into his mind, his stunned consciousness. He did not move away, her words rooting him to the ground. There was eeriness in his stillness, as he stood tall, looming and motionless, life slowly draining from him, the spirit leaving his body. His huge frame seemed to fill the smallness of the room, stiff and straight, like a huge, tall tree about to be felled.

His silence screamed back at her. She had expected him to explode, welling out lava of fury, venting out his betrayed anguish. His stillness was like the calmness without wind, the agony of frozen fury, like the hush of death.

'Please,' she whimpered. 'Please, say something. I am prepared for anything—your hate, your contempt, even your curse! I deserve it!'

She clutched at his hand in despair. He flinched, her touch thawing him back to life.

'How could I curse you?' he whispered, his voice hoarse. 'You have taken away that power too, for I love you too much...'

He stared at her as if he was looking at her for the first time. 'Love...love?' he muttered. 'Was it ever real, Menaka? In all this pretence, these lies, the deceit, was anything real between us?' he faltered, his face dazed. 'Was it?' he asked more forcefully. 'Or was it just a bewitchment?'

He spoke in short sentences, not trusting himself to speak longer. 'All that I felt for you, was it also a sham, an emotion beguiled by your bewitching? Was it Kama's arrow that did the deed and not my heart? Did my heart betray me too?'

Menaka shook her head violently. 'No, I know your love is genuine. Don't degrade it, Kaushik, for it is the depth of your love that made me realize how shallow I am! I was the imposter, who tried to feign it,' she beseeched. 'But I cannot bear to live this lie any longer. It is killing me, it is killing me to see you so blinded that you don't realize you are falling! I can't watch your fall from glory anymore! I can't take on the burden of my deception, your depravation. ..'

He gave a short laugh. 'Don't say it anymore, Menaka. It sounds stale, wilted. Your words are as pretty as you, as intoxicating, as captivating ...don't speak, for it's only lies that emit from your lovely, lying lips!' he said viciously. 'I don't know what to believe, what is true and what is not. You are a fake, a mirage, a deadly false illusion. Go away before I do you any harm!'

He had said it; she had made him say it at last.

'I shall,' she said quietly. 'But not before letting you know the truth. I owed it to you.'

'You owed it to me?' he barked. 'Do you know you have destroyed me? Destroyed us? Destroyed whatever we had, whatever we did, whatever we felt, whatever we made—this child?' he lashed out.

It was her turn to keep silent; she had no words of protest, no argument for exoneration. Her silence was provocative, whipping him into a cold rage.

'Easy for you to confess and walk away, is it not, my beautiful Menaka?' he taunted. 'You are that beautiful tempest that shows no mercy! Why did you confess anyway or does it feel good to feel to be a martyr?' he asked savagely. 'I could have lived in ignorant bliss if you had allowed me to. But now I shall despair in shame that I ever loved you so foolishly!' he struggled with his emotions. Love was curdling into hate, affection into agony, trust into distrust. He paused, looking at her searchingly. 'But why are you telling me all this now?'

She flinched, looking at him resolutely. 'I could live with you, but not with myself with this deception!'

'Selfish!!' he snapped. 'You considered your conscience and your happiness, but not all what you have wreaked on us! Because you are not just a damned heartless whore from Heaven who makes love for gains...' he mouthed deliberately, watching the blood seep from her lovely face, '...but you are a conniving coward too! You say you had the courage to tell me the truth. Which truth, Menaka? That truth is a lie too. This is another game of yours to abandon me with our child while you slip off to Heaven leaving me with the baby so that I never get back to my work. As apsaras always do!!' he spat.

Menaka paled, as his venom scathed her soul. He was beginning to hate her. She was his offence and his offender. Repulsed, he had nothing to turn to but his unfinished dream. His work would be his shield, his saviour. She could see that he was contemplating turning to it, to retrieve his usurped glory, to seek his lost goal. Menaka felt a strange vindication—her plan was working.

'You could not have planned it better, Menaka!' he smiled painfully. 'You desert me, you desert our child. Oh! I do forget, you have done it before, so you have mastered this art as well. You are a mother, Menaka, how can you?'

His words were meant to stab and she braved each knife thrust, ignoring the pain.

'As a father, you can?' she asked evenly.

His brows knitted angrily. 'Righteous still, are you? Or are you forcing me to disown our child?' he raised a sardonic brow. 'Like you, I have done it before! I seem to be good at deserting people. I left my family for a dream which I dumped for you, and now you leave me! You taught me a lesson from my own book and a lot more...' he sighed, clearing his throat. 'Shakuntala was ours, yours and mine, a result of our love, but that was a deceitful pretence and so is the child. You made her a tool of your treachery. I can never keep her! She is a reminder of my failure, my gullibility and my stupidity of loving you, believing you, trusting you. You make me hate you, you make me hate our baby! What are you turning me into, Menaka—monster??'

Menaka trembled, the fire of his wrath and hate was singeing her.

'Don't hate her for what I did, please!' she implored. 'I shall take her away. But give her your blessings, don't disown her. She is your daughter, Kaushik!'

Her frantic entreaty seemed to touch a raw nerve. He suddenly looked haggard, deflated of his anger, defeated and tired. He looked down at the sleeping, curled form of his daughter, her thick lashes curled serenely on her pink, chubby cheeks. Not for the first time he saw how closely she resembled her mother.

'You know that you can't keep her. Mortals are not allowed in Heaven. Nor can I keep her...or ever hate her,' he muttered inconsolably. 'She is mine, ours, a symbol of our love, our marriage, our loss and our hate. I shall never be able to forget you each time I look at her. She will remind me of you and all what you meant to me, all what you did. I can't have her! Though she is as much a victim as I am,' he paused and looked at her with narrowed eyes, dawning to a new, brutal realization, 'as much as you are, Menaka.'

Menaka bit into her lower lip hard, to stop emitting a soft gasp of horror.

'We are all victims, aren't we, Menaka?' he said hoarsely. 'Indra made a plan, you were part of it and you pretended to be in love. But your pretence became a reality, your lie the truth. Is that what you want to make me believe? And is this confession of yours to be the last pretence before you leave me forever?'

Menaka could not answer; her throat choked with emotion and panic. He had always been astutely insightful; now he was uncannily, dangerously close to her truth. He was analyzing her motives, subjecting her to intense scrutiny. He could not bring himself to hate her, and he was searching for a plausible justification to not let go of her. But she had to leave him for his sake.

She would have to wound him with crueller words. She turned around and said, 'I was fed up with you, I was fed up of staying here!' she lashed out. 'What have you given me, Kaushik? If not wealth, I was expecting some prestige, but you are ashamed to acknowledge me as your wife. You prefer hiding in this miserable hut you call a home, saddling me with a daughter I am bored of nursing! I am tired, Kaushik, tired of this drudgery with you. I want to go back to Heaven, in my life of luxury...'

'Stop it! Stop your lies, Menaka!' he shouted, his face a sickly pale. 'Whom are you fooling? I cannot believe what we felt for each other was false. I have seen you, Menaka, you have worked here like a menial slave!' he said. 'The most scheming apsara could not demean herself that much, she would be too self-loving to do that!' he added acidly. 'I have seen your wild passion and I have also seen your tender love, your selfless devotion that could not have been an act. It would be far easier for me to believe that you are an exemplary actress. My anger, my hate would help me deal with your betrayal far better. Your words were meant to wound me, anger me, and they did. I lashed at you with words you wanted me to say. What is it you want—me to hate you, Menaka?' he looked at her sadly.

To give me up, she wept silently. Menaka could hear the desperation in his voice, spurring her to convince him of her infidelity. 'I am telling you the truth now. You are no longer the man I loved!' she cried, watching him flinch. 'You were the famous Vishwamitra, but who are you now? Just a silly, faded rishi cavorting with an apsara. You talk about Vasishth and Arundati, but can you ever give me the respect that they command? I have been lying to you since the beginning, I am like any other apsara, Kaushik, the ones you so despise. I was sent as a seductress to strip you of all your powers. And I stand here before you guilty. I do confess.'

Vishwamitra looked at the woman he had loved for so many years. 'You are again telling me your half-truth!' he charged, his eyes contemptuous, yet begging her to say otherwise. 'What is your motive? To lie for a greater good?' he asked shrewdly, seeing her lips tremble. 'Don't make a fool of me again, Menaka, for you can betray me but I cannot be betrayed of my feelings for you. They were real! And so were yours! Why are you blurring them? How do I know what you are saying is not a lie either?' he paused. There was a new quality in his voice—mockery, aimed at her, at the feminine world, at the liars. 'Women are supposed to be these loving, fragile creatures at the best of times, but you made me just realize that they are hard, moved by desires unknown by the men that place trust in them,' he said bleakly. 'All I know is that you don't lie to the one who trusts you and never trust a person who lies to you. And you are a very good liar, Menaka, but please, what is your whole truth? You owe me that.'

'That I pretended to love you,' she said tonelessly, refusing to divulge further. *Make him hate me, please*, she prayed. *Make him spurn me.*

'And if you would not have admitted to it now, I would never have known,' he said evenly. 'You could have carried out this lovely subterfuge forever. Why didn't you? We would have lived happily together bringing up our daughter. So, then why are you confessing now? Why?'

His soft tone was disquieting. She would have preferred him to rage, to rant, hurting her as much as she had hurt him. This cross-examination was unnerving. He was getting closer to her truth.

'Because I want to go! Because I never loved you and I can't suffer that guilt any longer,' she cried, desperately, vainly hoping he would believe the last of her lies.

He nodded slowly, the weight of her words, crushing the last vestige of his hope.

'Do you know I love you?' he asked unexpectedly.

'Yes,' she nodded painfully.

'Then why did you do this? Why are you so determined to end it? What is that truth you are lying to me about?'

Menaka shook her head. 'I have told you all. You just don't want to accept it. But you will have to!'

'No, you have again admitted to a half-truth! Your partially true statement is meant to fool me, intended to mislead!!' he exclaimed vehemently. 'You have told me never to believe you. You have said enough to lose my trust in you. And when I don't trust you, how can I love you? Is that what you want?'

Menaka felt a helpless fear grip her. She was losing ground; she could never match his wits. She tried her last, desperate attempt. 'I did what Indra told me to do,' she said tonelessly. 'I am just an instrument of his plan. I was simply following his instructions.'

Vishwamitra's face tightened, his eyes flaring. 'Oh, he shall suffer for it!' he said softly, his tone quietly menacing. 'I have enough powers left still to put a curse on him...'

'Don't!' she exclaimed. 'Don't curse him!!' she said quickly.

'Why?' his eyes narrowed. 'Is he your lover too?'

She recoiled as if he had slapped her. 'No, but by cursing him, it'll do you more harm than him,' she cried. 'It'll sap you of the powers you have left, and you need to conserve all what you have got!'

His brow cleared. 'Aha, so the lady cares more than she shows!'

Menaka clenched her lower lip between her teeth. He saw the gesture and turned away. 'But I curse you, Menaka, I shall curse you!!' he said and turned back to look at her, his eyes pools of despair. 'You stand before me, not Kaushik your lover or your husband, but Vishwamitra. You had the temerity to betray his love and his trust. And yet you don't cower in fear or dread. You have nothing with you but your beauty, your courage and your wits. All of which you have constantly used against me to ruin me. And so I curse you...' he breathed, his eyes burning into her pale, beautiful face.

Menaka closed her eyes to take in his wrath, waited for him to pronounce his deathly words. The air grew still, there was an uneasy calm. Her eyes flew open. Her breath stuck in her throat. He was standing close to her. But he did not touch her. She could feel the heat of his body, the smouldering intensity of his eyes, the fevered breath coming though those beautiful, generous lips about to spout his final malediction.

'...I curse you that we never meet again after this!' he said softly, his tortured face close, each word scorching her ears, her mind, her heart. 'That is the only curse I can think for you, my Menaka!' he rasped, his breathed plea barely audible. 'I can never wish harm upon you, never! Nor shall I invoke any evil to drain me of my powers, as you so wonderfully reminded me. But I shall make you endure the same grief you have made me suffer, which I shall grieve all my life,' he paused, his tawny eyes pouring into her soul. 'We are to never meet again. This is the punishment for falling in love or call it the retribution of my folly.'

Menaka started, her face sallow, sagging with the blow of his words and partial relief; the damning comfort of a load been taken off. He had admitted to what she had provoked him to say. He had stopped holding on to her, he had released her. He was a free man again.

She stepped back, turning to walk towards the cradle.

'Don't! Where will you take her?' he asked sharply. 'You won't be allowed to take a mortal to Heaven. Neither can you live in this Hell called Earth. Don't even think of not returning to Heaven and looking after her all by yourself. You will end up being a harlot to some debauched nobleman or be part of a harem of a decadent king!' he said cruelly. 'Our mortal world is an ugly place, and you won't survive here, my beautiful Menaka. And neither would I wish my daughter to be an entertainer in Heaven!'

Menaka nodded. 'Yes, I know,' she whispered bleakly and looked hopefully at him.

'You'll keep her with you?'

'I can't, just as you can't take her to Heaven. I won't have the time for her now,' he said dully. 'She needs proper care and education. My friend Rishi Kanva, as you know is childless and is very fond of her. I shall request him to look after her. He will be a better father to her than me, I am certain!'

Menaka felt bereft; she could no longer have any claim on her daughter, no say in her future. But this was how it was to be. Vishwamitra was deciding, but it was her decision. Like him, she would have to let go of her child for her sake. There had been a reason for wanting this done. There had been a purpose for achieving this, for obtaining what she had lost—their interest, welfare, benefit.

She dropped her hand listlessly, never to hold her baby again. Menaka felt a hot rush of agony and she turned away abruptly, almost running to the door to escape from the welling anguish deluging her.

'Menaka,' his voice stopped her again. She paused but didn't turn her head. She did not trust herself anymore. 'Tell Indra, he lost. I shall win this war too!!' She could hear the savage fury, the determination back in his distinctive baritone.

'And go back to Heaven, don't wander around here on Earth to escape it. Heaven is your destination. It always was,' she heard him pause, his voice strained. 'Vishwavasu will return to you. He will be redeemed by Lord Rama, an incarnation of Lord Vishnu to be born very soon. Go, Menaka, and wait for him...' he said gently, drained of all his venomous anger. He said as though it were his concern to comfort her, as though her eyes were the ones bruised with tears.

Menaka spun around, seeing him for the last time through the thick glaze of abashed tears. She wanted to fling herself in his arms, to stop this charade and love him madly as she always would. But she stood still, pressing her fingers together so hard that she could feel the skin break and caught the last glimpse of him. His eyes infinitely sad, he gave her his last smile—bleak, but that same craggy, beautiful smile that made her melt and stop her heart. Today, it broke her heart. She felt a sob building against her throat.

'Forgive me!' she whispered. 'Please, forgive me if you ever can!' And then she was gone.

Hating Love

$\mathcal{S}$ometimes he would wake with a sense of pain, sometimes with pleasure. But often, he felt only hate. Vishwamitra lay on the bed thinking, dreaming, recalling. There was the memory that kept him from sleeping—of her lifting her thick, chestnut hair off her creamy shoulders, pinning them quickly in a neat coil; the soft swell and shape of her breasts, the feel of them, snug in his hands; the fevered feel of her silky thighs brushing against his, and the agony that she was gone; that burning need he still felt for her. It was that memory that kept his mind feverish and stopped him from sleeping. She was not for him. She couldn't possibly be for him anymore. He was crazy to remember her, but he could not wrench her out of his mind. He couldn't sleep, like so many, interminable nights since she had left him.

Vishwamitra was not aware of how many days had passed. He had handed Shakuntala to a visibly surprised, but pleased, Rishi Kanva. He had retired hurriedly from the ashram, not once looking at his beautiful daughter's smiling face. He had failed as her father; he would never be able to face her, look at her straight in the eyes. He had felt a physical pain, tearing through his chest, hot and bloodless.

He had come back to his hut, his home for the past many years with Menaka. The thought made him wince. Her absence was like a dull pulsating ache, hurting right through his soul. He felt her near him, saw her humming as she sat at the fireside; as she fetched the water, some of it spilled on the front of her, drenching her fetchingly. He lay on the empty bed, inhaling her fragrance, remembering the feel of her soft body crushed against him, her slim arms around him, her fingers in his hair, clenched hard, staring triumphantly into his ragged face, flushed with a hot flood of bursting desire for her, fully knowing the power she had over him...

He sat up in his bed, his body broke in cold sweat. She still had that hold over him. He was trying to distance his pain by going about his usual routine; he did his daily prayers, his long hours of meditation, but the mind could not be calmed.

Love, Vishwamitra despaired, *took long to work itself out, as did hate*. He would have liked to have left that past alone, but he felt all his hatred returning. *Hate seems to flow in the same blood as love: it even evoked the same passion, the same actions*, he thought, sardonically. He struggled with the wild hope that the mental sight of her would awaken love, a softer sentiment, a tender memory which he might work on to survive. But it did not. It was just hate, lust and rage. He had those mad, furious moments when he wished that if he could have her just once more, swiftly and roughly, and then he would be at peace again. He could purge her out of his desires, his imagination. *And then I would leave her*, he thought bitterly.

Hate was akin to that mad, tossing, physical love, hot and pounding. It has its frenzied peak and then its dull spell of serenity. Now had been his orgiastic moment of hatred. He lay there on the empty bed, sweating, spent and frustrated. It was she who was inside him, not he inside her, driven to a crescendo of passion. He was generous enough to feel sorry for her, trapped in that prison called Amravati. She had falsely committed nothing but love and now she had none to give. Or did she? Jealousy, hot and livid, seared through him. Was she with some gandharva, some deva or even that handsome fool Indra?

Jealousy was the worst feeling of all; it made lovers insecure and vicious, twisting love, corroding it, poisoning trust. In his violently beleaguered mind, Vishwamitra considered every man as her potential lover. Vishwavasu wasn't back so whom was she with now—Uranyu, her pining admirer or that lusty Kama? Suddenly he wanted to strech out his hand and touch her, slipping his fingers in her thick, fragrant mane, feeling her smooth, bare body lying beside his, he wanted to turn his head on the pillow and speak to her, he wanted to savour the almost imperceptible smell and taste of her skin. He closed his eyes, seeing her in his mind again—their act of love was over, he had spent everything he had, and was lying back with his head on her soft, flat stomach and her taste persistent yet elusive in his mouth.

He recalled their conversations, every little lie of hers he magnified into a betrayal, his poisoned mind doubting even her most open statement, deciphering new, hidden implications. He could not bear the thought of her even talking or touching another man, even now when he had lost her. *Did she smile invitingly, did she gesticulate charmingly when she spoke in that measured, soft voice of hers or did she bite into her luscious, lower lip as was her habit which never had failed to arouse him?*

That was the worst period of all—his jealous imagination. He had never thought himself a jealous man or an imaginative one. But he evoked lifelike images in his tormented mind, which were vivid and graphic—Menaka making wild love; Menaka with some deva; Menaka with some naked, handsome gandharva, doing the same things that they had done together; Menaka kissing in her characteristically delicious way, arching voluptuously in the act, her white throat bare and inviting, whimpering a moan of pleasure, uttering that gurgle; Menaka in untamed abandonment, her eyes gleaming as she led her man to the frenzied gush of ecstasy. He saw them through the day and through the bleak silence of the night. Only the daily chores were a forced distraction and for a few minutes between the stillness and the crescendo, his mangled mind would be clear of her. Weeks lapsed into months and the images were yet as distinct and frequent and endless. His impotence angered him, hating her, loving her more.

Jealousy, he had always believed, coexisted solely with

desire. Yet he had never been jealous when she had been by his side all those years. He had implicit, unwavering faith in her, loving her with an earnest abandon, which he thought had been reciprocated. But her absence filled him with jealous wrath. Even his desire now was nearer to hatred than love. He saw in his fevered mind all the broad, bare-bodied men in her past and all the possible men in the future, throwing long, entwined shadows on his mind. Vishwamitra survived on an irrational hope that he could kill any physical desire for her. And yet, more than often, he yearned simply for her companionship—the way she caressed his cheek, her finger trailing lightly over the cleft of his chin; the sparkle of her eyes as she watched him have his meal; watching her swim tantalizingly in the river; see her pluck the flowers to dress her long, fragrant hair; tenderly feeding a stray deer; their long, lazy walks together with their arms entwined, their bodies cleaved in a soft, swaying motion like the whistling breeze around; her comforting, constant humming in this very room, soft and sweet...

He lay there unable to sleep, one fragment of memory after another stinging him with hatred and desire. Hate should have killed lust, but it seemed to fuel it. He would have given anything to sleep, even for a moment however fitfully.

But his churning mind could not let her alone. He hated her because he wished to think she did not love him, had never loved him. By thinking the worst of her, he hoped he could get her out of his tortured mind as she had from his life. *What grievance*, he wondered now, *have I got against her, whether she loved me or not?* It did not matter. She was gone. She had been loyal to him all through those years, and she had given him so much pleasure and passion that he had been exhausted in it. She had put up with his whims, his vile moods, and what had he given her in return? He had come into this relationship, their marriage, knowing in his heart that loving an apsara was a dream, that one day it would slip away, waking him alone and lonely. And she had ended it in a nightmare. That anger, the grief, the swamp of insecurity, the illogical hope in a hopeless future made him feel helpless in his misery, all these emotions crashing on him like a tidal, melancholic wave.

Is this the end, he wondered, *this crazy imaginings, this wishful re-enactments of their past together?* There was no need ever to go back to it. It was futile and perverse. He had another insane thought—more than anything in the world he wanted to hurt Menaka, also the intrusive memory of her. He wanted to take a woman back with him and lie naked with her on that same cot, the same places where he had made love to Menaka. It was the only way to hurt her and to hurt himself. Then perhaps, he would not love enough; he would just be secure and content, his self-pity and hatred would cease to walk hand in hand across the darkening sunset every day.

But he knew it was absurd. He thought how strange it was that he felt no desire for another woman at all. It was as if quite suddenly after all the wanton, passionate years with Menaka, he had woken up sterile and impotent. His insatiable passion for Menaka had killed simple lust for ever. Never again would he be able to enjoy another woman.

Theirs was not a love story or a story of passion, it was a tale of hate. But Vishwamitra was not convinced of that either. Perhaps his hatred was as deficient as his love. He looked at the mirror he had given her, peered into his reflection and caught sight of his own face in that gilded mirror, the features blurred with his breath. What had he done to himself, what had she done to him? Was he seeing a reflection of hate? He saw a haggard face, the thick lines of pain drawing his face into a hard mask. But there was in those tired eyes as he stared with intense longing was a bright, weary hope that he would get one day that unobtainable person he was pining for.

He had the security of possessing nothing, not her and his daughter. When she had left him, he could not bring himself to do anything. He could only brood and reconstruct what they had said to each other, his slow grief burning in the embers of anger and remorse. He had wanted the love to last. But if love had to die, he wanted it to kill it quickly; he wished to wring its neck and squeeze out the life with his bare hands.

He finally woke, bleary with the sadness of her tortured face, her anguished voice begging for his forgiveness. Her stricken eyes still rested on his mind. Within minutes of waking her voice, her smell, her presence fanned the pain again. She created at once the absolute love he had lost with every separation of the dream from reality.

'I've never loved anybody more than you.' Her whispered words seem to mock him now. It was as if, she was resting on his chest, her soft, milky breasts crushed against him, her hands around his waist, her fingers absently scorching his skin, her feet caressing his ankles, abandoning herself as completely as she had done, some months ago on the hard mud floor.

She had not been lying either when she murmured huskily through swollen, parted lips, 'Nobody else. Ever again.' Those were, he knew ironic contradictions of the heart that existed on pure, emotional idealism. He loved her but even in his blur of hate and anger and pain, he knew that she had so much more capacity for love than he had.

If I hated her so much, how could I still love her? Can one really hate and love? Or is it myself that I really loath? That I had allowed myself to be set up to be seduced by a woman I fell so hopefully in love with but who had meant only to destroy me, lead me to this ruination. He hated his body that had been so aroused and had so enjoyed her. And he despised his untrusting mind. But there is an end of hate as there is an end of love.

Menaka had long since gone now, dead for him. He could not go on loving the dead with the intensity one loves the living. Not for him. 'I mustn't believe that she's alive,' he reminded himself now as he sat for his prayers and closed his eyes and he tried to focus, to be reasonable. He looked up at the sky as if she was looking down at him. *See, how I can get on without you. It is not so hard*, he told her. Only his hatred could make him believe in her survival and his. Hating Menaka was like loving her. And suddenly, she did not seem worth hating or loving.

He was a man in love once, but today he was a man of

hate. Hate also for the man who had made it happen—Indra—the culprit to whom Vishwamitra had always been afraid of losing Menaka. Unconsciously, he had been her guardian, her protector, like a soldier, protecting himself and her from any assailing intrusion. He had been prepared to take on Indra if he had to. But the coward never challenged him in an open battle, luring her away as insidiously as he had infiltrated her in his heart. *I wanted Menaka for a lifetime and you took her away, Indra*, he swore with vengeance resurfacing him within him. *With your great schemes you ruined our happiness like a storm trampling the forest, uprooting it relentlessly. I hate you, Indra, I shall make you pay for it in such a way you shall be forever wretched in your existence. Hatred is in my mind now, in my soul. Not just in my heart. It is not an ache. It is revenge.*

His old vengeance had returned. But this hate and suspicion, this passion to destroy went deeper. The unconscious worked wildly, pushing him to insanity, until one morning he woke up and knew, as though he had planned it overnight that from that day on he was going to forget her. For the first time since long he thought of Hemavati; she must have endured the same ripping, bleeding agony he was writhing in now. He had broken her heart; Menaka had shattered his. This was his punishment, his turn for penitence.

He lived through the shallow glibness of the days. He was like a blind-folded man, wrapped with darkness and despair around him, without any light or a ray of hope. But there was. And it was in him. Was it the tenth day or the hundredth, he was not sure. But he had now decided on his course of action.

Heaven and Home

$\mathcal{T}$here was nothing wrong with the present. The truth had come out. Lies were no longer part of her life; they had deserted her and Menaka felt strangely happy without them, yet so bereft. She was in Heaven again, turned away from the world, living in an endless dream. She could barely remember how she had managed to travel back to Heaven, to drag herself here to her palace. It had been waiting for her, not given away to someone else in her absence. It was as if Indra had been sure she would return here, someday.

He had been shocked to see her, and more shocked at the state she was in. She was on the verge of collapse, crumpling more in despair than physical exhaustion. She remained silent and mute for days, but the hopelessness in her eyes spoke volumes. For once, it moved even Indra's hard, selfish heart. He was overjoyed she had come back but, she had changed. What had happened? Why had she returned, when the last time they had met, she had made it amply clear that if she came back, he would have to face the fire of Vishwamitra's fury. He had braced himself, quietly preparing his army of devas and his allies. But six months down, there was no sign of the incensed rishi at Heaven's door. He had sent Kama, Varun and Surya to search for him, but they had returned explaining the rishi had long left his own ashram to retire to the Himalayas for further penance. *That blasted rishi was back to what he was at best—meditation*, Indra scowled. *But what had happened between him and Menaka? And where was the baby? How had Menaka given her up so easily?*

The thought of Menaka, for once, did not fill him with a warm suffusion of desire, but a niggling anxiety that was slowly deepening into a constant worry. She remained listless, barely speaking, and when she did, it was in dull monosyllables. Two people were her constant companions—her friend Tilottama and Uranyu, who was still hopelessly in love with her. But she had soon driven Uranyu away, much to Indra's jealous relief.

She rarely met anyone, cloistered in her palace, sequestered from the probing world. And she refused to reveal the past which had forced her to come back to Heaven, a place she no longer considered her home. Yet, she had come back.

Menaka was staring out of the window, into the emptiness of beauty of the garden exploding with flowers. *So lovely*, she thought dully, *and bursting with life*. Life was sunlight on the struggling sapling of the rose bush she had planted at the ashram, the leap of the heart when she saw Kaushik and the tug of the hand of her baby. Life was his mouth pressed down on her, pulsating with unrestrained energy. *What sense does the beauty of flowers have for me, when I am dying here?* she thought as she drew the thick curtains to block the lovely sight.

The agony of being without him had long started and she wished she could have the luxury of death. She just wanted him like she used to in the old days. She wanted to be able to eat her meals with him, and sleep with him in their bed in their tiny hut. She wanted Kaushik. She wanted ordinary, corrupt, human love. Not pain, she implored in the thick mist of misery. She could never die, but what she felt now was worse than death. Death ended and started a new life. This was an endless anguish. She was not in peace, she was not at rest.

All her life she had tried to live in the illusion of beauty and admiration. It allowed her to forget that she was a heartless woman, always fake. Yet Vasu and Kaushik had loved her despite that. She might be immortal, but did she have that loveliness of the immortal soul of all people? It was in Vasu, as he was always gentle and good. She had found it in Kaushik, who was arrogant yet kind. *But in this heartless woman how did they find anything to love?*

'Why did you leave him?' Menaka was startled not at the bluntness of the question, but by the identity of the owner of the voice. *Urvashi*, she registered, even without turning her head to acknowledge her. *Why had she come now?* Menaka was thankful her visitor was not Uranyu. She had pushed him away, not allowing him to hope any longer. She could never be his, she told him gently, because she was too tired to play this game of love anymore. He promised to love for both of them, his eyes burning with an intensity she was determined to douse. She had thrust him away, forbidding him to ever enter her palace. She knew that he deserved better. She had brutally driven all love out, and she would see to it there is no lust for her either. *What am I expected to do now? Where do I go from here?*

Urvashi seemed to answer her unspoken question. 'My biggest regret was that I did not fight for Pururav as I should have,' she sighed. It was rare to see Urvashi remorseful. 'But I and all the apsaras thought that you would fight and manage what none of us had yet succeeded in—live happily on Earth.' There was a poignant wistfulness in her voice, and Menaka simply shook her head.

Menaka did not want to think of him anymore. But she had willed this situation to occur—to make him leave her—she had prayed for this. *Give him a chance; let him have his happiness, his dream. Let this happen and I shall never ask for anything else. I love him and I'll do anything for him, even live away from him. I promise I shall give him up for ever, only let him live with a chance, with a hope, a renewed purpose.* She would lose him, but her loss was his victory. *People can love without seeing each other, can't they?* she questioned herself painfully.

Urvashi was gently shaking her arm.

'Talk, Menaka, speak up! I don't know what happened, but you did what you had to...' she gave Menaka a quick, searching look. 'You did not take it so badly even when Vasu was thrown out...' she continued uncertainly. 'Or is it that you suffered the same loss twice?'

Menaka kept silent, her eyes vacant. She clearly did not hear her or believe her. 'You still blame me for his dismissal? That I allowed an innocent man to be punished.'

Menaka chewed on her lip, turning her head away. She felt tired of this dull, niggling pain; she had lost Vasu, she had lost Kaushik, and her two daughters. When she was with Vasu, she had loved him with abandon—free, brazen and unfettered; With Kaushik, it had always been a strategy, a plan, a deception. But he had loved her, totally. Even at their last fateful time together, when she had revealed her truth to him, he had lashed out, yet he had loved her enough to let her go, to go back to Vasu. She was back and his memories were starting to haunt her. She had loved Vasu, fought for him, grieved for him. While she had loved Kaushik, she loved Vasu and now she did not have either. *Was it possible to love two men*, she sighed. *Though, I don't have any love to give to anyone now.*

'I feel guilty about Vasu, I should have cleared his name,' Menaka was interrupted by Urvashi's confession. Urvashi had the grace to look ashamed. 'I can say it now, Menaka. My silence confirmed the accusation made by Rambha...I have not been at peace since. Nor has Rambha. She suffered a worse fate; she lost Tumburu to a curse ironically like Vasu. And she was raped!!' It came out baldly, without her usual flippancy.

Menaka turned around, her eyes widening. 'Raped?' she whispered, her voice, low and dry. That unforgivable, crime of forcing a woman to submit against her will, was what Rambha had accused Vasu of. It was a fleeting thought, all Menaka could register was the horror of it.

Menaka stared uncomprehendingly at Urvashi. 'How was an apsara raped??' she gasped, her own anguish abandoned.

'While visiting Nalakuber at Kuber's palace, Rambha was stopped by Ravan, Kuber's half-brother. Even the fact that she was his nephew's betrothed, did not stop him from ravishing her,' explained Urvashi, her voice clear and expressionless. 'He raped her in Kuber's garden and walked away...'

'Walked away?!' exclaimed Menaka. 'Kuber allowed it??'

'Kuber is too scared of Ravan, who wouldn't be able to lift a finger to help himself against his brother. How would he help Rambha??' asked Urvashi contemptuously. 'It was Nalakuber who was ready to go and kill Ravan, but again his father stopped him, warning him of the outcome. Impotent with fury, Nalakuber is said to have cursed Ravan that the next time he forces himself on any woman who does not desire him, he would die, breaking his head into pieces. The devas, even Lord Brahma and Lord Vishnu were delighted and they rained a shower of flowers.'

'Did they?' scoffed Menaka. 'Then why was not Ravan punished? Were they too cowardly to fight him? Or did they think Rambha, being an apsara, was not worth defending?'

Beneath the contempt was a pounding anger that Urvashi could feel emanating from Menaka. 'Don't apsaras have a dignity, an honour worth protecting? Or are we mere sexual embellishments of gratification?'

Menaka was beyond her own grief, it suddenly seemed too trivial and selfish. She felt a stronger emotion, familiar and not forgotten—anger. Unfiltered fury at the apathy shown by the devas, who had not stood for Rambha and her humiliation, coursed through her body. Were they scared or selfish? Ravan had dared to attack a woman in Heaven and the devas had kept quiet. Unchallenged, this emperor of the three worlds had taken over Lanka, ousting his brother Kuber from his golden kingdom and was virtually the most formidable king on Earth now. *But, one day, this powerful man who had humiliated a woman, would die because of a woman*, Menaka thought grimly.

'Rambha is the queen of the apsaras, and the devas, for all their might, could not protect her; what sort of help and hope do the lesser immortals expect? We are just slaves!' she cried, a deep rage fanning her face but she expelled a deep breath to calm herself down. Fury was futile.

'How is she?' Menaka asked, her heart going out for Rambha.

'Beautiful and more bitter!' shrugged Urvashi unfeelingly, snatching a glance at Menaka's face. She could not get over Menaka's outrage, her concern for that wretched woman who had been responsible for her unhappiness. It had been Rambha who had plotted with Indra to falsely frame Vasu, oust him and make him live his years of misery on Earth. It was Rambha who had snatched Menaka's happiness, colluded and calculated, manoeuvred and manipulated. But for this same woman, Menaka had spoken up, waking from her self-imposed stupor to battle for her sake, for a cause which should least affect her.

Menaka found Urvashi's callousness abrasive. 'What Rambha has gone through cannot be wished on your vilest enemy!'

'Mercifully, my dear Menaka, you do realize she is your enemy even though you don't consider her one! Rambha is incorrigible. She preened at my downfall, instigated and gloated at your loss and...'

'That makes us no different from her then!'

'I am not crowing, just letting you know that she got back what she deserved!'

'By being raped?' Menaka looked incredulous at the malicious satisfaction Urvashi was deriving.

'Yes,' said Urvashi solemnly, her eyes flinty. 'One who is heartless enough to feign that horrific humiliation and accuse an innocent of it, deserves nothing worse than that. She should know what an assault means, be it on your body, your reputation, your very soul! Menaka, I confess I don't feel sorry for her. She was responsible for Vasu's doom! She ruined your happiness. She accused Vasu of being drunk and trying to molest her, she now knows what molestation means, what all you have had to endure! She is licking the wounds she inflicted on others!' she added fiercely. 'Your sins always double back!'

Urvashi could not have put it more brutally. The incongruity of what was expected and what had occurred was too grisly. Rambha's crime had been a crime of the heart, a transgression not punishable by physical law. Yet, she had been punished. But Menaka could not bring herself to rejoice. She was too weary of all the wickedness.

Urvashi gently touched her shoulder. 'I am guilty of the same, Menaka. I may not have stooped so low as Rambha to indulge in false allegations, but neither did I refute it, knowing Vasu was innocent. My silence was as vile and violent as her attack on his character. But I could never get myself to forgive him, and I felt vindicated. I am sorry, Menaka, I finally gathered some moral courage to tell you that. That is why I came here before my nerve failed me, and I hope you can forgive me some day.'

Menaka gave her a sad smile. 'Forgiving oneself is always more difficult, but I am sure you will be happier now. More relieved, less bitter,' she pressed her hand reassuringly. 'And if it makes you feel better, let me tell you what I had hated letting you know. That Pururav had been cursed with separation from you right from the start of your romance. You resented Vasu, but it was Tumburu who had once cursed Pururav during an altercation between them.'

Urvashi gave Menaka a look of bewilderment. 'Why would Tumburu do that? And Pururav never let me know!'

'During a dance session, Rambha was finding one particular step particularly trying. Tumburu was extremely patient with her but watching them, Pururav laughed scornfully and teased Rambha about her clumsiness. Pururav continued to boast that you had a more nimble foot and could never commit such silly mistakes. A furious Rambha questioned him about his credentials to pass such a judgement. Pururav retorted that he had learnt more about dancing from you than Rambha ever could from Tumburu. At which, Tumburu lost his temper, cursing Pururav that he would never have his loved one whom he was so arrogantly proud of!'

The flare of temper in Urvashi's eyes glittered dangerously. 'So Tumburu deserves his fate too!' she said viciously. 'He is the one who is accursed as the demon Viradha. When would he be relieved from it?'

Menaka wondered too. Would Lord Ram release him too as well as Vasu from their cursed avatars? 'Curses, our life seems to be full of them! So convenient for others, so complicating for us!'

she sighed, recalling how she had stopped Kaushik from mouthing one on Indra, the culprit of this senseless cataclysm of events.

Kaushik, she called his name silently. By cursing her, he had cursed himself too and they could never meet again. Urvashi had the momentary joy of meeting Pururav once a year, she had lost Kaushik forever, never to be able to catch a glimpse of him. They had always been doomed. Menaka recalled how early she had begun to realize this—when she had first conspired to use Kaushik as her escape plan, when she dared to do the impermissible, when her remorse had started to corrode her hollow. Love had curdled into a misery of guilt. Her love and fear had acted like conscience, suddenly making her believe that their love was cursed.

She balled her fingers into a fist, her nails biting into the soft flesh of her palm. Why was she not blessed with a prolonged loss of consciousness that would make her forget her loss? Was she to suffer it forever or would time quench the pain into a bearable dullness? Today, she found, she had nothing left except memories which gave her strange solace. She was thankful for it. *Give it him too*, she prayed, *give him my peace, Kaushik needs it more.*

'Why didn't Pururav tell me?'

Menaka was interrupted from her waking reverie. She noticed the perplexed expression on Urvashi's face. 'Pururav took his curse lightly so as to not have bothered to discuss it with you,' said Menaka kindly. 'He wanted to protect you from the ugliness of it.'

'Or the fact that he was supremely confident that we would never part...' said Urvashi, her eyes sad and soft. Menaka had glimpsed a rare, weak moment of the apsara.

'But you do get to meet him once a year at least,' said Menaka consolingly, further words clogging in her throat.

She would never be able to see Kaushik now, never. Not just because of the curse he had laid upon her, but because he never wished to see her again. Even that flare of happiness she had given him was drained out of him like blood. He had to choose between her and his goal. And she had made the choice for him. *Make him believe in himself again*, she prayed. *And make me believe in myself too*. She glanced at the apsara sitting next to her, probably as unhappy as her, but who hid it from the world in her mask of devilish insouciance.

'You wouldn't have had nine sons from him if you couldn't!' she chaffed, trying to make Urvashi smile again. 'Pururav saw to it that you weren't separated forever. He endured a lot to dilute the curse. He went all the way to the mountains, the Badarikasrama, and meditated to Lord Vishnu, who was pleased and ordered Indra to return you to him. Thus, you can still meet him once a year.'

'Those seem to be his only moments of sanity, he goes crazed with grief each time I leave him. They call him the mad king; roaming the forest, screaming my name, walking like a deranged man ...Oh Menaka, what sort of love do these mortals endure? They love so intensely, why can't we?'

'Because we are too selfish and uncaring. We can't love anyone but ourselves,' replied Menaka.

She did not want to talk further, recalling the anguish that did not seem to age with time. *I don't feel anything but pain*, she reminded herself frantically, grabbing at some vestige of sanity. *If I don't come alive again, I'm going to destroy myself quite deliberately. Every year, I shall be more used. I'm going to be just a wasted apsara*. Would she be like those apsaras who laugh too much and have three men with them, touching them without intimacy? *I'm falling in pieces already*, she cried silently. She wanted to forget the absoluteness of her pain, lose all their memories for ever. It was as though by this separation that she wanted to rob a part of herself, to lose her individuality. It was the first step to her own death that she would live on forever with the memories crumbling like the broken pieces of her heart. *What happens if you cast away all what makes you?*

Hope and Resurrection

Vishwamitra was in two minds—should he stay in his ashram or revive Vasishth's challenge? He recalled his last humiliation at the hands of the rishi. He had decided to pick up where he had last left, at the debate over King Harishchandara's honesty. And he had to get away from the ashram and the torturous memories of Menaka; thinking of her gave him a sick, dry feeling. Vishwamitra decided to tackle the dormant challenge with all his pent up aggression. He needed to vent out his ire, be it on Vasishth or Harishchandra. He left for Ayodhya and headed straight for the palace; he had to prove Vasishth wrong and this good king a liar.

On Vishwamitra's arrival, the king had graciously welcomed him. 'O most respected sir, I had heard your new ashram is in my kingdom, and I was set to pay you a visit myself. I am honoured, sir, but let me know the reason for your presence and I shall serve you in the best way I can.'

'I wish to perform a special yagna here which requires immense wealth,' stated Vishwamitra. 'And I have heard you are a wealthy king. I hope you can help me.'

'Certainly, sir, pray what all will you need?'

Vishwamitra looked squarely at the king and simply said, 'All your wealth.'

The king looked unfazed. After a moment's thought, he nodded.

Vishwamitra decided to push through nevertheless. 'Will you be able to supply me with that huge a heap of gold, which would drown the height of a man standing on an elephant at the top of your highest hill?'

'I shall do my best,' said the king, his head bowed and his eyes unfaltering. He ordered a huge heap of gold to be presented and soon his royal coffers were empty and as expected, yet it fell short of the required amount.

Vishwamitra waited for the king to slip and speak a lie. He did not. 'I have given you all what I had, my personal wealth as well as the one in the coffers,' he said, not a crease of worry furrowing his brow. 'We are running short but I relinquish my land, my kingdom to you.'

Vishwamitra pretended to be angry. 'You lie, o king! I don't want your kingdom, as it's not yours to stake. It also belongs to your subjects. Do you mean to say that you have gambled them as well?' he pursued relentlessly.

The king was at a loss of words and taken aback. 'I shall never harm my subjects,' he said. 'I have nothing else to give you but my family. I stake them.'

'Are they for sale, o king?' asked Vishwamitra. 'You hand your wife and son to me, but again what use are they to me? I need money, sir, not servants!' he added cruelly.

The king to keep his promise, sold all what belonged to him—his kingdom, his wife and only child. And last, he sold himself to Veerbahu, a keeper of a cremation ground. But his woes were far from over. His son, Rohit, died of snake bite. His wife Chandramati did not have enough money to cremate him. Forced to take to begging to collect those dues, Chandramati found herself accused of murder for which she was to get capital punishment. On the orders of his master Veerbahu, Harishchandra was to execute the punishment of beheading. But as he brought down the axe, to cut down his wife's neck, Vishwamitra halted him. He had tested the man enough. He had lost but he was won over by Harishchandra's tenacious honesty. The wife and son were resurrected and his kingdom returned. The torture by

Vishwamitra and the tribulations suffered, to test the good king was all a maya, an illusion.

'I have no complaints, no reason for hurt, honoured Vishwamitra,' said Harishchandra simply. 'You brought out the best in me. I shall be forever known for this because of you, sir.'

He might have got out the best in Harishchandra, but it had brought out the worst of mine, Vishwamitra had to admit to himself, feeling slightly ashamed. Harishchandra made him feel small. Once again, Vasishth had made him taste defeat but in that quick, deep moment, Vishwamitra realized his grouse against Vasishth too was petty. He had indulged in a pointless test of will when instead he had a larger goal to follow—to be the Brahmarishi—and to be crowned a Brahmarishi by none other than Vasishth himself.

Vishwamitra returned to his ashram in the Himalayas, a deeply perturbed man. Though his respect for Harishchandra had doubled, his loss of face before Vasishth made him inadequate. *Was I not fit to be a Brahmarishi?* The thought tormented him. His pride, his defeat and his supposed achievements made him ponder what he had and what he had lost. But what shocked him most was his own heartlessness and latent cruelty, at the violence he was capable of. It cut him deep and viciously. And now he knew what Harishchandra or rather Vasishth had done to him. It was not Vishwamitra who had put Harishchandra on trial, but the other way round where he was put to test, and he had failed miserably. He neither had the generosity nor the kindness needed to be humane. So how could he ever hope to be the great soul he was striving for? For all his knowledge and wisdom, he was a cruel, arrogant ignoramus.

He counted his defeats, each one forcing him to reflect. Even with Menaka, it had been a surrender of his wanton desire, to fall flat before her in all his weakness. 'Am I but a slave to desire, anger and ego? Can I and will I ever acquire the goal of becoming a Brahmarishi? How am I ever going to fulfil my dream?'

And strangely, he heard an echo from the past; Menaka's voice pleading with him to go back to his purpose, and to leave her and their child. 'We shall wait for you,' her words now taunted him. But he had not listened to her. He had lost his dream, her and their daughter. He cursed himself; what had he done?

He had succumbed to his bloodlust and allowed himself to stray from his resolve. Yet it was not he, but she who had brought him to his senses. And another hard truth crashed upon him. It was like a snarling wave, devouring him in its hungry tide. It left him overwhelmed, drowning him in a vortex of his own emotions. It was not hate or anger, but it was remorse and regret. He could see Menaka for what she was—selfless in her love, beautiful in her final gesture of abandonment. He recalled how often Menaka cajoled, fought, argued, persuaded, and begged him to follow his dream. But he clung on to her in his selfish concupiscence till she had to wrench herself away from him. She had that moral courage, he did not. He put his head in his hands and wept, the tears welling deep from within, from his bleeding, weeping heart, the wail ripped from his mind, bruising his soul, tearing at his eyes and coursing down unchecked down his weary face.

Seeing Harishchandra sacrifice his wife and son had been like a knife in his heart. Harishchandra's plight reminded him of the desperate Menaka, when she had told him she would leave him. He had hated her for that, never seeing her love, her final sacrifice. In Harishchandra, he had seen Menaka, forsaking him and their child for a greater cause—his goal which he had forgotten to follow, his target he had lost sight of. It was Menaka who had forced him to see the truth, the truth which he had demanded from the wretched Harishchandra. Vishwamitra could feel his face wet with tears. He was crying for his wise love, who had shown him his path at last.

He made a short frustrated gesture as though he wanted to touch her, beg for her forgiveness, grovel at her feet, just hold her close and sink his head into her arms. *Menaka, what have I done*, he shouted bleakly. His eyes had an abstract tenderness just thinking of her and a tortured anguish of all what he had lost.

The realization made him feel weak. He felt drained of all his hate, his anger, his jealousy, his grief. Love gushed in and so did remorse. How could he ever believe that his love had petered out? Harishchandra had shown what a monster he was. The king was ready to kill his wife for the sake of honesty, and he had done the same out of hate and distrust. The end of the trial was not what he had expected, it had been his trial as well. He had been found guilty, convicted of the most terrible crime—of killing his love, strangling his trust, murdering his dreams.

He was struck senseless by this unusual clarity. Hate and suspicion and envy had driven him so far away that he had misread her words. Love never mattered in his time of hate. He even used to pray in hate, the shattering obliteration preventing him from thinking any good. He thought he had caught her out in her lies but when she had spoken the truth, he had believed it to be a lie. That had been the shallowness of his trust, and the depth of her love. He had piled evidence against her and yet now all of it pointed against him. Here in this trial was the complete answer of what he was. Her soft voice tauntingly hummed around him, making him believe in it, believing in her love again. In his mind, he leafed through their story, the pages thick and profuse. He read them slowly, till the end to make sure. The last chapter was not the end of his story as he had assumed. It was the beginning of another one. He had to start again. He was bereft of hate, cleansed of his anger. Eternity was not the end, it was the endless prolongation of the moment of love. And that was the moment he chose now that moment of absolute love, of absolute trust, of complete submission. He was spent of his hate. He had only her love to live on.

He closed his eyes, happy calm, settling down on him and began to meditate. He desired loneliness and solitude, and he made a final effort and began severe penance. He found it disturbingly difficult. He kept wavering, either distracted or unsettled with some random intrusion, unable to concentrate. Then he remembered why and for whom he was doing this and he slowly but certainly collected his thoughts, and reined in first his senses and then his wide, expanding mind.

As days passed his tapas became more vigorous, more austere. He gave up food, and the air which he barely breathed was his only source of nutrition. He did not feel anything, not the cold, not the heat or that heat emanating from his own body, as every cell in his body became purified. His body shrank, gaunt and cadaverous, but glowed with a strange light, like the red of the burning embers. And if touched, one would have been scalded as if by a hot iron. His face shorn of its cosmetic handsomeness, lost its pride and hauteur, was replaced by an illuminating humility, spreading as a halo, confirming his exalted state. And in such a state, for days together, he lapsed into a catatonic state of meditation.

But in Vishwamitra's mind there was a shining, single thought that this time his penance was not just for himself, but for his Menaka, who had given up everything for him. Her love filled his being, his soul. It was beautiful to discover and to believe again. Their love was immortal.

When two people love each other, they cannot disguise a lack of tenderness in a kiss, in a touch or even in the trickle of news about them. Even after so many years, Menaka yearned to glean whatever she could about Kaushik and Shakuntala. Her baby must be fairly grown up now, a young girl. But was she shy or spirited, mild or mercurial? Menaka had watched her over the years, hidden amongst the tall groves of Rishi Kanva's ashram. The ashram looked far prettier than she had last seen it but Menaka's eager eyes searched for her daughter. She was not there but Menaka was sure she was the reason why the ashram was lovelier now, dotted with the steady burst of flowers in vibrant clumps. It reminded Menaka of their ashram on the Mahi, small but pretty, and how she had planted the rose bushes, how she loved plucking the jasmines to wear in her hair and wrists...

Menaka blinked, shutting those memories again and stared at the lovely expanse in front of her. From a distance, Kanva's ashram beside the River Malini looked like a scene from Heaven.

Menaka's searching eyes kept seeking a glimpse of her daughter. She saw her at last. She looked tall, slim and lovely...

and forlorn. Menaka's heart skipped a beat. Shakuntala seemed visibly sad, the dimpled smile wiped off her radiant face, her dark eyes no conger flashing with humour and happiness. She had her father's attractive, heart-warming smile, the deep dimples, his strong nose and the aggressive jut of his chin. Menaka felt a twist in her heart, she could not disown her past, the intruding flashes of nostalgia. They were not just memories, they were sentiments, which were hungry, yearning and full of longing. Menaka sighed. But these good memories were bad: they hurt you the most. From what little she could gather, Shakuntala was a little of all, more like her father and better than her mother.

'You watch her like an angel; why don't you reveal yourself as her mother?' Rishi Kanva had asked her, his eyes as gentle as his voice. 'Over the years, you have been watching her grow from a toddler to a lovely woman. You are her mother, Menaka, come forward and claim that.'

'No, you are her sole parent!' Menaka quickly protested. 'Besides, she wouldn't want to meet a mother who abandoned her,' she added wryly. 'The fact that I get to see her occasionally gives me some joy...' her voice trailed away.

'Tell her, you will feel better. So will she,' coaxed Rishi Kanva. 'She is aware of the truth of her birth...'

'And she is but bitter about it,' she reminded him.

'No, not really. She is quite proud that she is the daughter of famous parents!' he smiled. 'She is a lovely girl, smart and sensible. Meet her, you'll be proud of her as well.'

'I am,' said Menaka simply. 'And I thank you for it, sir. I am indebted to you. Vishwamitra knew when he handed her to you that you would provide her with the best education, values, discipline and love, which we as her parents could not do. What does she want to do now?'

'She wants to run this ashram!' laughed the old rishi. 'I told her she is too sheltered, and should go out and see the world. But she insists to stay, she is happier in the woods with the flowers, the trees, the animals. She is Nature's child, Menaka. She is fearless, loving, wild and passionate; has the frailty of the softest flower, and yet she is as fierce as a tigress. She has the strength that knows how to bend, courage to trust and knows the silence that knows how to be eloquent.'

Menaka nodded, her eyes shining with pride. 'Yes, I have seen her, how she mingles with man and animal, the forest and the river, the worldly and the spiritual. She is innocent yet knowledgeable, but not arrogant. She does not know what treachery is, what weakness is. She has received the best possible upbringing in an atmosphere of love, kindness, truth and fearlessness,' said Menaka, with pride. She felt a pang of sorrow when she realized that for her daughter she was a stranger, who familiar but unacquainted, a mother who did not belong to her or her world.

She smiled faintly at the old rishi. 'Her power comes from her integrity, her knowledge. You have taught her to be proud of herself, refusing to be cast in any shadow of inferiority. She knows she is a woman, the creation of the same Deva who made Man, Nature, Earth and the Heavens.'

Kanva's eyes were grave. 'Shakuntala does not believe she was born out of sin, but out of love and true passion. She is not ashamed of her birth, so you should not feel guilty either, Menaka. And like you, she is a gem, shining bright and beautiful. And there's something new going on in her life—she is in love with a king! They got married too!'

The news came as a jolt. It didn't flood her with excitement and joy as expected. Menaka looked disconcerted. 'That means she has truly grown up!' she tried to smile. 'When was the wedding? But then why is she still here in the ashram?'

Kanva nodded. 'Yes, she has not yet joined him. He will return and take her back to Hastinapur,' he said, and noticed the puzzled look on Menaka's face. 'To make a long love story short, Shakuntala met King Dushyant when he was out hunting here in these woods. I was not here at the ashram then. He stayed at the ashram for a few days during which they fell in love and got married in the gandharva tradition...'

Menaka felt a faint stirring of unease. 'But why indulge in

this secrecy of a gandharva vivah? And why did they not wait for you to return?' she insisted. 'What was the hurry?'

Kanva looked slightly taken aback at her imperativeness. 'Dushyant had to rush back to his kingdom soon afterwards for...'

'Then he could have set the marriage for a later date, and married in the presence of all, especially you! You are her father!' argued Menaka, getting more apprehensive about this unknown man. 'Strange for a king to have time for love, but not the time to marry properly. He seems like more of a man in a hurry.'

Kanva was quick to note the sharpness in her voice. 'You are not pleased?'

'I am anxious,' she frowned.

'Those are just a mother's fears about a daughter stepping into a new world!' said Kanva, with an easy shrug. 'Shakuntala is a married woman now, and she will be returning to Hastinapur soon. Don't worry. You make him sound like some pleasure seeker, a king devoted to the pursuit of pleasures.'

'He seems to be one, reckless and irresponsible,' she retorted tartly. 'Dushyant seems to me like a man moved not by love, but purely by lust!'

Kanva flinched.

'If it was love for her that Dushyant felt, he could have and should have, waited until you returned to the ashram,' maintained Menaka, worriedly. 'He is a king who should know his duties. He falls in love with Shakuntala, but hides it from the world with a secret marriage and a hollow promise that he shall return to take her back to his kingdom as a queen! His intentions appear questionable.'

'He'll be back soon,' said the rishi assuredly, hoping to soothe her. 'I trust Shakuntala and her choice.'

Menaka cast a bemused look at the old rishi. 'Perhaps you trust her too much,' she said. 'You gave her so much of freedom that she did not know allow herself to be tied down by it.'

Kanva felt a flash of annoyance and a surge of protectiveness for his daughter. 'Menaka, be more kind to her. She is your daughter.'

Menaka shook her head. 'Please don't get angry with me, reverend rishi, I am not criticizing her or you. But trust is as strong as it is fragile. You say you trust her, but how is that she agreed upon this gandharva wedding when she knew you were not there? Did she not wish her father's blessings? Why could she have not waited for you and told the king that she would marry him later?'

'Because, she was a girl in love.'

'Yes, and they were in a hurry to consummate that love!' corrected Menaka. 'Shakuntala is naive, she is not familiar with the ways of the world, but this man, this king, he knew better. Had he been an honourable man with honourable intentions, he should have informed you of his feelings and intention of marriage and then left. Instead, he left in a hurry as if to escape before you arrived, assuring Shakuntala of a flimsy promise. That's why I fear he simply took advantage of her, the situation and made a promise he had no intention of fulfilling.'

'No!' Kanva looked horrified.

'I sincerely hope not!' said Menaka tersely. 'When is he supposed to come here to take her back?'

'I don't know. She is waiting for him...' he said uncertainly.

Menaka bit her lip, her anxiety making her vaguely exasperated. She prayed her fears were unfounded, and that her cynicism would be proved wrong.

'Why don't you talk to Shakuntala?' suggested Kanva, appearing uncertain and worried himself.

'I can't!' she shrugged helplessly. 'I am a virtual stranger to her. She would resent my intrusion. Anyway, I think you are right, I might be over-reacting. Dushyant will come back soon and take his bride away!' she added, forcing some optimism in her remark.

Kanva was not fooled. 'You are scared to face her, Menaka.'

'Because I am ashamed of myself,' confessed Menaka, lowering her eyes.

'Is that what's been eating you all these years?' wondered the rishi, amazed. 'That is worse than repentance, it is a crime! You gave up your husband and your child for their welfare, their well-being, so how do you call yourself unfit to be a mother? You were a good wife, you are a good woman. And like you, Menaka, your daughter inherits her soul from you—independent, assertive and most importantly, who can take responsibility and accountability for herself. You are an apsara, Menaka, but also a shakti, who gives strength and protects. You did that through selfless sacrifice of your happiness,' he paused, deciding to be honest with her. 'You may not have realized it, but you are neither faint nor feeble. You do exactly what you want, sure of yourself, sure of the choices you have made even if it means suppressing your personal happiness or your defiance at being branded ruthless. You have—which is quite rare—that hunger for an alternative. You keep seeking your choices; vacillating between acceptance and struggle. That is the war within you.'

Menaka made a movement.

'Hear me out, Menaka. No one seems to have told you some truths about yourself. Don't deride yourself so harshly, so easily. You are protective and passionate; a loving, giving woman, not just an apsara, enticing and entertaining. You are, an intelligent woman, your knowledge coming more out of your own experiences than formal education. Through your own experiences and decisions, you have debated on the meaning of life with the best of philosophers—Vishwavasu and Vishwamitra.' Kanva saw her start at the mention of both the names. 'They were not merely your lovers, they were your gurus as well, teaching your profound lessons in life, which even the wisest teacher might not be able to teach his disciple. They helped you explore the mysteries of existence just as they themselves did. If they composed literature of the sacred, that knowledge of the soul and of the flesh, they learnt from you! You are the personification of spiritual ecstasy and sexual longing that the world will always remember you by. And like you were once, your daughter is lusting for life, eager for adventure, a fearless wanderer in life's vast fields.'

Menaka did not how to react. She was slightly overwhelmed by pride. Her daughter was what she had hoped she would be and more.

'Menaka, why do you think yourself undeserving?' asked the rishi astutely. 'You loved and lost, but won in the end. One who participated in all the aspects of life, not a as man's equal, but in fact superior to him. Vishwamitra might be the greatest rishi today, but he would not have been so were it not for you. You castigate yourself unfairly that you were the cause for his downfall. But you were also responsible for resurrecting him to his current glory. Today Vishwamitra is an encyclopaedia of knowledge, the only person in the world to have evolved in himself the special 108 chakras, unlike the usual seven we all have, and connected them to the seven planes in the material cosmos,' explained the rishi. 'But through perseverance and penance, Vishwamitra has realized the higher plane of these un-manifested universes, which emanated from the original entity—the mula brahman. He is on the verge of becoming a Brahmarishi, Menaka, just as you persevered.'

Her heart lurched each time the old rishi uttered his name. *I don't know where he is.* They were not in touch, and they never would be. But her ears, her mind, yearned for some news of him. It was like stumbling and falling blindly in a desert, both seeking each other, both lost, both searching for their oasis. But it would be a mirage if they were together.

I sometimes have that mad, threatening will to break my promise and his curse, she thought wretchedly. *I dare not. I should not.* Menaka closed her eyes, momentarily engulfed in the darkness of hopelessness. *I won't gain anything from it. I was allowed to transgress, but the fruits of my sins were taken away, even our daughter.*

Menaka turned instead to the rishi. 'Is he?' she asked hesitantly, afraid her wish might jinx it. She had wanted Vishwamitra to be happy and successful and he was. She had left him for that very purpose, she had wanted him to follow his dream. He was close to achieving it now. 'Will he get it?'

Kanva's smile was reassuring. 'Yes, he shall. And that day is to come very soon.'

Rivals

$\mathcal{T}$ilottama threw Menaka a quick, nervous look wondering how she was to break the news.

'What is it, Tilottama? You look like a frightened doe,' Menaka's voice was soft and gentle as always.

'It's about Vishwamitra!' she blurted, her eyes anxiously scanning her friend. 'They are about to make trouble...' she explained flustered. 'He has become invincible once more, and Indra is feeling threatened again...'

Tilottama did not need to finish her sentence. In a flash, Menaka understood what she was going to say and what it portended. *Indra would never declare an open war*, she thought contemptuously. He would again use some apsara to fight his battle.

'Whom is he sending this time?' she asked sharply.

'Rambha.'

Menaka could not believe her ears. *Why would Rambha agree for this suicidal seduction?* Menaka was confused, angry and apprehensive—angry with Indra and Rambha, and scared for Kaushik. She felt an ominous twinge, lingering long in her frightened mind, refusing to let go. Rishi Kanva had told her that Kaushik was very close to his goal. He would be a Brahmarishi soon, but he was again to be thwarted by the wiliness of Indra. *Would Kaushik be able to save himself from danger this time?* Her heart beat wildly. Could she let him know of this peril? She wanted to, but his curse stopped her from meeting him. Not that it mattered she thought fiercely; she would miserably live his curse than allow him to come to any harm, to save him from a certain doom. But her reckless defiance sagged as quickly. She could not warn Kaushik when he was so deep in years of uninterrupted meditation. Her presence would break his meditation instead.

The fact that Indra had not approached her, implied he no longer trusted her, presuming correctly that she would refuse his preposterous proposal. He had instead taken the help of his old ally, Rambha, for his new plan. Again, Menaka felt a damp, cold feeling of premonition. It clutched at her heart icily, freezing reason and sanity, making her shiver with the uncertainty and the evilness of the scheme of things to come.

She had to meet either of the two, or both. But that would not be wise; they would never listen to her, putting them swiftly on their guard. Out of the two, meeting Rambha alone made more reasonable sense.

Tilottama saw the emotions flit through Menaka's eyes, which finally hardened with resolution. 'Dont!' the urgency in Tilottama's voice stopped her. 'Menaka, don't contemplate the absurd! She dislikes you and openly resents you. She would not heed to whatever you have to say!'

'What else can I do?' snapped Menaka. 'Rambha is in danger too, though I am not too sure if she realizes it. There is always a severe punishment to pay if you break a of a rishi's meditation. And Kau...Vishwamitra's fury is well known. He will destroy the person who attempts to challenges his tapas now.'

Tilottama nodded and could not help smiling at Menaka's quick self-correction. 'You have never thought of him as Vishwamitra. It's always been Kaushik—the young, arrogant, infatuated king whom you glimpsed for a short time when Vasishth summoned you down to Earth!'

Menaka blushed. It seemed eons ago but the image was still alive. 'Oh, you remember that!! It was the first time he saw an apsara so...'

'...he was bound to be besotted,' grinned Tilottama, 'and not just by any apsara, my friend, but you!! He always was smitten. That was another reason why Indra chose you to seduce him, Menaka.'

Menaka looked surprised. 'Oh, Indra saw through this as well? Most mortals are fascinated by us. Kaushik wasn't an exception.'

'Why do you think Indra agreed with Varun to have the Saptarishis called at the Sudharma Hall?' said Tilottama impatiently. 'Because he had to appease Vishwamitra in some way and he made sure Vishwamitra caught a glimpse of you sometime, somewhere in Amravati.'

Menaka could not believe her ears. 'But I barely moved out of this room, let alone met visitors!'

'But Vishwamitra did see you, Indra cunningly arranged it. You were grieving over Vasu, bound to your chamber and Indra knew you would never agree to step out. He re-routed Vishwamitra's chariot specifically all around your palace, twice. First, at the welcome and next when Vishwamitra left Amravati in a huff after his disagreement with Vasishth. Vishwamitra saw you standing at your balcony.'

'Indra is impossible, and I was a fool! He had it all worked out so neatly, as early as then...!' Menaka could not shake the incredulity from her voice.

'He always works on people's weakness. Vishwamitra's weakness was always you. And yours was always...' Tilottama hesitated.

'Vasu?' she breathed, expelling a deep sigh.

'Yes,' nodded Tilottama. 'But Vishwamitra has always been your strength. He lent you an intensity, a certain depth of character. After that heartbreak and leaving Shakuntala behind, you couldn't have survived otherwise!' she remarked candidly. 'And that is why now Indra dare not ask you for the same request twice.'

'What are his plans with Rambha?' asked Menaka, uneasily.

'It's all rather furtive. Not even Kama has been informed, in case he snitches to you. Indra is aware of how fond Kama is of you and he wouldn't risk it.'

'Rambha plans to seduce Kaushik without Kama's help? That would be a sure disaster! Without Kama, Rambha can never succeed. Kaushik would reduce her to ashes the moment he opens his eyes!' she said worriedly. She gave Tilottama a look of desperation. 'I have to warn her, Tilottama. She has to know what she is getting into!'

'Menaka, she is our queen. She well knows what she is doing,' said Tilottama calmly.

Menaka was amazed at Tilottama's detached composure. Tilottama was a woman of few words but when she decided to advise, it was always pearls of wisdom. Menaka knew she was protective about her, glancing affectionately at her friend. Tilottama was exquisite. There were so many wild stories about her dusky beauty which drove not manavs and asuras but arousing even the triads of devas—the Trimurti—to mad desire. One popular story was how Lord Shiva got smitten by her when she visited him to seek his blessings. He is said to have developed four visible faces as she circumambulated him. Noticing her husband developing a head in each direction to catch a glimpse of her, his wife, Devi Parvati, got visibly annoyed and covered his eyes immediately with her hands. The world and the universe were instantly enveloped in darkness and it was then Lord Shiva developed his famous third eye, to bring light to the world again. All because of Tilottama's eye-catching beauty!

But it was a more belligerent Tilottama standing in front of her now, firmly forbidding her to meet Rambha, for whom she did not hold much affection or admiration.

'Rambha is quite likely to presume the opposite!' cautioned Tilottama. 'Learn to be more wary of her.'

'I am not doing it for her,' she replied. 'It's for Kaushik.'

Tilottama had been right, thought Menaka a day later, as she stood in Rambha's grand chamber, where she had been made to wait till Rambha made an appearance, making it clear she was not pleased to see Menaka at all.

'The queen deigns to meet me!' she smirked. 'And pray what may be the reason for this honour?' She detached herself from her dressing table and came towards Menaka, cold-eyed, acquisitive, predatory.

Menaka thought it best to ignore the pointless sarcasm, but it made conversation difficult to proceed. She would have to tackle the matter head on and quickly.

'If what I have heard is right, you are being sent to Earth to break off Vishwamitra's tapas,' she started, not sure how blunt she could be with Rambha.

She saw two spots of red suffusing Rambha's high cheek bones, darkening her smooth, dusky skin. 'Your spies informed you well,' she said in a hissing spurt and her eyes glinted. 'Is the spy this particular apsara in whose arms you prefer to be rather than poor Uranyu's these days?' she smirked watching the heightened colour on Menaka's pallor. 'But yes, Menaka, your lovely spy heard correctly that I am being sent to seduce Vishwamitra. And I am looking forward to meeting your man!' she drawled in her smoky voice, that deliberately, grated Menaka's already frazzled nerves.

'It will never come to that!' retorted Menaka. 'The moment he opens his eyes, he will destroy you.'

Rambha flushed angrily. Suddenly the little spurt of vicious anger rose again on her chiselled face. Menaka realized she had said it all wrong. It was meant to have been a word of caution but it came out as a threat, a jealous retort.

'What is this, Menaka?' purred Rambha dangerously. 'Are you plain jealous that I shall be seducing Vishwamitra? Or are you insecure that I might be better than you?' Rambha gave her a mocking smile. 'Making love to an earthly man would be a novelty. Mortals are said to be ardent lovers and your Kaushik more so. How good was he, Menaka?'

It was her turn to feel the heat of colour rising on her face. Menaka immediately imagined the two of them together, their lips fastened, their sweat-slicked limbs entwined, writhing in ecstasy, he moaning deeply in her mouth as he filled inside her full and warm... She felt an aching knot of desire and shut off the image brutally as she knew it would never happen. She looked squarely at the imposing figure of Rambha.

'It's not about you versus me,' she explained quietly. 'It's not about us at all.'

'Yes, I know. It's about your lover whom you are so desperate to shield!' said Rambha waspishly.

Menaka decided to ignore the other woman's petty petulance. 'This plan is dangerous. Vishwamitra will not spare you. Please, Rambha, don't venture anywhere close to him.'

There was a perceptible change on Rambha's beautiful, hard face. 'Is that a warning?'

'It's a plea!' gushed Menaka. 'Vishwamitra's wrath is lethal. Don't try this game on him. He is already furious with Indra, and this time he won't spare him or anyone who hinders him. He is sure to curse you! You are not even taking Kama with you for protection!'

Rambha narrowed her eyes. 'Kama might get reduced to ashes himself like he did the last time, when he tried to play match maker for Lord Shiva and Devi Parvati. Lord Shiva had burnt him alive in his rage. It's an old story, but I guess, Kama has learnt his lesson too!' she laughed scornfully. 'And his dumb darts wouldn't have worked anyway. I don't need him,' she sounded dismissive. 'Not after last time's fiasco when you were made to fall in love with your prey. Indra made that huge mistake.'

Rambha rounded on her belligerently. 'And why would you care about my well-being, dear?' she asked caustically. 'You haven't been much of a gracious subordinate. You didn't bother to apologize for maligning Tumburu in open court. Nor did you pay me a visit when you returned from Earth after your assignment with Vishwamitra. Nor offered your condolences,' she accused. 'I am your superior, you are to come and meet me not the other way round.'

She gave her a supercilious smile which gurgled into a giggle— harsh, uncontrolled and malicious. The sound reminded Menaka of her own discordant self, a chaos of discomfort and anxiety and was flooded with a wave of panic, feeling the urge to run away from the room.

This was going worse than she imagined it to be; Menaka frankly did not know how to respond. She wished she had listened to Tilottama and not come here at all. *Whatever I have to say was likely to be misconstrued by Rambha*, Menaka sighed. She would try one last time.

'I was in a mess myself, Rambha,' she supplied shortly. 'It was only when I heard about this new scheme that I decided to meet you. It's suicidal, Rambha!' she added desperately, hoping to make sense her fear. 'Indra is sending you to incite anger, not desire in Vishwamitra. That's why Kama is not being sent with you, why don't you understand?'

Rambha pursed her full lips thinly. Again, she had said the wrong words.

'I understand your intentions perfectly, Menaka. You are protecting your lover. Or perhaps, you don't want to share him with me, as you did Vasu!'

She looked strange; her obstinate face was twisted into a mask of smiling spite.

Menaka's eyes widened in genuine surprise. She asked, 'Is that why you resent me that I took away Vasu from you? And now by having Kaushik, you would be squaring the issue?!'

Rambha was looking at her with spiteful eyes and grim smile. Menaka felt her face tighten in shock.

'No, no, Rambha. This is not what it seems!' Menaka's eyes were frantic, her protest loud. 'I don't know what your equation with Vasu was, but I do know that you plotted with Indra to oust him out of Heaven, either to punish me or him, or both,' she said strongly, her voice strengthening with each word she uttered. 'But now I ask, Rambha, why did you falsely accuse Vasu of a crime for which he is still suffering?'

'Because he chose you over me,' said Rambha calmly.

Menaka looked blank. She had intuitively known it all along, but yet when Rambha admitted it, it still did come as a shock. And what was more shocking was the venom of a spurned heart, poisoning so many lives. She was repulsed by the ugliness of it all and it showed amply on her face. She had a mad urge to slap this woman but she had long given up on her. But the evilness frightened Menaka; the grotesqueness of the situation was repugnant.

Menaka was finding it hard to conceal her emotions, and her thoughts must have flitted clearly on her face.

Rambha stared back at her balefully. 'Don't you dare pity me!' she snarled. 'Look at you, Menaka, what have you got? You had two daughters and lost both of them. Vishwamitra was never yours to lose and Vasu might never return!'

'So might Tumburu!' Menaka shot back, her eyes flashing. 'You used him in your vile games and see where it got him! He is enduring all what Vasu is, for your mistake! And...'

'...and I got raped because I falsely accused Vasu of doing the same, is that what you are saying?' shouted Rambha.

Menaka was stunned and momentarily speechless at Rambha's vicious vehemence.

'No! I would never wish that on you, never!' said Menaka, her face white. 'You used people but you were used yourself! Why are you helping Indra in his war with Vishwamitra? Just to get back at me? Rambha, Indra is the one who started it all. He resented Vasu and threw him out through you. If you are his friend, how did he allow your rape to go unpunished? And more importantly, how could anyone rape in Heaven? Indra is the one who was supposed to protect you against Ravan, he was the one who should have punished Ravan, but he was allowed to walk free, remorseless. You are colluding with this man who was too much of a coward to fight your offender. He is our king, Rambha, it his duty is to defend us!'

Rambha's face had gone ashen. No words spilled out but a long, strangulated sigh slowly bubbling into a whimper. She suddenly seemed to crumple before Menaka's eyes. She sank her head in her hands and broke down in a shudder of sobs.

It was a terrible sight to behold. The tears streamed down her lovely face, smudged with naked grief and poignant hopelessness. Her shoulders were slumped in undisguised defeat, surrendering to her despair. Menaka had never felt so helpless before. In front of her was a woman in torment, broken and bereft. There was a raw inhibition in the emotions exposed, and Menaka felt like an intruder. But she could not leave Rambha alone. She walked slowly up to her, the woman who once so proud, arrogant and dangerous was now relegated to a whimpering bundle of misery.

She laid a hesitant hand on Rambha's shaking shoulders, allowing Rambha to weep, waiting patiently for the storm to subside.

'Drink this,' she said, placing a cool tumbler of water in Rambha's shaking hands. She pressed them reassuringly, forcing the trembling to stop.

'I have never felt so humiliated, so...so...bruised, so invaded!' cried Rambha in a cracked whisper. She looked straight into Menaka's eyes, letting out the emotional anguish churning within.

'Make me forget that terrible night, Menaka!' she cried hoarsely. 'For all our powers, our immortality, I has lain, ravaged and broken and bruised, screaming, pleading to that monster to leave me, to stop...' she choked, her tears thick with remembered anger and humiliation.

'No, don't say any more!' urged Menaka.

'Let me speak! I want to talk about it...I have to talk to someone!' said Rambha fiercely. 'I couldn't say anything to Nalakuber, as he was so crazed that he would have killed Ravan if he could. But I begged him not to! Ravan would have killed him in a second. I was more scared of losing him than grieving over myself!'

Menaka kept silent, allowing Rambha to well out the dormant words, long interred, waiting to erupt. Rambha sat tense, her body rigid and upright in her chair, her lips tight, clutching the tumbler, while forcing the words out. 'It was a cool, pleasant evening, as I walked towards Nalakuber's palace as I always do. There was nothing out of the ordinary about it except that hidden in the shadow of the foot hills was Ravan,' she shivered slightly. 'He stepped out, startling me, but I ignored him and continued to walk. He stopped me. I looked at him enquiringly, even a little coldly. I didn't know who he was and had no intention of talking to him. "I am Ravan," he introduced himself. "You are an apsara, aren't you?" He said it so casually that it was almost insulting. "I am the queen of the apsaras," I said pointedly.

'But that did not impress him much. He remained undeterred. "But of course, this Heaven has only men—the handsome devas and the gandharvas, and my cowardly brother Kuber! The only women here are the apsaras; the wives are tucked in some safe place!" he added lasciviously, moving closer. "So for whom are these wet lips meant for? They look hungry enough to be kissed."

'I fumed at his lewd bluntness, but he seemed to enjoy my anger. "For my husband," I retorted, "Nalakuber."

"My precious nephew!" he raised his eyebrows. "Apsaras don't marry and even if they do, it doesn't count!" he said dismissively. "They are made for pleasure," he said, while his eyes raking my body. I have always been proud of my body, flaunted it, used it on unsuspecting men, but at that moment I felt as if my soul had been ripped from that very body. I felt ashamed of it, wanted to hide it from his lecherous eyes. His hands suddenly grabbed at my angavastra and again, I have never felt more naked in my life. I felt sick. His groping hands were at my waist, pulling me closer. And for the first time, I was frightened. "I am your nephew's wife, which means I am your daughter-in-law. Please let me go!" I begged and I hated that tone in my voice. I was pleading with him. I looked around me, but it was now a stark, dark night of solitary isolation. The hills which I crossed everyday did not look beautiful anymore. And evil was right in front of me, his face close, leering, the flesh mottled grey, the mouth crumpled and damp. And I was struggling in his arms, his uneven breath staled my face, my neck. My skin crawled with repulsion, I felt defiled! He threw me onto the soft, green grass which I loved to walk on, and pinned me down by my shoulders. "For me you are just a harlot of the Heavens made to make me happy. So make me happy! Make love to me, apsara!" he shouted at me, pressing heavily, his face sickly with excitement.

'That was all that I remember, I don't remember anything after that except me screaming. I don't know if I screamed or was it just in my mind,' Rambha's mouth twitched. 'All I know that I was being plundered, violated, crushed under him, helpless and in pain, imploring for mercy...' she sobbed convulsively, her eyes dark and blazing, reliving each horrible moment. 'Menaka, the rage, the humiliation, it was like a fire and I was burning in it, so damned powerless and pathetic. I couldn't even help myself!'

Menaka saw she was trembling. Fear, hate, fury, pain—Menaka could feel the emotions emanating from her. Rambha closed her eyes shut, so tight that the lashes quivered on cheeks that were now raddled.

'And worse was when Nalakuber was made to feel as helpless, impotent in his fury,' she croaked hoarsely. 'All he could do was cast a curse that Ravan would die the moment he forced himself on any woman!'

Ravan should have gotten this curse a long time ago, then possibly women could have been saved like Rambha or the seer Vedavati. When he had caught Vedavati by her hair in an attempt to molest her, she had saved herself by self-immolating herself, but not before uttering her last ominous words, 'I shall be born again for your destruction!'

Ravan was a paradox. The asura king was the son of the famous Rishi Vishravas and the grandson of the revered Rishi Pulastya, one of the ten Prajapatis (sons of Brahma). He was considered a scholar himself; famously known also as the mahabrahman. But for all his knowledge, he lacked in wisdom and humility. The irony was that it was not his immense wealth that made him so arrogant, it was his pride of knowledge. As a Brahmarakshasa, he had best of both—the knowledge of the brahmin and the warrior power of the asura. But Ravan misused it openly. He was a maestro of the Veena, the author of *Ravan Sanhita*, the complicated book on Hindu astrology, besides being a scholar of Ayurveda and political science. That such a man could do this, was beyond Menaka's comprehension. *How did a scholar become such a monster, by breed or by his deeds?*

'A nephew cursing his uncle!' shuddered Rambha, her hand curling around the empty tumbler. 'That's all Nalakuber could do. He could not fight him as his father stopped him on time! Ravan had already vanquished Kuber, ousted him from Lanka and chased him in Heaven too.'

Menaka had got to know of the incidents, which had occurred while she was away from Heaven with Kaushik. It had all started when Ravan through his deep, single-minded devotion to Lord Shiva got the nectar of immortality from him. Once that was in his belly, he sacked Kuber from Lanka, the city specially designed by the prolific Vishwakarma, the celestial architect for his asura grandfather, Sumali. Ravan won back his grandfather's golden city from his half-brother, Kuber, who was forced to flee to Indralok and who later became the treasurer of the devas.

Vishravas, the disillusioned, defeated father, advised Kuber to surrender, as Ravan was now invincible with Shiva's boon of immortality. Kuber fled to Heaven but not before severely censuring his brother publicly for his vulgar greed. Incensed, Ravan is said to have chased his brother in Heaven, plundered his celestial city Alaka, defeated him and the devas and taken control of the three worlds. But his most savoured moment of revenge was when he insulted his defeated brother in the presence of all the devas. Ravan was known to be a kind, good ruler, where even the poorest in Lanka could boast of a pot of gold. But when it came to his brother Kuber, Ravan was a different person. His hate was all-devouring. Was his rape of Rambha, his brother's daughter-in-law, his very last act of vindictiveness?

Rambha had composed herself quickly, wiping her tears and the last traces of her painful reminisces. She got up gathering her skirt and her lost dignity, checking her face in the mirror, removing the dark smudges. She put down the mirror, masking her face, hard and beautiful as she always ought to be.

Menaka tried one last feeble attempt. 'Don't try this, Rambha, please!'

Rambha gave her a queer look, her eyes distant, her lips tremulous. 'I won't risk any other apsara. I am the queen, Menaka, I shall go.'

Fury and Fate

Vishwamitra felt a presence, but he ignored it. Yet, the presence wouldn't go away, it hovered closer. He frowned mentally. It was intruding, trespassing into his mind, his senses, entering his consciousness uninvited. He slowly became aware of his surrounding, his eyes still shut but his mind open, rudely awakened from his long slumber of meditation. He lost control of his body and mind, he was with the world again. He sensed it was dawn, he could feel the weak rays of the struggling sun. He felt faint moisture on his parched skin. Was it drizzling? He felt a light moving flickering feebly like his unsteady, wavering mind. He felt the sting of the cool breeze blowing around him, swirling with an exquisite fragrance. It was achingly familiar, and Vishwamitra became alert. He immediately thought of Menaka. *She was back!* And his heart leaped with joy, but he swiftly stemmed it. *It could not be. She would not break her promise and I had not withdraw my curse upon us.* He had wished so often to take it back. But words once uttered could not go unheard or unheeded. He had learnt this from his own mistake. By cursing her, he had cursed himself to never see her, to never be able to feel her, inhale the scent of the woman he loved. And yet that feminine fragrance was assailing him again. Vishwamitra frowned, a wisp of anger licking him, *if not Menaka, who was this woman threatening my peace of mind?* She was suffocatingly close, stifling his senses with her erotic vapours.

Vishwamitra eyes flew open, flashing with a fire that lit up the darkening forest grounds. He saw a woman—a beautiful woman, in conformity with his expectations, but not Menaka.

'I am Rambha,' she breathed through her crimson mouth, confident yet coy, sure that he could not turn away from her. No man had done that, no man could resist her.

Vishwamitra felt a rage he thought would explode through him. *Rambha! That queen of apsaras, who had caused Menaka so much grief.* Like before, she must have hatched a plan with Indra and must have been sent by Indra. Vishwamitra was reminded of a similar, familiar experience. He could still visualize it—a wet evening, a waterfall, a drenched Menaka and him being drawn powerfully into a vortex of lust and desire, against the conflicting tide of reason and caution...

But he felt no desire as he stared at this woman. He felt no flame of arousal devouring him. He was not even attracted by her sultry beauty, in fact he was revulsed into anger. He was meant to be trapped in it, to desire her, to forget his tapas, his prayer, his worship, his work and in the pleasure of the flesh, abandon his life's mission again. He felt hot burst of fury burning in him instead. He parted his lips, dry and cracked and whispered, 'Rambha'. His hoarse voice sent shivers down Rambha's curvaceous back.

Rambha looked at him, and two swift thoughts ran through her panicking mind. First, she knew now why Menaka had fallen so hopelessly in love with this man. And the second was that her end had come, because in his eyes she saw her death.

'Rambha, for this audacity you shall suffer. You, who are so proud of your beauty and prowess, shall turn into a stone for a thousand years, and will woo endless time, howling wind, the beating sun and the relentless rain. I leave you with them,' he pronounced in his rich, deep voice.

He saw Rambha tremble, quailing before him. She was about to say something, but before the words spilled from her mouth, she was inured forever in dull stone. Standing before him was a beautiful statue, a stone sculpture of what she once was.

After he witnessed his curse come to fruition, he was not pleased and felt no relief. He had acquired enough control over his senses to resist Rambha's amorous charms, but not adequate restraint over his rage. With his curse on Rambha, he again had squandered whatever spiritual prowess he had gathered till now. Indra, if not to lure, he had used Rambha to weaken him. He wanted to end this man once and for all but he heard a faint echo of a plea. He recalled Menaka's warning ,'Do not curse him, it will harm you more than him!'

Yet again, he had not listened to Menaka's sane advice; his curse on Rambha had already harmed him. He had ruined another innocent woman, who was just doing her duty. A wave of regret washed over him as he stared at the stone figurine in front of him, her mouth still open, as if trying to tell him something through her remaining unsaid words. *What had she been trying to tell me?* Her last unsaid words, screamed in his mind. *Or had it been her last vicious invective she wanted to throw at me?*

He gazed at the beautiful face in stone, fearful and panicking, the words wrenched out, even in her last throes of death as life had draining out of her. Had he thought she said 'Go to her!' Was this a trick, a last attempt to fool him? Or maybe it was 'Go to Hell!' But he saw again that mad desperation in Rambha's dying eyes, imploring him. Why had she shown such extreme urgency, fraught with intensity and frustration? Was Menaka in some danger? Vishwamitra heart froze, his breathing becoming shallow as he felt an ugly fear suffocating him. *Menaka*, he shouted in despair. But the cry was in his mind, ripped from his aching heart.

He could not go to her ever. He could not. He was helpless in the curse he had inflicted upon them. Breaking his curse would undo everything, meeting her would be the end of all he had aspired for, all he had striven for. He knew that if he met her, he would never be able to leave her again. He would hold on to her like a drowning man, to save his life. And Menaka knew that well.

Their separation was not an act of providence, it was his consequence of foolishness. The evilness of the curse was not what it portended but the inherent bleak hopelessness of it that they would have to live forever without each other. *That* was their curse, their tragedy of loss.

He closed his eyes, willing his powers to be able to see her. And he saw her. There was a sad etherealness about her. Did sorrow make a person more beauteous, toning that loveliness with an edge of elegance and pain? She looked hauntingly exquisite, her dark wine-coloured eyes darkening into shades of deep purple, profound with an unspoken pain in them. Her lustrous, auburn waves, not decked with flowers, but flowing loose and listless, like a dark shroud over her. Her lips, oh those delicate, delectable lips, were pale and bloodless. He imagined her biting them, her pretty teeth sinking mercilessly into their full, lush softness... Vishwamitra forced his eyes to open, to wake him into the present. She could have been by his side now but for his rashness...

And he had behaved impetuously now as well, the stone statuette of Rambha mocked him. He still had no control over his anger, his most volatile emotion. He clenched his hands. He had lost, allowing Indra his victory.

Anger still reigned in him, he would have to rein it in. His flaw and his focus lay somewhere between his rage and the serenity in his mind. He had to find that path.

Vishwamitra cast the statue a last look. He had to depart for his new journey—to the higher heights of the frosty Himalayas, the abode of snow.

ψ

'After Rambha, I anoint you as the new queen of the apsaras!'

Indra's announcement failed to impact Menaka, rather she seemed almost glacial in her dispiritedness. She knew it was a weak way of appeasement, of making amends of a bad decision yet again.

'I want nothing from you! Not your crown of thorns!' she said quietly.

'You have to do something here in Heaven!' retorted Indra in mild exasperation. 'You have vowed not to perform till Vasu returns,' his voice was silky. 'And now after this Vishwamitra episode, you refuse any more assignments.'

'Seductions,' she corrected him, her eyes cold. 'Yes, I shall *not* entice anyone astray nor try to woo the love or sexual favour of someone.'

'Then what do you wish to do here? You have to do something!' he expostulated. 'Be reasonable, Menaka. Accept the position. I am being generous!'

Kama tapped Menaka lightly on her shoulder. 'Take it, Menaka. You might not realize, but it will do all a lot of good. Starting with you!'

Menaka looked listlessly at both, uncharacteristically quiet.

Kama persisted. 'Menaka, someone has to look after the apsaras. With Rambha gone, it would be wise to take her place. You can always return the crown once Rambha is back.'

'That I will,' she replied, 'only if I agree to accept it.'

'It's not as easy to relinquish as you assume it will be,' warned Indra, smiling craftily. 'Just like Chitrasen will have to hand back the title of king of dev gandharva, once Vasu returns. But both of you'll make a more handsome pair—Vishwavasu, the king of the gandharvas and you, Menaka, the queen of the apsaras!'

Menaka was quick to grasp Indra's insidious politicking. Contempt gleamed in her cold eyes. 'You think you can do and undo us anytime by pitting one against the other?'

Indra's face tightened. He knew she was not talking about herself or Vasu, but referring to Rambha. He glanced at Kama. He did not look pleased either. The news of Rambha had reached Amravati fast enough to plunge it in anxious confusion. Indra was deeply unhappy himself, angry at the turn of events. He stood defeated again. *Vishwamitra*, he mouthed the dreaded word silently, feeling a bitter taste in his mouth. He had lost Menaka to him, and now Rambha. But there was hope. By giving vent to Rambha's curse, Vishwamitra must have lost most of his tapas powers again. Rambha had been vain enough to believe she would successfully seduce him, unaware that Indra had sent her to rouse him into anger, not desire.

Kama knew better, and he was outraged, which he demonstrated in full force.

'Why do you need my advice now? Did we discuss before you sent Rambha to Vishwamitra?' he demanded. 'I would have been against it. Or is that the reason why you kept it from me?' he guessed, observing Indra's reddened face. 'I should have been with her. She couldn't have done it alone without help. But who is to convince two egotists who believe they are the best?' he said, his face grim. He gave his friend a brittle, probing look.

'What is it about Vishwamitra that brings out the worst in you, my friend?' he paused. 'Till now you have taken all the wrong decisions, and he has beaten you each time, and each time the loss has been enormous.'

He waved his arm towards the silent Menaka. 'Rambha's lost to us for eons now; and Menaka is as good as gone, she is wasted in every way. You killed her very spirit! As you so eloquently explained, she cannot be used any more for any good...she is worthless as an apsara! And that's why you want to make her a queen, now so that she is of some *use*. It's not your generosity!' Kama accused, unimpressed. '...as you used Rambha but lost to Vishwamitra's curse. What did you achieve, Indra? You lost-lost everything!'

Indra listened to his friend's tirade, his face defeated but the last words injected him with renewed fervour. 'No, all's not lost! We have one last chance by pitting Vishwamitra against Vasishth and let them ruin each other!'

Menaka gave a faint smile as if unsurprised at his words. But Kama looked at his friend with disbelief. 'Haven't you done enough harm already? End this matter. Yes, he is a mere man who challenged you. You lost, he won. Now offer a truce and give up on this obduracy. We need peace in Heaven, not tragedies! We lost Vishwavasu, Tumburu, Menaka, Rambha, and both Uranyu and Nalakuber are as good as gone, too grief-stricken to function properly. And all for your war with that man! Our best apsaras and gandharvas have gone, who else would you want to gamble on?' he almost shouted. 'Are you not surprised that Vishwamitra could have cast a curse on you as well, and made you suffer the same fate as Rambha? But ironically enough, he has done that; through these defeats, he *has* cursed you! He proved to you that he is superior to you and that is the reality you have to live with. That is his curse for you.'

Every word his friend uttered was like a whiplash, stinging him with hurtful truth. Vishwamitra had fought a fair game, beating him openly, destroying every arsenal Indra threw at him. And his weapons of war had been his apsaras, but he had used them badly.

Menaka made a slight movement, like a frozen, beautiful marble statue come alive.

'These were his last words to me, "Tell Indra, he shall lose and I shall win this war!!"' said Menaka. 'They have come true.'

There was no malice in her statement, no vicious sense of glee. Just immeasurable sadness and looking at it reflected in her eyes, for the first time Indra felt a twinge of regret. He had overreached himself, he admitted resignedly to himself. Vishwamitra had routed him completely and had come out better in the conflict, and come out a better person as well. Unlike him, he had lost; lost his best people, lost their faith, lost the respect they had in him.

'We, your apsaras, my lord, were so made exclusively on that element of desire, and that was how our sensuous beauty was used,' said Menaka quietly. 'We accepted it as a part of us, as our work, as our profession and there was a voluntary affirmation of this religion given to us. For we were made to believe that our innate sexuality was associated with sacredness, it was not amoral. We were not to be concerned with principles of right and wrong. Nor were we to conform to standards of behaviour and character, we were free but we were to simply follow your orders even at the risk of our lives. We could not be killed but we could be destroyed, we could be stopped. We were vulnerable to curses and assaults, we could be burnt, cursed, turned into stones or monsters but we lived through all that and came to Heaven, back to the fold, taking the divine orders of seducing the next unsuspecting victim. Like all of us, Rambha too knew what she was getting into and what it implied. And she agreed, despite me warning her against it,' she added, watching Indra pursing his lips, his frown deepening. 'Yet she did go because she said this was duty; she had to do it. As the queen, she did not want to risk some other apsara to face Vishwamitra's wrath. She protected us. You are our king, my lord, should you not be protecting us too?'

Indra was at a loss of words, as he always did with Menaka. He could not outwit her in argument. It was with royal might and the powers as a king that he could subdue her. And that was what she was questioning now.

'A king besides throwing orders and expecting his subjects to obey, also defends them. That is his duty as well,' she continued, her face expressionless but a wealth of emotion loaded in each word she enunciated. Each was an accusation of his incompetence. 'Or are we your slaves?' she added tightly. 'To be used and thrown away, subjected to your random whim and royal orders? You ordered Vasu out of your Amravati, you ordered me to entrap Vishwamitra and now you sent Rambha to a certain death, knowing Vishwamitra would be provoked not into desire but a fit of anger to essentially dissolve his powers.'

Indra flushed hotly. Menaka had guessed his intention.

'Nor did you save her from being raped by Ravan! How could you allow him to go free for what he did?'

Indra's face went white, and then the blood rushed to his pale face. It was as if she had struck him, the imprint of it and its sting, lingering for long.

'Ravan had defeated us, we could not fight him. We were the lost side,' he muttered.

'And that assured him that he could take any apsara against her will in your very heavenly kingdom?' she taunted. 'Was that not violence, was that not an assault, was that not a crime? She was the queen of the apsaras, one of the most powerful women in

Indralok, yet you made her a victim of rape by a plunderer whom you allowed to roam free! You couldn't save her which as a king you should have. After your wars, we are the tokens of truce, a gift from the devas, trophies to be offered to the winners. You have used us in every possible way, my lord, even as distractions for the devas from their wives! Remember?' she mocked. 'The celestial star Tara preferred to live with her lover, Lord Chandra than return to her husband, Rishi Brihaspati, the guru of the devas. But he was hell bent on getting his wife back. Tara had refused to stay with a husband she did not love anymore, arguing she preferred to live with Chandra. In desperation, you had offered me to Chandra so that he would be deflected from his infatuation. But Chandra did not waver and remained with Tara and she was furious with you and me as well. How often are we to be your weapons of war, to pamper those mad ambitions! Which apsara do you intend to sacrifice next to propitiate your ego?'

The cold sharpness of her words seared through but the old desperate pride persisted.

He was defeated, but he told himself: 'I'm not going to lose!' But even in the final blow of his defeat, the contempt of it, Indra felt his arrogance resurface, remaining overpoweringly strong but warning him not to make a scene. His acute embarrassment of failure had more terror than force, it stifled cries of his frustrations, it even urged him to agree quietly.

But he wasn't running away, he had a plan. He would have to fight Vishwamitra himself, one day, face-to-face.

The Father, the Mother and the Daughter

Vishwamitra had not stirred out of his ashram for years. He had almost stopped breathing, and he had already given up food a long time back. The devas trembled with apprehension, knowing that Vishwamitra was capable of doing anything. But to become a Brahmarishi, Vishwamitra knew he had to master the meaning of brahman—the ultimate truth, the highest reality. Having attained this divine power, he could claim he was the ultimate expert in religion and spiritual knowledge. And he would not keep it to himself; he would collect and compile it as hymns or treatise to be handed down for generations of mankind.

Vasishth had a series of such hymns compiled in the Rigveda. He still had none, Vishwamitra acknowledged with a humble awareness of inadequacy. But he persevered and lapsed into a coma of profound, deep thought. All the devas seem to filter in his body, his mind assimilated the vidya of each. He could feel Agni, brahmana's reigning deity, the energy and the source of usable power; and also Shakti the spiritual strength, the life-giving breath. He felt calm, the flux of emotion and thought froze still, unmoving, constant. He felt himself shrinking, compressed and condensed to a particle. His self, his soul, the atman rushed eagerly towards the brahman, like a water droplet falling into a sea of water, the ripples churned into a vortex, yet there was a magical tranquillity, a calmness of sudden realization, the serene bliss of actualisation. Thoughts crystallized into a murmur of soft syllables 'aum'. And the rest flowed serenely.

> *Aum bhūr bhuva svaha*
> *tát savitúr várenyam*
> *bhárgo devásya dhīmahi*
> *dhíyo yó naha prachodáyāt*

(Let us worship the supremacy of that divine light,
The deva-head of truth and enlightenment who illuminates all, who recreates all,
From whom all shall proceed, to whom all must return,
Whom we invoke to direct our understanding aright
May he enlighten our minds, inspire our intelligence.)

He saw a light, a sliver of brightness, slowly expanding to a bright haze, almost blinding him, his eyes shut but open to the vision unfolding in front of him.

'Gayatri,' whispered Vishwamitra, recognizing the vision of the devis—Shakti, Durga, Saraswati, Lakshmi—the combined female source of the energy of the Creator, the Preserver and the Destroyer; the Maa Devi of them all.

'Gayatri,' he repeated. 'To you, oh mother, I devote this prayer—the Gayatri Mantra—meant for all and anyone, beyond the Vedas, yagna, charity and tap. This mantra is one of righteous wisdom, a prayer for oneself and his personal connection with devas. One does not need siddhi and sadhana, just the faith in this mantra, a faith in oneself.'

'You have created the mother of all veda, the core mantra of self-actualisation that shall benefit all forever,' she smiled. 'You have liberated knowledge from rules. This mantra is the worship of true knowledge you have made available to all. A deed none of the wisest have been able to achieve, a deed incomparable.'

Vishwamitra bowed his head, feeling a ripple of excitement going through him.

'But you are close to your goal,' she laughed softly, clearly reading his mind. 'To be a Brahmarishi like the wise and generous

Vasishth, you have but one hurdle—your ego. You *are* great, Vishwamitra, for you have achieved your greatness solely through merit. Temper it with some humility and compassion, and you can be the greatest. Until then...' she smiled as the light slowly faded away, but her words rang in his disappointed mind.

He was still not a Brahmarishi. He might have created another Heaven, created harmony and goodness with his new mantra, the ultimate blessing to mankind. But he was still not qualified. Vishwamitra turned calmly back to his meditation, the crease of his furrowed brows clearing to settle into a new determination. He will do it. He will be a Brahmarishi.

♦

What Menaka had dreaded through almost a lifetime was going to come true. She would have to meet her daughter; not glimpse her furtively through the hidden foliage of the woods, but confront her face-to-face. She gnawed at her lips, thinking of some way to escape from it. *Escape*, she sighed, *I have been running away from this eventuality since the day I had left my daughter in Kaushik's arms.*

But Rishi Kanva had arrived a few days back, scared and confused.

'You were right, Menaka!' he started disjointedly. 'Dushyant still has not returned!'

There was a turgid incoherence in his plea but Menaka drew her own, quick conclusion—Dushyant had deserted Shakuntala as she had feared.

'How has Shakuntala taken it?' she questioned anxiously.

'Bravely, but she won't tell me anything!' cried the perplexed father. 'She silently goes about her daily chores as if nothing untoward has happened.'

'Untoward?' repeated Menaka, with a frown.

'Oh, I forgot to mention this to you. Shakuntala is pregnant!'

It gets worse, Menaka grimaced, a spurt of anger welling up against this man she had not seen. A dastardly rake, her lips curled contemptuously, who was not worth her daughter.

'Please meet her, Menaka! She is stubborn and almost unseemly in her reaction. She refuses to meet the king and sort out matters. I tried telling her in so many ways, but she says she is content bringing up the child on her own, arguing as I had when she was a baby. But how can she? She is a child herself, Menaka. Oh, please come and talk to her! She needs her mother as never before, she needs to talk to a woman!!'

'...whom she trusts,' Menaka reminded him gently.

'Please, don't refuse this time!' implored the old man. It was a father in distress, more anxious than angry. 'You are her mother after all!' he added accusingly. 'She needs you, though both of you don't seem to see it!'

Menaka was unexpectedly stung at his words. She was a selfish woman, he seemed to chide, a selfish mother. That cut her to the core. She would have to meet her daughter; she could not avoid it any longer. It would be her trial, she knew, the fear was so strong that she could taste it in her dry mouth.

Menaka recalled her tempestuous meeting with Pramadvara, her other daughter as decisively abandoned as Shakuntala. But it had been a dying girl Menaka had held in her arms and her grief had given her the strength to take on even Lord Yama. But this time it would be so different. She would be facing the wrath of a spurned child—open and livid, the hostility fresh and face to face, masked by no lies, the truth welling out like an angry river.

Menaka stood outside the neat hut, willing herself to enter. Clenching her fists and her resolve, she did. It was spotless, as neat as the ashram outside. Again, it reminded Menaka of the small hut down by the river with Kaushik, their home had been as clean and orderly as this one.

'You are my mother.'

The curt statement took Menaka by surprise. Not the suddenness of it or the sharp, bitter veracity it contained, but more because Menaka had not seen the speaker till then. She turned sharply to her right to see her daughter standing tall and straight, not ungainly because of the soft swell of her belly, her tawny eyes looking unwaveringly upon her.

Menaka sucked in her breath. She felt like a thief, caught red-handed. The sight of her daughter heightened her dormant fear, flowing alive, hot and fervid, scalding her to force her to face the consequence of her most hard-hearted decision—deserting her daughter.

Menaka could merely nod, her lips parched, her voice and throat drying up painfully.

'Father told me that you had had reservations about Dushyant. He keeps telling me how wise and right you were!' started Shakuntala. 'But you would, wouldn't you? You know so much more about men.'

Menaka winced. The words hurtled at her were almost insulting, but Menaka was quick to catch the hidden disappointment in her daughter's voice.

'Do you intend telling Dushyant about his baby?' she asked instead, not mincing words of politeness, serving the matter the urgency it deserved.

'No.'

Menaka waited for her to expand on the short reply. Shakuntala remained silent.

'I agree,' said Menaka. The man did not deserve any truth.

Shakuntala smiled unpleasantly. 'Your opinion does not matter. I have mine which should suffice for both me and my baby. Just as you made the decision about me when I was a baby,' she reminded her bitingly, one brow raised.

Just like her father, Menaka realized with a pang, when he was in a belligerent mood.

Menaka bit her lip. She had lots to explain, but nothing to say.

'I can only ask for your forgiveness,' she said, her voice stronger than what she was going through. 'I don't expect it, but I hope for it someday.'

Menaka glanced at her daughter's unrelenting, defiant face. 'And you are not me. You are a far better person, and braver,' she added gently. 'I didn't have the courage to bring up a child on my own like you plan to do. Leaving you with Rishi Kanva was an easier option, I admit. But I don't regret that decision,' she sighed. 'You turned to be a finer person than what I could have.'

Shakuntala sneered, her lovely face distorted in open scorn. 'Words, however noble, cannot hide the cowardliness of the act.'

'As my daughter, would you have liked it better being a courtesan like me in the heavens?' asked Menaka brutally. 'An apsara?'

The colour drained out of Shakuntala's face, her eyes wide and shocked.

'That's why apsaras are not allowed to keep their children. Besides, mortals are forbidden in Heaven,' said Menaka. 'And you are a mortal, Shakuntala, a princess. You were deprived of our love but not our concern. By keeping you with Rishi Kanva, Kau... Vishwamitra wanted you to have the best—love, care, education, respect which we might not have been able to provide.'

'Then why have me?' demanded Shakuntala. 'If you knew you couldn't keep your child, why did you bear me? I am but a tainted fruit of lust!'

It was like a physical blow and Menaka reeled under the impact of the harsh words. The shock reached the pit of her stomach and she felt it tighten. She had to take in her daughter's savage rage. Shakuntala was standing stiff, very pale and her stare was all inward. Menaka doubted whether she saw her at all, so blind was her fury. But it appeared however that she was listening, and Menaka went on, 'Because I loved your father, and I wanted to have his child,' she said simply. 'I wanted a family. I wanted all of us to be together. I wanted...oh, so many things!' her voice faltered, but she quickly gathered herself. 'I understand what it means to have a child by the man you love. But I didn't understand it till I loved the man...'

'You loved Vishwavasu too,' lashed Shakuntala, vehemently. 'And you had a child from him as well—your first daughter Pramadvara,' she reminded her caustically.

'...whom I was forced to forsake too,' explained Menaka, her eyes steady. 'Vasu was taken away from me. I had no one, that's why probably I yearned again for love, a family, for another child, a child from your father. But the fact is that I had a child from a man I loved but could not keep...' she trailed off, glancing at her daughter's glacial expression.

Shakuntala turned her dark, abstracted gaze towards her and spoke in a tone of feeble sarcasm, 'Go on!' she hissed out the word venomously. 'It is a great revelation to me, this long talk from such an experienced woman of ...er...emotions.'

Menaka was in a trough of exhaustion. She felt so tired, and all of a sudden that fatigue was like a whirlpool, pulling her down, dragging her arms and legs in a swirl of weary pain. She sank slowly onto a stool, fighting waves of tiredness.

'But it was not to be. I was a foolish woman. You are not, Shakuntala...' Menaka stopped.

Shakuntala nodded but Menaka could not make out whether she agreed with what she had said or whether it was a thought so obvious she did not want to hear it said.

Shakuntala gave her a twisted smile. 'I think that however smart a woman may be, a woman in love is a foolish woman. I am. But were you? You seduced my father; it was you who deceived him. You left him and me.'

Menaka flinched at the savage bluntness. 'I had to. For his good and yours as well,' she said simply, drained of further justification. 'As I said earlier, you are a braver person than I was.'

She watched Shakuntala, hoping her words would calm her. Shakuntala had turned her face away, trying to breathe deeply. She added softly, almost a whisper, not meaning to say it, 'I loved him.' It was an appeal.

Shakuntala's voice grew louder. 'But he didn't. He used me and left me,' she said bitterly. 'And I stupidly trusted him to have his child, with the hope that our son would be the heir which he agreed and promised to do. It was on that one condition I allowed him to touch me!'

Menaka gave her daughter a look of utter amazement. 'You made him promise that? You made love to him on that single assurance?'

'Yes!' her daughter retorted spiritedly. 'I needed some sort of a surety! Something that would make him assume responsibility, not just a secret marriage...'

'But if he didn't keep his word of returning and declaring you his wife, what assurance do you have that he will acknowledge this child?' asked Menaka, bewilderment giving way to anxiety.

'I know he won't, that's why I would rather keep the child and bring him up on my own,' answered Shakuntala with a grace Menaka could but only admire.

'Do you realize it's not going to be easy'

'Nothing really is. Was it easy for you to give up your child? Was it easy for me growing up without you?'

Menaka made an impatient movement. 'Your decision is momentous and exceptional, but mine wasn't. It was an act of cowardice, not owning up to my actions, my responsibilities, which is why probably, I let go of you too easily. Yours will take enormous, uncommon courage, as you will be taking on the world, Shakuntala. No woman has dared to do this before. You would be the first mother to single-handedly bring up her child on her own.'

'I shall be his father and mother,' said Shakuntala defiantly. 'He shall never feel unwanted, orphaned in the world I shall bring him into.'

Menaka grimaced. Every word was like a barb, questioning her credentials as a mother.

'I am not out to prove anything,' said Shakuntala more quietly. 'I simply don't want to disown my child or go to a father who refuses to acknowledge me as his wife. If he can't return to his wife, will he accept our child? I don't need him. Dushyant is the son of the famous King Ilina and Rathantara, and the kingdom he inherited from his father is believed to be panning from Gandhar to the Vindhyas and from Sindhu to Banga. But I don't want his wealth or his status. I want nothing for myself! But for my child, I shall fight when necessary...' her eyes flared momentarily with a tawny glow, which reminded Menaka a chisky of Kaushik.

'If he doesn't love me enough to make me his wife, his queen, so be it. Having taken his pleasure with me, he did not find it necessary to keep his word. Is a lie, told while making love, supposed to be excusable?' she asked artlessly.

'No, it shows the truth of the person,' replied Menaka, moved by her daughter's astuteness.

'Surely enough, the fact that he never returned proves it. He deserted me and I shall not beg for acknowledgement. I shall not go to him and convince him otherwise. Never!' she said fiercely, angry pride shining in her golden eyes like her father.

'Not even for your child?' asked Menaka acutely.

'For my child, I would do anything!' she shot back furiously. 'As a wife, I don't want to be his queen but yes, as a mother, I shall not allow my child be usurped of his rights.'

Menaka saw her daughter in a new light. She was not a naive sentimentalist and had not got carried away by Dushyant's flattery after all. She had validated her self-choice of her secret marriage by making him accept her condition before she allowed him to make love to her. Her son would be king, her daughter a princess, neither abandoned nor rejected. And that single demand demonstrated her wariness as well as her shrewdness concerning the first man she had met in her life. With a foresight that deceived her age, she had quickly grabbed the opportunity through the child she might conceive, assuring it of his royal inheritance. Yet the girl in Shakuntala had not been impressed by his royal lineage to submit to his seduction blindly. She had ensured that she did not get relegated as his paramour or worse, his mistress, but be considered his wife, a queen. She had turned his momentary weakness into a life-long relationship for her and her child, strictly legitimate.

Menaka realized she barely knew her daughter to sufficiently understand her. Possibly, Shakuntala had never allowed herself to forget that she was an orphan, the fear relentlessly haunting her, making her promise herself that she did not ever wish the same for her child. Shakuntala had been extremely careful of her position, unimpressed and not deluded by the unctuous attention of a royal playboy. She treated him never as a superior. He might be a king but so was she of royal blood, tempered with the sagacity of the seers. Menaka was astounded by her daughter's astute intelligence.

'When the day comes, I shall confront him if need be,' said Shakuntala quietly. 'But not now...I...'

'Then come with me to Indralok,' urged Menaka. 'I shall look after you and the child. If it's a boy, he shall be trained by all the devas to be a warrior, like a prince should...'

'And what if it's a girl?' asked Shakuntala softly, and Menaka heard a trace of uncertainty in her voice. Menaka felt a frantic need to protect her daughter, shelter her from the worst.

'She will be a princess, learned in art and warfare. Not an apsara!' assured Menaka quickly. 'I couldn't do it for my daughter, but for my daughter's child, I will provide the best!' She could well imagine Indra's consternation but she would fight him again if she had to.

Shakuntala shook her head. 'But aren't mortals forbidden in Heaven?' It was a statement, not a question. 'No, Mother, don't worry about me, I am happier here.'

Menaka held her breath, not daring to breathe, not daring to believe her ears, her heart contracting in sweet pain and then bursting with immeasurable joy. She barely heard the rest of the sentence. Her daughter had called her 'mother'. It was like a sprinkle of water on parched earth, soaking in every drop for her sustenance, quenching her long desired thirst. Menaka felt a strange calm settle in her heart, her mind nourished with renewed hope. She was her daughter's mother at last.

'I am a child of the forest, Mother,' explained Shakuntala. 'Here, we are ruled by the instinct of survival, of free will. We know the beauty and horror of Nature, it's power and its preservation. We respect it and we revere it. And it has made me strong. I really don't know your world, or what's outside this jungle and am not accustomed to the rules of society. In that world, possibly having a child without the father is a slur. I consider it my right, my choice. I want to bring my child to the world which I belong, not a society of unfair mores. We forest-dwellers follow our own regulations. You know that, mother, you have experienced it too. I met a man, fell in love with him and gave myself to him in all trust and pleasure. He did not reciprocate, he ran away. But now I shall have his child solely for myself. Not because it is expected of me. Not because it is not done. It is neither an act of rebellion nor an appeasement. It's an option I choose for myself. From a girl, I became a woman and now shall soon be a mother. It's my decision and I want it as I would have wanted it. I would rather stay in the forest and make my child a warrior and scholar, be it a girl or a boy, better than any prince or princess in the kingdom!' she said proudly. 'And for that he doesn't need his father's legacy. He shall do so on his own merit like his grandfather Vishwamitra did!'

Menaka's heart contracted. Her words echoed of Kaushik's prophecy of his grandchild. Would it come true? Would their daughter's child be the founder king of a huge nation? Menaka gazed at her daughter and again in her, Menaka saw the fierce obduracy of her father. Yet she was sensible and self-assured enough to fight for her rights, blessed with an innate wisdom to plan out her future and her child's, and fight for its legitimate inheritance, all without help from anyone. Rishi Kanva was wrong; Shakuntala did not need her mother. Shakuntala did not need anyone, as long she had her child. Her child, Menaka knew, would always be her weakness.

'And anyway, am I not a princess too, Mother?' smiled Shakuntala. 'And when I have my child, I want my child to grow up in the palace, as the son of a princess should! I shall not desert my baby for societal conventions I don't care to know!'

Menaka kept silent; she had got her answer. She had wondered why her daughter had given herself so easily to Dushyant without waiting for Rishi Kanva to return. She knew now. It was the same insecurity of being an abandoned child. She had fallen in love and wanted to have him at all cost. In Dushyant she saw romance and a reprieve. His royalty was an assurance of her child's future, unlike what had been hers. Although being a princess, a royal child of the king-rishi Vishwamitra, she had been made to grow up innocuously in an ashram. She was adored by

Kanva and the others, but she never let herself forget that she was a foundling, belonging to none. She did not want the same fate for her child. And to ascertain that, she wanted to marry the right man. Dushyant was her answer to her prayers. The man she fell in love with at first sight. Insecurities did make us do strange things. Menaka could not rid herself with another thought, it was because of her that her daughter nursed it. It was a questionable legacy a mother had bestowed on her daughter.

Ignorance and Enlightenment

$\mathcal{V}$ishwamitra thought he heard a cry for help. It was not a cry, almost a hoarse whisper of a dying man. Vishwamitra was startled; frowning, he thought *was the man dying?* The thought forced Vishwamitra to open his eyes and look around him. He did not notice him at first, but then looked down to see an emaciated, weeping man was almost grovelling at his feet.

'Help me, please! I need some water!' he whimpered, his breath coming in short gasps.

Vishwamitra quickly emptied the water from his small kamandalam, into the trembling, open mouth of the prostrate man. The lips were cracked, bleeding through the deep dry welts. His tongue was curled and snaked out eagerly as the first drop of water fell on it. Vishwamitra saw that the man was a priest, poor and grimy, and his clothes torn. Clearly, he had fallen on bad days. He was thirsty but drinking the water slowly and carefully, not allowing a single drop to trickle down to get wasted. He finally finished drinking, relishing the last drop as much as the first and handed the empty pitcher back into his hands. The water seemed to have given him some vestige of strength..

'I am forever indebted to you, o kind rishi, you saved my life!' he croaked, his words still hoarse, but getting stronger with every word he uttered. He paused and took a deep breath, a hesitant look hovering in his tired eyes.

'May I have some food?' he asked, tentatively. 'I am hungry. I haven't had food in the last ten days.'

Vishwamitra nodded. He pulled up the plate, his disciple left for him every day, with the hope that he would break his fast and have a morsel. The plate was full but the food was frugal— herbs, fruit and a little rice and dal.

The old brahmin was about to snatch a morsel, when he looked at his filthy, calloused hands and the grubby nails.

'I cannot eat without washing my hands,' he said.

Vishwamitra patted his hand. 'All the water I had in the kamandalam is finished. But there is a river nearby...' he said, pointing behind the man's stooped back. 'You can have a wash there. But do you have the strength to do that?' asked Vishwamitra dubiously.

'Cleanliness is paramount. A clean body helps clean the mind. It's the first step to enlightenment,' said the man, while struggling to get up.

Vishwamitra took his hands and helped him up. The man swayed slightly, but straightened his slight shoulders and took a determined step towards the river.

'Come quickly or the food will go cold,' Vishwamitra called after him.

The man nodded and quickened his steps.

Vishwamitra looked at the food. He felt nothing, not the faintest pang of hunger. He sighed and muttered to himself and got back to his meditation.

The man carefully washed his hand, scraping each nail clean, rubbing his palms strongly to rinse out the filth and washing the entire length of his arms clean. Then he looked at his feet. They were worse. He washed them thoroughly, generously splashing water over his thin, trembling legs. He felt a lot cleaner.

He turned back towards the rishi. He still felt slightly weak and took some time reaching the huge banyan tree under which Vishwamitra sat. He saw the plate and was surprised to feel the food still hot. His mouth watered and he quickly gobbled down the food. Satiated and full, he looked at the rishi at last to voice his gratitude again, when he noticed the closed eyes of the rishi. He was back to his meditation, his eyes shut in deep contemplation.

The old man stared at the rishi, wondering what he should do now. He touched the other mam's aim, not lightly but almost prodding him.

Vishwamitra did not respond immediately. He felt another shake at his left shoulder. He slowly opened his eyes to see the man standing before him.

'Welcome, Devendra,' said Vishwamitra, with a quiet smile on his lips. 'Hope the weather on Earth was kind to you.'

The man was startled. His fingers closed in a fist and rested them on his hips, as was his habit. Indra gave Vishwamitra a look of utter exasperation. This man had beaten him at every step, each time proving his superiority over him. He had been outmanoeuvred, again but Indra could not bring himself to acknowledge trounce.

'You are not defeated, o king of the devas,' said Vishwamitra.

Indra looked annoyed, but didn't say anything.

'You were but doing your duty. You had to protect your Heaven, as I protected my interests,' continued Vishwamitra calmly.

Indra looked at Vishwamitra in disbelief. There was not a trace of anger in his voice, nor a furrow of irritation on his serene face. Vishwamitra had won his final test. He had not just won over his hunger or his basic needs, but he had full control of his mind, even his treacherous anger. Indra had tried to trick him to make him lose his temper as he often easily did. But Vishwamitra had not caught the bait, as he had once with Menaka. But Vishwamitra had survived the betrayal and come out stronger. He had neither ranted or raved or languished away a broken hearted loser, as Indra had wrongly assumed. By sending Rambha, Indra had hoped that Vishwamitra would succumb to anger and curse her and undo his years of penance.

But not this time, as Indra looked into the calm eyes of the rishi. The great rishi, Indra corrected himself mentally. The man who had challenged the devas, carved his own Heaven, threatened to install its own Indra, forced the devas to descend on Earth to attend to whichever yagna he so desired, changed the equation between Man and Deva, mortality versus immortality. He had fought the holy rishis for his right for knowledge and acquired it through aggressive perseverance. And finally, in his quest of being the Brahmarishi, he had created the Gayatri Mantra, bequeathing the name of the divine entity in the content itself; the meter in the verse so composed so as to enlighten and bless the whole of mankind. Vishwamitra was the first among his exalted peers to have understood the actual brilliance and meaning of the 'Gayatri' and created a mantra from his knowledge to share it with the world, even the most common and the poorest man. The mantra was meant for all the faithful, not a prerogative of the privileged. Again, he had bestowed a larger good to the world, proving to a class-driven world, that virtue always won over vantage.

And for the first time, Indra felt a shiver of fear snaking through him. He, Lord Indra, the king of devas was at the mercy of the greatest rishi living in the universe. In that long, drawn out moment, Indra accepted his defeat, accepting finally the greatness of this man, the mortal he had vowed to vanquish. Indra grudgingly realized that the rishi had powers greater than his, and that he could not stop him anymore. Indra wanted to rush back home, in the safe precincts of his Indralok, but fear and dejection rooted him to where he stood standing still, uncertain and surrendered. What would Vishwamitra do to him now?

Vishwamitra felt a strong, enormous power flow through him, as he realized that he was finally in complete control of himself. He cast Indra a curious glance, the one who had given him immeasurable grief and clashed with so often; the one who had made him lose his Menaka forever. Vishwamitra momentarily closed his eyes, welcoming the wave of calmness to assuage him. But then, it was because of Indra that he had met Menaka, if not by chance, by connivance. She was a quiescent sentiment now, soothing yet nourishing his soul. He had irretrievably lost her, but she lived indelibly in him. Indra could never snatch that from him.

Vishwamitra's face remained unperturbed, even as the emotions surged through him. 'I am most honoured to meet you face-to-face, Devendra, albeit in disguise,' said Vishwamitra, glancing at Indra's true form.

'I should have guessed you knew when you kept the food hot for me and got back to your meditation,' shrugged Indra. 'You preferred not to challenge me or did you not wish for a confrontation?'

'What is it that you wish to fight for now?' asked Vishwamitra evenly. 'I don't need your Heaven, Indra. You tried to break me in several ways, several times. It was a test of wills. But yes, you did succeed in breaking my concentration again today though for which you must have a good reason, again,' he added good-humouredly.

'What do I say, yes, am guilty as charged,' acceded the divine king, his handsome face crumpled in surrender. 'And I bow to you, sir, in all humility and shame, for I have done you wrong.'

'I forgive you,' said Vishwamitra. 'As Menaka once warned me, I shan't waste my curse on you.'

He saw Indra flinch at Menaka's name. 'You caused me a lot of grief, but what you did to Menaka was wicked,' said Vishwamitra quietly, a nerve twitching in his cheek. 'I should punish you for it but I shall listen to my Menaka's good advice, though you don't deserve her kindness. I am not sure if you have learnt your lesson though. You play games too often, playing with too many lives. One day, it'll come back to haunt you or worse, dethrone you from your divine stature. Beware, Devendra, beware. You are your own enemy.'

Indra missed the significance of the statement, so relieved was he that the mighty rishi had not laid a curse on him. He sighed with evident respite. 'Hindering you was not my sole motive, sir,' he explained hastily. 'I am here as a messenger as well, or rather, as a mediator.'

Vishwamitra remained silent, allowing Indra to continue.

'You are near your objective; you are almost a Brahmarishi now. All the devas and even the triumvirate acknowledge it...'

'I am humbled,' interrupted Vishwamitra. 'But I await the great Rishi Vasisth's blessings. I wish his acknowledgement. That would be my humblest, my supreme moment—to be granted that status by the best himself.'

'He cannot come to you. He is too deep in sorrow with the death of all his sons...' said Indra, watching Vishwamitra slyly.

Vishwamitra clenched his jaw.

'I hear that you were in some way responsible for their deaths...' insinuated Indra, his tone disingenuous.

'Don't ferment trouble, you rabble-rouser,' warned Vishwamitra, without raising his voice. But his eyes were hooded, his lips pursed in a thin, unhappy line. Indra's innuendo was not unjustified. He *had* been responsible for the death of Vasishth's sons. It had happened so unexpectedly, that he had not been able to control the sudden tragic turn of events.

The Ikshvaku king Saudasa, also called Kalmashapad, while traveling through a forest, encountered a young rishi. The path was unusually narrow to allow just one and the king assumed the ascetic would make way for his chariot to pass. But Rishi Shakti, the hot-tempered eldest son of Vasishth, thought otherwise and argued that a warrior should give way to the rishi, conforming to the social hierarchy. Furious, the king lashed at Shakti with his horse-whip. More humiliated than hurt, Shakti cursed the king, changing him to a flesh-eating asura. Before he could realize the danger of his folly, Shakti was devoured by the monster he had created through that curse. Hungry for more, the asura tracked down the other sons of Vasishth and killed them all.

Long before the incident had occurred, Vasishth and Vishwamitra were embroiled in a power struggle for the coveted title of the rajpurohit, the position of the royal priest. Vasishth was the appointed royal priest, but King Saudas was none too pleased with him and was contemplating selecting another, preferably Vishwamitra, and while he pondered over his decision, the king further aggravated the hostility between them.

On that fateful day, Vishwamitra was passing by the same forest, witnessed the brawl and saw an opportunity to get back at Vasishth and King Saudas. Hearing the two young men quarrelling, he had stopped to watch silently, behind a tree, reluctant to mediate and diffusing the tension. He had not gauged it would to end in the mass murder. He could have prevented it, had he intervened on time.

Indra was observing him carefully. 'With all his sons dead, Vasishth is prostrate with grief. Lost to sorrow, he has given up food and water, and is preparing for samadhi, imploring the holy waters of the River Saraswati, to carry him away,' he paused, at the shocked concern on Vishwamitra's face.

'Is he that unwell?' muttered Vishwamitra, frowning hard. It was the first time Vishwamitra felt any empathy with the old rishi, his most formidable rival. But revenge was diverse an emotion, lapping in its vortex anger, jealousy, pain, everything perverse and destructive. The suddenness of the double tragedy had shaken Vishwamitra. Their war had gone on too long, too bloody. It had to end.

Indra noticed the look of determination on Vishwamitra's face. 'If there is still a last shred of misgivings for Rishi Vasishth...' he started to be abruptly interrupted by Vishwamitra.

'Don't instigate, Indra! You have done enough damage,' cautioned Vishwamitra again, his voice tight. 'You have gone too far every time, but each time the devas and the others have been too kind to you. Frankly, you don't deserve to be a deva, forget the king of gdevas. Let me say this Devendra, you are worse than Man. Wily and malicious even to your own people,' he accentuated, his eyes narrowing. 'You don't just use them, you abuse them.'

Indra felt the blood rush to his face. Vishwamitra clearly meant Menaka and how Indra had shamelessly used her against him. Indra's heart constricted, panic flooding him again.

'And you are dangerous only because of the power you represent, the power consented upon you. Take care of it, because without it, you are nothing. Not even a lesser mortal!'

Scorn dripped from every word. Indra's fair face turned a mottled crimson. He had tried to incite Vishwamitra to anger as a last bid, but he had been thoroughly castigated himself.

Vishwamitra was not done. 'You pride yourself in being divine, don't you, Indra?' he said, his voice dangerously soft. 'It is your crowning glory. But Man has it in him too; he just does not realize it. It is deep down inside him, buried in his vanity, ego, pride and greed. But he has to seek it, find it himself and search for it. And through that search, he discovers himself. When each man finds his divinity, Earth will become Heaven. But that is what you do not want, and that is why you strived so hard to stop me from attaining my goal, and my divinity, as you prefer to call it,' he said testily. 'You have yours, Indra, hope you can retain it.'

The silence was not the only chasm between them. Indra knew each word Vishwamitra had uttered could be an omen for him. Looking suitably subdued, he said hastily, 'I am but a messenger today, sir. I was to let you know about Rishi Vasishth. Now I take your leave,' he added stiffly.

Vishwamitra smiled, he knew Indra disliked people who were superior to him. *It was a petulant reaction but then, Indra was incorrigibly immature to tackle any situation or serious sentiment, incapable of finer wisdom*, sighed Vishwamitra as he treaded his way along the long path to Vasishth's ashram.

The moment he reached the cool valley, Vishwamitra spotted the ashram, nestled within the snowy folds of the Himalayas. As the cold air stung his craggy face, Vishwamitra felt a sense of familiarity to the place and the situation. *Here it was where it had all begun. The game of power, the clash of honour and pride, our empty, angry words falling on deaf ears, yet aggrandising our egos. It had led to war and bloodshed, grief and gore, ruin and regret. Their venom and vitriol had flowed long and strong, spilling onto innocent lives as well.*

As Vishwamitra approached the hermitage, Vasishth's students stared at him with trepidation. *What now? Would there be a bloody battle again? Would Vishwamitra attack a dying, bed-ridden old man?*

Vishwamitra politely asked to be led to the rishi. A white-faced student directed him to Vasishth's hut. The moment he entered the small, airy room, there was a stunned silence.

Vishwamitra did not know where to look, especially avoiding the misty, aged eyes of Arundhati. He would have to gather courage to face her or bear her accusation. She was a mother mourning the death of her sons but right now she looked more worried about her sick husband. She was placing a compress on his fevered head, ignoring Vishwamitra's presence in the room. Possibly that was her way of showing her resentment for him. Vishwamitra could barely glance at Shakti's young widow, Adrsyanti, cradling her baby in her arms. But the baby was smiling beatifically, his brown eyes already shining with innate wisdom.

'What's his name?' he asked quietly.

'Parasher,' replied the mother uncertainly, looking at him with frantic eyes.

'Please don't fear me, lady, forgive me if you can,' started Vishwamitra, a hard lump in his throat, but he placed his hand on the baby's head and blessed him. 'He shall grow into a famous rishi and his son more so. He shall be remembered for thousands of years for his exceptional literary achievements.'

Vishwamitra heard Vasishth give a weak chuckle. 'You are talking about Vyas, aren't you? Telling us about our future! When did you get into fortune telling, Vishwamitra?'

His humour was still intact, smiled Vishwamitra to himself as he ventured close to the narrow, coir bed where the rishi was resting. He looked wan, his wrinkled face as dry as the bark leaves on which he wrote the scriptures. But his eyes, weary and stricken, still shone with an inner knowledge.

'I come in all humbleness, great sire. And regret. I come here to ask your forgiveness,' stated Vishwamitra, the sight of the ailing rishi robbing of him of speech momentarily. Is that what he had done to this man? And Vishwamitra was forced to concede to another ugly truth about himself that he was the cause of this man's plight.

Vasishth managed a weak smile. 'Aha, you have arrived at

last...' he croaked, his voice as dry as coarse sand. 'I have been waiting for you.'

Both Vishwamitra and Arundhati looked startled. Vishwamitra broke the short, thick ensuing silence with a perplexed query. 'Were you waiting to forgive me?' he said hopefully.

'You don't need my forgiveness, you want my blessings,' replied Vasishth, flatly. 'You had to come back to face your enemy,' he smiled weakly, 'and your demons. You had to show me how great you have become through all these years...'

'No, no, I haven't come here to flaunt or seek revenge! Forgive me, sir, my stubborn pride has inflicted more harm than good to everyone...'

'Forgiveness for what?'

'I am responsible for the death of your sons,' said Vishwamitra, in a cracked whisper.

'My sons died the death they deserved,' said Vasishth. 'It was wrong of Shakti to have cursed King Saudas in his rage of arrogance. He turned Saudas into a cannibal, and he became his first victim. He created the monster which eventually killed him and his brothers. That is what often Man often does, though he never seems to realize it. And often the monster lies within him...' he sighed.

'There was a monster in me too,' said Vishwamitra slowly. 'And I am responsible for that!' he blurted the guilt tearing into him again. 'As I was for your sons' death. I could have stopped the cannibal from devouring them, but my irrational desire for revenge stopped me!' he choked, shame stifling further words. 'Forgive me, sir, forgive me, if I am worth being pardoned for I have committed the worst crime, bloody and dastardly.'

Arundhati made a movement. Vishwamitra looked at her with imploring eyes. 'Don't curse me, mother!'

Her gentle eyes flared with pain, slowly fading to a dull glow, her eyes bright with unshed tears. 'If this is what was meant to be, so be it. Let them rest in peace,' she murmured, her face lined with elegant grief. 'And so should we. I have no anger or hatred towards you, Vishwamitra, for you were just a catalyst in things to happen. You came to our ashram once as a guest and lots of bitter water has flowed since then. But, today, you are here again and with different intentions. I honour you.'

'Do not make me feel more ashamed of myself. Please do not honour me as your guest but as a culprit, who has come here to beg for forgiveness...'

'I have already forgiven you,' said Vasishth. 'For I know that your actions were not just an outcome of our enmity, it was your anger against the injustice inflicted upon you by me and the rishis, by denying you the right to knowledge and wisdom. It is not the perquisite of us rishis but others as well. Be it a warrior, a king, a merchant or a sweeper, education should be universal, not limited to class and colour, the fortunate and the famous, the moneyed and the mighty alone. You showed the light of this path that is right. I learned my lesson too and you taught me where I went wrong. Knowledge cannot be denied to anyone. And so is forgiveness, son. Why just you, I have forgiven King Saudas too. He was not responsible for his deeds, Shakti was. When I met Saudas, I broke the curse and set him free. I am sure he shall rule is kingdom justly, and never insult anyone anymore, be it a rishi or a beggar. For a king, all subjects are alike, isn't it so, Vishwamitra? You told me that once, remember?'

Vishwamitra bowed his head. 'I would add further—treating all with compassion and respect distinguishes a man from a monster. And you made me a man again, sir. Please do not forsake your life for all what I have done. Live again and break this stubborn fast of yours. I beseech you to take some food. You cannot give up!'

Vishwamitra poured some water in a brass glass and took it to the frail rishi's quivering lips. He sipped slowly.

'I have had a long life, son,' breathed the elderly rishi, resting his head back on the pillow. His pale, transparent skin was covered in fine gauze of wrinkles, each one recounting an epoch of wisdom and philosophy. His eyes shone with a dull brightness, the innate specks of knowledge glittering from within. 'My sons have gone, but the knowledge and the legacy of my thoughts has been passed to my disciples. That is how knowledge shall spread—by them. It doesn't have to be through our off-springs, does it, Vishwamitra?' he questioned with a knowing smile. 'You should know better. You did it. You don't need sons to carry your lineage, your own integrity carries on the good name. You disowned your sons as they were worthless and instead chose your nephew Shunasef and all your disciples to spread your word to the people.'

'I was not worthy too,' said Vishwamitra softly. 'How can I forget that I deserted Hemavati, and my innocent Shakuntala? That I never understood Menaka for how noble she was?' interrupted Vishwamitra, the anguish raw in his voice. 'I have been cruel to all the women in my life. How can they ever forgive me? How can I ever forgive myself?'

'You shall atone for it; your day of reckoning with them will come to pass too,' smiled the old rishi. 'You left Hemavati for yourself, but Menaka left you for your own good. You abandoned your family for your selfish reasons; Menaka forsook you out of selflessness. That realization is your remorse, your penitence is your penance. Vishwamitra, you are your own teacher, your learnt from your mistakes. You were not a rebel, you were a true liberal. You did not fight because you were provoked, but because you were thwarted. For you, gaining knowledge was a free right, entitled to every man on Earth. That is why you challenged me, you challenged the rishis, Indra and the devas. You were defying a system that says you are not born a brahmin but have to earn it. And you did it, Vishwamitra. You showed the world, the devas, and all of mankind that merit outshines entitlement. And for that, all shall always be indebted to you, o Brahmarishi Vishwamitra!'

Vishwamitra started. He was too stunned to comprehend Vasishth's words.

'Yes, you became a Brahmarishi a long time ago, Vishwamitra, you just did not realize it. You wanted more,' smiled Vasishtha.

A swift look of disbelief crossed Vishwamitra's face. He was dumbfounded.

'You were always a famous and a great king, the regenerate

warrior, but your single-mindedness conquered all—the world and the Heavens, and lastly, yourself,' said Vasishth. 'You vanquished all. But it took a while to overcome your pride and anger,' continued Vasishth, gathering strength as he spoke, '...and each test I hurled at you, you lost but came out more determined to reach the top...'

Vishwamitra threw him a look of surprise. Vasishth's show of strength and supremacy had been pretence?

As if tracing his line of bewildered thought, the old rishi spoke aloud, 'Or how else would you have met your own challenge?' he said gently. 'You are a rare person, Vishwamitra. You were a king, a mighty, famous, good and prosperous king—an emperor could be a better word—but you dared to do the unthinkable, which is gain knowledge. You had power and prestige but you sought a higher version of it. And you persevered. You battled. You won some, you lost a lot, but you never gave up. This determination was powered by a will to succeed and through it arose the wisdom you were lacking. You have it now, Vishwamita. You have it all. Believe it, you are now a Brahmarishi, the wisest and the most powerful of all.'

Again a sudden silence descended in the room and in his heaving mind, but the words kept echoing in his ears. Vishwamitra heard them in abject wonder, the words he had battled so long and hard for. Brahmarishi Vasishth himself was declaring that he, Vishwamitra was now one like him. His words took time to sink in. But as they percolated through his numb mind, Vishwamitra realized he felt nothing. There was no sense of elation, of triumph, or a certain thrill of achievement. The words were but words, and it fell on him, bouncing off without affecting him.

'You *are* a Brahmarishi, Vishwamitra, rejoice!' said Vasishth and as if by cue, the gusty wind outside blew a shower of flowers in the room. 'The devas have acknowledged it and so have Brahma, Vishnu and Shiva. Do you not feel it?' he asked tenderly.

Vishwamitra closed his eyes, he saw a calm before him as it always did and through it he saw the holy trinity blessing him. And then he felt it. An acute, deep overwhelming emotion of humility; a certain subdued submission of one's self to a larger, higher consciousness.

Vasishth folded his hands in salutation. Vishwamitra felt a lump in his throat watching this great man bowing before him. Vishwamitra threw himself at the old rishi's feet. It was his last surrender to the man who had made him what he had aspired so long to be. But through the happy haze, a sneaking cold evasive thought crept up, making him wince. He would not be what he was today but for her, for Menaka.

Failed and Fulfilled

*M*enaka was perplexed by the news she had just received. *Why had Rishi Kanva called for me now? It must be concerning Shakuntala again, or Bharat.* Menaka's forehead creased in a slight frown, thinking hard. Her grandson rarely fell sick. He was a sturdy adolescent, cheerful and strong, very tall for his age, an all-round warrior having mastered all four types of mace fighting and excelling at elephant and horse riding. *He would be,* smiled Menaka fondly, *having teachers like Indra, Surya and Varun as his teachers besides Rishi Kanva, who had acquainted him with the Vedas and the Upanishads like he once had groomed Shakuntala.* And having been raised in the forest, he moved around with the wild animals, fearless and agile. He rode the wild animals and often made a sport of opening the mouths of lions and tigers in order to count their teeth, much to Shakuntala's annoyance.

'Animals are not for sport, and hunting them is devious if not dastardly!' she scolded, her eyes glittering with anger.

'It's Man's mindless bloodlust which they term as royal leisure, dear, get used to it...' Menaka had reminded her. 'You are now the Queen of Hastinapur!'

Menaka had reached Rishi Kanva's ashram. It was as quiet and charming as always, the River Malini gurgling softly, the flowers still in full bloom, the young rishis of the ashram going about their work efficiently. Menaka bit her lip and wondered if Rishi Kanva was unwell. She entered his hut and stood still, a small gasp freezing in her throat, her face white, leaked of colour.

'Don't faint on me, please, or can apsaras faint?'

That voice with distinctive, deep baritone with gravelly, measured tones, which still echoed in her memory, reliving each talk they had. This was no dream. It was him. Standing as tall as he always did, the added years had not allowed his broad shoulder to stoop, though they had left their mark on his hard, hewn face. It was again well-hidden by a luxuriant beard, elegantly grey-streaked now. But his eyes were the same, twinkling with sardonic humour making his otherwise dull, tawny eyes sparkle; and so was that blood-thumping, heart-wrenching smile.

It was as if time had stretched, prolonging the moment to a lifetime. The words clogged in her constricted throat, thick with un-felled tears. She could only stare back at him, her thirsty eyes drinking in the sight. She dared not blink, dreading he would vanish away like a mirage, so illusory and unattainable was he.

Gradually she felt the strength seeping back into her weak legs, her thudding heart beating at a more sedate pace, her skin, still pale and glistening. She still did not trust herself to speak, scared that a mere whimper might break the spell. It was not the dream, which had visited her every day, through the waking hours and sleepless night hours. He was here. *He had come to meet me*, her dancing heart wildly sang to her. He did not hate her, he was not angry with her, for she saw not a hint of either in his soft, mellowed eyes, but just love.

Menaka dug her teeth into her trembling lips, to steady them. She would not cry, she had never cried in front of him and now would be no exception. She walked slowly towards him, still unable to believe her dazed eyes and as she approached him, he seemed to change. It wasn't Kaushik standing and waiting for her anymore, it was Vasu, his golden eyes warm and smiling...

Menaka gasped. She gave a start and found herself awake, her eyes wide open, giddy and afraid, staring at the sway of the glistening ceiling, grappling with the image just shattered. *It had been a dream after all*, she sighed, still trembling. Menaka sat up slowly, her heart beating wildly. Kaushik and Vasu, again. *Why do they keep intruding her dreams, into her inner most consciousness,* she thought wretchedly. *When would I attain peace again?*

'You are up late today. Should we go for our dance practice?' she heard Tilottama enter her chamber. 'As the queen, you can give it a miss!'

Menaka was still disoriented, missing the playful jibe. But she was genuinely surprised to see her friend.

'Did you not go with the others for the wedding of Ram and Sita?' she muttered, expelling the last vestige of sleep and the lingering dream from her mind.

'There were already so many of us going, I decided to stay put, like you.'

'Another chance to fan the rumours about us!'

Tilottama shrugged her slight shoulders. 'Rambha viciously started it when I spoke for you against Tumburu. And since I am unattached, without some gandharva chasing me or me hot after some deva, makes it all the more...er...seem correct!' chuckled Tilottama. 'Anyway, they will be more excited about this wedding right now. The whole of Amravati is down there at Mithila now!'

'Are they? Did Kama and the others survive the previous nights' orgy?' asked Menaka dryly, her lips twitching into a wide smile. 'But they wouldn't have missed the wedding. It is one of the happiest times on Earth today. And all the devas must have gone to shower their blessings on the couple.'

'Brahmarishi Vishwamitra is said to have arranged that marriage,' started Tilottama slowly, casting a sidelong glance at her friend. Menaka gave a slight start. *That name. That man. Now he had the coveted title.* Menaka felt a glow of pleasure and pride mingling through her. He had done it.

'Ram and Lakshman were his disciples, and they helped him kill the demon Taraka and her son Subahu who were harassing Vishwamitra with his yagna,' supplied Tilottama. 'So pleased was he with these two extraordinary princes, that he is said to have given them the ultimate knowledge of the brahman and the mother of all vidya—the bal and the atibal—for everlasting vigour and vitality, to fight hunger, thirst and fatigue. He is said to have imparted all his sacred, his secret knowledge to these two princes to carry forward the gems of wisdom. And then he got them to Mithila to introduce them to their future brides. He initiated the entire romance and marriage. He is said to have claimed that is his last good work he has done on Earth.'

A small smile touched Menaka's lovely face. 'So he ended it all with love; he still believes in it,' she murmured. She did not need Tilottama's explanation, as she kept herself abreast with the smallest detail about Kaushik, Shakuntala and Vasu. The mention of Ram had flared a new hope in her. Would Ram free Vasu from Indra's curse to return to Heaven?

Tilottama threw her a sharp glance. 'Vishwamitra didn't come to meet you ever, did he? And neither did you make any attempt to meet him. You didn't go for this wedding because you knew he was there.'

'How would it benefit either of us if we did meet?' shrugged Menaka, heaving a tired sigh. 'We don't have anything more to say to each other.'

'Because both of you did what the other requested. You pushed him away, towards his vision and he became a Brahmarishi. And by cursing you, he saw to it that you returned home to Heaven, your rightful place, back to Vasu. He knew too well that you had used him to forget Vasu,' Tilottama paused abruptly, noticing the pain smudging her friend's eloquent eyes. 'He didn't come for his daughter's wedding for the same reason. He will never meet you for he does not want to deprive you of your last chance at happiness—Vasu.'

Menaka stared at her hands, turning inwards on herself as she often did. 'Even Shakuntala senses this, and that's why she has no anger against her father,' she explained. 'She gracefully accepted his absence at her wedding. But he did meet her later, after the wedding, she told me. Father and daughter have been reunited too. It had to happen. Shakuntala was his one joy, who would instantly gladden his heart. He was angrier for having to abandon her than me betraying him,' recalled Menaka. 'He didn't allow me to take her knowing that she would be in kinder care with Kanva, his friend who was pining for a child. It all happened for the best, I presume.'

Tilottama gave her friend's hand a tight, reassuring squeeze. 'All's well, Vishwamitra eventually did become a Brahmarishi and Shakuntala got the grandest wedding when Dushyant finally decided to marry her,' she grinned. 'This wedding of the Ayodhya princes seems to be as big as the one Shakuntala had years ago!'

Menaka's face brightened immediately. 'That was a huge affair and not without its share of controversy,' she remarked. 'Shakuntala made sure of that.'

'She is your daughter, after all!'

'No, she is smarter!' Menaka gave a wry smile, 'and braver. Unlike me, she decided not to desert her child but instead bring him up on her own. She is the first mother to do that!' Menaka could not hide the pride in her voice. 'That the wedding took place is a wonder. I was surprised when Shakuntala finally decided to let Dushyant know that they had a son. She was content bringing him up on her own. It was only when Bharat started asking pertinent questions about his father that she decided to introduce him to his father. That's when she approached Dushyant at his palace at Hastinapur after so many years.'

'Where she was treated so rudely by him! Dushyant called Shakuntala a whore!' fumed Tilottama.

Menaka felt a hot flush of anger. "You are like your mother, he said',' said Menaka, through gritted teeth. 'Shakuntala had to suffer the stigma of being my daughter. Not that she took it lightly. She proudly proclaimed she was the child of famous parents, and if she was a whore, then Dushyant was a cowardly debauch who did not keep his promise of marrying her. She reminded him she was an orphan, not an illegitimate child and though she once might have loved him, she would not accept his insults or a single harsh word that would go against her dignity.'

Tiltottama nodded thoughtfully. 'I have met her when she used to get Bharat here. She has your beauty, Menaka, your gentleness and yet she is as fierce as a tigress!'

'Like her father,' said Menaka.

'No, that's like you too,' Tilottama corrected her. 'You know when to fight back and show your claws and snarl! You fought for Vasu's honour!'

And Shakuntala had to fight to regain her own. Dushyant had not kept his promise of taking her back as his wife, but instead of pining and waiting for his return, she had given birth to their child in the ashram. She had named him Sarvadaman, which meant 'the all-conqueror'. She had brought him up like a prince in exile, teaching him everything fit enough for royalty. But Dushyant had refused to acknowledge her or the son, and had ordered her to leave, branding her as a whore and the mother of a bastard child born of lust. Menaka had winced at the harsh words, more angry with herself for making her daughter exposed to such a filthy character assault. Dushyant had not spared Kaushik and herself either; accusing both for being shamelessly wanton to carry on an unholy liaison. And with such parents, it was not unsurprising that their daughter Shakuntala had spoken like a common whore at his court.

Enraged, Shakuntala had rushed to protect her son and her reputation. She had realized that this was the man to whom she had lost her heart and herself to, the man she had chosen for herself thirteen years ago. This was the man who had made her pregnant with his child and left, promising to bring her back as his queen but he had reneged shamelessly. And now he had the temerity to insult her in open court, maligning her and their son.

'My Shakuntala was a naive girl who grew up in an ashram, who did not know what fear was, living amongst the wild animals and dangerous jungle. But here was a man who was far worse,' said Menaka, the contempt still apparent in her voice. 'Shakuntala had never experienced treachery or betrayal. Or, what weakness was. All through her growing years she had been showered with love, kindness, respect and dignity. That is why she could lash back at Dushyant in the only language she knew—simple truth. And she battled to clear her name and mine,' recounted Menaka, her eyes darkening with remembered pain at what her daughter had endured that day at her lover's royal assembly.

'You feign ignorance of not knowing me and brand me a whore for having known you,' she had corrected him, her voice dripping with venom. 'By not acknowledging me, I do not become a whore, but you become a coward and a man lacking principles and culture. I am your wife, whom you married in the ashram of Rishi Kanva, in the gandharva tradition, but which you saw as an opportunity to use and disown me. Yet I am your wife, if not your queen,' she continued contemptuously. 'A wife who deserves her husband's love and respect. But all I got is your insult, a right I have not given you. And as a king, neither do you have a right to insult your subject. I demand respect that is my due.'

Tilottama listened as she heard Menaka speak; her daughter's humiliation was hers as well.

'Shakuntala's eloquence stems from the power of fearless truth,' observed Tilottama. 'She knew her status and her rights and she did not hesitate to demand it. Menaka, you did the same when you fought for Vasu at Indra's court. Both of you fought for the people whom you loved—you for Vasu, Shakuntala for her son. But more importantly, both of you did it for your self-respect. You were not the whore, it was Indra and Dushyant who sold their soul with their lies and allegations for their personal gains. It was their honour which was at stake. Not yours.'

Menaka smiled proudly; it displayed great dignity and elegance. 'Shakuntala is a wise girl, you know. She reminded Dushyant that she had not visited him at court to beg for his lost love or for his charity; she did not need either,' remarked Menaka, coiling up her hair absently as she continued to narrate her daughter's story. 'She had lived happily without it in her ashram all those years and did not desire his wealth or status, which were as hollow as him. What she demanded was justice which was hers by right. And it was not for her, she wanted it for her son. And that was her sole purpose that he acknowledged his son. "My truth is my only weapon, my only defence. And your wisdom is in your honesty to accept it. Truth is what even a thousand ashwamegha sacrifices cannot mask, truth is not in just the study of all the Vedas or bathing in the sacred waters of the Ganga. Truth is answering your conscience," she sneered. "And it is that truth that you, o king, are denying by refusing me and our son. By calling my parents unpardonable words, they do not become what you have accused them of. Vishwamitra shall always be respected as a revered rishi and my mother as the beauteous apsara, the daughter of Brahma, created with the world. She, whom my father had married, will always be known as the love of Vishwamitra, his wife, and the mother of his child, Shakuntala; never as the heavenly whore, as you so shamefully accuse a woman and call me the same!"

'Saying that she turned to her twelve year old son and said, "You wanted to know who your father was. Let me introduce him to you!" she announced with elaborate disdain. "A man who abandoned us and assumes we have come here to seek his status and crown. Fear not, king, my son does not need your kingdom to become king. He is accomplished enough to carve a kingdom for himself, just as my father carved his own future. My son shall always be remembered as Vishwamitra's grandson, if not as King Dushyant's son! He will rule over the world as Bharat, without your name, legacy and recognizance."

'And hurling those last scornful words, Shakuntala had turned to leave the court with her son and had it not been for the intervention of the devas and celestial rishis, Shakuntala would have returned to her ashram. They reprimanded the king and made him confess that she indeed was his wife and Sarvadaman was his son.

'The rishis renamed the young prince Bharat, "the cherished one" and that was what everyone calls him now,' said Menaka thinking fondly of her teenaged grandson.

Her initial reservation about Dushyant had mellowed but she admitted that she was not as fond of him as she was of Rishi Ruru, who was still devoted to Pramadvara. Now theirs was a sweet, simple love story, tempered not just by passion, but honesty and respect. Menaka gave an inward sigh; she was a fine one deciding about honesty.

'You don't like him much. You never did!' stated Tilottama, sensing Menaka's doubts about Dushyant.

'He made my child suffer, I can't get myself to forgive him,' confessed Menaka. 'That he deserted her, made her wait those twelve years, humiliated her and her twelve-year-old son in the presence of his nobles and ministers, I cannot respect him. He claims he was forced to decide against accepting Shakuntala and their son because his subjects would have questioned him about the legitimacy of the marriage and the child. There was no witness for either, he dared argue,' said Menaka hotly. 'He accepted her because he had no other choice! Some rishis warned him that he might seek the wrath of Vishwamitra.'

'That must have done the trick!' laughed Tilottama, and Menaka could not help smiling.

'Kaushik's reputation is still fearsome! Dushyant came to his senses soon enough. Not that Shakuntala had any illusions about him or their marriage, she married him not for love but to give her son his royal rights!' she remarked with a cynical twist to her smile. 'Shakuntala had lost her faith in him long ago. Dushyant will have to earn it back, and he is valiantly doing so now. I don't think she takes too kindly to the definition of that emotion called love,' rued Menaka. 'But yes, she is now the queen of Hastinapur, if that is any consolation.'

'The rightful queen,' corrected Tilottama. 'She deserves the title, if not the man! How could she trust a man like Dushyant? What would have happened if the rishis had not intervened?'

'She would have come back to the ashram and trained her son to be a king nevertheless!' retorted Menaka. 'She made her choice on her terms. But yes, what happens when a woman, is thus maligned and accused by her man?'

Tilottama nodded thoughtfully. 'She realizes that he does not deserve her. Considers him a bitter mistake and forgets him,' she added spiritedly. 'Didn't you do the same, Menaka, you tried to forget the men you so loved, though they were good men?'

Menaka made an impatient movement, hinting an unspoken

but clear determination not to discuss further. 'Why is it always women are defined by the men?' she said, her face alive with self-critical irony, her eyes sad and truthful.

Tilottama did not reply. Her friend's tone was too vehement.

'Men,' said Menaka softly. 'Were they my mistakes, Tilottama?' she asked painfully, in appeal.

'Vasu and Vishwamitra were mistakes?' repeated Tilottama gently.

'Things which don't go right are mistakes...' sighed Menaka suddenly, her face changed. 'An understanding, a realization, that is not correct. But yet I don't regret,' she declared, more firmly.

'What are you trying to say?' asked Tilottama cautiously.

'That there are certain episodes in our lives that give you so much happiness, but which go bad for some reason or the other and yet we don't get over them,' she said, her eyes smudged with memory. 'Possibly that's why we tend to obsess over unfinished relationships!'

Tilottama glanced at Menaka keenly. 'You never got over Vasu either, did you? To escape the grief of his separation you ran away, deliberately into Vishwamitra's arms. And then you gave him up too, for his own good, and not yours. You could have had him forever if you had kept the truth to yourself.'

'I couldn't have continued living a lie. Guilt kills happiness. That was the difference between Vasu and Kaushik. With Vasu I was content, loving him unconditionally. With Kaushik, I felt burdened with my own guilt. In every way, he was better off without me,' said Menaka, a faraway look in her eyes. 'Without trust and with that guilt, we could never have been happy for long. The bitterness of separation—one was taken away from me, the other was abandonment by choice—does not make the grief worse or better. And I know I loved them both, lost them both.'

'You haven't lost Vasu, he'll come back, I am sure!' interrupted Tilottama quickly.

'Yes, he might. He shall one day,' agreed Menaka, breaking into a sad, pensive smile. 'But will he be the same Vasu I loved? I am not that same Menaka anymore. Would he still love me?

There are so many "if", too many "when". I don't dare hope anymore and there is no point in waiting. We are unfading, we shall never die, Tilottama. But Death, to me is a release, meant for our greater good. But we celestial beings are unfortunate not to be blessed with it. As immortals, our life is an evergreen river, flowing slow or fast, taking us with it, forever and ever, changing course when there is an obstacle but never reaching our sea...' Her eyes were staring, softly sombre. 'Vasu and Pramadvara, Kaushik and Shakuntala; two men I loved and with whom I had my two daughters. I feel fulfilled, not failed.'

It was a satisfied statement, without rancour, remorse or regrets. She sounded almost content. 'Failed relationships do not mean failure. I didn't fail them and they didn't fail me. It's a loss, but not failure!' she repeated, more fiercely.

Tilottama nodded. 'You haven't failed, Menaka. You have tided over the worst. You are in command now as the queen of the apsaras, using hope and not fear as Rambha did. And for what you gave up your all for, Vishwamitra did become a Brahmarishi eventually! You saved your daughter's life and Pramadvara is now happily settled with her family. So are Shakuntala and Bharat. And they love you,' she added.

'I got their respect, that's more important' said Menaka, a wistful look in her eyes. 'I never thought I would, and it's their greatness which makes it so, not mine. I feel small in their generosity to forgive,' she said, chewing on her lip thoughtfully. 'It's important a child respects his parent. I would hate to see shame in their eyes because of me, and I had given them enough reasons and occasions to give them that.'

'But they don't. You have a family, you are a family,' assured Tilottama, scrutinizing her friend closely. She sat pale and beautiful, with her intelligent, critical smile.

'Let's go for the wedding!!' said Tilottama suddenly.

Menaka gave a start.

'Yes, Menaka, let's go. You can meet him there. It's your last chance!' coaxed Tilottama urgently.

Menaka froze.

'After this wedding, he is going to the Himalayas. He says his last good work on Earth is done. He has served Lord Ram, and he wants to retire, to relinquish all. He's going, Menaka, he may never return. Go meet him, please, get away from here!'

Menaka felt her heart hammering wildly, feeling warm and then hot, the heat spreading fast. *I can see him, hear his velvet, rich voice, look into those questioning eyes caressing her.*

'You are worried about that curse or him? '

Menaka shook her head, trembling. 'No, I never was. Nor was he. It wasn't a curse, it was caution. A circle of fire, where I couldn't get out and he could not enter.'

'You might not get to meet him ever after today!' pleaded Tilottama.

Menaka clutched her fingers tightly together, steadying her quivering hands, her racing heart and rising hope. She again had a choice...

Tilottama waited. Then time slowly ticked by, thickening the silence in the room.

'No!' exhaled Menaka. 'No!!' she repeated in a hoarse sigh, her voice stronger in volume and certainty. 'We'll undo each other!' she whispered brokenly. Moments later, her voice low, she spoke with effort 'No, I could have always met him, and he could have met me. But we didn't. We won't. It is done.'

Tilottama felt a hot prick of unshed tears, as she watched her friend regain her composure, a small, brave smile resurfacing through her clenched lips, her violet eyes once again clear and confident, seeking a truth beyond tradition, living her convictions beyond convention.

'You are extraordinary, you know.'

'No I am not!' retorted Menaka, startled into laughter. 'I am an apsara!' and began to laugh irresistibly, looking outside.

It was unsurpassably beautiful; the sun rising fast and high, leaving a flaming, quivering glow of its presence, the wide-branched trees straightening up as if to salute it. The flowers swayed gently in the balmy breeze, ruffling the settled dew on the soft petals, making the long, winding, grassy paths prettier in the thin warmth of the morning light, welcoming a fresh day with new promise, renewed optimism. The colours of this paradise were extraordinarily beautiful and vivid, but nothing was permanent. But she was enclosed by them, their dry, vivid colours. This was Amravati. This was her home, her haven where she must shed burdens; she could not escape from it.

She had to stay here, alone or not.

Epilogue:
Menaka's Legacy

The world did not allow Vishwamitra to retire to the mountains. Under him flourished a generation of new seers and rishis—irrespective of their birth and background.

Rishi Richik's predictions turned true. Vishwamitra's grand-nephew Parshuram, the son of Jamadagni though born a rishi, turned into a blood-thirsty warrior, a kshatriya-hater, born to annihilate generations of royal dynasties. It was during Sita's swayamvara that these two unique rishis met at King Janak's court—the grand-uncle Vishwamitra as Ram's teacher and Parshuram, the grand-nephew who threatened to kill Ram for having broken the Shiva's bow.

Vasu returned to heaven, freed from his curse as Kabandh by Ram's blessings. Indra accepted him as the Devagandharva but not his friend, never forgiving him for marrying Menaka. But Vasu, indifferent to Indra, was more anxious to reunite with Menaka.

Though Rambha remained frozen in time and stone for a thousand years, she inadvertently helped Sita. It was because of Nalkuber's curse on Ravan that stopped Ravan from touching Sita in captivity. He desperately tried to woo her instead.

Menaka's words, eventually, came true for Indra. He lost everything—his kingdom, his pride, his wife. In a fit of arrogance, he killed a seer for which he was banished from Heaven and a new king was appointed.

Vishwamitra and Menaka's grandson Bharat became an emperor whose sprawling empire was later called as Bharat. He was a unique representative of both the solar and lunar dynasties of those times. As the son of King Dushyant, from the chandravanshi line of kings and mother Shakuntala, a suryavanshi daughter of Vishwamitra, Bharat was a descendant of both royal families. Moreover, like his grandfather, Vishwamitra, he believed in worth not birth, and his sons were not the natural heirs to the throne. He adopted Vitath, an orphan as the scion to a new lineage.

As for Menaka, she was reunited with Vasu and led a contented life in Heaven, but she never forgot Vishwamitra. Vasu though having noticed the subtle change in her—didn't say anything but loved her as he always did—quietly and strongly. And Menaka, touched by his sensitive astuteness, loved him all the more.

Menaka never got to meet Vishwamitra ever. He was her last seduction.